THE TEXAS OIL FIELDS BROUGHT WEALTH TO SOME . . . AND AN EARLY GRAVE TO OTHERS

LEE TEMPLE: Cowboy, drifter, jailbird with a past, but still as fair a friend as anyone could wish, and a quick learner. His creed was never to pick a fight, but never to leave one. He taught Frank Loman a thing or two, and saved young Harry Hargrove to boot. If he was ever to start fresh, the boomtown of Emilia was as good a place as any. . . .

HARRY HARGROVE: Smart, engaging, noble . . . it was hard to believe that he could have ever been sired by the likes of Cotton Hargrove. A diamond in the rough, he fought against many of the things his father stood for, yet he always gravitated toward the family hornet's nest. . . .

FRANK LOMAN: They nicknamed him "Buffalo" with good reason—he was a towering brute of a man who took what he wanted. A rival of the Hargroves, he despised each individually—Cotton for his power, Harry for his privileges, and Elizabeth for her independence. And if Lee Temple was a friend to them, it was just too damn bad for him. . . .

COTTON HARGROVE: Scoundrel, rogue, thief—those were just some of the milder terms his rivals used to describe the savage, tyrannical patriach. He struck it rich in the oil fields, and didn't care who knew how. Much of the land was his, and he wouldn't stop until he had it all. . . .

ELIZABETH HARGROVE: She inherited her late mother's striking good looks—and her father's ruthless disposition. As wild as the gushing wells that liberated her, she drove cars at breakneck speed, smoked cigarettes, and was above inhibition in both mind and body. . . .

THE CHIEF: The grandson of a Comanche chief, Robert L. Randall worked for Cotton Hargrove, mixing nitroglycerine to be dropped down the wells. When a sniper took aim at Hargrove's wildcat oil well, the Chief's keen instincts would save an innocent man—but his quest for vengeance would touch off a devastating wave of destruction. . . .

TALKING TOMMY ELLIS: Personable, clever, and perceptive, Talking Tommy was well named. It was said that anybody in town would give you twenty dollars if you ever caught him with his mouth shut. Hargrove teamed Ellis with Lee Temple to ride shotgun in the fields, and to find out whatever he could about the former cowpoke. Ellis obeyed his orders gladly, lest someone start chipping at his own mysterious background. . . .

Praise for
WAYNE BARTON
and
STAN WILLIAMS

and the thrilling Western classic *Manhunt*

"Equal parts classic Western and classic whodunit . . . a page-turner spurred to full gallop. . . . Here's dialogue that snaps like a hot fire, and a poker deck of memorable characters. . . ."

—Bruce H. Thorstad, author of *The Gents*

". . . a Western with a strong mystery twist that will keep the reader turning the pages and guessing until the very end."

—Elmer Kelton, five-time Spur Award–winning author of *Slaughter*

"Catering both to the Western buff and mystery fan, *Manhunt* is well worth the price for a few hours' entertainment."

—*Topeka Capital-Journal* (KS)

"Plenty of action and suspense in this novel that combines the best elements of the classic Western and the classic detective yarn—all of it seasoned with sound and believable characters. Barton and Williams surely are a pair to ride the river with."

—T. V. Olsen, author of *Westward They Rode*

Books by Wayne Barton and Stan Williams

Wildcat
Shadow of Doubt
High Country
Manhunt
Live by the Gun
Warhorse

Books by Wayne Barton

Return to Phantom Hill
Ride Down the Wind

Published by POCKET BOOKS

WILDCAT

WAYNE BARTON
AND
STAN WILLIAMS

POCKET BOOKS

New York   London   Toronto   Sydney   Singapore

This book is a work of fiction. Names, characters, places and incidents are products of the author's imagination or are used fictitiously. Any resemblance to actual events or locales or persons, living or dead, is entirely coincidental.

Portions of the article "Successful Writing Team Puts Up with Hassles for End Result" by Georgia Todd Temple, copyright © 1993 by *The Midland Reporter-Telegram*, are reprinted by permission.

An *Original* Publication of POCKET BOOKS

POCKET BOOKS, a division of Simon & Schuster, Inc.
1230 Avenue of the Americas, New York, NY 10020

Copyright © 1995 by Wayne Barton and Stan Williams

ISBN: 0-671-74579-4

First Pocket Books printing October 1995

11 10 9 8 7 6 5 4 3 2

POCKET and colophon are registered trademarks of Simon & Schuster, Inc.

For information regarding special discounts for bulk purchases, please contact Simon & Schuster Special Sales at 1-800-456-6798 or business@simonandschuster.com

Cover art by Ben Perini

Printed in the U.S.A.

Authors' Note

Lee Temple, the young New Mexico cowhand who comes to the Emilia oil boom, is fictional. But in 1918 a young Texas farm boy did come, green as a gourd, to the roaring boomtown of Desdemona. He was fifteen years old. Desdemona—called Hogtown, perhaps because it was near Hog Creek—wasn't the best place for a teenage boy, but he found a man's job and stayed a year. Then, because his mother thought he should finish high school, he went back to the farm.

In 1921 he left home for good. For the next fifty years he followed the Texas oil fields, first to the Corsicana boom, then to Mexia (pronounced, usually, Ma-HAY-a), Ross City, Otis Chalk, Big Spring, North Cowden, Odessa, and other places that have vanished from both map and memory. He worked as a roustabout, a rig builder, a tool dresser and driller on cable tool rigs, a nitro shooter, an operator, a switcher, and a pumper.

His two sons grew up understanding the term "oil field trash." Each of them did his own share of following the oil fields, one to New Mexico and the northern Rockies, the other to the last boom on Alaska's North Slope. Finally the logic of oil country brought them both back to West Texas, where they'd begun.

Wildcat really started with that farm boy and the things that happened to him and his family and the people he knew in the oil fields and the boomtowns. His name was John Sam Barton. He was the father of one of the authors, and a lot of his stories have found their way into this book.

We, the authors, owe particular thanks to Edward Rowland, former Director of the Petroleum Museum, and to Betty Orbeck, the museum's Director of Archives, for their help and their generosity in allowing us access to the museum's files and facilities. Located in Midland, Texas, the Petroleum Museum houses a unique collection of exhibits and archives recording the past and present and pointing to the future of the oil industry.

The Boomtown Museum at Ranger, Texas, a 1917 boomtown that looked a lot like our fictional Emilia, provided information and encouragement, as did the people of Ranger. Also due a thank-you are Bob Barton and Scotty Bray for filling in background and detail on events and ways of doing things from the boomtown days; Doug Grad, our editor at Pocket Books, for his patience and forbearance when things were looking doubtful; and a final thanks goes to our wives, Jill Williams and Margie Barton, for putting up with a lot while the book was in progress.

WILDCAT

Chapter 1

LEE TEMPLE SWUNG DOWN FROM THE DOORWAY OF THE RED-painted T&P boxcar. The half-mile-long freight train of which the boxcar was a small part sat on a siding waiting for faster or more important traffic to pass. Down toward the front of the train where the locomotive bled steam from its vents, Temple saw a compact depot of reddish-brown brick. Thurber, the name on its sign read.

Temple had boarded the boxcar that morning in the Fort Worth stockyards. Now he frowned, trying to visualize a map of western Texas. The frown didn't fit well on his lean, long-jawed face, and after a moment he shrugged. It really didn't matter. He was six hours west of Fort Worth, six hours on his way to nowhere in particular. Maybe on his way to Thurber, he thought, looking across the tracks toward town.

Most of Thurber seemed built of the same brick as the depot. The business block boasted three or four solid two-story buildings, one of them with a tall brick smoke-stack from which a wisp of white vapor trailed in the light easterly wind. The nearest building looked new, and was. Its sign read: TATUM'S GROCERY AND MARKET, EST. 1913. Temple ran a hand over the blond stubble, almost long enough to be the start of a beard, that covered his cheeks and chin.

Mentally he counted the coins in the pocket of his jeans. A store, he decided, was just right.

He reached into the boxcar and touched the polished leather of his saddle. It should be safe enough for the few minutes he'd be gone. The other riders in the car were a family that had been there when he'd boarded that morning—a couple who looked a few years older than he, and a little girl of four or five. They'd huddled at their own end of the car, not answering his greeting, and he hadn't intruded on them. The girl was watching him now. Temple grinned at her, but she only drew in her thin shoulders and closed her eyes.

His decision made, Temple tilted his Stetson down against the hot afternoon sun and walked briskly toward Tatum's store. His boots crunched on the cindered right-of-way. Inside, he paused by the doorway, blinking as his eyes adjusted to the relative darkness.

"What'll it be, kid?" a squat, unkempt man who might have been Tatum asked.

Temple looked over the shelves slowly. His last meal had been supper at the Tarrant County Jail the night before, and he was surprised how the sight of food sharpened the hunger he'd felt off and on all day. It was his own fault. He might have stayed for breakfast, but he'd been in a hurry to put the jail and everything about it behind him. He swallowed the rush of saliva that came into his mouth and said,

"I was wondering. Is there any work to be had around here?"

Tatum, or whoever, gave him a second look, then shook his head. "Nothing in cowboying, mister," he said, revising his estimate of age. Temple was used to that. As his whipcord leanness made him look taller than six feet, his wide blue eyes made him seem younger than his years.

"It doesn't have to be cowboying."

"Still nothing."

The storekeeper frowned at him. Temple could see him turning suspicion in his mind like an ox chewing its cud. Temple was used to that, too, though he'd never understood it. Some people reacted to him that way, like city dogs scenting their first wolf. It's almost like he knows, he thought, but that was silly. Tatum couldn't know anything about him, nor about his father. After a moment the man tugged at his beard.

"We's mostly farmers around here, and times is pretty slow," he said. "And the mines is shut down." He pondered a moment more, then said, "Might be some jobs on west at Emilia, but it ain't anyplace decent folks would want to stop. There's an oil boom going on. Like Sodom and Gomorrah, them boomtowns. The scum of the earth follows the oil fields."

"Thanks," Temple said. "I'll keep that in mind." He nodded toward the big orange-yellow wheel of cheese on the counter. "What do you get for your cheese?"

"Dime a pound."

The whistle on the locomotive across the way sounded its long call. Another answered in a complicated pattern of long and short hoots. The drum of wheels on the rails drew closer until the sound settled into a steady rush.

"How about crackers?"

"You can have a handful free with the cheese. A box is fifteen cents."

"Milk?"

"All you want. Got to charge you ten cents a quart. Unseasonable hot lately. Ain't easy to keep milk fresh in this heat."

"Ten cents. Does that come with crackers, too?"

Tatum's suspicion rushed back into his dark face. He frowned and leaned forward on the counter. "Listen," he said, "you trying to be funny?"

"Not me." Temple saw the man's hand drop beneath the countertop, and he took an easy step back. The storekeeper might have anything from an ax handle to a shotgun under there, and Temple wasn't looking for trouble with a living soul. He did some quick figuring. "I'm just after a bite to eat. I guess I'll have two pounds of the cheese, a box of crackers, and about half a gallon of milk."

"Let's see." Tatum's heavy brows drew together. "That'll come to fifty-five cents. Being I ain't so sure about that milk,

I'll give you the lot for four bits. Throw in a jug, too, since I see you ain't carrying one."

"Nice of you," Temple said.

The other man hadn't moved. "Maybe I ought to see your money."

"Sure thing." Temple came slowly to the counter, well away from the bearded man. He spread a handful of coins on the counter, looked at them, drew back a dime and a quarter. "There you go. Fifty cents."

"Just barely." The storekeeper almost smiled. "Two pounds, you said." He reached under the counter, drew out a foot-long butcher knife, and cut into the cheese with surgical precision. "I'll wrap it for you. Crackers is over on the shelf there. Some of these here canned beans or tomatoes might go good with your cheese. Or maybe a slab of bacon."

"Not today,"

"All right." Tatum used a long-handled dipper to fill a big mason jar with milk, sniffed at it, then screwed the top on tightly. "Get you a gunnysack to carry all this. If you'll take a word of advice, I'd drink up that milk pretty quick."

The drum of the passing train faded, sinking toward silence as suddenly as it had come. Its engine gave a final wailing cry, and then another locomotive hooted in the near distance.

"Sounds like they're calling me," Temple said. "Much obliged."

"Pleasure's mine." This time Tatum did smile, carefully, as if he had only so many smiles to spare. He turned the butcher knife idly in his big hands. "Enjoy your trip, cowboy."

Temple strode back toward the freight, his bag of plunder slung over his shoulder. He put his mind back over the conversation in the store, tried to see what had set Tatum so much on his guard. In the end he gave it up. Maybe Ma was right, he thought. Maybe it shows—what Pa was, what I am. A phrase from the newspaper article rose to his mind, and he absently touched the pocket where he kept the much-refolded scrap of paper. *Killer's eyes.*

Up by the depot, the engineer and two other men stood on the platform, deep in discussion. A burly brakeman in a blue uniform moved slowly down the train, rapping occasionally at the wheels of a car with a heavy wooden club. Ignoring him, Temple swung aboard the boxcar. In the doorway with his feet dangling, he opened the sack and began to lay out his supper.

He had his jackknife ready to shave off a slice of cheese when he sensed someone behind him. He turned quickly, gripping the knife. The little girl crouched on hands and knees three yards away. She scuttled backward at his sudden movement, but immediately began inching toward him again. She wore a dirty flour-sack dress. Her straw-colored hair hung limply around her shoulders. The only life about her was in her eyes, rapt and full of wonder, fixed on the jar of milk. Slowly, as if she were afraid it might disappear, she reached out toward it.

"Sarah Louise!" the woman who must have been her mother called from the end of the car. Her voice was thin and harsh. "Sarah, sweetie, you come here. Don't you bother that—gentleman."

Sarah looked back over her shoulder, then turned again to stare at the milk. The life died out of her face and she shut her eyes. Clenching her hands into fists, she put them to her mouth and began to cry. She cried almost silently, big tears squeezing past her tightly closed lids.

"Sarah Louise."

The man came quickly up behind her. He was lanky and big-eared, clad in patched overalls. A flat gray cap partly covered hair the same color as the girl's. He couldn't have been older than twenty-five or -six, but strands of gray already showed below the cap. He glanced almost fearfully at Temple. Then he saw the food on the boxcar floor, and his Adam's apple bobbed as he swallowed. He bent and picked up the child.

"You come back here with us, Sarah. Come on, now. That don't belong to us, baby. Go to your mama."

Temple looked at the three of them. They sat with their backs to him. He could hear them whispering to the girl. She put her head down in the woman's lap, her shoulders still quivering beneath the thin cotton dress. The woman stroked her hair. Temple looked at the crackers and cheese and milk sitting on the white butcher paper from Tatum's store.

"Well, hell," he muttered.

Then he gathered everything into the butcher paper and walked to the back of the car. The woman started and gave a little cry when he set the bundle down beside her.

"I brought this down for you all," he said. "Thanks for watching the saddle."

The woman's eyes reminded Temple of a stray dog he'd tried to feed when he was a boy in New Mexico. The dog had bitten him.

"Oh, please, don't make fun—" she began.

"Listen, mister," the man said at the same time, "we can't—"

Temple waved a hand. "Mine's in the other car," he said. "Plenty to go around. If you'll take a word of advice, though, I'd drink up that milk pretty quick."

He heaved his saddle to its familiar place on his shoulder.

"God bless you, mister," the woman cried from behind him.

Temple nodded, not looking back, and dropped lightly from the car's doorway onto the cinders.

Harry Hargrove climbed down from a cattle car and stretched himself. It wasn't the most comfortable accommodation in the world, but it suited his personality. He'd spent most of the ride from Fort Worth listening to the oil field yarns of a pair of boomers fresh from Oklahoma. Not as sure of their welcome in Thurber, they stayed in the car while Harry dropped off to ease his cramped muscles.

Keeping to the near side of the cars opposite Tatum's, Harry walked the length of the train to the engine. He saw very few other riders. A family of three, man, woman, and little girl, sat in the far doorway of a boxcar apparently studying their dangling feet. Looking at them, Harry felt a twinge of guilt. He traveled by freight because he chose to; obviously, they had no choice. A lanky cowboy had left their car or one near it, and Harry watched him walk in a long loose gait across to Tatum's.

At the front of the train, fireman and engineer greeted him with a respectful "Afternoon, Mr. Hargrove." Mick Singleterry, the brakeman, was more reserved or more sullen. Harry thanked them for the railroad's hospitality, shook hands all around, and headed for his car, feeling like a hypocrite.

You've said you won't use the money, he thought. His money. Principles. But it's just fine to use his name and influence. Yeah. Some principles.

The cowboy was returning to the train with a brown sack over his shoulder. For a moment Harry was tempted to go and talk to him. Maybe he was related to the farm family—a brother, say. Maybe they had a story to tell.

When he got back to the cattle car, a half-dozen new passengers had found places inside. They'd cleared the straw from one corner and were playing cards. Shooter and Chief, the two he'd met, were in the middle of it, and nobody seemed to notice his return. Harry smiled and went back to his corner of the car. He settled in the straw with his back against the slatted wall, took a copy of *The Eyes of the World* from his suitcase and lost himself in the book.

After two chapters he woke to his surroundings with a start. The train was moving. Something had struck his foot hard enough get his attention. He squinted upward against the slanting evening sun. The air was dusty. Above him loomed a tall, heavy hulk of a man. At first Harry thought it was his father. "What?" he said.

"*What*, hell!" The big man drew back a boot and kicked Hargrove again. The man was not Harry's father.

"Loman?" Harry said. He was confused. Loman had not been in the car when Harry started reading. He realized he should have been more watchful, but it was too late for that now. "Hello, Frank. Did you get on at Thurber?"

The answer was another kick, aimed higher up this time. Harry rolled with it, dropping the book, letting himself go an extra turn so that he could scramble to his feet some distance from Loman.

Some of the men in the car were becoming aware of trouble, beginning to stare at Loman and Harry. The lanky cowboy—Harry hadn't seen him come in, either—was asleep with his hat tipped over his eyes. Shooter made a move to get to his feet, but his Indian sidekick put a hand on his arm to stop him. Most of these men were Loman's hands, Harry realized. He couldn't count on help from anyone.

Heavy through the shoulders and neck like a buffalo, Frank Loman glared down at Hargrove. Harry smelled the taint of liquor on his breath.

"I knew you'd run out," Loman said. "I thought you were gone for good."

"I'm back."

"Better for you if you'd stayed gone."

"Probably. But it can't be helped."

"All right, rich boy," Loman said, "I think I'm going to bounce you around the car awhile and then throw you out."

"Why?" Hargrove asked. He kept his voice as light as he could. He knew he should be afraid, but he wasn't.

"I don't like you, and everywhere I go I see you."

Harry laughed, surprised at how easy it was. "You're not my favorite person, Frank. But we can live and let live."

The Buffalo blinked, looking at an idea that hadn't occurred to him before. "I can't do that," he said slowly, seriously. He rocked with the motion of the train. "I can't let you live."

Chapter 2

HIS MIND ON HOW FOOLISH HE'D BEEN WITH HIS FOOD, TEMPLE didn't think to look before he jumped out of the boxcar. He almost landed on the brakeman, just coming down from the head of the train. Startled, the man backed away fast, brandishing the club in his hand almost by reflex. He didn't swing it. Instead he sized up Temple with a hard, bright stare.

"Ought to watch where you're going, cowboy."

Temple lowered the saddle, holding it in both hands across his body. The brakeman looked about the same age and height, though he was bigger through the chest and shoulders. He wore a thin moustache that looked oddly out of place on his round, beefy face. He still held the club poised. It was two feet long, turned and tapered like a baseball bat. Someone had varnished it to bring out the grain of the wood, but it was scuffed and dented from thumping against the iron wheels of the cars. A leather thong held it to the brakeman's wrist.

"Name's Temple. Sorry, I didn't know you were there. No harm intended."

The brakeman studied him a second longer, frowning as Tatum had frowned. Then he lowered his arm, letting the bat tap against his boot. "No harm done," he said. "But this ain't the orphan train. You want to ride, you got to pay."

"Didn't know you sold tickets."

The brakeman frowned again and shifted his hand on the handle of the club. "Don't come off smart with me, cowboy," he said. "It's a risk, letting you ride. It's against railroad policy. Now, me, I don't want to see nobody throwed off a train. But I've got to have some little something for the risk."

"About how little did you have in mind?"

"A dollar, say?"

"How far does that take me?"

The man grinned at one side of his mouth. "My run goes clear to the Pacific," he said. "San Diego, by way of El Paso and Albuquerque. You ever seen California?"

"Don't figure to." Temple inclined his head toward the door of the boxcar. "What about them?"

The brakeman looked. "Yeah." He turned his head, spat tobacco juice beneath the car, wiped his mouth with the back of a striped canvas glove. "Farmers. Starved out. Heading for California where there's money growing on every bush." He shrugged. "It's where they want to go, but I don't see how they can get there. Not on my train."

"What I need," Temple said, "is a job. You heard of anything along the line?"

"Cowboying? Might be they're hiring out toward Gallup. Same dollar'll get you there. Navajo country. You know it?"

"Been there. But I was thinking of something closer— around here, maybe. It doesn't have to be running cows."

"No?" The man looked at the saddle Temple held. "Well, you're taller'n you need to be, but I guess you're strapping enough. You willing to leave off nursing cows and do real work, then?"

"Anything inside the law."

"Yeah? Funny talk from a man hoboing—no offense." He considered. "Might be something at the next stop. Oil field work."

"Sodom and Gomorrah?"

"Emilia. But you won't be sitting that saddle."

Temple heaved the saddle into the doorway of the car, balancing it so that the tooled skirt and stirrup leather hung down. He untied the saddlebags and draped them across his shoulder.

"I was thinking about that. You're not looking for a good roping saddle, are you?"

The brakeman took a step back and raised the heavy bat, slapping it into his gloved palm.

"Listen, mister, I never heard of no cowboy parting with his saddle. You steal it?"

"Nope. Got my initials branded into it, if you want to see."

"Hell, I don't know your initials." He hesitated, fiddling with the bat. "What did you have in mind?"

"I'm figuring to take on another line of work. Thought you might trade this for the fare."

"Hell. I'd owe you about twenty in change—and I ain't giving you no money."

Temple nodded again toward the door of the car. "For them, too," he said. "Far as they want to ride."

The brakeman began to laugh. "Cowboy, I had you

figured wrong," he said. "You don't look like the Salvation Army." Then he sobered. "I'm telling you, I've seen their like before. It won't make no neverminds whether they're throwed off here or down the line or they ride plumb to California. It ain't like they think out there."

"The saddle's worth more than their fares. Maybe you could keep them from starving along the way."

Down the line the locomotive's whistle gave a long, mournful howl. "About to pull out," the brakeman murmured. He looked speculatively at Temple. "Law's on my side here. I could knock you cold, take the saddle if I wanted. Those saddlebags, too."

"Might be you could," Temple said.

"Or I could make the deal, then kick those sodbusters off anyway. You'd never know anything about it."

Temple nodded. "Right enough," he said. "But why would a man want to do himself that way?"

The brakeman looked at him a moment longer. *Wolf.* Then he grinned and dropped the club so that it hung loosely from his wrist.

"Cowboy, I've not run across another one like you. I'll do what I can for them. Here go." He dug in his pocket for a stub of pencil and scribbled on a page torn from his tally book. "Name of a man in Emilia, next stop. He runs contract gangs and does hauling. You tell him Mick Singleterry sent you. Got that?"

Temple folded the page into his shirt pocket without looking at it. "I'll remember."

The whistle sounded again. Steam hissed into the locomotive's cylinders and the drive pistons began to thump. The brakeman lifted the saddle awkwardly, staggering as if it weighed more than he expected. Carrying it, he turned and trotted toward the caboose.

"Cattle car about ten back got some more boomers in it," he called over his shoulder. "Might want to make their acquaintance." He laughed again, though Temple couldn't see the joke. "So long, cowboy."

Temple waited by the track as the freight ground into motion. He hadn't understood much of what the railroad man had said there at the end, but it didn't really matter. Maybe there would be a job in Emilia. Maybe he'd thrown away a good saddle for nothing. Either way, he'd manage.

A half-dozen boxcars drifted by him, then two gondolas loaded with gravel, then a cattle car with an open door. He snagged the handrail and swung up, the train's motion throwing him against a squat, toad-faced man who stood by the doorway. Without speaking, the man put out a steadying hand and answered Temple's word of thanks with an impersonal nod. Half a dozen other men lounged on the dusty straw, talking, playing cards, sleeping. One was deep in a book. None of them paid any special attention as Temple found a place, sat, and tilted his hat down to rest his eyes from the dry, hot sun. He was asleep before the last car cleared the water tower at Thurber.

He awoke to the sway of the car and the sound of angry voices. A minute passed before he remembered where he was, before he got the face of a dark-eyed young woman out of his mind. "Amy," he murmured, and the sound of his voice woke him to his surroundings. He took off his hat, shook his head to drive away her image.

". . . new-money trash, I said. Trash with money is still trash."

The train swayed in a long, climbing curve across the face of a wooded hill. Late afternoon sunlight flowed between the slats of the cattle car's sides, striping the floor and walls and the men inside with shifting patterns of liquid gold. Dust motes danced and swirled in slanting bars of golden light. Where the dust rose thickest, two men faced each other, shifting their feet to keep their balance in the dry hay. Temple squinted at them against the glare.

"Speak up, Hargrove. What do you have to say to that?"

One was slender, tall, young, good-looking. The one speaking was not much older but fifty pounds heavier. The slighter man swayed easily to the train's motion, his body relaxed. He was treating the whole thing as a joke, though Temple could hear the tightness in his voice.

"Trash is trash, Loman, with money or without. What kind of trash would that make you?"

The card game had stopped. The other men in the car still sat or sprawled on the floor, not looking at the pair. Tension lay over them as real as the barred sunlight.

"Rich kid," Loman sneered. "You think any workingman is trash, right?" He jerked his head toward the nearest of his silent audience—the toad of a man Temple had noticed earlier. "How about it, Shooter? You mind him calling you trash?"

Shooter studied the two of them with round, expressionless eyes. He gave a pleasant, frog-mouthed smile. "Oil field trash is the kind I am," he said in a low voice. "My own dear mother said it last time I seen her. Never known her to lie." He nudged the man next to him. "What do you say, Chief? Is that the kind of trash we are?"

The man called Chief pushed back a black hat with a silver concho band. His face was lean and sharp, hook-nosed, with hard black eyes and a sparse moustache that drooped past the corners of his mouth. Sunlight barred his high cheekbones like war paint.

"White man's fight," he muttered, and tipped the hat back down. "No business of poor Indian."

"Let it go, Loman," the slender man said. "I'm whatever you want me to be. I don't want to fight you."

Temple found himself nodding agreement. That made sense. Fighting ruined friendships, hurt people, could cost a man his freedom—or his life. *Killer's eyes, killer's heart.*

"Especially not over a woman."

He realized he'd spoken the thought half aloud only when the two glanced his way. Then the big one—Loman—turned back to his opponent.

"That makes you a coward, too," he said.

Temple tensed, but the one called Hargrove only smiled. "If you say so," he said.

"And your old man's a back-shooting son of a bitch."

"Tell that to him."

"And your sister's—"

"Listen, Loman—"

"—a whore. No!" The big man laughed. "No, that's wrong. A whore—"

Hargrove's right fist caught him on the cheekbone hard enough to rock his head back.

"—gets paid, but—"

Hargrove pressed in, swinging with both hands in blind anger. His opponent wasn't angry. The big man gave ground under the sheer fury of the assault, but Temple saw his mouth sketch a satisfied grin. Hargrove landed once more to the head, but Loman closed with him, taking the rest of the flurry on forearms and shoulders. Then he shoved with both muscular arms, sending the smaller man hurtling backward.

His feet slipping on the dry hay, Hargrove crashed against the side of the car, stumbled forward, fell to one knee. As he started to rise, Loman took a shuffling step toward him. The big man's right arm came up as if he held a hammer, then smashed down across Hargrove's neck and shoulder. Hargrove fell on his face in the hay.

"—but Liz gives it away for free!" the Buffalo cried.

Lee Temple stood up. Hargrove braced his hands and lifted his face clear of the straw. Loman kicked at the younger man's head, missed, dug his boot hard into his chest instead. He had drawn back for another kick when Temple put a long hand on his shoulder.

"He had to hit you," Temple said. "You fixed that. No reason to kill him over it."

Loman turned to stare at him, white-eyed. "You, Cowboy," he said thickly. "This ain't your business."

"That's God's truth. But this young fellow got me curious with the riddle he raised a while ago."

"What riddle you talking about?"

"Back a few minutes ago, he was trying to get it straight what kind of trash you are."

Loman's eyes narrowed. He gathered his strength and started to lift his massive right arm.

"I believe I've got it figured out."

Loman swung the arm like a slaughterhouse worker felling

a steer. But Temple was no longer there. He had leaned to his left, dropping into a half crouch that took him down and away from Loman's hammer blow. As the great fist slashed past, he came upward again, driving his right hand past Loman's open guard with all the power of his legs and back behind it.

The punch struck Loman's jaw with a force that jolted Temple to the toes of his boots. There was an audible crack—he wasn't sure if it came from Loman's jaw or his own hand—and the big man dropped like a steer in the slaughterhouse.

Temple leaned over him. "I'd say you were the kind who'd miscall a man's family to make him fight. That's the kind of trash you are."

Loman's eyelids fluttered. He muttered thickly and pawed a big hand across the front of his face as if to shoo away some insect.

"Hooo-eee, Cowboy, you pack a wallop," Shooter said. The toad-faced man was smiling. Even his silent companion had tilted back his hat to watch the fight. "Not many could put Frank Loman out that way."

"Lucky."

"Trouble is, he's not likely to stay out long," Shooter added. "And the chances are you haven't improved his disposition one bit."

Temple looked out the car's doorway. The train was just breaking over the crest of its climb. Not yet gathering speed down toward the wide valley, it was moving little faster than a man could walk.

"I reckon we could do something about that," he said. He got a good grip under Loman's burly shoulders, half dragged him to the slatted doorway of the car, and rolled him out. Loman fell loosely, raising a little puff of dust when he hit the dried grass alongside the tracks. The last Temple saw of him, he was on his feet, rubbing one uncertain hand across his mouth and lower jaw.

Hargrove wasn't dead. When Temple touched his shoulder, he opened his eyes, frowning in a puzzled way. He tried to sit up, slumped back against the side of the car, then made it the second time.

"Who—Where's Loman?"

"He got off."

Hargrove blinked, looking as if the words took a long time to reach him. Clawing at the slatted wall until he found a handhold, he pulled himself to his feet. He frowned groggily toward the open doorway and his face took on a startled look.

"Good Lord. Did you kill him?"

"Nope. Don't think a person could, short of using an ax or a Winchester. Your head all right?"

"Where is it?" Gently, Hargrove touched his fingertips to the left side of his face. Blood oozed from a cut in his eyebrow. A swollen bluish bruise ran from there down to the point of his jawbone.

"Don't remind me," he said. He looked at his fingers, wiped the blood on the leg of his trousers, and offered the hand to Temple. "Harry Hargrove, and very pleased to meet you."

"Lee Temple."

A pattern of long and short blasts on the train's whistle almost drowned Harry's next words.

"Cowboy? New Mexico?"

"Used to be both. Now I'm figuring to find a job in Emilia."

Harry started to grin, but winced and changed his mind. "Well, you won't have long to wait." He waved a hand toward the open doorway. "There it is."

Chapter 3

TEMPLE STEPPED TO THE DOOR OF THE CATTLE CAR. AT FIRST HE could see nothing of Emilia. The fore part of the train and the track ahead faded into a drifting black curtain. A shuddering roar, even louder than the noise of the train, grew in intensity until its power vibrated through his bones. The car slid into the curtain, and Temple felt a fine mist of lukewarm liquid settling on his face and arms.

"What in hell . . . ?" he tried to ask Harry over the throbbing cascade of noise.

Harry grinned. His face and hands were streaked with oil. As he wiped it away, more settled on his skin and clothing, soaking in, darkening the khaki of his shirt and pants. Temple wiped a hand across his own face and his palm came away black. The heavy pungent smell of oil was everywhere. He tasted its slick saltiness on his lips.

"There!" Harry shouted, pointing.

Slitting his eyes against the mist, Temple made out the shadowy wooden skeleton of an oil derrick not twenty yards from the track. A solid column of dark liquid shot upward from it, feathering out into tiny droplets on the gentle west wind. As the train car rolled past, it came out of the cloud of windborne oil. Temple could see better now, the derrick and a group of men clumped like bees on its floor trying to stem the flow. Beyond it was a railroad station and beyond that a town, much as Thurber had been except that dozens of wooden derricks loomed like strange bare trees in every open space. A pall of smoke and steam hung over everything, dimming the sunlight. In the gloom, tall yellow flames flared from iron poles.

"Emilia," Harry shouted. The noise of the well was dying

17

away as they moved into the station. He grinned again, showing oil-stained teeth. "Welcome to the boom!"

"Is it burning down?"

Harry's laugh rang through the racket. "Gas flares," he cried. "Gas comes out with the oil. It's not worth anything, so they burn it. Gives us better streetlights than Dallas."

The others in the car had gathered eagerly behind Temple and Harry, jostling for a look out the doorway.

"What do you think, Indian?" Shooter asked.

The hook-nosed man peered intently at a pool of oil in his cupped hand. He sniffed it, then ducked his head and tasted it, smacking his lips.

"Sweet crude. Tastes like the Gunsight Limestone. It's going to be a good place for shooters. We stay."

"We stay. Yee-*hah!*" Shooter slapped Temple on the shoulder. "Hey, Cowboy, come along with us if you're minded to stop over. You look like you'd be good to have around when things start to howl."

Harry put a hand on Temple's arm. "Sorry, Shooter," he said. "I've got first claim on Mr. Temple. He's coming home to eat a steak with me."

"I couldn't do that," Temple said quickly.

"Sure you could. You just cut it up into pieces and chew it. I'll show you. I owe you a meal, at least."

All Temple knew about Harry was that Loman had called him a rich boy. Still, a man riding the freights surely couldn't afford steak. "Forget it," he said. "You don't owe me anything."

"Then I like your company." The train was sliding to a stop amid the squeal of brakes. "Got your gear? Here, let me find my suitcase. My sister'll be waiting for us."

Temple thought of the name Loman had called Harry's sister. "Will she?"

"Watch for her. Yellow hair. Yellow roadster. You'll know her when you see her."

"Will I?"

The train had lurched to a painful stop. Without answering, Harry dropped off onto the cinders beside the track. The sides of the boxcars were spotted and streaked with greenish-black runnels of oil, as if they'd been painted by a giant with a frayed brush. Following Harry, Temple picked his way across a tangle of tracks and sidings. Men bustled about, unloading boxcars, piling crates and oddly shaped boxes onto motortrucks. Busy with the sights, Temple had to leap aside as a tubby switch engine, hooting impatiently, hustled past pushing a string of dirty black tank cars.

"Watch it," Harry laughed back at him.

"Busy place."

"It's quieted down some since I've been gone." Harry swerved around a flatcar where a gang of workers were rolling lengths of steel pipe down onto a long, wide-tired wagon drawn by what seemed dozens of mules. "This way. Yellow hair, yellow roadster."

In front of the station two angry and oil-stained trainmen faced three men in blackened khakis and heavy boots. Like everyone else in Emilia, all of them seemed to be shouting at once.

"—reckless endangerment—"

"—gol-dangedest stupidest thing I ever seen, driving your gol-danged train right through that blowing oil—"

"—damned jarheads knew the railroad was there when you put up that damned rig and started to drill—"

"—gol-danged locomotive's gol-danged firebox had set it off, you'd've blowed us all higher than a gol-danged Georgia pine, you gol-danged—"

"—set the Rangers on you for encroaching on the railroad's right-of-way. No more damned brains—"

Temple edged past, trying to keep up with Harry. The slender man was bouncing along indifferent to the commotion, craning his neck as he looked along the platform.

"Her auto's a Mercer."

"I wouldn't know a Mercer from—"

"Just look for yellow. Remember. Yellow hair, yellow roadster."

"I remember," Temple said. He wouldn't know a Mercer by sight, but he thought they were expensive. Again he wondered about the Hargrove family, wondered why Harry had been deadheading on a freight car. "The lady standing over that way has yellow hair, best as I can tell. But her auto's green."

"Not Betty, then. Where?" Harry stopped so suddenly Temple almost fell over him. "Oh, by the baggage wagon. Well, I'll be damned. Betty's gotten herself a new car."

The young woman caught sight of them at the same moment. "Harry!" Stretching herself on tiptoe, she waved her yellow scarf. "Harry, over here."

Harry ran to meet her, dropping his suitcase at the edge of the platform and sweeping her into a hug. Temple followed more slowly, his eyes on the woman. She had the same slenderness as her brother, and the tightly fitting green dress she wore emphasized the clean lines of her body. Her hair was not yellow but a deep honey-gold, bobbed short and mostly covered by a small green hat.

Beneath the hat her face seemed thin, tapering to a pointed chin in a way that reminded Temple of his favorite pony when he was a child. Then she looked past her brother's shoulder, fully at Temple. He saw dark eyes, deep and lively and curious, full lips curving into a smile that was half pout, and he knew that Betty Hargrove was the most beautiful thing he'd seen since he left New Mexico.

Since Amy, his mind warned. Temple stopped abruptly, but Betty's attention was no longer on him. She had drawn back from her brother's embrace.

"Harry, for God's sake." She brushed at the front of her dress, laughing. "You look like you've been rolling in oil. And so do I, now." Ignoring the oil, she hugged him again, then pulled back and looked into his face. Her expression changed. "What . . . ?" She reached up and touched his bruised cheek with her fingertips. "Harry, what happened to your face?"

"Nothing. An accident on the train."

"What kind of accident? If you'd ride the passenger cars like a normal person—"

"Now, Betty."

"'Now, Betty,' hell!" Her gaze shifted to Temple, dark eyes filled with concern and suspicion. "Did you do this?"

"He helped me. Betty, this—"

Temple heard the patter of feet behind him, beating on the platform like quick hands on a drum. He turned in time to see the little girl from the boxcar running toward him.

"Mithter!"

He went down on one knee as she ran into him. She threw both arms around his neck and kissed him wetly.

"Thank you," she said. "And my mommy and papa thank you, too."

She put her pink hand on his face and stared into his eyes for a moment. Then she turned and ran back toward the father. He scooped her up, lifted a hand to Temple, then hurried back toward the freight, which had begun to move.

"Well," said Harry.

His sister laughed. "A ladies' man," she said. "Do you always pick them so young, Cowboy?"

"Betty, behave."

"Harry, hush."

Temple stood up, watched the train roll slowly past on its way to California. Last chance, he said in his mind, not sure where the thought came from. Then the train began to pick up speed. Temple took off his hat and turned back toward the Hargroves.

"I came back as soon as I heard," Harry was saying. "Betty, I'm sorry. Sorry about Roy, and sorry I wasn't here."

For a second Temple saw her eyes narrow as if from a blow. Then she laughed. "Didn't miss a thing," she said. "Not even a funeral. Can't have a funeral if there's nothing to bury."

"Betty—"

"No. I want to know about your face. And about your cowboy." She looked past Harry. Straight on, Temple could see the hurt still in her eyes, but her voice showed none of it. "Hello, Cowboy."

"Hello, lady."

"Betty," Harry said, "meet Lee Temple. He saved me some trouble today."

21

Betty held out her hand like a man. "Elizabeth," she said. "My friends call me all kinds of things. Only my big brother calls me Betty."

She smiled, but her eyes stayed dark and thoughtful on Temple's face. Her smile reminded him fleetingly of Amy's. But her smile was wider, closer, brighter. He wondered if this could be the sister Loman had called whore. He didn't think so.

"Pleased to meet you, Miss Hargrove," he said, taking her hand.

"I've invited Lee home to supper," Harry put in. "But he's been arguing about it. See if you can persuade him, Betty."

"I appreciate the offer," Temple said, "but I have to see a man about a job." He drew the paper from his shirt pocket. "I'd take it as a favor if you could tell me where to find him."

Harry unfolded the note, read it. He looked at Temple in surprise. Then he began to laugh.

"Something funny?"

"Just a little." Harry held up the paper. "You haven't looked at this, have you?"

"No. A train man gave it to me at Thurber, and I hadn't thought to. Why?"

"And this is the man you've come to Emilia to ask about a job?"

"Well—yes. Do you know him?"

Harry began to laugh again. "Sure do. So do you. Maybe you'll reconsider our offer of supper." He waved the paper at Temple happily. "The name here's Frank Loman. You just threw him off the train."

"It's a Reo Torpedo," Elizabeth Hargrove said. "How do you like it?"

Harry was tying his suitcase onto an open wire rack behind the single seat. It was a pigskin case, expensive but much-scuffed.

"Not much of a place to put luggage."

"I'd've brought Daddy's touring car if I'd known you had

22

company." She made a face. "But it always smells of dog. Not to mention those big cigars he's taken to smoking."

"Look," Temple said, "I don't want to be any trouble. . . ."

"Then give me your saddlebags. There. Now, get in. And hang on, if I know my little sister's driving."

"But—"

"Oh, sit down, Cowboy," Elizabeth said. "You should've learned by now how stubborn Harry is." She swung into the low green car, seemingly unhampered by the tightness of her skirt, and patted the seat beside hers. "Here. Harry can crank. Not many people have ridden in this one yet. I haven't even worn the new off."

"I thought you liked the Mercer," Harry said.

"Liked it swell." She laughed. "Bastard got stuck in that mud sink at Franklin's Corner. I told Zeke Randolph where it was and took this one."

Harry bent to the crank, looking at her across the sloping hood. "Papa know about that?"

"Maybe. If Zeke's told him by now." She clicked a lever on the steering column. "Ready."

"Does he know the kind of language you use?"

"Learned it at his knee. Are you going to crank?"

Harry spun the crank. The engine coughed, caught, accelerated to a roar. Harry trotted around to where Temple stood uncertainly.

"Get in. Hurry up, we'll get left."

Temple slipped into the low seat, folding his long legs awkwardly into a space made for someone much smaller. He looked for something to hold onto. Elizabeth shifted gears with a clash and started backing the car around as Harry leaped onto the running board. She hauled the car backward in a tight circle until its nose pointed southwest, then shifted again and fed it gas. The Reo leaped like a startled jackrabbit, slid wildly across a stretch of dirt and grass where the gushing oil had sprayed, bounced slantwise across a ditch, and finally skidded onto a graveled road leading out of Emilia.

Temple took off his Stetson and held it in his lap. He heard Harry Hargrove's laughter in his ear. He didn't feel like laughing himself. Harry crouched on the running board, clinging to the spare tire's mounting like a monkey to a palm tree. He grinned.

"There was an easier way, Betty," he yelled over the ping and spatter of flying gravel.

She laughed joyfully. The wind had swept her green hat away somewhere, and short golden hair whipped about her cheeks. Looking at her, Temple felt a lump start to form in his throat.

"Just like a man," she called across to Harry. "Always looking for something easy."

Temple saw Harry Hargrove's smile disappear. "I wish you wouldn't talk that way," Harry said.

Elizabeth laughed again. Temple didn't like it. He didn't like her. But she was striking to look at. He looked at her and wanted to touch her and didn't like wanting to and thought that maybe Loman had been right about her after all.

Then, as if she'd heard his thought, Elizabeth Hargrove turned suddenly and covered his hand with one of hers. "I'm sorry," she said. "Sometimes I forget. I forget who I'm with, how I'm supposed to behave." She looked across at Harry, real concern in her eyes. "Hell, Harry, you know I'm just teasing."

"Sure." Harry freed a hand to touch his bruised jaw. "I know."

"I take it back. I forgot the cowboy was your friend. Hey, Cowboy, I take back what I said to Harry, hear me?"

"I hear you."

Under the direct gaze of her dark eyes, Temple found it difficult to remember he disliked her. Her voice was soft now, too soft to carry over wind and motor.

"Sometimes I forget, that's all." He read the words off her lips. "Sometimes I forget who . . ."

She had taken her attention off her driving as she talked, so that the car had slowed to a speed Temple thought almost bearable. Now she pressed the throttle again and the Reo shot down a long hill like a runaway locomotive. She took one hand from the wheel and fumbled in her purse while the car verged onto the edge of the road.

"Here, Cowboy, hold the wheel for me."

"But I don't know—"

She didn't listen, and Temple didn't finish. He grabbed the wheel because she'd released it. Hoping the car responded the same as a horse, he tried to follow the curves of the road. The wheels jolted and bounced over clumps of grass and brush, first swerving to one side and then the other, while Elizabeth found a package of factory-rolled cigarettes, took one out and lighted it.

"That's good. Thanks," she said, taking back the wheel. "Lord, Cowboy, where'd you learn to drive?"

"I didn't."

"Oh." She blew a long breath of smoke into the wind and frowned seriously at the two of them. "Want to tell me what really happened on the train?" she asked. "The business to do with Loman?"

"How'd you know that?"

"Then it *was* him. What happened?"

"He was on the cars. Wanted to fight. He called Papa a killer."

Elizabeth took her eyes off the road and stared at him in open disbelief. "You fought him over *that?*"

"He called me a coward."

"No better. One truth and one lie." She shook her head firmly. "I know you, big brother. What was the real reason?"

Harry shrugged, not meeting her eyes. "Didn't have much choice. He wouldn't take no for an answer."

She was silent a moment. Temple barely heard her next words over the howl of the wind.

"He meant to kill you."

"What? No, nothing that serious, I'm sure. He was just surprised to see me again."

"I'll bet."

"And Lee helped me out."

"Then Lee saved your life." She looked quickly at Temple, and there was more depth in her gaze than he'd seen there before. "You did, Cowboy. Thank you. I mean it. Thanks."

"It wasn't so bad as that," Temple said, though he wasn't sure he believed it. "Harry would have done all right."

"He's not a coward."

"Cut it out, Betty," Harry said. He leaned in closer. "You haven't been drinking, have you, in the middle of the day?"

"He *is* brave," she insisted. "I don't know anybody as brave as him, Cowboy. I've known him all my life. I've seen him jump in the deep bend of the creek, smoke grapevine, fight bullies."

"Betty, quit it."

"And I can see from the look of his face that he put up a good fight against that buffalo, Loman."

"He did," Temple said. "He hit Loman about six times before the Buffalo could blink."

Elizabeth gave him a sidelong pouting smile. "I don't think I believe that."

"I don't remember any of it," Harry said. "Except feeling like I'd been trampled by the Buffalo."

"I do believe that."

They were bearing down on a yellow roadster, half buried in a mire of sticky red mud. Two men were working on the car, one burrowing in the mud at the front while he tried to hook a chain around the axle, the other backing a span of mules into position to haul it out. They glanced up as the Reo sped nearer. The one holding the mules waved a lazy arm to motion the car to stop.

Elizabeth's laugh rang out over the noise of the motor. She pressed down on a button and the electric horn blared. The first man dropped the lines and waved both arms frantically. The mules bolted. The man in the mud scrambled up, poised to run, his eyes wide and disbelieving as the Reo bore down on him.

Just as Temple closed his eyes for the crash, Elizabeth stepped hard on the brake and pulled the wheel over to the right. Waiting until the Reo skidded almost broadside, she slammed the car down into first gear and hit the accelerator.

The tires clawed for footing, slung mud and loose gravel toward the men and mules, finally caught. The car bounded over the low gravel bank to the right of the road, fishtailed through tall grass, and swung back onto the road beyond the mudhole.

"Good Lord!" Harry murmured.

Temple opened his eyes. "Amen!" he breathed. He felt sorry he'd parted with his saddle, because he never for damn sure intended to ride in another motorcar. He didn't try to look back toward the mud-spattered Mercer, but he heard the shouts behind them, rapidly growing fainter with distance.

"Betty, that was Zeke and his mechanic," Harry said.

"I know. They wanted me to stop."

"They'll raise hell to Papa, sure's you're a foot high."

She looked at him, rolling her eyes. For an instant Temple saw again in her face the woman he'd disliked so much.

"Oh, no," she mocked. "Not that! I'd never do anything to upset poor, dear Papa!"

"Betty, behave."

"Harry, hush."

The car shot over a rise and down the other side. Then the road curved south up a low, rocky hill. A stand of oak trees crowned the hill, and the road wound into its shade.

"Hargrove's oak grove," Elizabeth sang out. "Home's where the heart is."

Temple couldn't tell from the tone if she was happy or angry. Before he had time to give the question much thought, Elizabeth braked the car into a side lane.

"Betty, watch out!"

"I am watching out, Harry."

The trees opened out into a wide clearing. Near its highest point, a tall, unpainted house loomed against the evening sky. In the dying light and with the dark trees around it in every direction, it looked unfinished, unused, as if the builders had given up and gone away before they were quite done with the job and the owners had never moved in.

"You're all so cute when you're puppies," Elizabeth shouted to him.

"What?"

For a second Temple had the crazy thought that it was all a joke, that brother and sister had connived to bring him out to the local haunted house. As he shook off the idea, Elizabeth slid the car to a rattling, dusty halt.

"Betty!"

"Home again, home again," she said. This time Temple was pretty sure. She was not happy.

Chapter 4

ELIZABETH HARGROVE WAS NOT HAPPY AT ALL.

"Hargrove's oak grove," she sang out. "Home's where the heart is." But her heart was not there.

She had been looking forward to seeing Harry again. Her happiest times had been spent with him. With him, she could sometimes forget all the bad things. But now it was spoiled. The bruises on Harry's face had spoiled it, the knowledge that this was more of the same old trouble. Even the gawky cowhand hunched in the seat beside her spoiled it.

It's Papa's fault, she told herself. Papa's. Like with Roy. It's always him. She held to that thought. She didn't want to examine her suspicion that Harry's beating had something to do with *her*.

Being rich was easier for her than for Harry. He was older, but she was the one who remembered the slights and taunts and closed doors that had faced the children of a man who shot people from ambush. Now their papa was an important man. People didn't forget what he really was, but they silenced their whispers. They bowed to him to get a loan, sell a car, make a deal. No matter what Elizabeth did to outrage the people of Emilia—and she did everything she could think of—they silenced their whispers and bowed to her—and to her papa's money.

It would be different if Roy were here. She held to that thought, too. But Roy wasn't here. Roy was dead. Besides, she might have been just the same even if he'd lived. Maybe Roy was her excuse. Maybe she really was what the town called her.

And even with Roy, the town would still be there. She knew they hadn't forgotten her, any more than they'd forgotten Papa.

"Betty, watch out!"

She leaned on the hand brake. "I am watching out, Harry." For both of us, she added in her mind.

She was the one who'd inherited Papa's ability to shoot people. She hated the idea of being like him—Harry wasn't—but it was true. Harry adapted by looking at higher things, by finding good causes that needed Hargrove money. Harry would never seek revenge for having his head banged. He had all the nobility. She wondered if it had come from their mother, if he'd gotten all there was—while she had her father's brooding knack for holding a grudge.

Now Harry had picked up another stray puppy, this tall cowboy with the soft voice and the strange eyes and the baby face with the hardness behind it. She stole a look at him, wondering how much Hargrove money he would want, how deeply he would bow for it, how soon he'd see them for what they were.

"You're all so cute when you're puppies," she shouted to him.

"What?"

I could do it, she thought. I could shoot Frank Loman and leave him lying until someone scooped him up with the trash! And then I could sob and shake and tell in court how terrified I was when I saw Papa kill him. That would be the funny part, the real justice: if they hanged him for taking his son's part—something he'd never do, still less for his daughter. *And I could do it all.*

"Betty!"

She swung her head back in time to see the house looming in the windshield. Home again, home again, jiggety-jig. She remembered a woman's voice singing to her in darkness, singing that rhyme. Her mother's? Why couldn't she remember more about her mother? Why didn't she know what had really happened?

Elizabeth slid the Reo to a stop with its radiator an inch short of the green iron hitching post.

"Home again, home again," she cried.

The Reo slid to a halt with its radiator looking down at a green iron hitching post. Temple wondered if Elizabeth or Harry felt the same urge he did to tie the car's reins to the post. Before he could ask, they were out of the auto and up on the porch. Elizabeth threw the stub of her cigarette into the untended flower bed.

"Come on, cow puppy," she said. "See what life's like among the rich."

"Betty, behave."

"Harry, hush."

Temple climbed out of the car, relieved to be on solid ground again, and followed them the few yards to the porch. From that vantage he could see a half circle of rocky ground, more like a natural clearing than a yard. Cows grazed along the boundary. Beyond it the dark shadows of the trees circled the house like the palisade of a fort.

The porch itself seemed the most solid part of the house. Eight feet wide, it ran the full width of the front and turned each corner. Square wooden pillars rose from brick columns every ten or twelve feet to support the roof. Close up, everything about it was level and plumb. Temple couldn't account for his earlier idea that it had looked unfinished, half built. He wondered again why no one had ever bothered to paint the house.

"Looks like dear Papa's not home right now," Elizabeth said. "His auto's not in the drive, and we haven't been attacked by that beast of a damned dog he keeps. You'll have to wait for his greeting to the Prodigal Son."

"Someone's home. There's Laurel Jean."

A woman had come out onto the porch, peering toward the car. Laurel Jean was five feet tall, probably two feet wide. Her brown face was unlined, though her hair shone silvergray in the light from the doorway. She wore a dress that might have been fashionable at the turn of the century. Below its sweeping skirt she wore long, wide, men's shoes that turned up at the toes.

"Elizabeth Hargrove, the very idea," she scolded even before she reached the edge of the porch. "And you're smoking, too. I just don't know about you children. Who's that with you? You know your papa doesn't—" She broke off, frowning. "Harry? Good lands, Harry!"

Harry bounded across the porch. Laurel Jean caught him in a hug, then immediately pulled back to arm's length.

"Harry, good lands. When you finally do come home, you look like some roustabout. What have you been doing?"

"Rolling in oil, Laurel Jean. Celebrating where our money comes from."

"Good lands—" She stopped and raised a plump hand to the bruise on his face. "That's not all," she said in a completely different voice. "Harry, are you all right?"

"Just fine, Laurel Jean. Nothing to worry about." He waved a hand toward Temple. "I've brought a guest for dinner. He'll be spending the night, too."

Temple took off his hat. "Ma'am," he said.

She gave him a close, searching look. "Don't 'ma'am' me, young man. I'll fix up the upstairs bedroom, soon's I'm done with supper. And your room for you, Harry."

"Don't go to any trouble, Laurel Jean," Harry said. "I'll only be staying the night. After that, I intend to get lodgings in town."

"Good lands," Laurel Jean murmured. She made a shooing motion at them. "You boys get out to the wash house and scrub off that oil. And give me those clothes—good lands, I'll never get them clean. And be quick about it, you know how your papa hates to wait supper."

"I know," Harry murmured. Then he laughed and aimed

31

a swat at Laurel Jean's skirts as she turned away. "Come on, Lee, we've got our orders."

Elizabeth said, "Since I wasn't invited to join your party, I'd better do something womanly. I'll help Laurel Jean with supper." She gave Temple a pouting smile. "Unless you need help washing your back, Cowboy."

"Betty, behave."

"Harry, hush."

Temple got his saddlebags from the car. Harry guided him around the corner and along the wide porch toward the back of the house. At the very highest point of the hill, a windmill stood, its vanes turning with a slow metallic groan in the light breeze. Beside it, a boarded-in tower supported a wooden water tank.

"Does—" Temple hesitated over the name, then settled for the one Harry had used. "Does Betty cook, then?"

He didn't like it. It didn't fit her. Whatever she was, she wasn't a Betty. She'd called herself Elizabeth. Loman had called her Liz. *A whore gets paid, but Liz gives it away for free.* He no longer doubted this was the sister Loman had meant.

"No," Harry was saying. "I'm not altogether a coward and Betty's not altogether lazy. But she doesn't cook. Laurel Jean does our cooking, laundry, cleaning. Keeps us about half civilized." He unfastened a rough slatted door in the tower, then paused for a second, looking at Temple. "Listen, about what Loman said—"

Temple wondered if all his thoughts were that easy to read. "I didn't pay him much attention," he said. "I was asleep right up until you two started knocking each other around."

"It was him doing most of the knocking, I'm afraid." Harry waggled his jaw carefully and winced. "But I did hit him first. It was what he said about—"

"Ought to be careful, letting somebody that big hooraw you into a fight."

You ought to listen to your own advice, Temple told himself. His mother had warned him often enough. *Your father's temper. You'll end up just like him one day.*

"I didn't mean to let him make me fight. But—"

"You might have had real trouble with him. If you're going to tackle people that big, you need to learn more about fighting."

"Yeah." Harry rubbed his jaw and smiled. "Or maybe I should carry a Winchester or an ax. Come on, let's get cleaned up."

Inside, it was almost dark, the cracks between the boards admitting only the faintest gleam of evening light. Harry found a lantern and lighted it. The single room was square and tall, tapering up to the underside of the platform that held the water tank. A tangle of boarded-in piping came from the bottom of the tank down to the concrete floor, where the pipes separated to run out in different directions. A rough stand in the middle of the room held a cast-iron sink, big enough to use as a bathtub, with a brass hydrant jutting out over it.

"Here you go. Nothing but cold water, I'm afraid, but there ought to be some soap around."

Temple found a bar of soft, strong lye and began soaping his hands and face. Then he laughed and pulled off the oil-stained shirt, extending his scrubbing to his back and chest. Harry had stripped to his union suit.

"Do you need another shirt?" Harry asked. "You're too stringy for mine, but one of Papa's would probably do."

"Got my own in my saddlebags. Doesn't look like the oil got into them." Temple unstrapped the bag and found his one clean shirt and a fresh pair of jeans. "That oil blowing out—does that sort of thing happen very often?"

Harry grinned at him. "You don't know much about a boomtown, do you? Happens all the time, though that was the first time I've seen it by the railroad track. Downtown and in the cotton fields and the creek bottoms and even the cemetery, but not by the railroad."

Temple looked at him. "The cemetery?"

Somewhere outside, a dog began barking in a deep-chested, threatening tone.

"Papa must be home. Supper in a minute." Harry finished drying himself on the rough towel and began to dress. "Is this Wednesday?"

"Yes. Listen—"

"We'll have chicken, then. I'm sorry I promised you steak. What we'll have is chicken. Potatoes, probably peas. Laurel Jean is completely predictable. Let's get inside."

"Listen, you were joking about the cemetery, weren't you?"

Harry opened the door, waited for Temple to go through. "You'll learn."

Chapter 5

THEY WERE STANDING AT THE TABLE WHEN COTTON HARGROVE came heavily down the stairs. Wherever Harry and Elizabeth had gotten their slenderness, it wasn't from him. He was wide and solid as a Percheron. The glass in his hand reminded Temple of a thimble caught in the limbs of a tree. He lumbered out of the hall into the dining room, stopped like a bull at a new gate, and stared at Harry and Temple. Then he drank off the last inch of whiskey in his glass and set it on the table.

"So." He ignored Temple and Elizabeth, looking at Harry. "I thought you were gone for good."

Harry smiled. "I've been hearing that a lot, lately," he said. "It's good to see you, too, Father."

"Yes. I *am* glad you're here. I could've used you sooner, especially if you've gotten all that nonsense about writing out of your head."

Harry shook his head cheerfully. "I haven't. And that's not why I came back."

"Then why did you come back?"

"I heard about—" Harry glanced at Elizabeth. "—about the accident at the rig."

"Terrible thing." Cotton shook his head. "Wrecked the drilling rig and cost us a month's work to get the well killed and plugged. Cost a fortune, too."

Elizabeth's laugh rang like a bell. "Yes," she said. "That's the important thing, isn't it? The money."

"You'd think so, missy, if you didn't have it to spend. Where did you get—"

"Father, this is Lee Temple," Harry interrupted.

Cotton Hargrove turned a glare on Harry, then aimed it at Temple. "I don't—" he began, but decided not to finish. He looked hard at Temple, frowning. "Temple, you say." He held out a big hand to his guest. "Damn glad to know you, Temple."

Hargrove's powerful grip almost pulled Temple off balance. He nodded and returned the pressure with all he had. It was barely enough for self-protection. Apparently the big man decided not to break his hand. Hargrove let go.

"Well, let's eat. Laurel Jean, damn it," he said.

Laurel Jean came through the kitchen door carrying a platter. "Here it is," she answered as if she had been waiting for his odd summons. Temple was struck at once by the flat, lifeless quality of her voice, quite different from the way she'd addressed Elizabeth and Harry.

Harry winked at Temple. Supper was a big baked chicken, steaming green peas, scalloped potatoes covered with a layer of bubbling cheese. Laurel Jean placed each dish on the table to some formula of her own. Last, she set the platter holding the golden chicken in front of Cotton Hargrove's place. After a moment she returned with a big pitcher of tea, poured their glasses full. "And you?" she asked of Hargrove.

"Hell, no. You know what to put in my glass."

"It's dinnertime," she said. "You have company."

Hargrove paused, holding a big two-pronged fork and a glistening carving knife suspended over the chicken while he stared into Laurel Jean's wrinkled face. His eyes narrowed. He pointed at the woman with his fork.

"Laurel Jean, damn it."

She disappeared into the kitchen again, came out with a labeled bottle of whiskey, set it beside Hargrove's glass. Her back stiff with disapproval, she shuffled back to the kitchen and closed the door behind her.

"Temple, how about some chicken?" Hargrove sliced the bird with as much speed and enthusiasm as if it had been an enemy, put a big section on Temple's plate. "I knew a Temple once. You the one that walked on Harry's face?"

"No, sir."

"Of course he's not, Father," Harry said, holding out his own plate.

Elizabeth smiled over her serving of chicken. Her eyes glittered as she said, "Buffalo Loman did that. The cowboy walked on Loman's face."

The big man studied Temple with renewed interest. "So you're the one. Never can tell." He shook his head like a Percheron troubled by flies. "Loman. Damn him. That man just doesn't want to get along. I can't understand it."

"No. You make it so easy for people to get along."

Cotton Hargrove looked at his daughter as if he wished he didn't know her. "Eliza."

"Yes, Papa." Elizabeth looked at him as if she had more than once asked him not to call her Eliza.

He looked at her as if he had more than once asked her not to call him Papa. "Where the hell'd you get that green car?"

"At the getting place."

He pointed at her with the carving knife. "Where's the yellow one?"

"Franklin Corner mudhole."

Harry said, "Looked like it had a broken axle."

Hargrove ignored that. "You hadn't had that yellow car two months. There's not enough money in this whole county to keep you in cars!"

She made a face at him. "I thought we had most of the money in the whole county. That's the only reason people here will have anything to do with us, the money."

"Listen—"

"Anyway, I traded them the yellow one. How much difference could it cost after just two months?"

"You'll take that Reo back to Randolph at dawn tomorrow morning."

"That'll be hard to do—"

"You'll do it or I'll—"

"—since they don't open until eight o'clock."

"—I'll put you out of this house!"

Elizabeth laughed. "Well, I guess I can find somewhere to go," she said with a slow smile. "Of course, it might not be somewhere you'd approve of for the daughter of an important man like Cotton Hargrove."

"Listen," Harry said. His face had darkened with embarrassment. "I'll get it straightened out in the morning."

"I want her to straighten it out. She's the one that got it crooked."

"Papa."

"I don't want to say it again."

Harry dipped himself some potatoes. "Dad, didn't you offer me a car once?"

"You know damn well I did. I've offered you everything a father could offer a son."

Elizabeth laughed.

"And you've thumbed your nose at me every time I've tried. You know you have."

"I know I have. But now I've changed my mind."

Elizabeth took the bowl of potatoes from Harry.

"What? All of a sudden, after all this time, you'll take something from that dirty oil money?"

Elizabeth passed the potatoes to Temple. He thanked her, served his plate, offered the bowl to Hargrove. Hargrove scraped half the potatoes onto his plate and put the bowl down beside the chicken.

"I want a *green* car," Harry said, "and I want some chicken."

Hargrove snorted. "So that's your idea, is it? Ha-ha-hee. To let your sister have her cake! Ho-me!"

Temple watched Hargrove's face purple into heavy laughter.

"All right," the father said. "Ha! Good enough for me. You children! Here, you, Harry, carve this damn chicken." He shoved the platter toward Harry. Then he poured himself a fresh inch of whiskey.

Harry finished carving the chicken, naming each piece in his own way as he served it to his tablemates. Elizabeth passed the peas.

After dinner, they took chairs out onto the porch. The sun was gone, the woods dark all around them, the June night clear and cool. Stars arched overhead—almost as many, Temple thought, as on the New Mexico range. He thought of Amy, her hair down, her face turned to him in the starlight. Rising abruptly, he turned his back on the sky and the night, staring at the lighted doorway of the Hargrove home.

"Mr. Hargrove, you mentioned knowing another Temple. Where was that?"

"None of that 'Mr. Hargrove' business. Call me Cotton." Hargrove tipped his chair back. "Temple. El Paso, oh, pretty near thirty years ago. Tall, rangy, yellow-haired kid, kind of like you. Matthew Temple."

The big man's face was mostly hidden by shadows. To Temple, it seemed he wore a queer half smile.

"Know him?"

A moment passed before Temple could answer. When he did, his voice sounded strange to him. "That was my father's name."

"You don't say!" Hargrove smiled, tipped his chair forward again, jabbed a finger at Temple. "Well, it's a small world! I've often thought about him. Where is old Matt now?"

"He's dead," Temple said. "He—died—back when I was just a kid. I—"

Laurel Jean brought coffee and sliced cake on a platter with cups and small plates. "Here," she said.

Cotton said, "Laurel Jean, damn it, that looks almost good."

The woman looked at him with clear suspicion. "Oh?"

"It does."

"Good lands."

She turned and went back inside. Temple took a breath, trying to phrase a question to ask Hargrove. Before he could manage it, the big rancher turned and leveled a finger at Harry.

"Loman," Cotton Hargrove said. "Loman. Tell me about that business on the train. How did he know to look for you there?"

Harry shrugged. "Pure bad luck, as nearly as I can tell. I caught a freight out of Dallas, found a carload of boomers coming this way. I guess Loman and his men got on at Mineral Wells. They were bringing back a load of drill pipe, keeping an eye on it, but they didn't move to my car until . . ." He looked to Temple. "Where, Lee?"

"I got on the train in the Fort Worth stockyards. Changed to your car in Thurber. That must be when Loman moved there, too."

"Lucky for me, wherever it was," Harry said. "Anyway, Loman must have been drinking. He got louder and louder, trying to push me into a fight. Then——"

"Talking about us, was he?" Hargrove interrupted. "What kind of things did he say?"

"Only what everybody knows."

"What does everybody know?"

"That I'm a coward."

"You are not!" Elizabeth cried.

Hargrove only grunted. "What else?"

Harry lifted his eyes and looked straight into his father's face. "That you're a back-shooting son of a bitch," he said.

"Yeah? What else?"

"Nothing else." Harry hung his head, looked at the warped flooring of the porch. "Wasn't that enough?"

"Enough to make you fight? Not likely." He shifted to aim his words toward Elizabeth. "I just thought your little sister might want to know how near she came to getting you killed."

"Father——"

Elizabeth was on her feet. "What? Harry, you didn't tell me that." She turned to Cotton Hargrove. "Someone's told you about it. One of your spies. Was it about me? What did Loman say about me?"

"Only what everybody knows."

"What does everybody know?"

"That you behave like a cheap whore. That you're a disgrace to this family."

In the dim light, Elizabeth's face went pale. "Disgrace? To *this* family?" She laughed, the sound hard and clear as diamond. "I thought I was a chip off the old block. Haven't you always said our mother—"

Hargrove was quick for his size. His slap cracked like a pistol shot against the side of her face, snapping her head to one side. Elizabeth put her hand to her cheek but otherwise stood motionless, silent.

Temple came out of his chair, but Harry was already past him. He shoved the older man, forcing him back a step with furious strength.

"If you ever touch her again, I'll kill you."

The big man's arms shot out in a driving two-handed blow that reminded Temple of Loman's rush. His forearms smashed into Harry's chest and hurled him backward against the wall of the house. The porch seemed to tremble from the impact.

"Coward?" Hargrove barked a laugh. There was a kind of pride in his voice. "No, I guess not. Not you."

Harry straightened, started to step toward Hargrove. But Elizabeth shot between them, her arms straight at her sides, her fists clenched. Her face pale and cold, she stared up into her father's eyes.

"If you ever touch him again, I'll kill you."

Hargrove looked from one of them to the other. After a moment his face darkened—not with fury, as Temple first thought, but with his heavy laughter.

"Ha! Ha-ha-hee! Just like you've always been! Stick up for one another, right or wrong. But as long as you're in this house—"

"That won't be a problem," Harry said. "I'll live in the little house in town."

"That two-room shack?" Cotton Hargrove stared at him a moment, then nodded abruptly. "Good enough." He resumed his seat as though nothing had happened and poured himself a new ounce of whiskey. "You, Temple—Lee, is it? I understand you're looking for work."

"That's right."

"I might have something for you."

Right then Temple would rather have worked naked in a den of rattlesnakes. But Hargrove had known his father. Maybe the big man could tell him what kind of a man Matthew Temple really was, what he'd been like, what kind of thing inside him had led him to the end of a rope.

You're just like your father. If you're not careful, one day you'll end up the way he did.

"I'm obliged to you," Temple began. Then he caught Harry's quick look of warning. Harry shook his head emphatically.

Temple hesitated a second, then said, "I'm obliged to you, but I think I'll look around a little first."

"Suit yourself," Cotton Hargrove said. He hunted in his pockets until he found a white business card. "At least you'll let me put you on to a fellow who might could use you. Name of Brace Bremerton. Ask around town about him if you want to. He'll play you fair."

"Well—"

"I couldn't do any less. Wouldn't be right." He scribbled on the back of the card and handed it to Temple. "There go. Better have a sip of whiskey with that cake."

"No, thank you."

Hargrove looked at his guest with an edge of suspicion. Then he took out his watch, turned it to the light, put it back in his pocket. "Make yourself at home here," he said to Temple. He finished his cake in one bite, strode to the front door, reached inside and brought out a short, heavy rifle. With it in one hand and his bottle in the other, he went down the steps and off to his right.

After a moment Temple heard an engine backfire and catch. Almost immediately Hargrove came around the house at the wheel of a long Pierce Arrow touring car. The car's top was folded back, its headlamps blazing. The glowing coal of Hargrove's cigar flamed like a small running light. He drove the way his daughter drove, gunning the engine and clashing the gears. Obviously he had taught her to drive.

At first Temple thought there was a second person in the front seat with Hargrove. Then he realized the dark figure was a huge black dog, its heavy shoulders almost as wide as a man's. As the car roared past Temple, the dog swung a blunt-muzzled head his way and gave a deep bark of warning. Then auto and man and dog were past, leaving behind a fine film of dust in the red glow of a tail lamp. Temple had to wonder where his host was going and why he carried a rifle.

"He carries it everywhere," Harry explained.

"Even to church," Elizabeth said. She laughed with new enthusiasm. "He doesn't darken the door without it!"

Harry smiled. "Papa doesn't darken that particular door often. Just when he wants to remind people how important we Hargroves are. At least that's how it's been since Mother—"

"Since Mother died," said Elizabeth in a different voice.

She turned to stare into the dark woods. Temple thought she was looking much farther into them than he could see. He turned his own eyes in that direction, expecting perhaps a small private cemetery. All he saw was the darkness of woods at night.

Harry said, "You look as tired as a man that puts buffaloes off trains. I'll show you your room when you're ready to turn in."

"I'll show him."

Temple would rather have spent the night in that same den of rattlesnakes. "I couldn't. Thanks all the same."

Harry said, "You didn't think you could eat dinner, either, until I showed you how. You'll be able to do this, too."

"Harry helped you with dinner. I'll help you spend the night," Elizabeth said.

"Betty—"

42

"Anyway, all the respectable folks are in bed by now. There's nothing open except the Line." She pouted a smile. "I could take you there. Ever seen Sodom and Gomorrah, Cowboy?"

"Can't say I have—though I thought Fort Worth came pretty close."

"If you won't have it any other way, I'll run you to town in a little while," Elizabeth said. "I can show you how to have a good time on the Line."

"Betty. Behave." Harry meant it this time. Temple heard it in his voice, saw it in his eyes, those eyes that blazed at Betty and fell harshly on the guest as well.

"Harry, hush!" Her eyes blazed back.

Harry said, "Listen, Lee, I guess we haven't been very good hosts here, but stay here with us tonight. I'll take you into town first thing in the morning and help you get settled."

Temple looked at it. He was down to his last nickel and his last pair of jeans—the others were in Laurel Jean's wash basket. Rattlesnakes or no, he wasn't going to get any better offers tonight. And the idea of repeating the drive to town in the dark was too much to face. No, there were good reasons he had to stay. The idea of sleeping under the same roof with Elizabeth Hargrove had nothing to do with his decision.

"All right," he said. "I thank you."

Harry smiled, finally, and waved that away. "No need," he said. "You've more than paid your way."

The three young people ate their cake. Elizabeth had coffee with hers. Then she lit another factory-rolled cigarette.

Temple got a wisp of her smoke on the breeze. It reminded him of his father, of Amy Forrest, who did not smoke. One whole problem was that everything reminded him of Amy Forrest with long dark hair framing her face, of Amy with her bright blue eyes, of Amy with her perfect white cheeks— for Christ's sake!

"What?"

They were looking at him. "Cake," Temple said.

Elizabeth was staring at him.

He tried to make her believe it. "Nice cake."

"Would you care for another piece?"

"No. No, I just meant that it was very good. Very good cake."

Temple did not sleep as well as a man who had been putting buffaloes off trains should have slept. He had not been in bed ten minutes when he heard Elizabeth start her car, wind the new engine up to a fever, and roar away in a shower of dirt and gravel. He thought he could smell her cigarette for a good long time after she was gone.

Chapter 6

"WORST FARMLAND IN TEXAS, AND THAT'S GOING SOME," HARRY said. "Too dry for cattle. There's almost enough vegetation to run goats on. Or there was, before the boom."

"And all of it belongs to Papa," Elizabeth added. "Every single rock and rattlesnake and badger hole, and don't you forget it."

Temple and Harry and Elizabeth stood on the lower edge of Hargrove's oak grove, looking down on the broken and rocky bluffs above Emilia. Left to itself, the Reo panted softly behind them, quivering now and then like a nervous cow pony. During the wild ride of the evening before, Temple hadn't taken much notice of the countryside. Now he silently agreed with Harry's assessment.

The bluffs seemed dry and lifeless. Massive gray-white teeth of limestone thrust up here and there through the flinty soil. Whatever the grazing had once been like, the ground was now barren except for a few hardy cedars and a straggling colony of mesquites growing back from their roots. Everything else had been bladed down to naked red dirt to make room for a forest of weatherbeaten wooden derricks. Steam engines chuffed and churned steadily. Heavy wooden walking beams rose and fell like the waves of the sea.

Crowded right to the edge of the bluff by a low earthen dike, a battery of three big redwood storage tanks loomed against the sky. Temple could see that the side of the tanks facing town had been scraped clean and carefully whitewashed. Huge letters, black against the white, read HARGROVE OIL. Close by them, a yellow flare of burning gas trailed like a flag from an upright iron pipe.

"They drilled more wells while you were gone, Harry," Elizabeth said. "I think there's thirty-four now. All Papa's." She slanted her head to look at Temple. "Envious, Cowboy?"

"No," Temple said without thinking about it. Half against his will, he'd been comparing the land with the rolling high plains of the Maxwell grant, belly deep in grass, with the blue bulk of the Sangre de Cristos hanging like a dream on the western horizon. He'd not seen anything in Texas to match that. "A man likes his own place best, I guess."

Elizabeth gave an odd little laugh. She looked tired. Beneath its careful makeup, her face seemed a shade paler than Temple remembered. He didn't know what time she'd come home, nor if she'd slept, but she'd been early at breakfast in the kitchen of the big house.

"Not the land," she said. "Those wells. They used to flow by themselves. Now they're mostly pumping. They pump about a thousand dollars a minute, I guess."

Temple looked at the ugly, angular derricks. She couldn't mean that, he thought. She's ragging me again. "That's a lot of money," he said.

"Not as much as Papa wants, but enough. Enough to make the good people in Emilia treat us poor white trash like we're aristocrats. Would you like to be an aristocrat, Cowboy?"

Temple shook his head. "Never tried it." He'd never

worried much about money, not even when he was planning to marry Amy. It hadn't seemed important. But then, he'd never seen money that flowed as freely as Elizabeth was hinting. "I doubt it would agree with me."

"Maybe you can try it. I'll bet you'd like a sample." She gave him a sidelong smile. "Of the money, I mean."

"Betty," Harry said. "Behave. What's wrong with you?"

"Me? Nothing. Just trying to make our guest feel comfortable."

"Betty, you weren't like this when I left. The accident—"

She laughed. "A lot of things weren't like this when you left. But don't think the town's forgotten you, either. Your face proves that."

"That wasn't the town. It was Loman."

"Same thing," she insisted. "You think it doesn't matter. But it does. The money's the only reason they tolerate us. If you think Harriet Jergin—"

"Betty," Harry said again. His voice held more anger than Temple had heard there before.

"I'm sorry, Harry," Elizabeth said at once. She shook her head. It must have hurt, because she put her hand to her forehead and brushed at her hair. "I can't help it."

"Yes, you can. You're hurting yourself, not the town."

"The money hurts them. Us having it. I like to rub their sanctimonious noses in it. And spending it hurts—"

"Only you. The way you spend it. It's bad for you."

Temple shifted his feet. Turning so that his back was partly to the two of them, he gazed down the slope. They seemed to have forgotten him. Then Elizabeth laughed.

"Yes, your way's better. Pretend the money doesn't exist. I can see that from your face—what the Buffalo left of it." She swung quickly away toward the car. "Come along, Cowboy. Since you're too good to work for the Hargroves—"

"I didn't mean—"

"—we have to get you into town—"

"Betty, behave."

"—anything like that."

"—so you can find a respectable job."

Elizabeth slipped into the Reo's low seat and raced the motor.

"Get in, damn it!" she cried. She banged her hand on the steering wheel. "Come on! Harry, you should drive. Now that you've got yourself a car, you'll have to learn to drive!"

"It wouldn't hurt *you* to take a lesson or two," Temple muttered as the car spun away. But no one heard him. He clung to the dash with one hand and held his hat with the other. Still, he had to grin at the adventure. It reminded him of his first time on the back of an unbroken horse, except that he'd had some control over the bronc.

The Reo whipped past the wooden tanks, then heeled over at an alarming angle as Elizabeth jockeyed it onto a narrow road down the face of the bluff. Below them, Temple saw Emilia spread out like a map. He leaned across to study the town as best he could from his swaying perch.

"Old Emilia and Oiltown pretty much run together," Harry shouted in his ear. "You'll see the difference when we get down. That along the creek is Ragtown—tents for the folks that can't find a place in town."

Near the patchwork of tents and lean-to shelters, Temple noticed another cluster of buildings, mixed with still more tents.

"What's that?"

It was Elizabeth who answered. "That's the Line." She took her eyes off the road and grinned at Temple. "Sodom and Gomorrah, Cowboy. You'll see."

"Betty! Watch where you're going."

Elizabeth zoomed past a lumbering motortruck that was just starting to climb the hill, then took the right-hand turn at the foot of the bluffs. She had to slow down almost at once. Traffic of all kinds jammed the road into Emilia. Autos, trucks, horses, and wagons all fought for space, the press growing heavier as the Reo crept into town. Parked vehicles narrowed the broad main street to a single lane each way. Pedestrians crowded the wooden sidewalks. Through shouted commands, shouts, and the blare of horns and the rattle of auto klaxons, Temple caught occasional snatches of music. He thought he'd never seen so many people, even in Fort Worth.

"Something special going on?" he shouted to Harry over the racket.

"Just another day. A year ago it was really busy. Wait till you see Oiltown."

The older part of Emilia was built of fieldstone and brick, with tall, roomy stores around the courthouse square. Side streets paved with brick rose gently to residential blocks shaded by oaks and pecan trees. A brick building with a tall tower, a school or church, stood sentinel on a low hill among the old houses. Above everything three big wooden tanks said HARGROVE OIL.

Except for the frantic activity, Emilia looked like a dozen ranching towns Temple had seen. Halfway along the main street, things changed. The brick paving ended abruptly in a sharp drop-off. The Reo bounced across it and seemed to enter another world—or at least another town.

On both sides of the rutted, muddy street, ramshackle, unpainted board structures jammed shoulder to shoulder without side streets or alleys. Everything seemed to be built around the tall derricks, some of them so close together their legs overlapped, the areas beneath them filled with tangles of rusty piping. Garish signs advertised three cafés, a barbershop, rooming houses, a land office, and what seemed a dozen different sellers of oil field supplies. As they passed one of the largest, Temple saw a familiar name.

"'Buffalo Tool Company,'" he read aloud. "'Frank Loman, General Manager.' Is that your friend from the train?"

"Big as life," Harry said.

"And twice as ugly," Elizabeth sang out. She leaned on the horn and edged past a huge, lumbering steam-powered ditch digger that almost blocked the street. "Want to stop and say hello, Cowboy?"

"Not just now," Temple said, but he turned in his seat, looking back at the building until a turn hid it again.

Harry directed the car up a narrow, muddy track, past

rows of clapboard bunkhouses with outside privies. Finally, he pointed to a raw-wood new building with a silly, flat roof and hinged side panels all the way around. A few of the panels were propped up with bowed boards to let in the morning breeze, but most were down and shut for privacy or protection from the insects. An unevenly painted sign proclaimed Irma Watson's Bed and Board. Elizabeth stopped so close to the front wall that the raised breeze panel would have crushed the hood if it had fallen.

"Here we are," Harry said to Temple. "Come on, I'll introduce you to the proprietor."

Harry Hargrove rapped smartly on the sagging screen door, then went in without waiting for an answer. Temple trailed behind him with Elizabeth bringing up the rear. Inside was a long, dimly lighted hallway. A door opened at the end of the hall, and a woman who might have been fifty or seventy peered out at them. After a moment she came out, wiping her hands on a checkered apron.

"Who's that? Young Harry Hargrove, is that you?"

Harry grinned. "That's right," he said, "and this is my friend, Lee Temple. Lee's looking for a job and a bed."

She peered at Temple over the top of rimless glasses. "No drinking in the house. No fighting." She looked past him at Elizabeth and sniffed. "No women. Dollar a day, that's for two meals plus I'll pack you a lunch. Week's deposit in advance."

Temple hesitated. A dollar a day was about the wages he'd been making in New Mexico. The seven-dollar deposit might as well have been ten thousand. He started to shake his head, but Harry cut in briskly.

"He'll take it. Put the deposit on our account."

The landlady nodded. She looked at Temple. "You'll be sharing the room. I can put you in with the Ballard brothers and Mad Dog Jack."

Behind them Elizabeth giggled. Harry shook his head.

"I don't know about that. He'd rather have a room to himself."

Widow Watson laughed widely enough to expose two hinged pink horseshoe plates of false teeth. "Everybody'd rather have a room to hisself, but there ain't any. He can choose his choice between bunking with Jack and the Ballards or getting a cot down in Ragtown along the creek. Myself, I don't know of another bed in town." She frowned and adjusted her glasses, peering at Temple. "Mr. Church, do you talk for yourself, ever?"

"Sometimes," Temple said. "The name's Temple, ma'am. And I'm accustomed to sharing a bunkhouse."

"There, young Hargrove, he talks pretty good on his own." She glanced back over her shoulder. "I've got to fix dinner. Room's the third door on your left down the hall. Bath's at the end. Bring in your gear whenever you like, but be quiet about it. There's people sleeping."

Temple slapped the saddlebags. "This is it."

"What is?"

"I was once in a courtroom without being asked this many questions."

"They find you guilty?" She didn't wait for an answer. "When you're done, there's still some breakfast. Young Harry, you and Miss Hargrove are welcome, too."

"I guess we'll pass on the breakfast, Lee," Harry said. "Want me to come along with you to see Bremerton?"

"Thanks, but no. I'll do that for myself."

"I have some shopping to do, Harry," Elizabeth said. "Can you keep busy?" She gave him a teasing grin. "Maybe you could find something to do at the library." To Temple she whispered, "Harry's quite a reader."

"Betty, behave."

"I'll be at Mayfair's. I've been looking at a new dress there."

"I wish you wouldn't go into the Oiltown stores, Betty. Most of Alice's customers are girls from the Line."

"That's why I like it."

Giving up on her, Harry turned to Temple and held out a hand. "Lee, good luck."

"Thanks," Temple said. "I'll pay back that advance as soon as I make a payday."

"I probably won't sleep a wink worrying about that. So long."

"So long, Harry, Miss Hargrove."

"So long, Mister Temple." She laughed at him. "Don't be a stranger."

The day had started out badly for Frank Loman. He'd awakened with both his head and his pride aching from the blow he'd taken the day before. Neither his breakfast coffee nor the short shot of rye he'd taken when he'd reached the office had helped. The rye helped less and less, he thought. No matter how much he drank, the liquor never seemed to reach the place in his soul that he wanted to deaden. And yesterday it had almost caused him to make a serious mistake.

"Buff?"

Clancy, his clerk, stood uncertainly in the office doorway. Loman looked up from the papers on the desk to glower at him.

"Don't call me that. What do you want?"

"Somebody to see you."

"Who?"

Clancy moistened his lips with the tip of his tongue. "Says his name's Temple," he said. "Dressed like—well, like a cowhand or something."

Loman shoved himself upright. The news that he'd been whipped had spread quickly, so much so that one of the hands had started the day by sassing him. Loman had knocked the man flat, then fired him. That should have shown people he didn't mean to take any ragging about it, even from Clancy.

Seeing the expression on his face, Clancy put both hands out quickly. "No, really, Bu—Frank. He's at the counter. Billings saw him come into town with the Hargrove kid and that slut sister of his. He—"

Crossing the room in two long strides, Loman shoved Clancy aside and plowed down the narrow aisle between crowded shelves. A dozen people filled the store, ordering from the clerks and haggling over terms and credit, but Loman saw only one of them. There was the cowboy, holding that damned big hat in his hand and looking curiously at a heavy pipe wrench lying on the counter. Loman slapped his hands down on either side of the wrench and faced him.

"What the hell do you want?"

The cowboy raised his head slowly. He was as tall as Loman, but skinny. Thin enough to snap in two, Loman thought, but his memory of the vicious uppercut the cowboy had thrown made him wonder if that were true. The innocent blue eyes that faced Loman showed caution, but no fear.

"To tell you the truth, Mr. Loman, I was hoping we could settle our differences."

Loman slammed open the hinged countertop and stepped out in front of the cowboy, his big right fist clenched. He saw Clancy watching from back in the shelves. Sudden silence fell as clerks and customers stared at the two men.

"You want to finish the fight you started, is that what you're saying—what's your name—Templeton?"

"Temple. No, sir. I'm saying I'd like not to have to finish it." To Loman's surprise, he smiled a little. "I'm not sure I'd get that lucky ever again."

Loman scowled. The blood pounding through his temples hurt his head, but didn't interfere with his thinking. It never paid to make an enemy you didn't have to make. And it never paid to warn an enemy until you were ready to finish him. Loman had made that mistake once already. With an effort, he stepped back and opened his hand.

"Temple." He marked the name down in his mind. "You think you've proved you're the better man? Is that it?"

"Nope." The smile faded. "I don't think I proved a damn thing."

"Are you working for the Hargroves?"

"Nope."

"I see," Loman murmured. He glanced at the silent crowd. "Fact is, Temple, you did me a favor. I'd had a drink or two, and I got plumb carried away when that young pup sassed me. I don't mean him any harm—" *Yet,* he added in his mind. "—and I'm glad you stopped me before I did him any."

Temple didn't answer. Loman thought the expression in the blue eyes hardened a little, but that was all. Still not scared, Loman thought. Be careful with this one.

"What I'm saying is I'll spot you that one punch. And if there's anything I can do to help you along your way, why, you just say the word."

"That's the thing," Temple said. "I'm likely going to be staying awhile. I'm asking for a job with Mr. Bremerton."

"So." Loman rubbed his chin and looked at Temple. "Well, Brace is a good man. If he asks, tell him it's all right between us." He stepped toward Temple and put out his hand. "Shake on it?"

"Sure."

Temple accepted the handshake cautiously. Loman tested his grip, found it firm, eased off. He was the stronger. Maybe he really could break Temple in two. Later, if it suited him, maybe he'd try.

"Far as I'm concerned, that squares us," Loman said. "I'll stay out of your business so long as you stay out of mine."

Temple nodded and put his hat back on. "Thanks, Mr. Loman," he said. "I'll surely try to do that."

After the cowboy left, the silence hung on for a minute, then dissolved in a babble of talk. Loman stepped to the big front window and watched Temple down the street. Clancy moved up beside him.

"See that, Buff?" Clancy said loudly. "He purely backed down. He as good as admitted you're the better man."

"Yeah." Loman rubbed his jaw again. In a tone too low to carry past Clancy, he said, "Listen, pull Billings off whatever he's doing. Have him keep an eye on Temple. I want to know how he spends his time." He raised his voice again. "And you get back to work!"

He turned away and started back toward the office. The pain in his head had lessened, but it was time for another drink all the same.

Brace Bremerton was a short, compact terrier of a man with great bushy eyebrows and bushy hair flushing out dark in all directions to end in gray curls.

"A job," he said. He considered Temple from behind the barrier of an untidy oak desk. "Well. You look stout enough, and you're not drunk yet this morning. Two points in your favor. Ever been in jail?"

"Yes, sir. In Fort Worth."

"Why?"

"Fighting."

"Um." Bremerton scribbled something on his desk pad. "What else can you tell me?"

"I have this note from Mr. Hargrove," Temple said, laying it atop a stack of papers on the desk. "He's the one gave me your name."

"Hargrove?" Bremerton pounced on the note as if it were a bone. "Hargrove. You're Lee Temple?"

"Yes, sir."

"Temple. Glad to meet you." Bremerton rose and shook Temple's hand as a terrier might shake a rat. "You're the man made Buffalo Loman walk home last evening. News travels slow. Didn't hear about it until this morning. Have a seat. What can you do besides fight?"

Temple drew up a hard wooden chair. *Fighting. That's how it starts. Just like your pa.* "I want to make it plain I'm not a fighter," he said.

"Had an accident, did you, with Buffalo?"

"Pretty near. But I hope to live it down. I've just had a visit with Loman. Tried to straighten it out."

"Good for you. Where'd you break out?"

"Pardon?"

"Where have you worked before?"

"Up to this spring, I was with Mr. Forrest on the Spread M, over by Wagon Mound, for two years. Before that—"

Bremerton gave a shake of his bushy head. "Not that," he said. "A real job. In the oil field."

Temple looked down at the desk, then straightened. "None. I've been a cowhand, and that's about all. But I'll give you a day's work and I'm willing to learn."

"Weevil, huh?" The oilman cocked his head to one side. "Cowhand. Good with animals. Horses. Horses?"

"Been riding since I was three."

"But a weevil. Can't start you at a man's wages. Say a hundred until we see how you'll work out."

Temple didn't understand. "Well, I'm not sure," he said. "The rent down at Widow—"

"—Watson's," Bremerton said. "Three of her boarders work for me. All right. Hundred and a quarter a month, and that's top dollar. You ready to start?"

Temple had made forty a month and found on the ranch. Even figuring his rent, he'd have double that—and Bremerton didn't consider it a man's wage. He realized, suddenly, that real money was involved somewhere in this business.

"Right now," he said.

"Got any money? Of course you don't." Bremerton pointed out the window. "Go across to Mayfair's Mercantile. Tell Miss Alice I said outfit you and charge it to me. Miss Alice likes to outfit young men." Bremerton thought about smiling but the message didn't make it all the way down his nerves. "I'll hold a little out of your pay until it's settled."

"I appreciate it. What sort of work will I be doing?"

Bremerton was already back at his desk, putting on his glasses, attending to his own work. "Whatever kind you're told."

"Sounds just like ranching," Temple said. He went back onto the street and across to the mercantile.

Miss Alice was six feet tall and looked strong as any man. She wore a green eyeshade like a bank teller, a green gingham dress with ruffles, and high-top button shoes. A green tape measure was draped around her neck with its ends tucked in her waistband. "Cowboy," she said, evaluating Temple. "Brace Bremerton send you?"

"Yes, ma'am."

"Don't tip your hat. Take it off. Let me see it."

"It was new Thursday in Fort Worth."

"Wouldn't matter if it was still in the egg. You'll need a hat you can work in. Was this Stetson the right size?"

"Yes, ma'am."

"Step right around behind the screen. Take those boots off. What size were they when they were new? Well, you'll need work boots. Try this hat. What size's that shirt or don't you know? Take it off anyway." Miss Alice was already measuring Temple with her eyes. "Hold up those arms."

She pressed the metal tip of her tape to his spine and measured across his shoulder and down his arm to the wrist. Then she took him in a bear hug and looped the tape about his chest. "Arms up. Look at you, tall but not much big around, eh?"

"Ma'am?"

She dropped the loop of tape to his waist and snugged it up tight at his back. "You eat regular?"

"Usually. Not so much the past few days."

"One thing you can say for Brace, he'll see you get fed right. Take off those old pants."

"Ma'am?"

"You speak English, don't you? Take them off."

"No, ma'am."

"No what? You don't speak the language or you won't take them off?"

Temple made a gesture with his hands. "Joost in from Roosia," he said. "No speak much the—"

"Listen!" Miss Alice said. "Don't make me take those pants down for you."

He took off his pants and handed them to her. "That's as far as I go," he told her, "in any language."

She laughed. "You better tell me, then, what size's that underwear? And just wait right here while I get your new duds. Who's that at the door now? Wait here, Cowboy."

The big woman went around the screen and glared toward the front of her store. "Oh, good morning, miss," Temple heard her say. "Have you decided about that chemise?"

"No," her customer said. "Can I look at it again?"

Temple knew the voice and suspected it meant trouble. He searched for something to cover himself with.

"It is pretty," Elizabeth Hargrove said. "I think I want to try it on."

"Screen's taken," Alice said. "Give me a minute here, and then you can try it."

But the young woman went right on back toward the screen. "I'll try it now," she said. "I'm not modest."

"I can see that," Alice told her, "but I have reason to think the gentleman is. Better wait your turn."

Elizabeth peeked around the screen. She winked at Temple. "Why, it's only the cowboy," she said brightly. "He and I are like brother and sister. Lee, move over."

Temple lifted the screen, moved it, kept it between them as they turned.

To Alice, the girl said, "I don't know what's come over Mr. Temple. Why, just last night we slept—in the same house. And now he's treating me like a stranger."

She kept trying to step around the screen, and Temple kept turning with it. They circled like partners in some clumsy dance until she was behind it and he was standing on the front side, his bare back to the window. He heard Measuring Alice's muffled snort of laughter.

"Damn you," he told Elizabeth.

"I'll bet you say that to all the girls." Unconcerned, she raised her arms and whisked her yellow dress off over her head. She tossed it up so it draped over the top of the screen.

Miss Alice said, "I thought you were bashful, Cowboy! But now you're showing the whole world your backside. While you're here, try on these boots."

"Boots, hell. Give me my pants."

Elizabeth tossed a lacy slip up over the screen to fall across Temple's bare shoulder.

He began to pivot again. The nearly naked Elizabeth turned with the screen, facing him and grinning. He stumbled and had to put down his burden, angled now so both of them could be seen in profile from the store window. Miss Alice laughed again.

"You make a lovely couple, but I don't know as my business can stand this kind of advertising. If your daddy were to come by here right now, he'd kill us all!"

Temple didn't doubt that for a moment. He kept shuffling his feet and twisting the screen. Just as he got it straight

again and had himself hidden from the gaze of Miss Alice
and an interested little boy looking in the window, Elizabeth
slipped past the edge and got behind it with him.

"Well," Temple said, "I will just be damned."

Elizabeth smiled at him. "If you had doubts about that,
Oiltown's just the place to settle them," she said. She leaned
back and looked at him frankly. She let him look at her just
as frankly before she slipped the new chemise over her head
and slid it down to cover herself. Turning her back to
Temple, she said, "Lace me up, please?"

"I never saw one of these before. I don't know how to
fasten it."

The girl laughed, looking back at him through lowered
lashes. "You expect me to believe you've never helped a girl
dress, Cowboy? It's like helping her undress, only backward."

"Whatever you choose to believe—"

"Here," Miss Alice interrupted. "I'll do it. It'll beat
listening to you two fight."

"You can damn sure have my place," Temple said. "Just
hand me my pants."

Chapter 7

BRACE BREMERTON LOCKED THE BACK DOOR OF HIS OFFICE AND
looked carefully around. A wagon drawn by four shaggy
draft horses blocked off the alley to his left. Three men
struggled with an awkwardly shaped crate. Bremerton
watched for a moment, then turned right. He waded through
tall grass and weeds, past several other buildings, until he
came to steps leading up to a recessed door.

He stopped to wind his watch while he looked around him
again. A drunk snored against the wall of a store a little way
up the alley, and a steady stream of pedestrians passed its

mouth. In Emilia, somebody was always around, but no one seemed to be paying Bremerton any attention. He climbed the steps and tapped at the door. Inside, a dog barked with hoarse ferocity. Cotton Hargrove opened the door, ushered Bremerton in.

The dog gave Bremerton one more growl, then went to his chair, hopped up and sat on his haunches. Bremerton said, "I hired the cowboy."

"Good." Hargrove sat heavily behind his oak desk.

"Don't know why you wanted a weevil. Seems like a good boy. But there's hands with experience I could hire."

"It's not your affair."

"Hell. It's my company."

"Only the sign. The cash box is mine."

Brace Bremerton ran a quick hand through his bushy hair. "Yes, sir," he said. "Temple. Alice's got him right now. I'll put him in the yard with a weed sling until—"

"No. Put him with Ellis."

"Ellis. Ellis?" Bremerton raised bushy eyebrows. "You want Ellis in the field? With what we're paying him? He's worth more—"

"Put Temple and Ellis together. I know—" Hargrove cut off whatever he'd been about to say. "I saw something in Temple," he told Bremerton instead. "I want Ellis to report on how he's shaping up—and whether we can trust him."

"Your money."

"Damn straight, and don't you forget it."

Hargrove poured himself an inch of whiskey. The dog growled at Brace Bremerton.

Bremerton didn't like it. He didn't like the dog. He didn't like Hargrove. He regretted the day he'd let the big man buy into his company. The company was much richer now, but Bremerton enjoyed it less. He wondered if Hargrove had made some sign to tell the dog to growl.

"All right. Tommy'll do the job for us."

"I know he will. You get back on the job yourself."

"All right," Bremerton said. When he stood to leave, the dog hopped down and followed him, growling. All right, Bremerton said to himself. All right. Both you sons of bitches can growl at me to your hearts' content. But the day either one of you bites me is the day you die.

Lee Temple fumbled on the clumping, high-topped work boots Alice Mayfair assured him were right for his new job. He doubted it. His jeans and shirt were rolled in a tight bundle secured by his wide belt with the silver buckle. He now wore drab khaki trousers and shirt and a shapeless gray canvas hat. He was threading his boot laces through innumerable hooks and eyes when the shop door opened again. To his relief, the new customer was male.

"Well it is, certainly," the man was saying, though Temple could not tell to whom. "It is a fine day, indeed."

He looked to be in his mid-forties. His round face was flushed, and he gestured freely with long skinny arms. He was neither large nor tall, but he gave that impression because his legs were long for his height. He crossed the room with a grasshoppery stride and bowed to Alice Mayfair.

"Morning, Measuring Alice, how are you today? And this must be Temple, our latest sacrifice on the altar of petroleum!"

"I'm fine, Tommy. Sounds as though you are, too. I don't know about this gentleman. We got so busy, I didn't ask his name."

"Didn't ask his name, indeed. Names are fine things. But then names can become things to be forgot sometimes in the evening, eh, Alice? Now, Mr. Temple, I'm pleased to introduce you to Miss Alice Mayfair, loveliest of Emilia's Mayfairs."

"Lee Temple, ma'am," he said, then realized that the leggy man already knew his name.

Measuring Alice smiled at Temple. "Meet Talking Tommy," she said. "Anybody in town'll give you a twenty-dollar gold piece if you ever catch him with his mouth shut."

"Tom Ellis." They shook hands. Ellis gave Temple a hard, measuring look, but the easy flow of his talk went on just the same. "A fine morning, but far along. Are you ready?"

"For what?"

"Work, my boy, work! You told Mr. Bremerton you were ready, did you not?"

"I did. I am."

"Then follow me. Your baptism awaits."

Leaving his old clothes with Measuring Alice and Elizabeth Hargrove still behind the screen, Temple followed Tommy out of the mercantile and across the street to a sturdy wagon.

"Mr. Bremerton's starting you out as a swamper with me. No doubt he wants you to benefit from my vast experience and philosophical perspective on life in the oil fields."

Temple grinned. "No doubt," he agreed, hardly causing a ripple in the flow of Talking Tommy's words.

"Now, as you've been a cowboy, you doubtless have a way with animals. Take this fine team of draft horses." He drew a breath and swung a sweeping gesture toward the four tall, heavy Percherons harnessed to the wagon. "Just you go ahead and look them over. Get acquainted. Befriend them, if you will. Myself, I'm more at home with a modern means of conveyance."

Temple started to speak, but Tommy was already climbing aboard the wagon. Temple looked at the team. He patted and rubbed them, spoke to them, inspected their broad, hairy hooves. He intended to do his best with them and his best for Talking Tommy Ellis and his best for Brace Bremerton. But he was a cowboy. He didn't know any more about Percherons than he knew about elephants. Still, they were horses, obviously more gentle and probably more intelligent than the jugheaded range ponies he was accustomed to. He would get along.

"First-rate team," he told Talking Tommy, craning his neck to look up at the tall wagon box. "Now what?"

"Join me on the box, my boy! I shall drive. For the moment, your duty is to sit attentively while I discourse on—"

"—life in the oil fields," Temple murmured. "You're not from around here, are you?"

Tommy Ellis glanced at him sharply. "What makes you say that?"

"You don't sound like a Texan."

"Oh." The long-legged man seemed to relax a little. "However great our earthly tribulations," he said, "there's always something to be thankful for." He slapped the seat beside him. "Climb aboard! Time is money! Is the brake loose? Then up, you steeds! Let's roll this rig! Ho, you horses!"

"Ho!" Temple echoed. He didn't intend it to look as if he wasn't trying. "Ho-o-o!"

Pretty well ignoring the shouts, the horses switched their long ears, broke their inertia, leaned into the traces and lumbered forward, carrying the heavy wagon into the press of Emilia's traffic in a swoop of dust.

"Ho-o-o," Talking Tommy cried again, almost drowning the indignant cries of a man scurrying out from under the Percherons' hooves. To Temple he said, "We'll take it somewhat easier once we get out of town. Mr. Bremerton likes to see his minions hustling. But the wise man knows that more is lost by haste than was ever won by speed."

"Right." Temple was glad to hear the reason for their hurry. He'd begun to think everybody in Emilia drove like lunatics for the sheer joy of it.

They rolled south and a little west away from town. Within the first half mile the mass of trucks and wagons thinned out, the other traffic turning right and left to other destinations. They passed other thickets of oil derricks, mixed with open tracts of farmland or pasture so far untouched by drilling. Remembering that they were his responsibility, Temple watched the Percherons cover the road. Like fine trotting horses eating the track, he thought. He studied them a good long while before he realized that Talking Tommy had fallen silent. Startled, he looked sideways at the older man.

"Will you testify?"

Tommy started, jerking his head up abruptly. "What?" he barked. "What's that?"

"Testify," Temple repeated, smiling to show it was a joke.

"Will you tell them I caught you quiet so I can get my twenty dollars?"

"Oh." Tommy stared at him a moment longer, then turned back to contemplate the road. After a few seconds he began to laugh. "No," he said. "I could not cast off my cloak in that fashion. But I will stake you to the finest lunch in Emilia, just to buy your silence."

They rode for a mile or so. Tommy frowned at the horses. Puzzled, Temple waited him out. After a time, Tommy coughed apologetically.

"A man gets a reputation," he said. He looked at Temple. "Perhaps you know what that's like?"

"Me?" Temple wondered if there was more behind Tommy's question than casual chatter. The smaller man's face was smooth and innocent, but his quick, darting eyes didn't seem to fit the personality he showed to Temple. "Why would you think that?"

"You can never tell about reputation," Tommy said. "Sometimes a man seeks it; sometimes it seeks him. Out here, a man doesn't have to talk all the time. He can take time to think. Air out his mind a little. Talking's fine, but most of us can't talk and think at the same time."

Temple said, "Right." Tommy had turned the question, but it suggested another to Temple. Cotton Hargrove had known his father—or so he said. Had Hargrove said something to Tommy? Or did Tommy have some knowledge of his own? Or, Temple wondered, was he himself too ready to read his own thoughts into other men's minds? "If it's a fair question—" Temple began.

"Never hesitate to ask a question." Tommy slipped back into his town manner as if it were a cloak he took off and put on. "Ignorance is an abiding sin. In the oil fields it can be a deadly one. The eighth."

He savored the phrase for a moment, seeming to taste the words with pursed lips. Then he jerked his head quickly toward the back of the wagon.

"No doubt you mean to ask about the job. We're delivering this load."

Temple hadn't meant to ask that, and he was sure Tommy knew it. He shrugged and said, "What are we hauling?"

"Nitroglycerine."

"What!" Temple twisted on the seat to stare back at the brown canvas tarp covering the load. "Do you mean to say—"

Tommy raised a palm. "My little joke," he said. "Having some fun. Initiating the weevil." He gazed seriously at Temple. "Funning you, boy, this time. But when a well's tight—doesn't flow as much as the company men think it should—they'll often loosen the formation up with a little nitroglycerine. We aren't the shooters, but we sometimes haul their soup."

"How little nitroglycerine?"

"Oh, not much. A hundred quarts or so."

"A *hundred?*" Temple gulped. "How do they set it off?"

Tommy chuckled. "My boy, with nitro the problem isn't how to set it off. The trick is to get to its destination *without* doing just that." He looked sharply at Temple. "Does the idea scare you?"

"Why, hell—" Temple stopped, thought about it. From the standpoint of the man on the wagon, the difference between one quart and a hundred wasn't that important. "Sure, it scares me," he said. "But if it's in the job, I'll do it. I'll go anyplace you will."

Tommy scowled, though Temple thought he seemed pleased. "Afraid of that," he said. "Not nearly as smart as you look." He shook the reins and the Percherons leaned harder on the traces. "Truth is, we're hauling two drill bits and several spools of drilling line—thick wire cable, very heavy, as you'll find when we come to unload it."

"Where?"

"Devil's Den Number One. That's the name of a well that Magnolia Oil is about to commence. A wildcat. That's a well in an untested area, looking for a new field. Down the road and through the gate and across the east pasture past the ranch house and over the hill and through the bull trap . . ."

Temple pulled the brim of his new hat down over his face and made a snoring noise.

After another mile or so Talking Tom coughed again. "Not to disturb your contemplation, friend Temple, but part of your job is to keep watch. In principle, we're safe during the hours of daylight, but—"

"Safe?"

"Safe as toads buried up in loam in dry weather."

"Safe from what?"

The longer Tommy talked, the more his face lost its lines of concern. "Unless somebody comes along plowing up the loam in the daytime, which lately has not seemed beyond the realm of likelihood."

"I'm just a weevil, remember? I'm trying to learn, but it's not all getting through."

"What's not?"

"What you're talking about."

Talking Tommy drew in a deep breath that puffed out his small torso. "I hadn't considered that," he admitted.

"Sorry to let you down."

"What I was hinting, in my circuitous way, was the danger of robberies and thefts and hijackings and killings."

Temple looked around. This part of the country might have been a thousand miles from the nearest oil well. The road was open, empty, dusty, rutted, orange-red under a hot mid-morning sun. It ran straight between barbed-wire fences. Fields of dark green cotton a few inches high stretched right and left to the foot of the bluffs. A half mile ahead a windmill turned lazily in a grove of post oaks.

"I doubt anybody could sneak up on us."

"True. But it's different in the dark."

Lee Temple couldn't dispute the logic; he noticed for the first time the slab-sided butt of a big automatic pistol showing above the talking man's belt. Seeing the direction of Temple's gaze, Tommy flipped a coat flap over the gun.

"This trouble's something you and I'll talk about only between ourselves. Is that quite clear?"

Temple hesitated. "I work for Mr. Bremerton," he said. "Doesn't seem like I could make a promise to hide something from him."

"Indeed you can't. Add him to the list."

"Any of the robberies happen to you?"

"I said 'hijackings and killings.' As you may notice, I'm still here. No, none of it's yet happened to me. Part of your job is to help me see it coming."

For a moment Temple didn't speak. I should have known, he thought. Everything looked so easy. But here it is again. "You mean I'm riding shotgun."

"You're riding shotgun." Tommy turned his quick probing gaze on Temple again. "Does that scare you?"

"No. It doesn't scare me."

"Then reach under the wagon seat."

Temple knew what he would find before he felt the smooth polished stock of a long gun.

"Nobody's in sight. Just pull it up and forward out of its rack. Get acquainted with it, learn to use it, be ready in case you need an iron friend."

Cautiously, Temple drew out a new Winchester shotgun. It was very long and very heavy, with an ugly, square-backed receiver and a bore that looked big enough to crawl into.

"Twelve-gauge," Tommy said. "Self-loader, model of 1911. It holds five buckshot shells that can cut the gizzard out of any hijacker who comes close enough to recognize."

Temple stroked a careful hand over the shotgun. It didn't break open. It had no lever or bolt handle or hammer. It looked like a grown-up version of the rifle he'd seen Cotton Hargrove carrying. Turning it over, he saw a hinged trapdoor just ahead of the trigger guard.

"This where it loads?"

"That's right."

"And this button's the safety."

"Good. I can see you're familiar with the breed."

"No. I've never fired a shotgun. I've carried a Winchester carbine as a saddle gun."

"Good shot?"

"Middling."

The team had reached the trees around the windmill. Talking Tommy swung them into the shade of the grove, set the brake, and wound the reins around the brake lever.

"Let's climb down a minute and give you a chance to

learn about it," he said. He led Temple farther into the grove, then picked out one big tree. "This should do. There's nothing behind it except open space."

Taking the gun from Temple, he held its muzzle to the sky and pressed the safety button. "Now it's ready to roar. See that lower limb? Here, stand on my other side. Shell's going to come out where your head is now."

Temple hesitated. For almost as long as he could remember, he'd been warned away from guns. First it had been his mother, then his stepfather, who had backed up his warnings with a strong arm and a ready belt. And at school, and later, there was always somebody ready to add to the warnings.

"Killer's kid. Probably be a killer himself." Or, *"Why's Mr. Forrest let his daughter hang around with that gunman's whelp? Just like his pa."*

The boom of the big twelve-gauge brought Temple back to the present. Ellis had raised the shotgun, pointed it for the first part of a second, and pulled the trigger. Under the drive of the recoil, he rocked on his legs like a grasshopper preparing to jump. The limb quivered as if struck by an ax. A shower of bark sprayed out around it.

"Your turn." Tommy reset the safety and handed Temple the gun. "Hold it to your shoulder as tight as if it was a pretty girl." He darted another look at Temple. "Which reminds me, wasn't that the Hargrove girl and you mostly naked behind the screen at Measuring Alice's this morning?"

"There's always something to be thankful for," Temple said. He raised the gun tentatively. "How do I aim?"

"Let that front bead fall on the limb where I barked it. Then shoot. It'll ride up on you no matter how strong you think you are. Pull the muzzle back down and shoot again until it's empty. Exceptionally pretty. Miss Hargrove."

Temple cinched the gun against his shoulder and cheek. The front sight seemed to nestle in the receiver groove as naturally as his old saddle carbine sights had lined up for him.

Not everyone had warned him against guns. Some, cowhands and drifters around Wagon Mound, had tried to get him to shoot.

"I'd bet on him—same eyes as his old man, always looks like he's looking at you over the sights."

Killer's eyes.

"When you're ready," Tommy said.

Temple drew the bead down on the limb and pulled the trigger. The noise shocked him, and the recoil punched him hard on the collarbone. Splinters flew from the limb a hand's breadth from where Tommy's shot had hit.

"Excellent!" Tommy said. "You're a natural shot. Got the eye of a predator."

Temple raised his head, but Tommy was intent on the target. "Now bring that muzzle down and shoot again, like a man that won't quit the first time he's hit. Keep shooting!"

Temple let the sight rest on the limb again, pulled the trigger, saw bark and splinters fly from the mark. The limb shook, bent. Temple manhandled the bucking gun, brought it to bear, fired in what seemed one endless roar. The limb fell free at his third shot, but he didn't care. He let go the last round anyway. He liked the roar the gun made, liked the rolling-cannon recoil that punched him hard and then pitched forward with the return of the barrel, liked the sense of go-to-hell freedom he got from shaking all those voices out of his mind.

"I'm in love. We got any more shells?"

Talking Tommy laughed out loud. "Treat it like a woman," he said. "And see it doesn't treat you the way a woman will. Better reset that safety." He turned serious again. "Always expect it to be loaded. And never put your hand around that port when the bolt's back! Not if you want to keep all five fingers."

Ellis took the gun again, pressed a button toward the rear of the receiver. The heavy bolt snicked into battery like a steam hammer falling. "See? You chamber a shell by pulling back on the barrel, there, until the action opens. Now, let's see you load it."

Over the next half hour Tommy drilled him in loading, cocking, and firing the gun, until Temple felt he knew it better than any friend he'd ever had. When only five fat red shells remained in the ammunition box, Tommy called a halt.

"You're ready for anything," he said. "Load her up, pump a shell into the chamber, and then feed that last one in. Be sure to set that safety. The better way's to put just four in its magazine and leave the chamber empty. But you and I're going to keep it jam-up full so when we do need it, we'll be able to use it that same day."

Temple hefted the gun. He liked shooting it. He wondered what it would be like if the target were a man rather than a limb.

"It likes me," he said.

"It'd better. It's your tool if we have to do any ugly work."

Temple frowned. The words brought something back, something far back in his memory.

"A gun's a tool, Laura. No more."

"A tool that'll kill you one day."

Laura. That was his mother's name. Had that been something his father had said? But it hadn't been a gun that had killed his father. Not directly.

"Tommy? Things like—like being able to shoot—you figure that runs in families?"

Tommy blinked at him. "That's one of the few things on which I can profess no knowledge," he said. "Blue eyes and fair hair, perhaps. I couldn't say about a shooter's eye."

"Or a killer's," Temple said, half to himself.

"What?"

"Nothing. We better get along, before Mr. Bremerton decides we're loafing."

They turned in at the Devil's Den main ranch gate a little after noon. Temple jumped down, opened the gate, and shut it when the wagon was past. Talking Tommy seemed to like his work. "I expect you're hungry," Tommy said. He hadn't spoken for half an hour.

"I'm all right."

"Sure! But I promised you the best lunch around Emilia. These jarheads down at the new rig don't look like much and don't smell like much you'd want to identify and can't carry on a very civilized human conversation, but one of them's a hell of a cook."

"That's after we've gone down the road and through the gate and across the east pasture past the ranch house and over the hill and through the bull trap?"

Talking Tommy looked at his swamper with a new interest. "Why, the Devil's Den! And here I thought you weren't listening." He rubbed his mouth and nodded slowly. "There's one mistake I won't make again, friend Temple."

They rolled on along a narrow road that had been cleared through low bitter brush, crossed a grassy mesa, and started down a long hill. Tommy rode the brake.

"They ought to have switchbacks here. Damn ranchers don't think of anything but horseback riders. Just hack out a straight little old dog-track road. Then we have to get their permission to come through with a crew to widen out their trails and fill in the worst of the holes. And after that, do you think they give us a word of thanks for building them a decent road on their own place?"

"No."

"Thank you. I couldn't find a stopping place."

Half a mile past the trap pasture the road widened into a broader area that had been cleared and leveled. A tall derrick, its wood raw and yellow in the noonday sun, stood in the center. A stack of unused lumber lay nearby. Sawdust crackled under the team's hooves. The smell of freshly cut pine was everywhere.

A swarm of men worked on the derrick floor, lacing a foot-wide leather belt onto the drive wheel of a new steam engine, chocking a blacksmith's forge into place, stringing wires and cables that Temple couldn't imagine the use of. Some distance from the rig, another Bremerton crew was unloading a big-bellied steam boiler, jockeying it carefully onto a cement base.

"About damn time you showed up," a man in a whipcord suit and a red tie greeted them. "We should have been rigged up for drilling an hour ago. Time's money."

"Undoubtedly," Tommy said. "Where would you like us to unload?"

"Lay everything on the rig floor. We can't pick up the bits until we get fire in the boiler. Unload. Then pick up that lumber, then get the hell out. We don't need spectators."

"Yes, sir. Just as you say."

Tommy edged the wagon up beside the raised derrick floor with practiced care. Temple wondered if the long-legged man was as ignorant of horses as he chose to appear. The man in whipcord watched for a minute, then stalked back toward the men on the boiler, shouting orders as he went.

"Company man," Tommy explained under his breath. "The company hires the services of rig builders and haulers and all the rest of us. And nothing annoys them more than poor planning on their own part." He slipped down from the wagon seat. "Now, friend Temple, we'll need a few of those long planks to help us unload. I'm afraid that lunch I promised you will be delayed."

Chapter 8

TALKING TOMMY BROUGHT TEMPLE TO IRMA WATSON'S BOARD-inghouse long after dark. The streets of Emilia and Oiltown glowed in a dusty yellow haze from the dozens of gas flares scattered through the town. The flares burned yellow or blue around the horizon, blocking out all but the brightest stars in the evening sky. In the flickering twilight, the streets and sidewalks seemed busy as ever.

"This one time, I'll stable the team," Tommy said. "But I'll see you here in the morning. Four-thirty sharp."

"Sharp," Temple agreed. Though he wouldn't have admitted it, he was as tired as a person needed to be. The trip to Devil's Den and back had been only the beginning of a long day of shuffling large and heavy items to points in and around Emilia. Temple hoped for a quiet evening and an early bedtime, to be ready for four-thirty and another day with Tommy.

Widow Watson stuck her head out of the far doorway as Temple came in. "Late for supper," she scolded. "I saved you a plate. The Ballards, too. Possum and sweet potatoes. You clean up out back. I'll get those clothes to the Chinaman's wash. Alice sent you over another suit of khakis for tomorrow."

"All right," Temple said. "If you can wait just a minute, I'll get changed."

She emerged completely into the hall. "Don't go in your room," she said. "Mad Dog Jack's asleep in there."

"Asleep? Pretty early."

"He's pulling morning tour, goes to work at midnight. Green as a gourd. You'll learn."

"I'm learning. I won't disturb him."

"Not but once you won't! You change out in the wash house. Put your cowboy suit back on. I'll see it gets cleaned tomorrow, too."

Temple was too tired to argue. "Thanks," he said. "Show me the way."

Two other boarders were just done with their washing when Temple got to the pump. From Talking Tommy's description, he recognized the Ballard brothers at once.

The Ballards were big, identically slope-shouldered, their hair shocked like wild corn silk and eyes black as hammered iron. Temple could see that they'd both been turned on the same lathe. They'd escaped before the maker had buffed them to a polish, leaving them rough-hewn and blocky. He guessed them a year on either side of thirty.

The older one took to Temple on sight. "I'm Bull, Bull Ballard," he said, thrusting out a hand. His leather and bone grip reminded Temple of a horse collar. "This is my baby brother, Ace High."

"Hell," Ace High said in greeting. His eyes and hands were smaller but just as quick as his brother's. His handshake was scaly and cold and uncommitted. It reminded Temple of one of those big snakes he had read about, one that tested blindly before it settled in to squeeze the life out of whatever fell into its grip. Ace High hadn't yet made up his mind about Temple. "You work for that bastard Hargrove?"

Temple considered the possibilities and settled for saying, "I'm working for Brace Bremerton."

"But you hang around with the Hargroves."

Ace High said it like an accusation. Temple looked at him steadily, then went about his cleaning up.

"I and Bull used to work for Hargrove," Ace High said, perhaps in grudging explanation. "We didn't much like him."

Bull laughed. "Maybe if you's to ask him, he'd say he didn't much like *us,* either!"

"Rides around in that big open Pierce Arrow with his rifle scabbard on the fender and his damn dog on the front seat. You see him and that dog together, you can't tell which's the biggest son of a bitch!"

Bull laid a ham-hock hand on his brother's shoulder. To Temple he said, "Don't seem to do him much good, all that money. I hear his son don't much like him."

"Neither do we." Ace High gave a muscle-bound shudder, trying to shake off his brother's grip. "But we like his daughter just fine. Don't we, Bull?"

"Just fine," Bull agreed. "Know what we like about her, Temple?"

"I don't—"

"We like her 'cause she was smart enough not to have anything to do with us," Ace High finished. He kept his dark little eyes on Temple. "You want to fight?"

"Not before supper. We might wake Jack."

Ace High moved his eyes to peer hard in one direction and then the other before he moved his head. "Is he up?"

Bull whispered, "I thought I heard him stir."

Ace High turned to look more carefully around the yard. Then he whirled back to Temple. "I don't much like you," he said in a whisper. "But I'll give you this advice for all our sakes. Let sleeping dogs lie!"

Mrs. Watson had been watching them from the hallway. "You boys look hot," she said. "Whyn't you sit in the breeze? I'll bring out your plates." She pointed them toward a long table under an arbor behind the boardinghouse.

"We'll help," Bull said. He set an example by taking up a tray laden with steaming dishes. Ace and Temple carried out their plates and glasses and a giant jar of tea.

Supper was hot. Big biscuits with butter, fresh corn on the cob, thick stewy okra with tomatoes and peppers cooked in it, deep orange sweet potatoes baked in their skins, and pieces of what Temple supposed was possum, dipped in batter and fried up to a crisp. Over the meal, Bull and Ace High argued the merits of pulling the Marines out of Vera Cruz versus marching to Mexico City and teaching that scoundrel Huerta a lesson. Temple concentrated on the food.

By the time Mrs. Watson brought out a dish of peach cobbler and a twelve-cup pot of coffee, Temple had begun to yawn. The strange half-light of the gas flares made the night seem earlier and brighter than it should, but he decided that wouldn't bother him.

He stood up, stacking his dishes to carry back inside. "I believe I'll turn in," he said. "Nice meeting you all."

"Oh, no," Bull said.

"You can't do that," Ace High echoed. "You'll wake Jack, and he'll raise the devil and Tom Walker!"

"We're headed down to the Line," Bull said. "Come along. We'll come back about midnight, after the dog's out of his kennel."

"I'd better not—" Temple began. Ace High shoved back his bench.

"I knew you was too high-toned to associate with us. Just you step out here in the yard—"

"—because I'm broke until I make a payday."

"That's no nevermind," Bull said. "We'll stake you this once, won't we, Ace?"

"Not with my damned—"

"Come on, Temple. Bring that big hat along. You've got to see the Line. It's just like—"

"Sodom and Gomorrah," Temple finished. By now he'd heard so much about the place that he couldn't resist a look.

Besides, he probably couldn't refuse without fighting Ace Ballard, and he'd resolved to give up fighting. He fell into step between the two hulking Ballards, wondering if he'd see Elizabeth Hargrove there.

The Line might have started out as a line, but it had grown into almost a small town. Temple and the Ballards crossed a swaying wooden bridge across the creek and came to a six-strand barbed-wire fence. The trail sidled along the fence to a gate where a bored deputy sheriff lounged with a pump shotgun cradled in his arms.

Bull Ballard nudged Temple. "Last law you'll see," he muttered. "They pretty much stay out of what happens on the Line. Best to go in with friends. Like us."

"He ain't my friend," Ace High growled.

"Don't mind him, Temple. Come on."

The fence enclosed a space of two or three acres, covered more or less at random with tents and ramshackle plank buildings. Near the center were a couple of more substantial structures, one of them with two stories. The whole area was lighted by flares and flickering double-wicked yellow-dog lanterns. Electric lights shone from the windows of some of the larger buildings.

A considerable crowd surged through the dust and mud. Shouldering his way along with the Ballards, Temple heard a low continuous hum of voices, a jumble of music pouring from different doorways, cries of barkers and shills, an occasional shout or curse or scream from somewhere nearby. He was inclined to stop and stare, but the Ballard boys hurried him along.

"Little place down here," he half heard Bull saying. "—good liquor, and they won't—"

The rest was lost in a burst of laughter from the crowd around a circle of tents on their right.

"Look there," Ace High said suddenly. "It's a doggone circus!"

It was a sideshow, at least. A barker shouted the virtues of the attractions inside the tents: the tattooed lady, a fire-eater, Siamese twins. A garish canvas sign pictured a gigantic spider with the head of a pretty girl.

"Aw," Bull Ballard said.

"A skeptic!" Picking the three of them out of the crowd, the barker pointed with his cane. "Right this way, gentlemen. Spidora the Spider Girl, marvel of the ages. If you doubt our veracity, just step inside that first tent. The attraction is free if you're not satisfied."

The Ballards hung back, but Temple pushed inside. It was darker there. He could make out a low counter with a web of crisscrossed ropes stretching back toward the canvas ceiling. A great black spider body, made of something like papier-mâché, hung in the webbing. The only lighted thing in the tent was the face of a pert, dark-haired young woman, apparently suspended, eyes closed, where the spider's head should be.

Ace High breathed loudly in Temple's ear. "It's a fake," he said. "That there's just a picture."

The woman's eyes opened. "Oh, yeah?" she said.

"Lord God!"

Ace High fell back a step, jostling against Bull. The woman turned her head, focused on Temple. She winked. Two of the stiff, jointed spider legs waved in his direction.

"Come back after the show, Cowboy. We'll catch some flies together."

"Lord God!"

"They do it with mirrors." Bull fed a coin into the box outside. "Come on, Ace High. You can use a drink."

Temple dropped in his last dime, grinning. Anything that hit Ace Ballard that hard seemed a good investment.

They came finally to a white, peaked tent that might also have come from a circus. A pear-shaped man in a grimy white apron came through the tent flaps, coughed as if it were to be his last act in this life, and spat in the trail. He nodded to the Ballards and tied back the flaps to leave a dim triangular opening that reminded Temple of the mouth to a cave.

Inside the tent lanterns glowed through a thick, smoky fog. A trio of musicians near the door played something with a vaguely ragtime beat, the music almost drowned by the clatter and jangle of a row of penny slot machines behind them. Each Ballard took Temple by an arm and steered him through a tangle of gambling tables and over a prostrate customer to the bar, which ran the full length of the tent's back wall.

The three bartenders had their own door flap since they had no access to the main part of the tent except over the top of the bar. Bull Ballard called for tequila. Ace High said he'd have whiskey. The nearest bartender poured them each a shot, called for four bits each, and looked at Temple.

"Tequila for him, too," Bull said. "He's with me."

"No, whiskey," Ace High argued. He slapped a coin on the bar. "That's a man's drink. And I'm paying."

The bartender shrugged, poured a shot from each bottle and set them both in front of Temple.

"Now, wait," Temple said.

"Men drink whiskey."

"Drink up, Temple. Ready for another?"

Bull had already swallowed his first glass of tequila. He sprinkled a teaspoon of salt on the back of his hand, licked it up in one pass, and downed the second glassful. He blinked, looked at his brother and snorted. "What is it instead of men that drinks tequila?"

"Ain't men. That's certain."

The bartender plunked two fresh glasses down in front of the Ballards and waited for his money. Bull Ballard gave it to him.

"Temple, you ain't drinking," Bull said.

"Too good to drink with us?" Ace High asked.

Temple picked up one of the glasses—he wasn't sure which. In unison the Ballards said, "Drink it down!"

Temple drank it; it was the whiskey. He was just getting his breath back when Bull took him by the shoulder and shook him. "My little brother was lying to you about that whiskey you drunk! Real men drink tequila. You be a man and drink yours down!"

The cowboy looked up into Bull's reddened eyes. Without hesitation he took up the tequila and drank it. His vision blurred, his life passed in front of his eyes. When he looked back at the bar, two fresh glasses were waiting there.

He wasn't sure exactly how many times that happened before Ace High said sweetly, "My brother's right about whiskey." A tear blurred his eye, rolled onto his cheek. "I've often heard our dear old mother call it the devil's drink. Mel! My friend and I are changing over to tequila."

Temple said, "Wait a minute." He wasn't a serious drinker at the best of times, and surely not for the past few months. He had an idea things were moving too fast.

Nobody paid any attention. Bull took the bartender by the wrist. "Melvin, if you give these two any of that tequila, don't ever offer me any more of it!"

Mel poured their glasses full of tequila. "All right, Mr. Ballard. What should I offer you?"

"I'll have whisseky."

"Whisseky?" said Mel.

"Whisseky?" Bull echoed. "All right then, by God, *I'll* have whisseky, too!"

"Drink your cactus juice," Ace High told Temple. "It's good for you."

Lee Temple leaned over the bar and looked into the surface of the tequila until he could see his own eye. He wasn't convinced it was good for him. But it was probably better than offending both Ballards. He was no longer quite sure which Ballard was which. Ace High sprinkled salt all over the back of Temple's hand and across the surface of his drink. Temple licked at the salt, then bent to put his mouth on the rim of the glass. He pushed his head back with the glass until its contents drained into his mouth. *"Salud!"* he said.

Bull said, "Don't talk Messican, Cowboy. Mel, pour Ace's friend a whisseky."

"No," Temple said. He shook his head, but nothing in his vision moved. He drank the whiskey.

Ace High said, "It's right nice of you to worry that way about Bull's feelings. I'm beginning to like you. Milk us another cactus, Mel!"

Bull glared at Temple. "Now that I see you drinking Messican liquor and talking Messican," he said, "you put me in mind of a feller in Tampico. We didn't much like him!"

Ace High laughed. "Maybe if you's to ask him, he'd say he didn't much like *us,* either!"

Temple laughed. Bull Ballard grabbed him by the shirt and yanked.

"You laughing at my little brother? Who you think you are, weevil?"

"No."

"He wouldn't do that, Bull," Ace High said.

"Then he must be laughing at me. Thass worse."

He shoved Temple backward. Temple caught himself gracefully, proud of the ease with which he kept his balance. He looked around and found he was sitting on the floor, his back against the bar. After some more loud talk above him, the two pairs of legs belonging to the Ballards wavered away toward the nearest poker table. Temple watched the legs.

"How'd she *do* that?" he said aloud. "Wave her legs, I mean. Spider legs."

Mel leaned over the bar and eyed the cowboy. "If you stay there," the bartender said, "somebody'll step on you. Else the Ballards'll be back, and they might remember you."

Temple peeked up at Mel through one mostly shut eye. "They looking?" he asked.

Mel shook his head.

Temple got to his feet.

Mel said, "Here, even yourself out with a glass of my owl-eye coffee. Men'll think it's whiskey."

Temple drained off the glass. It tasted a lot like the crude oil he'd ridden through—when?—sometime. "How'd that Indian know it was sweet?" he asked the bartender.

"I think I'll let you out the back door," Mel said. "You need to know the Ballards a little better before you try to drink with them."

"Better? They're old friends."

"I mean, you catch them sober and Bull's sweet as a virgin's kiss; it's Ace would bite off your nose. You catch them both drunk, Ace High's a kitten; it's Bull would tear your tongue out by the roots." He rubbed his chin. "What you'd hope would be to catch Bull sober and Ace High drunk so's they'd be as nice as choir boys. But you can bet the devil'd see to it you'd catch them the other way around."

Temple didn't really follow the conversation, but he saw some of its possibilities. "How was it you figured to get me out the back?" he asked.

"Wait until I give the word," Mel said. "Then vault over this bar like the devil was after you—which he may be! All right, now!"

Lee Temple leapt, skidded across the polished top and plopped as lightly as a watermelon onto the dirty floor behind the bar.

"That's just fine," Mel told him. "If I'd knew you were so agile, I'd've had you crawl under the bar. You've lit square on your head."

"That explains it."

"Can you move your feet and hands?"

"Where are they?"

The bartender got hold of Temple's belt and helped him up. "Out through that flap," he advised.

Temple went through the flap without ever straightening up as high as the bar top. He sucked in a gallon of almost-clear air, stood upright and looked for his hat. It was jammed firmly down to his ears. A familiar voice asked how he was doing.

He found its source. "Talk," he said. "Glad to see you."

Talking Tommy waved his arms like a startled grasshopper. "No, Billy. My night name is Radcliff. And this is Roxanne." He nodded toward the woman who clung to his arm.

Roxanne was six feet tall and feminine as lace. Temple looked for the tape measure, but it apparently didn't go with the maroon evening costume she was wearing. "Mr. Billy," she said. She gave a quick curtsy and smiled demurely at Temple.

Lee Temple thought about the waving arms. "Ma'am," he said. "Measuring Roxanne. Honored to meet you." He turned to Tommy, waved his arms. "Listen, Redbluff, I saw this girl tonight—"

Talking Tommy leaned closer to Temple. "Nor do we ever during the daylight refer to our nighttime identities. Not any of us. *Comprende?*"

Lee Temple nodded intently. "Never. But she had all these legs—"

"Maybe Billy will join us at the dance hall," Alice-Roxanne said. "I think he could stand to rest."

"I could sit to rest."

"A very good idea. Come along, young sir. We'll look in on the Parlor of Prance. This way."

The Parlor was one of the wooden buildings. Inside, the three of them took a table near the raised dance floor. A waiter with a towel over his arm took Tommy's order for white wine and three glasses and padded away. The place seemed much quieter than the tent had been, its air clearer. A five-piece band was playing a fox-trot while a dozen couples danced.

Temple blinked and felt his head clear a little. He looked around, wondering if Bull and Ace High had found their way there. He didn't see any Ballards, but at a table for four nearby, a squat, frog-faced man talked with a young woman in a bright green dress. The two bent so close that their heads touched. Across the table, Chief was looking gravely up into the face of the slender woman who sat on his lap. She wore his concho-banded black hat over her yellow curls. Temple counted six tall bottles standing on the foursome's table.

"Shooter," Temple said, nodding their way. "And that's his friend, Chief. I don't know their night names."

Tommy turned to look. "Yes," he said. "Suicide jockeys. Very well paid, but I've noticed their ilk drink much and often when they're off duty." He smiled at Alice-Roxanne. "Accompanied by two flowers of the twilight, eager to help them enjoy their money."

The band slipped into a hesitation waltz. Shooter rose from the table to escort his partner to the dance floor, Chief and the other woman following. Along the way, Shooter saw Temple and threw him a sketchy salute and a wide-mouthed smile.

"Perhaps Billy will excuse us if we do the same," Tommy murmured. "Billy—"

Temple wasn't listening. Looking past Shooter, he'd seen Elizabeth Hargrove among the dancers. She pressed very close to a tall young man in a fawn-colored sport coat and a black tie. As they danced, she looked up into his eyes. Tendrils of blond hair framed her face. She was out of place, Temple thought. He belonged here, and Tommy and Measuring Alice and the others. She didn't.

He started to rise, meaning to tell her so. His head swam. He took a sip of the white wine to clear his thinking. It didn't seem to help, so he took another.

When the music paused, the young man whispered something in Elizabeth's ear. She shook her head, her short hair flying. The man whispered again, and this time she laughed and squeezed his arm. Liz, Temple thought.

"It's her night name," he said.

"Billy? Are you all right?"

Tommy was shaking him. Temple frowned. In his mind the outline of Elizabeth's face blurred softly with Amy Forrest's dark hair and eyes and laughter, and both blurred into the face of the dark-haired woman from the sideshow.

"Listen, Raeburn," he began, "I met this girl tonight—"

He started to wave his arms, but then something like a great, soft hammer seemed to hit him. The blur in his vision spread until nothing was quite clear, and he was never sure what happened next.

Chapter 9

LEE TEMPLE HAD JUST GOTTEN HIS BODY BENT TO FIT THE AIRLESS upper bunk, had just shut his eyes and given himself over to the idea of sleep, when a fire bell began to toll. He sat up with a rush and hit his head soundly on a ceiling joist. It didn't seem to make much difference in the way he felt.

Mrs. Watson stood in the hallway banging at a big brass wash pan. Bull Ballard crabbed around in his bunk and blinked at Temple.

"Morning," he said. "Glad you made it back. How'd you and that little spidery gal do?"

"Huh?"

Ace High got up still wearing his hat. A red ace stood in the band like a proud feather. "Shut up that bell, old woman!" he growled. Then he caught sight of Temple and lost his good humor. "You still here, weevil? After breakfast I think I'll just kick your ass."

Temple looked in the other bunk for Mad Dog Jack, but that bunk was made and straightened neatly. It was enough to be grateful for. "No," he said, "not after breakfast."

"What?"

"You'll have to wait till I feel better."

"Aw hell."

Bull laughed at his brother. "Yeah, but no kidding," he said, "did you get along with her?"

"Who?"

Temple frowned. He remembered Alice and Talking Tommy and a confusion of names. After that he had only a vague, sick memory of Amy's face and Elizabeth's, then of dark eyes and a mouth and long slender legs that didn't seem to belong to either of them.

"That spider girl."

"She better have been worth it," Ace High said, pulling on his work pants. "Cost us a day's pay, and I'm halfway minded to beat it out of you."

"He'll pay us back," Bull soothed. "Won't you, Cowboy?"

"Sure." Temple rubbed his head, hoping it might fall off. "Sure I will. I must've had a wonderful time."

Breakfast was scrambled eggs and grits and gravy and hot flaky biscuits. Temple had a hard time looking at it. He took the unoccupied end of the long dining table, grateful that the Ballards had settled at the other end. They were busy between bites, arguing politics with a couple of boarders Temple hadn't met. He half listened while he drank a first cup of coffee and thought about trying to eat a biscuit.

"I'm telling you it ain't Mexico we ought to worry about. Those countries in Europe are primed for a war, and they'll pull us into it surer'n hell."

"There's a whole ocean between us and Europe. Mexico, now—"

"Besides, them European kings and czars and whatnot is all kinfolk. They ain't fixing to fight one another."

Temple spread a biscuit with Widow Watson's blackberry jam, tried a bite, managed to keep it down. He was working on his second bite when Talking Tommy came through the dining room door, wished everyone good morning, and took the chair beside Temple's. Mrs. Watson's Waltham clock read four-twenty.

"Barely time for a cup of coffee," Tommy said. He speared a biscuit and slathered it with jam. "Good morning, young Mr. Temple! Pleasant evening? Sleep well? Ready to rip?"

Temple looked at him with one eye. "Sure."

"'Sure.' Indeed, there's the enthusiasm that makes this country great! Wake up, my boy. Taste the air. We'll be working daylights for the next week or two, so enjoy it!"

Temple opened his other eye. He almost felt he could survive a day of riding on the wagon seat with Tommy. "What are we delivering today?" he asked.

"Oh, no deliveries for us. Mr. Bremerton has a task for me around the office. As for you . . ."

"What?"

"Oh, some healthful outdoor work at the warehouse. Something to occupy the body, leaving the mind free to contemplate the universe and ask itself the important questions of life."

"What questions are those?"

The talking man took a big bite of the biscuit. "Who do you imagine could tell you that? And what good would it do if anyone else could?" He glanced at the other diners and lowered his voice. "Not to pry, you understand, but how did you get on with that young lady in the spider suit?"

Temple groaned softly and closed his eyes. "Mirrors," he said. "They do it with mirrors."

Harry Hargrove edged into the narrow seat of the green Reo and studied its controls. After a couple of tries, he started it and allowed the engine to idle while he thought out his next move. He worked through the gears carefully, testing out what Betty had shown him about the clutch. Finally he backed away from the hitching post, stopped, then lurched forward through the Hargrove oak grove to the main road.

By the time he reached Emilia, he could steer, shift gears, and watch the road all at once. Still, he decided not to challenge the traffic on the crowded main street. He idled along the network of gravel-topped residential streets until he was behind the town's library, then pulled the car into a grassy lot at the foot of a production rig. With vast relief he turned off the motor and went inside.

The library was a stone building, one of the oldest in Emilia. It had once stood in a spacious park shaded by live oaks. Now the trees had been replaced by tall angular derricks that crowded right up to the stone walls. While the wells were drilling, the library had shut down. When the wells went on production, the derricks were left in place. Bobbing walking beams nodded to Harry as he came up the library steps.

At the main desk a young lady was waiting as if she had seen him coming. "Harry!" she cried. "I was afraid you were gone for good."

"Harriet!" He went to her and leaned over the desk and kissed her. "But we aren't supposed to make this much noise in the library," he said.

Harriet Jergin said, "Not when anyone else is here. But that isn't often." She was a delicate girl, almost as tall as Harry. Harry thought her dark hair and bright blue eyes made a stunning combination. Thinking that, he went around the desk and took her in his arms.

"Hare," he said.

"People do peek in the windows," she said. "We ought to be a little careful."

He did not take his eyes off her face. "To hell with people." He drew her close and kissed her for a long time. "Listen—"

"This isn't the place." She drew away.

"To listen?" He followed her. "Don't say it isn't the time."

"Is it?" she asked. "Is it the time?"

"It is. Hare, I want you to marry me."

She stopped, let him take her in his arms again, tried to read the depths of his eyes. "Are you sure?"

"I'm sure. I'm the one doing the asking." He went down on both knees. "Here. Is this it? Is this what you'd like? Will you please marry me?"

"Harry! Get up, goose!"

"Well, what do you want?"

"I *want* you to get up. People are staring in the front window!"

"I won't get up until you give me the right answer."

"Yes."

"What? I couldn't hear that."

"Yes!"

He stood, turned, and went to the front window. He pressed his nose up against the glass and made a face at Gwenn Riddle and old Mrs. McCandless. He moved his mouth to tell them, "She said *yes!*" The two women looked at each other, shook their heads and went away.

"Goose," Harriet said again. "What will they think?" She put her hand to his cheek, kissed him.

Thank you, he thought. Thank you, my dear! Aloud, he said, "Set a date! How would tomorrow be? I'll get Lee Temple to be my best man."

"I don't know him."

"Then I'll tell you about him. He's a cowboy. We can be married on horseback."

"I don't think Aunt Minnie would approve."

"Where is your aunt? I ought to ask her permission."

"She'd like that," Harriet said. "She's up at the house, busy bringing culture to Emilia. I'm surprised you're not up helping—though I think the only reason you take part is to—"

He grabbed her and whirled her around the room. "To steal a moment alone with you, me proud beauty!" He kissed her again. "I'm going straight up to see her, then. Phone her if you'd like."

"Phone her yourself, Harry. That's what the phone is for."

"No it isn't. No, a matter like this a man must see to in person. Of course, I could have asked you over the phone."

She threw a book after him as he left. He didn't think she tried very hard to hit him.

Bremerton's warehouse was a solid brick building with a spacious storage yard. A hastily painted canvas sign with the Bremerton name hung above the door, partially covering the original sign set in the bricks. A high wooden fence surrounded the yard, its top ornamented with barbed wire.

"It's not as if we need that wire much," Tommy said. "There's always someone here except Sundays, and most often then. This is the operation. What do you think of it?"

Temple thought he'd never seen so much equipment he didn't recognize. Yard and warehouse held spools of wire stacked twelve feet high, spools of rope from lariat size to the thickness of Temple's wrist, spools of woven wire cable covering half the floor space. Five-gallon buckets of grease stacked four high in two different corners.

Bremerton had giant drill bits new in boxes, used ones lying helter-skelter, rack upon rack of steel pipe in thirty-foot joints. Half the yard was used for storage, the other half partitioned into corrals for mules and draft horses. Temple counted six wagons and four big blocky Nash Quad motortrucks, all in the process of being loaded. Men swarmed around the compound, all seeming busy on tasks of great urgency.

"Impressive." Talking Tommy answered his own question. "There's a change room and water jug inside the door there, but don't spend too much time there. You, Slick!"

The man Tommy had summoned was tall and lanky, maybe a year older than Temple, but already going bald. What hair he had was clipped close to his skull. He ran a hand across it and grinned at Tommy, then at Temple.

"Phil Porterfield, but they mostly call me Slick," he said, offering Temple a hand.

"I saw you this morning," Temple said. "Trying to tell the Ballards about Europe."

"Right enough. Getting an idea into Bull's head is like driving a wax candle into an anvil. Ready to go to work?"

"He is," Tommy answered for him. "Listen, Lee, Slick is the yard boss here. Do what he tells you and don't get into any card games with him. I'll see you directly."

"Thanks, Tommy." Temple looked at Porterfield, decided that he liked him, and asked, "Where's the job?"

"Right here." The foreman pointed to the nearest rack of pipe. It was obviously used, crusted with thick black grease studded with dirt and pebbles. "We need that cleaned up so's we can use it again. Any questions?"

"One. How?"

Porterfield grinned again. "There's a steam boiler in the shed there. You'll find a hose tied onto it with a nozzle so's you can spray steam and hot water about wherever you want. Drag the hose out to the rack, and I'll show you what to do next. Chances are that'll hold you for a week or so."

He went to attend to another summons. Temple thought over what he'd been told. Then he went into the change room, put his lunch in a locker and stripped to work boots and trousers. Shoving his gloves in a back pocket, he went to find the steam hose.

Harry walked along the crowded main street to Meadow-lark, turned north and uphill for a couple of blocks and stopped in front of a tall Queen Anne mansion with a wide veranda around three sides and a similar porch around the second story. The yellow paint of the trim was peeling, and cracks showed in the mortar of the two massive chimneys.

Harry twisted a crank bell at the front door and waited for Miss Minnie Jergin to answer it. She opened the door almost immediately.

"Come in, dear boy!" she cried. Her voice was like a broken brass bell, now clear and in the next word cracked or hoarse, depending upon which spot the clapper of her voice struck her vocal cords. She took his arm and led him through the large front room to the kitchen. "Harriet called," she said expectantly.

"Then I suppose she told you why I was coming."

"No-o."

"Really?"

"I have some lem-on-ade in the cooler."

He sat at the kitchen table and waited for her to bring the lemonade. "Aunt Minnie . . ." he said.

She poured the lemonade into two glasses and sat across from him at the table. "Yes?"

"Aunt Minnie, I . . ." He hadn't stopped to realize that it would be more difficult to discuss the topic with her than with Harriet. "I guess you may know that . . ."

She reached across to take his hands in her own pale, wrinkled, spotted hands. "Yes?"

"I care very much for your niece."

"Of course you do, dear boy. How could you help it?"

"I care so much for her that I want to ask her, to ask you if I may—ask her for her hand." When he finally got to the last group of words, he rushed through them in a single gulp.

The white-haired old lady looked at him with great round gray eyes which had begun to water. "Dear boy, Harry, do you really care for her?"

"I love her!"

"Yes, I know. But can you put her and her happiness ahead of ever-y-thing else—"

"Absolutely!"

"—and ever-y-*one* else—"

"She will be first in my life, always."

"—and ever-y-one else's happiness?"

"I give you my word! But why do you say 'everyone else's happiness'? Why should anyone else's feelings interfere between—"

"Wh-at do you call me?"

"Call you? Aunt Minnie."

"No, you never called me that until this morning."

"Well, then, I guess *Miss* Minnie."

She smiled and squeezed his hand. "Exactly. But once I had my young man. I did. Then, when the crucial moment came, he allowed the feelings of others to obscure his concern for my feelings. He lacked the courage to stand up to them."

"Aunt Minnie, I give you my absolute word. On the memory of my mother—"

"Just your word will do, dear boy. But remember this one thing for me. My young man let me down. My father should have killed him, but he lacked the courage also." She smiled but did not laugh. "I'm all Harriet has to protect her in this world. I welcome your help in that task. But if you let her down, Harry Hargrove, I'll act as if I were her parent—"

"Yes, ma'am."

"—and I have never lacked for courage."

"No, ma'am. I never thought you had."

Lee Temple spent the better part of a week steam-cleaning pipe, ending each day tired, dehydrated, his chest and shoulders streaked with black, sticky ropes of paraffin, his hands blistered through his gloves from handling the steam hose. Each day he scrubbed himself down with strong soap in the bathhouse at Bremerton's, put on his clean suit of clothes, and went back to Watson's boardinghouse without energy even to respond to Ace High Ballard's growls.

In a way, it was the best time he'd spent in months. Far from thinking about the important questions of life, he'd found that during working hours he didn't have to think about *anything,* not even lost love or lost friendship or the memories of his father—though too often he found himself thinking about Elizabeth Hargrove.

At the boardinghouse, he spent the evenings reading from Widow Watson's surprisingly big library and getting to know the other boarders. Best of all, he was tired enough not to be tempted when the Ballards or Porterfield invited him out to the Line.

On Saturday morning Tommy caught him as he headed for the change room.

"No free ride for you today, friend Temple. There's a wildcat spudding in on the C-Bar. I need someone who's good with Percherons."

Temple didn't understand a word Tommy had said, and he hadn't forgotten his misgivings about the big horses. But to earn a break from the steam hose he would have been ready to drive a team of alligators.

"I'm your man."

They went out of town with an eight-horse hitch pulling two huge, barrel-shaped water wagons. Temple drove. He'd never handled so many horses at once, nor pulled so big a load, nor dealt with the problems of a second wagon lashed tongue to tailboard behind the first. Fortunately the Percherons seemed to know their business perfectly well without any help from him. Once clear of town he even found time to ask Tommy for an explanation of their job.

"Forgot you were a weevil. Spudding in means starting a well. The C-Bar is a ranch out this way from town, owned by a citizen name of Carstairs. A wildcat is a well far away from established production. The water is intended to fire the boiler to operate the rig. There's neither water nor fuel at the location, so both will have to be hauled." The long-legged man stopped for breath. "Does that educate you sufficiently?"

"Almost. But why is it you riding shotgun today instead of me?"

Tommy Ellis smiled. "A matter of safety," he said. "First, we're safer with you handling these horses. Second, no hijackers, however greedy, are likely to steal a load of water."

The well location lay in a hollow a mile or so off the main road. Temple urged the draft team to the top of the rise above it, then paused to let them breathe before he started the wagon down. It was the first time he'd seen a well actually drilling. A lanky man in overalls was tending a black steam boiler set a good fifty yards from the derrick. A redwood water tank sat nearby. Steam lines ran to a chuffing steam engine with a single tall cylinder and a massive iron flywheel. The engine drove a wide leather belt, the belt turned a six-foot-tall wooden bull wheel, and the wheel worked the massive walking beam up and down. The thing that impressed Temple most was the great earth-thudding boom each time the beam came down.

Temple and Tommy Ellis stopped the water wagons well up on the hillside, then ran a heavy four-inch hose down to drain into the boiler's storage tank. That done, they left the team to doze and clambered down the slope to the rig.

"That noise is the bit hitting the rock," the driller explained to Temple. He paused while the ground shook and the tall wooden derrick supports trembled. "Hammering our way down, like driving a nail." He stuck out a hand as the world shook again. "Jeeter Sikes, and proud to meet you. This here's Oilcloth, my tool dresser."

Sikes was a tall man so narrow that his shoulder seams hung halfway down to his elbows. When he shook hands, his fingers wrapped nearly around Temple's hand. Oilcloth, back from firing the boiler, offered a gap-toothed smile.

"Jeeter," Tommy said, "how's the family?"

"Getting along. Cindy'll be starting school this fall, if the boom holds out. Y'all sit yourselves on the lazy bench. Ain't much for you to do while that tank's filling. Just don't smoke anywhere inside the derrick legs."

"We don't smoke, Temple nor me," Ellis said. "No bad habits to speak of, excepting Temple likes spiders some."

92

"Good policy. About smoking, I mean." Jeeter pulled out a pouch of Red Man, transferred a handful of long, stringy strands to his jaw, and held the pouch toward Temple. "Chaw?"

"No, thanks."

"Just this once," Tommy said and took a much smaller helping. "You boys going to find anything this time?"

"Wildcat," said Oilcloth. "Can't talk about it, or the company man will have a fit." He pursed his lips. "But we all is pretty good at oil finding, ain't we, Jeeter?"

"The Gunsight Lime's tight as a tick here," Jeeter said. "Won't give up nothing but a dab of water. That fancy geologist, wants to see what's deeper, down the next formation." He frowned. "That's for you, Tommy, not to tell all over town."

"How can you tell how deep you're drilling?" Temple asked.

Sikes laughed. "Ain't no mystery at the moment. We just started yesterday. But look there where I tied that rag."

He pointed up into the derrick. The drilling line, the heavy wire cable that whipped up and down with the walking beam's motion, had a piece of white cotton tied about halfway up.

"Eighty-four feet to the crown of the derrick," Sikes said. "Eighty-four feet back down to the floor, here. When that rag gets back to me, we'll have that much in the hole. Then I'll mark it in my tally book and start again." He squinted at Temple. "You know what's on the bottom of the line. Drill bit, like that one. Like a big chisel."

"Yeah. I've seen those. Carried a few."

"Well, you look out for the oil fields," Sikes advised. "It'll get in your blood till you're like Oilcloth and me—dragging around from one boom to the next until you die in some ragtopped old boomtown."

Tom Ellis laughed. "I expect you've got a few years yet, Jeeter." Temple saw Tommy's knuckles tap lightly on the splintery wood of a crossbeam. "Lee, best see about that water."

Oilcloth pushed to his feet. "Might as well go along," he said. "I ain't doing anything much right now. Might be I can help you spool that hose."

"Thanks, Oilcloth."

Watching the two of them go, Jeeter elbowed Tommy gently in the ribs. "Looks like Oilcloth approves your new man. Means he must lift his own end and be willing."

"He's all that," Tommy said.

"Also means he's bright enough to take instruction."

"He's that, too."

"That'll separate him from the run-of-the-mill hand."

"It does." Tommy frowned, pulling a thin worried crease between his eyes. "Reminds me of somebody I heard about once. But he can't be the same Temple."

"Might as well forget about him. If he's a good hand, you won't have him long. Somebody'll see him and hire him away from you and promote him on up the line."

Tommy laughed without smiling. "I must have been asleep not to think of that. You're absolutely right. I won't be able to keep him. Somebody has other plans."

"Seems likely to me. Judging by what's gone on in the past."

"A wise and judicious historical approach indeed," Tommy murmured.

"What?"

"I expect you're right." He changed his tone and gestured at the drilling line. "Looks like you'll hit a hundred feet before dark."

Sikes nodded. "Just like drilling a snowbank," he said. "Formation's soft as butter. If it stays this way, we'll be down inside the month."

Tom Ellis looked at the dresser and swamper discussing the situation under the shade of tree. "I guess we'll be on our way, then," he said. His eyes stayed on Temple, thoughtful. "Time to move Mr. Temple on toward his future. Wish I could remember where I ran across that name in the past."

Chapter 10

LEE TEMPLE HAD BEEN LUCKY ABOUT HIS PAY. HE MADE A PAYDAY at Bremerton's at the end of his first week. At the end of his third week they paid him again. Even after paying off his debts to Bremerton and Harry Hargrove and the Ballards, he was left with more hard cash than he would have gotten for two months of working cattle.

"We ought to celebrate," Harry told him over the supper Temple insisted on buying him at the Oiltown Elite Cafe. "Listen, there's a dance tonight at the Woodman Hall. Why don't you come?"

Temple grinned and shook his head. "Thanks, but I guess not," he said. "I get the feeling oil field hands aren't exactly welcome uptown."

"What makes you say that?"

"Maybe it was the policeman I ran into last night when I walked up to the square. Suggested I get myself back down to Oiltown and stay there."

"He had no right to do that. He doesn't speak for everybody."

Temple shrugged. "I can't say he's in the wrong. He lives here. I don't own a foot of Emilia and don't aim to. I'm an outsider, same's the rest of the boomers."

"It doesn't have to be that way. I wish you'd come. I want you to meet Harriet. And Betty would love to see you."

"Will she be there?" Temple asked before he thought.

Harry understood. "Oh, yes, she'll be there." He laughed. "She wouldn't miss an occasion like that."

Temple heard again something she'd said that first morning. *I like to rub their sanctimonious noses in it.*

"I'd like to see her," he said, and wondered if it was true.

He remembered her on the dance floor that night on the Line, looking up into another man's face with half-closed eyes, relaxed in his arms as though she belonged there. Maybe she did. "But I still think I'd better not."

That evening, Temple changed into his best clothes—none too good, but those he'd arrived in—and walked down Oiltown's nameless main street toward Emilia and the Woodman Hall. In the twilight of the gas flares, Oiltown was as busy as ever. Cars and wagons and motortrucks jockeyed for position, raising clouds of dust. Horns and the shouts of teamsters rose and fell to the accompaniment of snatches of music from the Line.

Temple stayed to the sidewalk, passing through a babble of voices: men in suits in front of one of the hotels, talking about leases and rock formations and profits; men in overalls in front of a tavern, laughing about a foremen, exchanging confidences on women, betting on which loaded wagon in Bremerton's yard across the way would pull out first; a street preacher, surrounded by a laughing crowd, talking about destruction.

"—and lo, the smoke of the country went up as the smoke of a furnace—"

At the great mudhole where the pavement started, the unofficial boundary between Oiltown and Emilia, he stopped. It came to him that he'd seen boundaries like that all his life, always from the wrong side. The last one he'd tried to cross had been in New Mexico.

"Of course I love you, Lee," Amy Forrest had said. "But marriage? I don't know. And what would Papa say?"

That didn't worry Temple. Mr. Forrest had always treated him well. Mr. Forrest had known his father.

"Your father likes me. I'll talk to him."

"Well, sure he likes you. But—Well, after all, you're . . ."

"Just a ranch hand? Do you think that'll matter to him?"

Amy hesitated a second, and Temple had the suspicion that wasn't what she'd meant at all. "No-o-o," she said finally.

"But don't talk to him yet. I'm just not sure I'm ready to get married." She reached up and drew his mouth down to hers. "Hush, now. Let's think about something else."

Temple hesitated a moment longer, then turned away from Emilia. He'd tried to cross the line, and it had earned him the loss of his job and a stretch in a Texas jail. Maybe he should stay on his own side. Maybe it was where he belonged.

He stretched his legs back along the bustling Oiltown street. The Line would be open. The Line was always open. If he wanted company, he could always find it there.

Near the depot, he heard a heavy truck moving slowly toward him. He thought nothing of it until it was even with him and he recognized Hargrove's Bulldog. It startled him to see it right in the town streets. The Bulldog was known as a soup wagon, rigged to carry nitroglycerine.

Temple recognized the driver, Charlie Osborn, alone in the cab without a guard. Temple started to hail him, then decided Charlie had enough problems if he was truly carrying a load. Maybe that in itself would be enough to scare off any hijackers. He couldn't figure Charlie's reason for heading out of town away from Hargrove Hill, but it wasn't his concern.

A woman's voice came to him from nearby. "Good evening, Cowbaby."

Temple turned. He thought what he should say to her, swallowed the words, smiled.

"Miss Hargrove."

"You were thinking awfully hard." She sat behind the wheel of the yellow Mercer in the deeper shadows of the side street. He'd forgotten how pretty she was. "Were you thinking about hijacking Father's truck?"

"Not tonight."

"A lost love, then?"

"No."

He turned and walked along the street. She drove along beside him.

"Then you must have been thinking about me. Harry said you wouldn't come to the dance. Still too good for the Hargroves?"

"No. But I don't belong there."

"Maybe you're right, Cowboy. Me either!" She laughed. He wasn't sure if she was laughing at him or at herself. "Deadly dull—the dance and the men, both." She patted the seat beside her. "Climb in," she offered. "I'm going down to the Line. We both belong there."

"No." He walked a little faster. "I was headed for the boardinghouse."

"I wish you would." She drove a little faster. "Your spider girl's gone on with the carnival, but I'm still here."

He stopped and looked at her, wondering how she'd known about that—and why she cared. "It's late." He picked up his speed.

"It is not. We could have fun."

"I have an early tour." He had to pull for breath.

"All right, wildfire, get in. If nothing else will do you, I'll give you a ride to Watson's."

"I'll walk. I need the exercise."

"Your wish is my dish, Cowboy. But your virtue would be safe with me!"

Then she fed her car all the gas it would take. The spinning wheels kicked dust and gravel back at him. Over the noise of the motor he heard her laughter as she roared away toward the Line. This time there was no doubt who she was laughing at.

Cotton Hargrove opened the door of his Pierce Arrow and waited for his dog. "Rotten," he said, "get in the car."

In the early summer twilight, the big dog whined hoarsely and bounded into the passenger's seat. He barked, put all four feet in the seat, sat straight up like a man and stared expectantly through the windshield.

Hargrove slipped his Winchester autoloader rifle into the leather boot he'd mounted on the fender just behind the spare tire. He settled in the seat, checking to be sure he could reach the rifle and that it slid freely in the boot. Then he stepped on the electric starter. After a few seconds he released the brake and roared out of the shed like an engineer pushing a locomotive. The electric headlamps he'd paid extra for blazed a path in the night. His fireman barked as they cleared the yard and turned south along the rough road toward Emilia.

Two miles down the way, Hargrove turned off. He followed a series of back roads until he was a few miles south and east of town. Then he pulled off the road. He shut his machine down, killed the lights, and waited.

He sat without impatience for a slow half hour. Just like the old days, he thought. Only tonight there was no Texas Ranger waiting along the river, watching for someone moving a stolen herd of cattle. *No Matthew Temple.*

"Temple," he murmured half aloud. He knew how Temple had finished. He'd even saved the piece from the newspaper, still had it somewhere. "Old Matt. Who'd've thought you had a kid?"

The black dog whined at the sound of his voice.

"Shut up, Rotten," Hargrove murmured. "Bad enough one of us talks to himself."

Sure he was alone in the night, he took a broom from the rear floorboard and swept the edge of the road where his tire tracks left it. Finally he drove without lights across the top of a domed hill to the shelter of a limestone outcrop. There he had a clear view of almost a mile of moonlit main road below, while he and his vehicle were completely hidden.

Hargrove smiled and drew the Winchester from its scabbard, cocking the bolt to seat a shell in the chamber. A lot of pepole didn't like the new self-loaders, preferring the lever action rifles Winchester had made forever or the newer bolt action based on the Mauser. Not Cotton Hargrove. With the self-loader cocked, he had ten rounds ready as fast as he pulled the trigger, and an extra magazine in his pocket. He wanted something that would shoot fast and hit hard, especially on a night like tonight.

"Come on, you worthless mutt." Hargrove motioned to the dog. "Earn your keep."

The big animal woofed softly and bounded past him.

Hargrove had trained the dog well. Twice he had to call it back from a short dash along the trail of some rabbit or coyote. The rest of the time, it worked a little way ahead of him, quartering back and forth across the hilltop. By the time Hargrove returned to the car, he was sure nobody else had been there that day.

Anyone closer to town would have heard the big bell in the Baptist church mark the hour twice while Hargrove waited. After a time, the dog leaped over into the back of the car and stretched out on the leather seat, its nose resting along its forepaws. Cotton watched the road. Half an hour after midnight, a short-coupled Bulldog motortruck came rolling south as gently as a baby carriage. Rotten sat up with an excited whine.

"I see him, damn it," Hargrove said. The dog surged up into the seat beside him, poised tensely.

All right, Hargrove thought. Charlie had made it safely so far. Others had watched the road from town, but Hargrove had picked for himself the best stretch for hijackers to make their move.

He laid the barrel of the rifle across the metal frame of the windshield. The dog whined. "Hush," Hargrove said softly. "There's nothing out here to hurt your ears!"

He could see the truck more clearly now. Its bobtailed bed was cut up by wooden partitions that resembled a big egg crate. Snugly cradled in each of the padded hollows was a shiny ten-quart nitroglycerine can. In the moonlight the cans winked and gleamed with the uneven motion of the truck. Twenty cans. Two hundred quarts.

"If that don't draw them," he told the dog, "there's nothing ever will. And they'll have to show themselves to get it." He felt in his coat pocket for his second magazine of fat, powerful .401 cartridges. He found it just as one of the shining cans exploded.

"Damnation!"

Hargrove leaped to his feet, almost as startled as if the can had really held nitro. Shards of tin flew sparkling in all directions. Liquid sprayed up from the truck's bed like a cloud of steam. The late report of a rifle boomed across from the opposite hill. The clatter of the Bulldog's engine rose to a frantic pitch and the truck bolted away down the road like a runaway wagon. Rotten stood with forepaws on the windshield frame, barking furiously. Hargrove was quick enough to find the muzzle flash when the rifleman fired again. He swung his Winchester to bear on the spot across the valley and sent two quick shots toward it.

He had lumbered twenty yards off to his right before an answering shot whined over his car. Rotten gave a growl and lunged out into the darkness, bounding away toward the far ridge. Hargrove banged three more shots at the rifle's flash, moved again, and fired until his own rifle was empty. Ejecting the spent magazine, he jammed the spare in its place. The firing from the other slope had stopped.

He was about to congratulate himself on being the best old man dark shooter in the county when he heard the sounds of a horse from the far side of the valley. "Damnation," he muttered. He listened until he couldn't hear the horse any longer. It sounded as if it had headed back toward Emilia.

He needed ten minutes to round up the black dog and coax it into the car again. He let the Pierce Arrow roll down the grassy hill onto the main road before he turned on his lights. His truck and driver were almost as hard to gentle down as the dog had been, but he caught up to them after four miles.

Charlie Osborn had brought the Bulldog to a panting stop. He leaped down onto the road as Hargrove drew up.

"Listen here, Mr. Hargrove," he said at once. "I ain't doing this no more. Being bait's one thing. Being a piece of raw liver tossed in a pool of sharks, that's something else."

Hargrove snorted. "You ever seen a shark, Charlie?"

"No. I ain't never seen the Pearly Gates, neither, and I aim to put off the pleasure long's I can. Working for you don't seem a likely way to do it."

"The pay's good."

"The good book says there ain't no spending once you're

in the graveyard. Had that can been full of real soup 'stead of water, you wouldn't have found enough of me to say grace over."

"It would've been real if you'd had your way. Best as I recall, you were the one telling me for sure that *nobody* knew about this run. I want to know who you told!"

"Me? Hell!" the driver said. "Don't put this off on me! Did you get the dry-gulching son of a bitch?"

"It was too far, too dark."

The driver swung back aboard the truck, mumbling something lost in the noise of the motor.

"What's that you say?"

"I said it weren't too far and dark for him to hit that soup can right plumb in the middle!" He slammed the vehicle in gear and let out the clutch. "I'm taking this contraption back to the yard," he yelled to Hargrove. "I'll be in tomorrow to pick up my time. I ain't doing this *no* more!"

Cotton Hargrove thought about it. As though Osborn were still there, he said, "He was a lot closer to you than I was to him." But he thought that the gunman had probably used a telescopic sight on his rifle.

Still, it wasn't sensible. He'd expected the hijackers would try to steal the load. Instead, somebody had tried to destroy the nitro—truck, Charlie, and all. That wasn't sensible, because there was no profit in it.

Cotton Hargrove knew he wasn't as smart as some nor as educated as others, but he'd learned always to look where the profit lay. Now, some of those smart and educated folks were grubbing around in the Hargrove shadow. And Cotton was just the man to rub his success in their bluenosed faces.

He was having his troubles. The last two wells at Hargrove Hill had come in dry, and some of the older ones were starting to cut water. Hijackers were stealing him blind. But none of that mattered. He was on top, where he'd always belonged. He meant to stay there. It would all have been perfect, if Harry had turned out better, and Elizabeth—

He cut that thought off where it stood and went back to his immediate problem. He knew to look for the profit. But an enemy out there in the night was after something else.

For one of the few times in his life, Hargrove was unsure of himself. He wasn't certain Charlie or one of the others hadn't tipped off the hijackers. That was the trouble with buying people. There was always somebody who could pay more. He needed a man, just one, he could trust the way he trusted Rotten.

"I could buy the Ballard boys or Mad Dog Jack, or maybe even the Buffalo," he told the dog. "But I couldn't be sure but what I was paying the very one who's bleeding me dry. Hell, I own Bremerton, and I'm not sure I can trust *him*."

Rotten looked up at his master, twitching one ear. Hargrove scratched the dog's head.

"No," he said, "but there's that cowboy. Temple. Old Matthew's boy. If he's the man his pa was, he can't be bought. God knows, I tried."

Cotton Hargrove reversed the car to back it crosswise in the road. Before he had it turned all the way back toward Emilia, he had his plan pretty much in mind. He laughed again.

"Hell," he told the dog, "even a fellow that can't be bought might follow a twitching skirt to perdition! I'm one that ought to know that. Why *you've* even proved it yourself."

The dog barked.

"You sure as hell have!" Cotton argued. "Remember that half-wolf bitch you followed into the woods last year? You didn't come home for two days."

The dog threw his muzzle toward the moon and howled.

"That's right! And Lee Temple ain't that different from you and me."

Chapter 11

FRANK LOMAN WAITED UNTIL CHARLIE HAD PULLED OUT OF THE Hargrove yard before he saddled his horse, strapped on his rifle boot, and headed south. As slowly as the Bulldog moved, Loman had no trouble getting ahead of it in time to choose a good spot.

He knew exactly where the truck was headed. To Hargrove's pet oil field, he thought. *The damned old fool's had the luck to find a real field. Well, we'll just see if I don't get it for myself in the end.*

Charlie. Loman had nothing against Charlie Osborn. He could drop a shot into the truck's engine, give the driver time to clear out. But then the explosion wouldn't look like an accident.

No. Charlie didn't matter. He'd be just another man gone. He'd picked the wrong man to work for, that was all.

Half an hour passed before Loman heard the truck coming along the road. One of its wheel bearings needed grease. He heard its faint squeak even above the racket of the motor. He smiled. *Dogs can hear it. Dogs and me!* No other man would have heard the bearing. Charlie probably hadn't noticed it yet, and now he never would.

In a few more minutes, Loman told himself, that dry bearing will be quiet. He smiled again to think that was his reason for being there—to quiet a bearing! "It's always the squeaking wheel gets the grease!" he said softly.

He lay prone beside a tree until the soup wagon was just where he wanted it. Then he set his sight on the moonlit top of the nearest nitro can and fired. Immediately he buried himself behind the tree, but there was no explosion. He heard the truck's motor thundering, the bad bearing shrieking.

Loman rose on one knee and tried a shot at the driver. A tree got in his way. He cursed it, knowing he'd missed. The truck was gone, and he was in a tight. Hargrove had sent out his nitro wagon without any nitro in it. That meant—

Above the road, from the other side of the valley, someone opened up with a rapid-fire rifle. The second bullet slammed into Loman's tree hard enough to make it quiver. Frank Loman took alarm. He scanned the opposite hill with his telescope until he found the blind eyes of the Pierce Arrow staring back at him.

"Cotton Hargrove!" he said aloud. He sent a bullet over the top of the car, trying for that black dog that always rode with the old man. He missed. The dog tore toward him, headed for his ridge. More shots came his way. He thought of Hargrove's short rifle and the big bullets it shot. Loman had never dreamed those bullets would sound so personal when they came through the trees looking for him.

He wanted to creep through the trees and across the road and find Hargrove and shoot him between the eyes. But it was too soon. He wasn't ready yet for Hargrove to die.

Instead he turned and ran to his horse. He let the animal walk until they were out of the trees. Then he put his heels in its flanks and set off along the trail faster than was safe even in daylight. He would need to get the horse hidden away and himself in his bed, just in case Cotton Hargrove happened to come checking.

In his dreams he sometimes wished Cotton would come checking on him. He would kill the rotten old man and have done with it! But no. No, he thought, I can't kill the old rooster until I've plucked his chicks. Nor until I'm sure about the legal lay of things. But once those little matters are taken care of, I won't let him live another day. All I'll want then is to tell him the truth myself, to see him sweat, to listen to him beg for his rotten life.

But he's a clever old bastard. I'll have to remember that so's I don't wind up being cooked in his pot. It was a pretty good trick of his—going to all that trouble buying the nitro cans from me and then hauling them full of water. Scared hell out of me when it *didn't* explode! But that was what he wanted, wasn't it? He may be headed for town right this minute to cut me off before I can get home.

Loman reined his horse onto a wider road and whipped it to a gallop. He would have to ride like a cyclone if he didn't want the old man to catch him. Then he had an idea. For the first time in his life he would get two birds with one stone!

As he came toward the edge of Oiltown, he urged his horse off the road and across a meadow into a thick stand of trees. He tied the horse, made his way on through the trees, and stood presently at the back fence of an unpainted frame cottage. He watched the shadows of figures inside.

When he was sure he heard no car or horse on either road, he went through the front gate like a ghost and rapped on the front door. After a moment, Talking Tommy Ellis opened the door wide and looked out at Loman.

The talking man showed no special surprise. "Frank," he said, "You're up late. Come in." Loman had never been inside the little house, never even stopped at it before.

"Much obliged," Loman said. He looked back along the road. Then he stepped inside in time to see the knob turn on a door at the far end of the room.

Ellis saw him see it. "How can I be of service, Frank? Would you care for a cup of coffee, piece of apple pie?"

Loman made a point of not looking at the bedroom door. "I believe the word for what I want is *advice,*" he said.

Tommy laughed. "Advice from a talking man?" he said. "Nothing easier. What is it you want advice about, your health or your love life?"

"Neither. I mean *advice*. You know, the way lawyers give advice."

"I'm not a lawyer, Frank."

"I think you are."

Thomas Ellis looked at his visitor and said nothing. Loman saw that he had the long-legged little man. He had the talking man caught, probably with somebody else's wife; and he had him nailed about his past. Loman was right! In his own world and under his own name, Ellis had been a lawyer.

"I'm not one to be stirring up the past," Frank Loman said. "All I want's a little bit of legal knowledge."

Tommy let out his breath. "You're mistaken, Frank. But I would truly like to be of service. Let me have your question. I'll look in some old books I have around. If I don't find the answer there, I might know whom to ask."

"I don't think it'll be that hard for you. You won't need a book or any help."

"Don't be too sure, Frank. I'm told that laws differ from one state to another."

"That may be, but—" Frank Loman stopped short. He listened to the exhaust of a heavy car roaring in from the south. He slid the curtain aside to see the Pierce Arrow slowing. Its big eyes swerved toward the house, lighting up the room through the curtain. "Hell!" he said hoarsely. "You got a back door?"

Without comment, Ellis guided him through the kitchen. Two cups sat on the table, two plates with half-eaten slices of pie. Ellis opened the back door and ushered his guest out into the comparative darkness.

"Listen," Loman said, "I was never here. You haven't seen me tonight at all. Else you'll be sorry."

Loman had time to see that the threat didn't frighten Talking Tommy. Then the Buffalo ran. Heavy but long-legged, he bounded over the back fence and ran toward his horse. He figured it was pretty much a standoff. Ellis had him in a vise because he hadn't wanted to be found by Cotton Hargrove. But Loman had a couple or three anvils hanging over Talking Tommy's head, too. Most likely they could come to an agreement.

Thomas Ellis closed his back door and returned to the front, where someone was knocking as loudly as a fireman.

"It never rains but it pours," he murmured, checking the pistol in his belt. Then he opened the door to admit Cotton Hargrove.

"Good morning," Tommy said. "It is morning, you know. You're out pretty early, aren't you?"

"Out late," Cotton said without any imagination. He came inside, still carrying his rifle. "Wondering if you heard any traffic out front in the last quarter of an hour."

"Yours is the only engine I've heard since midnight."

"This would probably have been a horse."

Tommy laughed. "The road's some distance, Mr. Hargrove. I doubt you could hear the Trojan horse from here."

"Trojan horse?"

"Really big, loud horse. No, I haven't heard any traffic over that way at all."

Hargrove began to remember his manners. "Truly sorry to disturb you, Tommy. I saw your light and thought you might have heard something. My nitro wagon was ambushed just a few miles down the road."

"Hijackers? Was anybody hurt?"

"No. But somebody tried to blow it up. No harm done. I was wondering had you boys had any interference lately—"

"No. We've been lucky."

"—since you took on young Temple."

"He's been like a month of rabbits' feet to me. I'm grateful to say we haven't seen a shadow of a hijacker. But I'm just teasing about Temple. He's a good hand."

"You figure he'd be any use if you fell among thieves?"

Tommy laughed. "Well, he's as green as a gourd—though not so green as he started out. He's a hard worker, wouldn't lie to save his life, and not afraid of Satan himself." He smiled at Hargrove. "Comes of having a clear conscience, I expect."

"What's that supposed—"

"If he can shoot men and horses the way he shoots trees, he'll be mighty useful."

Cotton Hargrove frowned and shook his head like a puzzled draft horse. Finally, he said, "So he's took to that new Winchester shotgun all right, has he?"

"Oh, yes." Tommy did not change expressions, but it

registered in his mind that Hargrove knew about the hideaway shotgun. "Like a duck," he replied.

"To water, eh? Ha. I figured he would. Well, sorry again to bother you. Not many lights on at—" He looked at his watch. "—two-thirty in the morning."

"Probably not."

"Talk, you would tell me if you knew anything?"

"Why wouldn't I, Mr. Hargrove?"

"Well, then. Be seeing you. Good night."

"Good night, Mr. Hargrove."

As Tommy Ellis shut the door behind Hargrove, he saw the black dog waiting patiently in the open touring car. Ellis went back to the kitchen, picked up the two plates of apple pie, and took them into his darkened bedroom.

Alice Mayfair huddled in the corner behind Tom Ellis's bedroom door, listening fearfully to men's voices in the front room. Having night visitors ruined their night-names charades. Alice didn't like it.

Frank Loman had come to the door first. He hadn't seen her, Alice thought. But from what he said, he knew things about Tommy that he ought not to know.

Alice thought of using a gun on Buffalo Loman. She thought how it would feel to hit him with a piece of lead pipe. Her thoughts made her tremble. In the daytime, when she had to be strong, she thought she might kill Loman the way she would kill a snake in the henhouse. But it was night and Alice was the soft and gentle Roxanne.

Like the snake, Loman was a threat. He threatened their happiness, threatened her Radcliff, her Talking Tommy, her Roger L. Barker!

There, she thought, now I've done it! I've let Loman draw Tommy's real name out of me.

And then she thought she had laughed out loud at the idea of Roger L. Barker being Rad's *real name!* As if that person existed any longer. As if Rhonda Jean Bergeron existed any longer. As if any of that world had ever been real!

Alice knew one thing for certain. She had to remember

that reality was here in Emilia and not back in Louisiana. No sooner had she allowed the ghost of that past into her mind than it played out on the stage of her mind that last scene of an earlier reality. She covered her ears and shut her eyes, but still she lived it all again. She saw Roger seem to stand a little taller, saw Willy Beauchamp pointing a pistol, heard Rhonda Bergeron scream, heard the terrible guns go off.

Alice Mayfair did not scream. She drew the curtain across that stage of reality past and huddled the more tightly into her corner. She waited in the dark, trembling like a woman with malaria, anxious to ask Tommy what the Buffalo knew, and filled with dread of what Tommy might tell her.

But Tommy had no sooner gotten rid of Loman than Cotton Hargrove came banging at the door. Alice thought of getting under the bed.

I'd rather take the Buffalo on barehanded, she thought, than be caught here in this house by the big Hargrove!

The tones of their voices suggested that Ellis and Hargrove were more closely acquainted than she would have expected. It's only because I never see the two of them together, she told herself. Of course they know each other. It's only business talk.

Finally she heard the front door close. She knew better than to peep past the shade to watch Hargrove leave, but she knew what she would see—his big touring car with the dog sitting up front like a slobbering statue. After a moment she heard the car leave, and then someone was fumbling at the bedroom door. "Radcliff?" she asked.

He murmured in response. She got to the door in time to help him. His hands were full of saucers and things. She took them from him.

Her voice quavered. "I'm frightened, Rad. It's been six years this July, and we still can't get away from it." Her shivering had stopped, but now it came back. *"Two* visitors in one night, Rad."

He put his arm around her shoulders, but she could tell his mind was still elsewhere. "No coincidence," he said. "One was chasing the other."

"Which? Why?"

"I believe, by a true coincidence, that it was nothing at all to do with us." He paused, frowned. "Nothing at all—unless that shotgun ties it all together somehow. I wonder how he knew about that. And Temple. The good Mr. Hargrove has an enormous interest in Lee."

"What do you mean, Rad?"

"I don't know. But I doubt it means anything good for Temple." He shook his head. "It's no good to speculate. As before, my dear, we must play out the cards as they are dealt. The worst of it is that the younger one has found out enough of our old life to be dangerous."

"I knew it! I could just feel it. I'll go back to my place for a few things right now! I don't need much. We'll pack tonight and move on while they're asleep. I don't care about the shop or the goods or the house or my friends, Rad! You ought to know by now I don't care about anything but you."

"You said it yourself, Rox. We've got six years here."

"But you said it *yourself*. Loman's found out. We'll have to fly."

"Or shut him up."

"Shut him up, Rad? How do you mean shut him up?" She caught at his arm. "You wouldn't do anything foolish again? Not on my account!"

"That'll depend on the Buffalo."

Elizabeth Hargrove pulled the yellow Mercer into its place in front of the big unpainted house, stopping with a clang and a jolt. She giggled.

"Too close," she said aloud. Holding to the fender, she worked her way around to the front of the car. The Mercer's bumper, a double ribbon of spring steel, wasn't damaged, but the iron hitching post leaned at a drunken angle.

"Little too close," Elizabeth said again. "Don't need a hitching post anyway. Don't even own a horse anymore."

She started for the porch, then paused. The round, silvery eyes of her father's big Pierce Arrow reflected back the moonlight from the doorway to the shed. A light burned in the parlor window.

"Damn," Elizabeth murmured, her concentration suddenly much sharper. But maybe he'd left the light on by mistake. Or maybe he'd gone to sleep in his chair with his damned big dog beside him.

She crossed the porch silently and eased open the heavy front door. Rotten barked.

"Damn," Elizabeth said again and slammed the door back hard. The black dog plunged out into the hallway, barking furiously at her. Cotton Hargrove came to the door of the parlor and glared.

"Where in hell have you been?"

"What do you care?" She pointed at the black dog. "Get that beast away from me. I swear to God, I'll take your shotgun and blow him into the next world."

"Rotten," Hargrove said.

The dog whined and ran back to him. Hargrove stepped past Elizabeth and held the door. The dog whined again, then raced out into the night. He paused for a second on the porch, then barked and rushed off on a circuit around the house.

"Silly son of a bitch," Hargrove muttered. "Eliza. Wait. I want to talk to you."

Elizabeth had started up the stairs. "Tomorrow," she said. "Late tomorrow."

"Now. In the parlor. Go."

Elizabeth hesitated. She knew his tone. By now she knew all his tones. If she tried to walk away, he would bring her back. "Damn," she said wearily and went back to the parlor.

Laurel Jean had laid out supper on the sideboard under a dish towel, now pulled aside. Elizabeth saw cold, tallow-marbled roast, a baked potato, green beans strewn with bacon, slabs of wheat bread and soft butter. Elizabeth turned away quickly, her stomach churning. A plate on the table by the big leather armchair held the remains of her father's meal. That was no better.

"What do you want?"

Hargrove settled himself unhurriedly into the chair, watching her. She fidgeted under his stare. He opened the cigar case and drew out a Dona Ana El Presidente.

"To talk," he said, biting off the end of the cigar.

"Talk. But don't light that thing. I'll be sick."

Hargrove laughed. She clenched her teeth together and stayed quiet. At least he put down the cigar.

"Where have you been?" he asked again.

"Bible class! You know where I've been. On the Line."

She read his response in his eyes. *On the Line. You and every other whore in town.* But he didn't say it. His voice stayed unusually mild. She was immediately wary.

"Eliza," he said. "How are you getting along with the Temple boy?"

"Boy?" She frowned. Her mind was still trying to wander. What could he want? "The Temple *boy?*"

"Lee Temple. Do you like him?"

"Sure." She tried to steer things back to his anger, back where she knew what to expect. "What of it?"

"Does he like you?"

She answered truthfully before she thought. "No."

Hargrove snorted. "Must make him the only man in the county, then."

That was better. "He is." She grinned, waiting for his anger. Still it didn't come.

"The only one that doesn't like you or the only one for you?"

She waved a hand, not liking the question. "Either," she said. "Both. It doesn't matter. I'm tired."

"I'm telling you it does matter."

"Damn," she said. "You warned me against getting tangled up with him, as I remember. That first night he spent with us? Why ask me now how I get along with him?"

"I'm interested in his welfare."

"Like hell."

That made Hargrove angry, but not in a way Elizabeth understood. He half rose from the chair. "What do you care why?" he snapped. "I'm not asking you to do anything you don't do every night of the world anyway."

"You haven't asked me to do anything yet. But I won't do it for you. Not with him."

"Not with *him?* There's only one reason for that. Hell.

You care for Temple. That's pretty good. You've tried to shine up to him and he won't have you. Is that—"

"Shut up. It's a lie!"

Hargrove laughed. "Well, damn my luck. You've had half a hundred men behind every bush in town—"

"I haven't—"

"—but when I ask you for one little favor, you tell me he's the *one man in the world* that won't have you!"

"No." Elizabeth began to laugh. She hoped it was laughter. "No, that isn't it. *He's* the only one *I* won't have. Damn your luck!"

Cotton Hargrove sliced off a bite of cold beef and put it in his mouth; with his fork upside down, he cut off a couple more bites and stacked them at the side of his plate while he chewed ponderously. "I wish you'd just be nice to him."

Elizabeth swallowed. She had to get away. "You be nice to him!" she snarled. Turning, she ran. He started to reach out for her arm as she came even with his end of the table, but she was too quick for him. As she raced up the stairs, her hand pressed to her mouth to hold back the sobs and the sickness that threatened to overwhelm her, she heard him laughing.

Chapter 12

LEE TEMPLE SLUMPED BESIDE TOMMY ELLIS WHILE ELLIS STEERED one of Bremerton's heavy Nash Quads out of town, bound for the rig on the C-Bar. Except for the stink of gasoline instead of the clean smells of harness and horses, Temple thought it was just like riding one of the freight wagons. The high spring seat was the same, and the cab was open except for a flapping canvas roof that afforded a little shade in daytime.

The roof wasn't needed tonight. Sunset had been no more than half an hour earlier, but away from Emilia and its constant gaslit twilight, the sky was as dark as it would get. The day had been close and humid, with low heavy clouds. At sunset a fresh breeze off the western plains had swept the clouds away, bringing a hint of coolness.

"A pleasant evening," Tommy said. "Good to be working nights again. For a man of my age, the sun seems to get a little hotter each year, the loads a little heavier, the pace a little slower." He sighed. "Indeed, as Shakespeare said—" He broke off and looked at Temple intently. "Am I boring you?"

"Huh? No," Temple said. "I wasn't listening anyway."

"Then listen to this," Tommy said. His tone didn't change, but Temple knew he was suddenly in earnest. "This could well be the time they'll hit us. Once away from town, we'll make some preparations. What we'll do right now is smile and talk and look as if we don't have a care in the world."

"Like this?"

"Oh, that's good. Very good, indeed. People are coming out of their houses to applaud the job you're doing."

Temple laughed. It was Saturday night. The Line would be crowded—the Line was always crowded—but Temple was glad to be away on a job. He thought of himself now as a veteran of the oil boom. He'd smiled when Bremerton had hired as Porterfield's swamper a youngster fresh off the farm—a weevil.

By all rights he should have been as happy as a pig in a mudhole, but the mood that had come on him a couple of weeks before had never quite gone away. He felt like a man in a dream, searching for something important, but not sure what he'd lost.

Except Amy, he thought. He was sure about losing her. *Not really. You never had her. You were just dumb enough to think so, but she knew better all along.*

And he'd lost more. He'd thought of Wagon Mound as home, of Mr. Forrest as a friend—almost as the father he'd hardly known. Mr. Forrest had known Matthew Temple, had employed him, spoke well of him and took on his son as a cowhand.

But not as a son-in-law. That was the rub. A man like Forrest might pay a debt to an old employee, might nurse his cub along; but when it came to the son of a killer marrying into the family, that was too much. He'd explained it all to Temple, carefully and unemotionally, that night in Fort Worth.

"Better if you don't come back with us, Lee. Amy knows what I'm doing. She understands. It's my intention to pay you off right here, with a six-month bonus for good work. And if I can write you a recommendation . . ."

Temple half smiled. He should have taken the recommendation, and the money. Instead he'd stormed out, had picked a fight with Curly Richards, whom he'd thought his rival with Amy, had seen his pay go for the fine, and had spent most of a month in the Fort Worth jail.

"Same eyes, same temper. Start out with fighting, and you'll end up just like your pa."

"Maybe Ma was right," Temple murmured.

"Pardon?" Tommy said.

With a start, Lee Temple pulled himself back to the night and the swaying seat of the truck.

"It's no trick," he said to Tommy. "All I have to do is sit like a wooden Indian. People expect me to do all the listening while Talking Tommy does all the talking."

Tommy wrestled the truck partly around and partly through a deep mudhole at the edge of town. Beyond, the yellowish glare of the carbide headlamps showed nothing but the rutted road disappearing into a tunnel of darkness.

"Well, listen then and quit talking so much yourself. When we've made enough distance to be pretty sure of being alone, I want you to bring out that shotgun and check its loads."

"I could do that now."

"We could hang a sign on the tailboard, if we wanted everybody to know we're alerted. Let's us be somewhat subtle."

"Be what?"

"Try to fool them. Appear nonchalant. Pretend we've never heard about somebody shooting up Hargrove's soup wagon."

"Water wagon."

"They didn't know that ahead of time, did they?"

"I don't know what they knew," Temple said. "Sounds like Hargrove was playing games in the dark and almost got his driver killed. Why *don't* we paint a sign on the wagon? No trespassing. Stay away or we'll shoot. Why don't we just warn the hijackers off?"

"Because Mr. Bremerton says to do it this way."

"Mr. Bremerton's not the one they might shoot."

Tommy was silent long enough for Temple to start feeling foolish. "Look, it's not that I'm scared—" he began.

"I know you're not, Lee." The leggy man laughed suddenly. "For one thing, you don't know enough to be scared." He thumped himself on the chest. "Me, now, *I'm* scared."

"You don't look it."

"A brave outward show, my boy. Inside, I'm a quivering mass of nerves." He twisted in his seat to look behind them and off to each side. "Time we armed ourselves. Draw out that shotgun and a box of buckshot shells."

The shotgun lay in its recess under the truck's seat, sheathed in a leather scabbard. Temple stripped the scabbard off and put it back. He held the shotgun with the butt resting on his thigh, the long barrel angled upward and out. He confirmed that its magazine was full of cartridges, then set the box on the seat beside him. Only then did it come to him that he likely wouldn't get to fire more than the five shells in the gun. If he should need to reload, he'd probably be dead. It struck him funny, but he didn't laugh.

"Ready to rip," he said.

Tommy suddenly had the big ugly automatic pistol in his hand. Letting the truck drive itself for a moment, he used both hands to draw back the slide, seat a round in the chamber, set the safety. He laid the pistol on the seat beside the shells, its muzzle pointing out along the headlight beams.

"Is it safe to leave it like that? With the hammer cocked, I mean?"

"Safe enough," Tommy said. "Your experience is with revolvers. Automatics are different. I'll teach you, but not tonight. Tonight, we need our wits together in case of trouble."

Temple thought about trouble. That brought his mind around to Cotton Hargrove, and the Hargrove name conjured up Elizabeth, blond and laughing.

"Hello, Cowboy."

He thought about her long enough to curse himself for refusing her invitation the last time they'd met.

"It's too soon for the hijackers to hit again," he said abruptly. "Especially since Hargrove was on to them."

"It would be too soon for you or me. No way to measure these people's motives and reasoning—if they are the same people. All we can do is to be ready for them."

"What are we going to do if they come looking at us in the dark with a telescopic sight at a hundred yards or so, the way they did with Charlie? You spoke of painting a sign. Whyn't you just paint sitting ducks on our backs?"

Tommy glanced his way, eyebrows raised. "You're in a sorry state tonight, Lee. Is something wrong?"

"It's—" Temple hesitated. He didn't know how to explain, even if he wanted to. And there was nothing to be gained by crying into Tommy's apron. "Sorry, Tommy," he said. "I'm just edgy. I'll be all right."

"Yes." The assurance in Ellis's voice startled Temple. "You will, indeed. If trouble starts, you'll be just fine."

"How do you know that?"

Tommy looked sideways at him, smiled. "I'm a judge of such things," he said.

It touched Temple's curiosity. "Sometimes, Talk, you sound like a gunfighter."

Ellis laughed. "When I belch, maybe, or when my bones creak." He shrugged. "I've had a wide acquaintance. Met some interesting people. That's all."

"You never let your gun show. You don't act like you're

looking to shoot anybody. But the closer we get to dark, the more you sound like you know the way of gunfights."

"Just a habit of mine. You know how I talk. Talking Tommy." He put a special emphasis on the name. "That's who I am, Lee. Nobody else. Do you understand me?"

Temple looked at him in the reflected light from the headlamps. Tommy's face was expressionless, his lips tightly closed. Slowly, Temple nodded.

"Sure, Tommy," he said. "I understand."

They rolled on toward the C-Bar, talking less, watching the road and the ditches more and more carefully every minute. At each curve, each clump of brush, each hilltop, Temple tightened his hands on the shotgun, certain that the hijackers would be hiding in the trees or blocking the road. As each menace passed, he sheepishly relaxed his hold, stealing a glance now and then at Tommy's serene face.

By his looks, Talking Tommy might have been thinking of a happy incident in childhood. But Temple saw the fine lines on Tommy's forehead, the unnatural stillness of his face. Only his eyes moved, and they moved constantly from the road to the darkness and back again. They were less than a mile from the C-Bar turnoff when his gaze suddenly hardened on a single spot.

"There," he said.

Temple squinted ahead. A pair of wavering yellow lights materialized on the road ahead, moving slowly toward them. Temple snicked off the safety on the shotgun.

"We make pretty good targets, here in our own light," he murmured.

"Let's give them something to look at, then."

Tommy pressed a switch. There was a hissing sound. A second later the big carbide spotlight on the truck's hood flared into life. Tommy swung the beam to center on the dark, humped shape behind the yellow lights.

"Hold up," he said. He laid the automatic back on the seat before Temple realized he'd picked it up. "That's Mr. Carstairs's Model T. He owns the C-Bar."

The Ford roadster crabbed over to the edge of the ditch and stopped, waiting for the truck to pull alongside. A comfortably heavy man with an old-fashioned gray moustache pulled himself up so that he was sitting on the back of the roadster's seat, almost on a level with the Quad's cab.

"Glad to see you, Ellis," he called over the noise of the motors. "Do you know what's going on down at that blamed oil rig?"

"Don't know as I do, Mr. Carstairs, but we're headed down that way right now. What's the trouble?"

"Mr. Carstairs, hell! Call me Buster. Everybody in the county does. Hell, I don't know what's the trouble. I was out at the green windmill just now and decided to drive by the rig—thought maybe they were getting oil all over my pasture. So I went to the hilltop for a look. Didn't see any oil, nor nothing else. No lights. There's not a sign of life anywhere around the rig."

"Oh?" Tommy's voice was still casual, but he leaned down toward the rancher. "Did you go down to see about it?"

Buster Carstairs looked uncomfortable. "Well, no. I knew they were pretty leery about visitors, so I stopped up on top of the hill." He shook his head. "Old Jeeter's flivver was there, and that walking-beam thing was going up and down, but I couldn't rouse a soul, not even with the horn."

"Hm. Maybe they couldn't hear over the drilling noise."

"That's another thing. Like I say, that beam affair was pounding away, but it didn't make near as much noise as I'd got accustomed to. I was headed in to call the sheriff. Thought maybe he'd come out and see what's what."

Ellis looked at Temple for a minute, then back at the rancher. "We'll check into it and get things hopping," he said. "No need to worry the sheriff just yet."

"I'd sure appreciate it." Carstairs pursed his lips under the thick moustache, then said, "Listen, I'll be glad to come with you."

"That won't be necessary."

"I mean, I don't know much about this oil drilling business. Don't want to. And I wasn't sure if they'd want me down there." He hesitated. "Nor I wasn't armed. I see you're loaded for bear."

"Buffalo," Temple breathed.

"Don't you worry about it, Mister—Buster," Tommy was saying. He smiled. "This sort of thing's our business, Lee's and mine. We'll see after it for you."

"Much obliged." With obvious relief, the rancher slid back into his seat. "I'll run on home. Don't go shooting any of my livestock, now."

"We'll take care, Mr. Carstairs," Temple put in, figuring it was about time he said something. "I've worked cattle myself, back in New Mexico."

"Well, you don't say! I'll rest easy, then."

The rancher put the Ford in gear and clucked away past them. Tommy looked at Temple.

"Wanted to be sure and show us he wasn't afraid," Temple observed.

"Well, he's unquestionably the only one who isn't!" This time Tommy sounded as though he meant it. "I don't like the sound of it, Lee. Not one bit. I think just for fun we'll go in the back way."

"You're the boss."

"Remember that." Ellis let out the clutch and the truck glided into motion. "It's probably nothing," he said softly. "We'll probably learn that they're out of something they need to make that rig hum. We'll give it to them, and they'll get the thing going, and then we'll all have a good laugh about it." But he didn't laugh.

They turned in under the C-Bar brand sign and drove a lonely half mile before they took a right-hand fork Temple hadn't noticed before. Tommy said, "The road's a little rougher, but it'll bring us in down by the slush pit. How are you at seeing in the dark?"

"Middling. Why?"

For answer, Ellis closed a valve. The spotlight and headlamps died with a hissing pop, and darkness flowed over the road like heavy oil.

"A little slower, but twice as safe."

"I always figured the hijackers would hit us out on the open road, if anyplace."

"Likewise. But it's a dark night. They could be waiting for us at the rig. Or anywhere."

"You're a cheerful and comforting companion," Temple murmured. He thought the air must have grown colder, because he had a tendency to shiver. He stared into the darkness until his eyes felt wide as an owl's, watching as the truck lurched slowly past clumps of cedar and mesquite. A low, panting sob grew in the air around them.

"Steam engine's still running," Ellis said. His voice barely carried to Temple. "And there's the rig."

Temple saw the dark spire of the derrick rising above the rim of the hollow ahead. Tommy followed the road around to the left and gently over the ridge. The rig lay just at the bottom of the long slope. It was running like a top, but as Carstairs had said, without the slam and jar of the heavy bit shaking its structure. The drilling floor was dark.

"It's not right," Tom Ellis said. "They'd've lighted the lanterns by now. And that engine's running almighty slow."

As if it had heard him, the steam engine gave a long, hissing sigh and stopped. For a few moments everything turned as before, the belts and wheels and the weight of the tools all seeking equilibrium. Then the walking beam creaked to a stop and the night was silent except for the steady throb of the truck's engine. Tommy immediately shut it off.

"We'll walk down from here. Keep that shotgun ready."

"We don't want to shoot Jeeter or Oilcloth."

"No. But Jeeter's got ears like a bat. If he was where he could hear us, he'd be turning out to see who we were."

"Maybe he's just dozed off." Temple didn't believe it, but he had to say something. Tommy gave a little snort that might have been a laugh.

"And Oilcloth, too? Well, that'll be our best hope. Come on."

He slipped down from the seat and started toward the rig, motioning Temple to the other side of the road. Temple did his best to watch his footing and to look in all directions at once. Try as he might to be quiet, his clumsy work boots scattered the loose rock of the road until he sounded like a cow coming down to drink. Like a herd of cows, he amended, cursing himself. He looked with envy in the direction Talking Tommy had gone, not quite sure from one moment to the next where to find him. The long-legged man seemed to drift from one pool of shadow to another, approaching the derrick as quietly as a spider.

They took shelter by the bank around the slush pit, paused there while they listened. In the hollow, the breeze was less. A heavy, sour smell made Temple want to cough. Timbers in the derrick creaked in the light breeze. Some loose piece of metal rasped against another as regularly as a clock ticking. From the brush behind the rig a night bird cried.

"Nobody there," Temple whispered.

"Jeeter'd die before he went off and left the tools running," Tommy answered. "Give me a minute to get over by the band wheel. You come in from this side."

Temple looked at the dark shadows under the derrick. When he tuned back, Tommy was gone. Temple licked his lips and gripped the cold metal of the shotgun, counting silently. At sixty he crossed the open space with three long strides and stepped onto the rig floor. He froze. Starlight coming through the wooden lattice of the derrick threw a dim, diffused glow over everything. Temple could make out dark shapes but nothing else. He waited, his pulse pounding in his ears. Then Tommy called from the far side of the floor.

"Temple?"

"Here."

"Stand still. I'm going to strike a light."

In the sudden glow of the match, Temple started and almost cried out. Oilcloth sat on the lazy bench within a yard of him. The tool dresser leaned comfortably against a wooden cross-brace, head tilted back, mouth open in a soundless snore. His lunch bucket sat beside him, opened. An apple lay near his boots where it had rolled from his open hand.

Asleep after all, Temple thought. But the surge of relief

froze in his chest. Tommy was bending over Jeeter's body.
The driller lay on the floor by the brake lever. A package of
Red Man, newly opened, was still in his hand, and flakes of
the tobacco spread across the wooden planks. Tommy
looked up at Temple, his face pale in the fading light.

"Oh, the dirty bastards!" he whispered harshly. He bent
as low as his legs would allow and came over to Temple. "I
suppose they've killed him as well."

Temple let out a little of his breath. "He's dead?"

Tommy touched the toolie's throat and arm with a gentle,
long-fingered hand. "Dead for hours. Dead, probably, before we left the yard."

The match burned down and he shook it out. In the new
darkness Temple said, "Nobody could have known we were
coming here before we left the warehouse."

"Apparently someone knew."

"Where are they, then? What are they waiting for?"

Tommy rubbed the side of his pistol barrel across his
cheek. "That's a very good question. It's also a pretty good
question how they got in here without making any tracks."

"What do you mean?"

Tommy struck another match, held it to one of the wicks
of a yellow-dog lantern. "Help me straighten this one out a
little. I want to know what killed him. You see a wound?"

Temple had already seen enough. He shook his head.

"Jeeter isn't marked, either. Maybe they were both bit at
the same time by a pair of vipers."

"No," Temple said at once. "I've seen snakebite. This
isn't it."

"Nor anything else I know of." Tommy peered into the
darkness outside the rig floor. "Let's have our look around
the whole lay of the location. You go around past the belt
housing. I'll meet you behind the engine house." He looked
again at Oilcloth, then blew out the light. "If you come
across anybody besides me, don't ask questions. Blow their
damned heads off!"

But their search found nothing. Twenty minutes later they
were back on the floor, the lantern lighted again. Tommy
covered the bodies with a sheet of canvas from the truck.

"The boiler's gone cold from lack of fuel," he said. "It hasn't been fired for quite a while. And the lanterns weren't lit. This happened before dark, just as I said."

Lee Temple rubbed his forehead. A dull ache throbbed behind his eyes. "Then nobody slipped up on them," he said. "It was someone they knew."

"Or something we don't know anything about." Tommy Ellis looked at the pistol in his hand as though he'd forgotten he had it. He reset the safety and shoved the gun into his waistband. "We have to get the law out here. We'd normally unload our wagon and take the bodies to town, but in this uncommon case, I don't believe we ought to move them."

"Right."

"One of us has to go for help. The other had better stay. Which job do you want?"

Temple had expected the question. The truth was he didn't want either job, but he knew what the answer had to be.

"You can handle the truck. I can't. I'll stay."

"True enough." Tommy hesitated. "Probably it'll be better if you put out the light," he said. "But you can suit yourself. And keep that shotgun close."

Temple almost laughed. "Don't worry!" Then he said, "Wait a minute. You can't go back without a guard. Maybe that's what the hijackers want."

Talking Tommy stared at him. "You might have something there." He glanced at the covered bodies, then at Temple. "Are you saying we should both go? Leave them alone?"

"Can't do that." Temple hated to say it, but again he knew the right answer. "We—knew them. And there are wolves and coyotes out here. But you better take the shotgun."

Ellis laughed harshly and touched the automatic in his belt. "I'll manage. And I hope to God they do jump me. Let's find you a place to keep watch."

Ten minutes later Temple stood below the skyline of the ridge while Tommy brought the truck engine back to throbbing life and edged the big Quad around. Up in the clean air, Temple's head felt better. The stars overhead shone clear and tranquil. The rig was peaceful now, quiet except for the small noises of the night—noises that sounded quite different to Temple now that he knew what lay beneath the steepled derrick.

Tommy leaned out of the cab. "Guess I'll run without lights for a spell," he said. "Take care, Lee."

"You, too."

The gears meshed and the truck crawled over the crest and away. Temple stood shivering in the warm night, holding the shotgun for comfort and contemplating those real questions of life that Tommy had once suggested he consider.

Chapter 13

"HIJACKERS, NOTHING." DR. THORNTON WAS A THIN, QUICK, nervous man, impatient with Temple's questions. He jerked a packet of factory-rolled cigarettes from his pocket, started to shake one free, then glanced toward the rig floor and shoved them back again. "Asphyxiation, pure and simple."

"You mean they suffocated?"

"Not exactly. Not mere oxygen deprivation. Inhalation of some noxious agent caused the deaths."

"Then . . . ?"

Temple couldn't think how he'd meant to finish. He was tired, maybe more tired than he'd ever been before. Dawn had brought a fresh wind before Tommy returned. He'd brought with him Brace Bremerton and two grim-looking Bremerton employees. The doctor and Sheriff Quinlan came along a few minutes later in the county police car, closely followed by a man from the drilling company and a couple of his hands.

"Told them we'd better come in first," Bremerton had said. "Weren't sure how edgy you'd be with that shotgun.

Except Tommy." He ran a hand through his bushy hair. "Tommy said you'd be all right. You look sick. Sit in the truck."

By now Temple wished he'd obeyed. Instead he'd watched from the lazy bench while Quinlan and the doctor poked around the bodies and the drilling floor. The investigation seemed to take a long time. Finally Quinlan consented to let the drilling company hands back their truck up to the rig and place Oilcloth and Jeeter in its bed.

"Noxious agent," Temple repeated. The words tasted strange in his mouth, as if he were parroting some foreign language. "Some kind of poison, you mean?"

"Sour gas."

That was the man from the drilling company. He was wide, graying, slow-moving and slow-talking. He stepped up beside the doctor and nodded toward the blanket-wrapped bundles on the truck.

"Seen it before. Likely they hit a low-pressure gas pocket just at the top of the Wichita. Gas bled out slow, bubbled up the hole so's Jeeter didn't notice the smell. Those low clouds yesterday held it right down in this valley with them. Sour gas."

"Then it wasn't hijackers?" None of it made any sense to Temple. "Sour gas. What's that?"

"Sulfuretted hydrogen," Thornton said. He frowned at Temple's blank look. "Hydrogen sulfide. Sewer gas. Does that tell you?" His frown deepened and he bent to peer into Temple's face. "Say, are you all right?"

"I'm just tired. And my head hurts some."

Thornton pulled Temple's hat off and tilted his head back to look into his eyes. "Hell!" To the pusher he said, "Here, help me with him. Over there, upwind of this damn death trap. Tell me, Cowboy, did you smell anything while you were out here last night?"

"No." Temple tried to pull away as the two men half dragged him away from the rig, but gave it up as too much trouble. "Well, yes. Something rotten." He shook his head as they eased him into the seat of Bremerton's truck. "It went away after a minute."

The doctor glanced back at the rig again, then pulled out a cigarette and lit it. He blew a puff of smoke Temple's way. "Smell that? I thought not. Paralysis of the nerves." He waved an impatient hand to shut off Temple's question. "Don't fret, it'll pass. Your friends might have smelled the gas at first. Then they didn't notice it anymore. Then they got sleepy, and then they were dead." He straightened. "Brace, Tommy! Over here."

"What's the trouble, Doc?"

"This young fool's the trouble. Standing guard." The doctor snorted. "Listen, Brace, you get him into town and put him to bed. I'll write up something to make him sleep."

"I'm all right."

Thornton ignored him. "Standing guard!" The doctor took another deep drag on his cigarette, then ground it under his heel. "It's fortunate you put him up on the slope, Tommy. If he'd stayed on the rig floor, we'd have three to bury. Bed rest and lots of liquids. I'll see him later."

Lee Temple opened his eyes in darkness. He was in his bunk. No one else was in the room. They had left him to rest and recuperate. He sat up. The room revolved around him in a slow, complete circle. It steadied. He found his clothes and boots, got dressed clumsily and crossed to the door.

Mrs. Watson caught him before he made it outside. "What are you doing out of that bed? I've even run Mad Dog Jack out of the house so you could rest up and get well."

"I thank you." He opened the outside door.

"Where are you going?"

"I've decided not to die in bed."

She stared after him. "There's worser places!" she shouted.

He turned and nodded to her. "I intend to find one of them," he said. The movement and the noise of his voice dislodged a boulder inside his head. It rolled to the front and became a terrific headache. He blanked out for a second, stumbled. Then he found his footing and went across the lot toward the Line.

Temple wasn't happy. He didn't like the idea of a nasty,

invisible, poisonous gas that sneaked out of the ground and murdered good men before they could run or curse or pray. It came to him that working in the oil field was a hell of way to make a living.

He went slowly on down to the Line, entering the first tent he came to. When he recognized Mel at the bar, he knew he'd been there before.

"What do you have for a headache?"

"All kinds of things to give you one. Nothing that'll make it better."

"One whiskey."

Mel set down a glass and poured a slug of amber whiskey. "Hope you won't be mixing your drinks tonight."

Temple put his money down with one hand and took up his glass with the other. He looked at Mel across the rim, tossed down the whiskey, and gritted his teeth. "Not likely," he said. He put down the glass and walked outside.

The sun was almost down. He wandered through the maze of tents until he saw a sign advertising Miss Sadie's Boardinghouse for Demure Young Ladies. Just what he needed, he decided. He still had most of a week's pay left. If he worked at it, he could spend the whole thing before morning.

Purposefully, he started toward the door. Before he got there, Elizabeth Hargrove came out, walking fast, carrying a cloth sack. Not even noticing Temple, she strode to the next tent, flung aside the flap and went inside.

He followed her with his eyes, then with his feet. She had stopped at the first table, leaning over to talk to the four people seated there. Shooter and the Indian were looking up at her with growing interest; their lady friends looked at her with mixed expressions of jealousy and surprise.

Elizabeth set her sack on the table with a solid sound. "Whatever you can," she was saying in answer to Shooter's question.

Chief wasn't sure about it. "And what will you do with this money?"

Temple could tell by the bounce of her blond hair that Liz didn't like the question. "I won't steal it," she said. "It's for the family. The company will handle Jeeter's funeral expenses, but his widow has four children to raise."

Chief let go his suspicion and reached into his coat pocket. He palmed an untidy fistful of bills into the cloth sack. "I meant no offense," he said with neither smile nor frown. Then he turned to the young woman beside him, grinned and said, "Honey, when old Shoot and me go, you won't need to raise funeral expenses. Big boom, no Indian."

She blinked wide brown eyes at him. "I wouldn't have none for you, anyway," she said seriously. "I'm not your kin. We're just—" She hesitated, pushing at the feathered hat she wore. "Just—friends."

"Business associates," Shooter murmured. He gave Elizabeth a salute. "I'm in," he said. "Jeeter was a good hand. Didn't waste his time down here on the Line. Didn't neglect his family." His eyes were not focused on anything. "Wasn't like some of us, fishing with the wrong bait. Asleep when we did have a bite and lost the finest fish we'd ever hook."

Elizabeth took up her sack and turned toward the next table, but Chief's woman stopped her. "Hold it, sister," she said loudly. "This *lady* you're collecting for—she too proud to take a whore's money?"

People at the nearby tables turned to watch. One of the onlookers snickered. "If she is, Liz'll have to get somebody else to deliver it."

Elizabeth's cheeks flushed. Temple couldn't say if it was embarrassment or anger. Whichever, she never took her eyes off the girl with the hat.

"I don't know how she'd feel," Elizabeth said. "But I'm not too proud." She opened the bag and held it out. "You're more than welcome to contribute, Georgette. If you want to, of course."

Georgette stared at her for a second, obviously startled that Elizabeth had known her name. "Well—I guess," she mumbled. Embarrassed at the attention she'd drawn, she quickly put in her money and fumbled for her champagne glass. "Sure. If it's for the kids. I love kids."

Chief neither smiled nor frowned, but he stretched a long

arm around Georgette's shoulders. Scooping up a bottle with his other hand, he refilled her glass.

"Thank you, Georgette," Elizabeth said.

"Well, sure, ah—Miss—"

"Liz," Elizabeth said with a bright smile. "All my friends call me Liz. Anybody else—for the kids?"

Temple watched Elizabeth as she moved directly from table to table, taking her collection. He was waiting for her when she came back to the doorway. So intent had she been at her work that she had not even seen him until then. He looked down at her with an Indian-even expression.

She opened the bag and held it out toward him as if he were free to contribute or take some of the money for himself. "It's for Jeeter's widow," she said. In her voice was none of the hard-edged teasing he was used to, none of the mischief. He put most of a week's pay in the sack.

"I didn't know you were acquainted with Jeeter. Nor his widow."

She met his eyes, and Temple was surprised to see she was close to tears. Then she grinned, and the hard, bright, defensive edge was back.

"Live and learn, Cowboy. There's lots you don't know about me. But I've offered you the chance to learn." She closed the sack and started to turn away. "Thank you," she said in a different voice. Then she slipped out through the flaps.

For a moment Temple hesitated. Shooter focused his eyes on him, gave him a wobbly salute. "Hell, fisherman," he said. "Don't let that one get away. She's a keeper."

Temple returned the salute. With military squareness of step he followed Elizabeth Hargrove out into the deepening shadows of evening. She was nearly to the next tent when he caught up to her.

"May I join you?" he asked her.

"Of course." She didn't look at him. Her voice was flat. "If you'd like."

"I would. Do you have time for a cup of coffee, glass of tea? Lemonade, maybe?"

She paused, looked up into his face this time, near enough

to smell the liquor on his breath. She smelled it, frowned. "Maybe. When we finish. Right now I want to see all of them before they've spent their wages."

Temple thought of all the money already gone to bartenders and gamblers and barkers. He was still thinking when Elizabeth reached the tent where he had bought his drink. While she started for the gaming tables, Temple went to the bar.

"Welcome back," Mel said. "Always like to see return business. What'll it be?"

Temple took off his hat and held it out toward the man. "How about five percent of what you've taken in tonight?"

Mel raised his eyebrows. The other bartender sidled over, reaching unobtrusively under the bar. "What the hell?" Mel asked. "You think you can hold us up right here in front of a hundred people?"

"No holdup. I'm with the lady." He pointed to Elizabeth with a feeling he recognized as pride. "We're taking up money for Jeeter's widow and kids."

"The hell you say."

"That's no lady," the second man said. "That's Liz."

Temple looked at him. "The *lady* is passing among your customers," he said mildly. "I'm asking you to return a little of your profit to the community."

Mel didn't know where to put that idea. First he bristled. Then he started to laugh. "You just stand right here a minute, Cowboy," he said finally. "I got to have me a word with the boss. Lou, here, will keep you company."

He went through a curtain to the right of the bar. Temple leaned on the bar. Lou stared at him morosely.

"Don't nobody never pass the hat when a bartender dies," he said.

"Too bad. Seems like somebody should." Temple nodded toward Elizabeth, busy among the tables. "Bet the lady would, if you left a family."

Lou considered the idea, watching as Elizabeth bent to speak to one of the card players. "Could be," he conceded. "Be pretty near worth dying, just to find out."

Mel returned in a couple of minutes. Without a word he reached under the bar and took out his cash box. He stared into it like a man inventorying the contents of his own stomach, then withdrew a stack of bills. "That's right at five percent," he said. "If it's not, it's a little more." He dropped the money into the hat as if he hoped Temple would give it back.

"I thank you."

"The establishment's sentiments and compliments to the widow," Mel recited carefully. He tugged his ear. "Boss says go shake down the Paradise and the Red Garter for the same cut. But take care. Life's more interesting with you around, Cowboy."

"I think so, too. Thanks."

At the Paradise Casino, Elizabeth protested. "Wait. I've already been here."

"Then you wait. Here, by the door. Who's in charge?"

"Why—Lester Banks. That's him at the dice table. The one with the little moustache."

Temple went hat in hand to the long green table. Bull Ballard and Ace High were among the players, both a little drunk.

"I'm with Miss Hargrove," he said, "taking up money for Jeeter's widow."

Bull said, "Hell, Liz just damn near cleaned us out. You reminding me makes me want to pull your head off."

Temple put his hat on the table in front of the dealer. "I'm not here to take your money," he told Bull, "but I haven't had supper and I'm just about mad enough about it to tie you and Ace together by the arms."

"Aw, don't talk so rough," Ace High murmured. "Bull don't mean no harm."

"I don't mean nothing but harm!" Bull put his hands on the arms of his chair to push himself up.

Temple leaned across close to him, kept his voice low. "If you come out of that chair, I'm going to embarrass you in front of all these people."

Bull frowned, blinked. He stared up at Temple for a

moment, and then he eased himself back into the seat. Temple turned to the dealer, who was rattling the dice in his hand impatiently.

"Now," he said, "you see the money in my hat. I'm collecting from you proprietors. The going rate is five percent of the evening's take—"

"Like hell!"

"—but you can give more—"

"More!"

"—if you'd like."

"Well, I damn well don't like!"

"And I wouldn't like to stand up on your table and tell all these good customers you're too tight to give the same as the other businessmen on the Line. But I will."

The gambler slipped a hand inside his coat. "You can't threaten me! What other businessmen?"

Two men pushed their way through the crowd to stand behind Temple. One of them reached for his shoulder. Bull Ballard intercepted the bouncer's wrist, wrapped it in his iron-hard hand, and squeezed. The man yelped.

"Temple's with Liz. Miss Hargrove, that is," Ace High said. "We're with Temple." He looked at the gambler. "Who're you with, Lester?"

Sweat ran down Lester's face. "How much is in your hat?" he asked finally.

"I haven't counted."

"I'll cut you high card for it. Double or nothing."

"We'll do it this way. You get the high card, you get the hatful. If I get the high card, I want five percent."

"Fair enough." The gambler produced a deck from somewhere in his coat, shuffled, offered it to Temple. Temple tapped it with a forefinger.

"You first."

Lester smiled. He flexed his fingers, squared off the deck, and lifted a dozen cards, showing the bottom one faceup. "King of spades to beat," he said.

Temple reached back and plucked the red ace from Ace High's hatband. He laid it across the deck. "I win."

"That's not fair play. You've got to draw from this deck."

Ace High rose to stand beside his brother. "I hate to admit it, Les, but that ace come from this deck," he said, leaning across to smile at Lester. "I palmed it out'n there myself, earlier tonight—same's you palmed your king just now."

The gambler looked at Ace High, then at both Ballards together, then at Temple, finally at the rest of the crowd, all watching with interest. He jerked his head toward the bouncers. They withdrew as smoothly as they'd come. Lester pulled out a cash box and began to count bills into Temple's hat.

"Five percent." He smoothed his thin moustache and nodded to Temple. "No offense taken, Cowboy. I like a man who'll push a bluff. If you ever need work, come see me." He smiled. "Have you run your traps at the Red Garter yet? Come back if they won't ante, and I'll send a couple of my boys with you to talk to them."

Temple said, "I thank you and the widow thanks you."

Bull Ballard said, "And I and Ace thank you, too, you son of a bitch! Do you mean to say that you've took twenty times that much from us just tonight? We may just pull your head off to see what you're stuffed with!"

The two bouncers slid back into position behind Bull. Lee Temple turned away through the crowd. Several people slapped his back, a couple offered to buy him a drink. A pretty, red-haired bar girl called, "Come with me, Cowboy; I'll take your mind off that widow." At the tent's doorway a lean, bearded man brushed past him on the way outside, and then Temple was back where Elizabeth waited.

She looked up at him with different eyes. "I didn't know you'd care."

"Yesterday, I might not. Today I know how sly death is. I know what the oil field is like."

"I'm sorry I said that. It's just that you were looking at me—earlier—like you wouldn't think *I* cared. I didn't want you to say it first."

"I didn't mean—"

"You should've. I know what kind of trash I am—"

"Don't say that. You're not—"

"I am." She stopped walking, turned to him. "You don't

know." She said flatly. "You don't know me, anything about me."

"You offered me the chance to learn. I'm taking you up on it."

For an instant he caught surprise, hurt, gladness all mixed together in her eyes. Then she grinned. "Sure, Cowboy. Why not? Now, let's get to the Red Garter before they hear you're coming and lock the doors."

"All right."

"The thing is, I'm tired of myself. You don't know what I mean. You've never felt that way."

Temple thought about his father, about the past that had dogged him all his life. "Do you think not?"

"You haven't," she said with finality. He didn't argue. After a moment she looked at him again. "Do you know what I wish sometimes?"

"No."

"I wish I could be somebody else. I wish I could just leave—leave—" She waved a hand. "—all of this, leave who I am, leave—me—behind. Even if it only lasted a little while."

"I wouldn't like that," Temple said.

She stared at him for a second, her eyes narrow and wary. "Sure you wouldn't. You and every other man in this place. You know just what I am and just what I need, don't you?"

"No," Temple said. He didn't tell her she'd become someone else, someone different from the young woman who'd been so concerned about Jeeter's family. He wanted that first one back. "But I don't want you to be anyone else—Elizabeth."

She flinched as if she'd been hit when he spoke her name. "Call me Liz."

"No." He shifted his grip on the hatful of money and reached out to take her hand. "I don't think I want you to be anybody else."

She didn't resist as he drew her gently up against his chest. She started to speak, didn't, put her free hand on his shoulder, stretched on tiptoe to meet him. His lips brushed hers as softly as the breeze playing across the blue plumage on a quail's head.

"Lee—"

"Now, ain't that right sweet," a heavy voice said from the shadows beside them.

In one motion Temple turned, spinning Elizabeth back and away, facing the man who'd spoken. He was no more than a tall shadow in the dark between two clapboard shanties.

"I wouldn't want to trouble you young lovebirds for all that money you've took up. Not unless you want me to trouble you. What I'd rather is for you to put it down. Walk away from it. No trouble."

Elizabeth shook her head enough to make her short golden hair whip across her face. "You can have it in hell!" she cried.

Temple moved in front of her. "No trouble," he said to the shadow. "We're not armed. Just step out here like a man, and we'll give it to you peacefully. What I can't do is leave it lying on the ground. People gave it to us in good faith."

The shadows bunched together, moved, came forward as a lean, bearded man with a gun in his hand. "Put it down."

"We'll put it on your grave!" the girl said.

"Easy," Temple told her. He dropped to one knee and set the hat on the ground, his eyes never leaving the robber. "Let's not have any trouble."

"Lee! You can't—"

"Shut up, missy! I'll have that money bag from you, too." He laughed. "And I might steal me a little kiss. If your big, brave cowboy don't mind."

"You touch me—"

"Reckon I wouldn't be the first. The money, or you'll be dead."

"One thing," Temple said, still kneeling. "She's leaving. Right now."

"Like hell."

The gun turned from Elizabeth to Temple, and he let out a tightly held breath.

"Thing is," Temple said, "a shot will bring folks out of these tents. They know Miss Hargrove. If they find out you've stolen their contributions to a poor widow, they just might string you up to the crossbeam of the nearest derrick before they got over being mad."

The robber stared at him, and Temple saw the sudden glint of fear in the man's eyes. "You stay right there! I swear I'll shoot."

"I'm right here. Here's the hat. Settle for that and be on your way, before somebody comes along."

The man took a step, then gave a sudden harsh laugh. "Sorry, Cowboy," he cried. "I'll have it all!" Drawing back the pistol, he swung it in a vicious arc at Temple's head.

Temple had been waiting. When he saw the robber's arm start to move, he uncoiled his long legs in a hard, driving surge. The gun hit him hard between neck and shoulder, sending a numbing wash of pain down his left arm, but he crashed into the lean man and slammed him back against the shanty wall. The whole structure trembled with the impact.

Temple kept his legs pumping, muscling the robber against the splintery wall. He'd lost track of the gun. He tried to grab for the man's wrist, but his left arm wasn't working right. He settled for clubbing his numbed forearm across the robber's face, then flung his weight on the man's outstretched gun arm, pinning it against the wall. He took a left-handed blow in the face and pounded back with his right.

He didn't know how long it took nor how many times the man hit him. Finally the sagging dead weight pulled him to the ground. He followed it down, still driving his fist home into something now jagged and wet. Someone was pulling at him, trying to pull him away, shouting into his ear. He shook his head to shoo away the annoyance and struck again and again until words gradually began to reach him in the dark place where he was.

"For God's sake, Lee, stop it! Stop! You'll kill him, if you haven't already! Lee! Lee Temple! Stop it!"

The voice was Elizabeth's. Temple realized she was

dragging with all her strength at his arm, trying to stop the blows. He looked at her, then at the still figure crumpled beneath him, then at his torn and bloody fists.

"Lee! Lee, are you all right?"

"All right. I've quit."

He bowed his head and drew a sobbing breath, then put both hands on the ground and pushed himself upright. He felt dizzy, sick, the way he'd been after the hydrogen sulfide. He leaned against the shanty wall and looked into Elizabeth's frightened face.

"Of course I'm all right. Did he hurt you?"

"Me? No. My God, Lee, what happened? The way you hit him. And your face. I've never seen anything like—"

"Good. He shouldn't have threatened you."

He pushed away from the wall and started to reach for the hat. Elizabeth was there ahead of him.

"I have it. The money. Come on, let's get away from here." She looked down at the robber, then looked away again. "Hurry. You need a doctor."

"I'm all right." Temple took a step. He was surprised when his legs started to give and he almost fell. Elizabeth caught his arm and he leaned heavily on her. "I'm all right."

"Sure you are, Cowboy." She was trying for the old tone, but he still heard the fear that shook her voice. "Hang on. I'll get you home. No, don't kiss! My God."

Chapter 14

THE TORPEDO WAS A TIN CYLINDER, SEVEN FEET LONG, WITH BRASS caps that screwed onto the ends. Each cap had a coupling on top so that another torpedo could be attached to the first.

"Just like pearls on a string," Shooter said. "We're shooting the well with a hundred quarts. We'll need ten torpedoes."

"Damnation! We know all that," Cotton Hargrove said.

They stood on the drilling floor of Hargrove Hill Number 43. Above them, shafts of early yellow sunlight angled through the wooden cross-braces of the derrick, throwing a spiderweb of shadows onto the floor. Across the silver length of the torpedo, Shooter and Hargrove faced each other. Pop Wooster, the rig's morning driller, stood a pace or two farther back. Behind him, the tool dresser and a couple of roustabouts watched with evident mistrust.

"We'll hang the torpedo in the wellhead so's it's straight up and down," Shooter went on in the same easy tone. "Then I'll fill it up, real easy, trickling the soup down the side." He smiled. "That's so's it won't splash and blow your pretty drilling rig all to toothpicks and crochet hoops."

The tool dresser, a lanky man with a big Adam's apple, swallowed and took a step farther away from the torpedo and from Shooter. Shooter saw him.

"Won't do you a bit of good." He nodded toward the light Ford truck parked just off the drilling floor. "There's ten cans of fresh-cooked nitroglycerine on there. If it goes, you'll be talking to Saint Peter before anybody hears the bang."

The tool dresser swallowed again, his Adam's apple jerking convulsively. "That happen very often?"

"Usually just once to a customer."

"You suicide jockeys are nuts," the man said. "All of you." He hurried to the edge of the floor, stepped off, began to move away. "Flat-out nuts!" Within a few yards he was running.

"Nervous sort of citizen," Shooter said.

Pop Wooster pushed back his hat and scratched at his thin gray hair. "Not much punkins as a tool dresser, either," he said.

"Time's money," Hargrove growled. "You going to get on with the job, or just stand here scaring us?"

"Let's understand this," Shooter said. "There's nothing going to happen in a hurry. We'll all go nice and slow and careful, or—"

"Time's—"

"—you can shoot your well yourself."

Hargrove stopped in mid-word. "No," he said. "I've tried that. Cost me a new rig and a ton of money."

"Plus two good men," Wooster murmured. Shooter looked at him. Hargrove didn't.

"Now, then," Shooter said after a pause, "I'll handle the soup. I need somebody to help couple the torpedoes together, and to ride the brake when we lower them in the hole."

Nobody spoke for a minute. "Why isn't that damn Indian here to help you?" Hargrove growled finally.

"Chief cooks up the soup. I shoot the wells. We take turns driving out the loads. We never work together."

"What's an Indian know about nitroglycerine?"

Shooter shrugged. Hargrove turned to his three hands. The two roustabouts found other places to look. They started edging toward the far side of the floor, the way the tool dresser had gone.

"Wooster?"

"Sure thing, Mr. Hargrove." Wooster took out a red bandanna and wiped his forehead. "If you say so."

Cotton Hargrove thought about it. "Hell," he said. "I'll help. Where do we start?"

They started by clearing everybody else off the floor. With Wooster and the others watching from a hundred yards away, they hung the first torpedo in the open mouth of the well. Then Shooter started toward the truck. When Hargrove followed, the nitro man shook his head.

"I'll handle it."

"Hell. I can at least help carry the cans up on the floor. Time's money."

Shooter stopped and looked at him steadily. "Haste is death," he said as finally as a shovelful of dirt on a coffin lid.

After a moment Hargrove muttered, "Hell." He went and sat on the lazy bench while Shooter carried the nitroglycerine cans, one at a time, up onto the rig floor.

"Now then," Shooter said, half aloud. Whistling under his breath, he gently unscrewed the two caps on the first can and began to pour. The clear, oily liquid flowed like syrup down the inner wall of the torpedo. When the cylinder was exactly full, he cut off the flow and set the can aside as gently as a feather. With surgeon's precision he screwed down the brass cap of the torpedo.

"You're doing just fine," he told Hargrove. "Now help me with the next one."

The two men used the rig hoist to pick up an empty torpedo, then nestled its lower end into place atop the full one. Hargrove, cursing steadily but quietly, held the weight while Shooter latched the coupling.

"Easy. Just like the safety pin on Sally Ann's drawers. There. I'll hold it now. You let off the brake. Yeah, let it down—yeah—until it's—right—there!"

The top of the empty torpedo was within an inch of where Shooter had hung the first one. The full one swung below it, down inside the well bore.

"That's good," Shooter said. "If you'll take your seat again, I'll fill us up another one."

At the end of two hours, all ten of the long metal cylinders hung in the well, heavy with their load.

"About damn time," Hargrove muttered. Then he glared at Shooter. "Wait a minute, you didn't put a timer in. How do you mean to fire it?"

"Very complicated."

Shooter was gathering the empty nitro cans, racking them with at least as much care as he'd given the full ones. When he finished, he reached into the truck and brought out a small wooden box. He opened it, took a device from a bed of white cotton, and bolted it swiftly to the topmost coupling of the torpedoes.

"Contact detonator," he said. "You can run it in the hole now. But be damn slow about it. I'm going to take a nap. Call me when Wooster gets it on bottom." He turned toward the truck, then paused and looked back at Hargrove. "He might not want to bounce it around much, going in," he said. "I wouldn't tell him that *time's money.*"

It was close to noon when Hargrove woke him. Shooter sat up on the truck's hard seat and stretched, rubbing his eyes. Chief was roosting on the truck's bumper, whittling at a cedar twig. "Hello, Indian," Shooter said.

"Indian decide see white man blow himself up." He pointed with the knife. "Ride out on iron horse."

Shooter looked. Chief's new Harley-Davidson motorcycle sat at the edge of the location. The roustabouts stood well back, looking at it admiringly.

"I didn't hear you ride up."

"Indian swift like arrow, silent like wind."

"Hell," Shooter said. "Save that wooden-Indian talk for the tourists."

"All right, damnit," Hargrove said. "Are you going to shoot this well or not?"

"Yes, sir, Mr. Hargrove, sir," Shooter said. "I'll be right there. Just give me a second with my partner here."

Hargrove snorted and stalked away. Shooter climbed down from the truck. From the big toolbox in its bed he took what looked like a three-foot length of iron pipe.

"Went fine," he told Chief. "I'll be just a minute."

"Perhaps I'd better move the truck away," Chief said. "Just in case Mr. Hargrove's well should blow in."

"Happy thought. I'll crank." Shooter spun the crank and Chief brought the engine to racketing life. "You think it will?" Shooter yelled over the noise. "Blow in?"

Chief shook his head. "I don't smell anything," he said and turned the truck away. Carrying his piece of pipe, Shooter walked to the wellhead where Hargrove fidgeted. Pop Wooster stood at the brake lever, waiting without impatience. The heavy wire cable of the hoist ran straight down into the well bore, dangling ten torpedo loads of nitroglycerine somewhere in the darkness below.

"Looks fine," Shooter said. He held up the length of pipe. "We call this a go-devil. Know why?"

"Get on with it," Hargrove said. "I already been to school. Wore out the dunce chair. I don't need lessons."

"Yes, sir."

Shooter fiddled with the piece of pipe. It had hinges down one side and a latch on the other. He opened it, then clamped it closed around the wire line, moving it up and down to be sure it would slide freely.

"This'll ride the line down. Weighs about five pounds. When it hits the detonator, the soup will go up." He turned to Wooster. "How deep's the well?"

"Twenty-six sixty."

"The torpedoes are seventy feet long, so their top's at twenty-five hundred ninety. Not quite half a mile." Shooter thought a moment. "It'll take the go-devil maybe fifteen seconds to fall that far when I turn it loose."

He released it. It shot down into the darkness of the well casing, rattling on the line as it fell.

"Damnation!"

"Fifteen seconds," he continued in the same unhurried tone. "We better go like the devil."

Wooster understood first. He locked down the brake lever and ran. Hargrove paused long enough to glare at Shooter, then puffed after the driller. Shooter grinned and sprinted along just behind them. They had reached Chief and the parked nitro truck when the ground seemed to hitch under their feet.

"There it goes," Chief said.

"And here it comes!"

A rumble started deep below, became a rattling rush that grew louder by the second. A solid column of liquid shot up out of the well, dropped off, pulsed upward again like blood from an artery, splashing out around the boards of the derrick, spraying to fine mist on the wind.

Hargrove yelled, "We got it!"

"I don't think so," Chief murmured.

"What's an Indian know about oil wells?"

The flow died back, pulsed. The spray didn't go quite as high. Its color was growing lighter, clearing up. The third time the pulse died, it didn't rise again.

"Nope," Wooster said.

Hargrove started for the well, Wooster beside him. Shooter and Chief exchanged looks, then followed. Murky brownish liquid welled steadily out over the edge of the casing to splatter on the floor. Chief dipped his hand in the flow and touched a finger to his tongue.

"Saltwater," he said. "No oil. Not a smidgen."

"Damnation," Hargrove growled. He turned and faced Shooter and Chief, holding out a hand to them.

"Thanks, boys. You did the best you could." He shook his head. "No two ways about it. Hargrove Hill's played out."

Elizabeth Hargrove heard the front door open and her father's heavy voice. She jumped up from her chair beside the bed where Lee Temple lay sleeping and hurried down the broad stairs.

"I saved you some supper," Laurel Jean was saying to Hargrove, "but you'd better—"

"I'll tell him, Laurel Jean," Elizabeth interrupted.

Cotton Hargrove frowned up the stairs at her. She had taken off her dress, stained with Temple's blood, and wrapped herself in a long kimono. She raised a hand to her throat, pulling the robe closed.

"Saw your car," Cotton said. "Surprised you're home. It's not morning yet. Tell me what?"

"Lee Temple's here. In the bedroom."

Hargrove raised his eyebrows. "Is he?" He barked a laugh that reminded her of the black dog. "Well, I asked you for him, but I didn't expect you'd drag him home like a bone."

"You *asked* me to—" she began. Then concern got the better of her anger and she gripped the banister. "He's asleep or—something. Hurt. Come up and look at him. Please."

Cotton Hargrove stared at her. He's never seen me this way, she thought. Maybe I've never been this way. Then he nodded. Without another word he clumped up to the spare bedroom. She saw him take in Temple's bruised face, the deep cut over his eyebrow where his head had slammed against the wall, the right eye swollen closed.

"Damnation! What happened?" He answered himself. "A fight. Over you?"

"No. Yes." Elizabeth couldn't think how to explain. "I don't know. I wanted to call the doctor, but—"

"Child, we can do anything for him a doctor could," Laurel Jean said from the doorway. "Good lands, it's not the first time I've seen bruises around this house."

Hargrove bent over the bed. His hands surprisingly gentle, he lifted Temple's left eyelid, pulled back the covers, felt the pulse in the throat. Temple didn't stir.

"Is he all right?"

"He's out." Hargrove straightened. "Been better not to let him go to sleep. But we won't wake him now. Laurel Jean, did you doctor those cuts and get him into bed?"

"I did," Elizabeth said. She felt her face grow warm under his gaze. "Hell," she said. "It's not the first time I've seen bruises, either."

Hargrove laughed. "Heat us up some supper, Laurel Jean," he said. "Eliza, come downstairs with me while I eat. I have a thing to say. Listen to me now."

She went down the stairs, looking back all the while. She didn't want to listen to him. She didn't want to talk about Temple. She shivered, remembering the way Temple had battered at the robber until she had waded in to stop him, remembering his face. Temple had looked like a different person. She supposed he must have looked that way when he pushed Frank Loman off the train.

"—wouldn't listen to me the other night."

She realized her father was talking. He took a seat at the head of the table and folded his hands, looking at her.

"I need your help."

She laughed. *"My* help? You?" She half turned away. "You've never needed anything from me. Or from any of us—Harry or me or our mother—not anybody!"

"I need it now," Cotton Hargrove said. He waved toward the far end of the table. "Sit down. Supper's coming."

She sat, watching him warily, while Laurel Jean set two places for them, then brought in fried chicken, mashed potatoes, English peas. The woman poured tea for Elizabeth. Then she sniffed and set a tumbler of whiskey beside Cotton's place.

"Thank you, Laurel Jean," Hargrove said. "Is Temple taken care of for the night?"

"I reckon. He's had right smart nursing."

"Don't worry about cleaning up tonight. We'll see you in the morning."

"Hmph. Good night, Miss Elizabeth."

"Good night, Laurel Jean."

Cotton Hargrove waited until Laurel Jean had closed the kitchen door firmly behind her. Then he took a sip from his glass and frowned across the rim at Elizabeth.

"Do you ever wonder why I let you run wild as a stray cat?" he asked. "Why I don't lock you up when you come in half drunk and half naked? Why I don't cut off your allowance, or just beat hell out of you?"

She hadn't expected the change of subject, but it didn't confuse her. This was her territory. "I know that last one." Her voice was cold and clear as her eyes. "I'd kill you if you ever touched me again."

He chuckled and helped himself to the chicken. "Maybe you would at that," he said. "But that's not the reason." He pointed a drumstick at her.

"You like showing yourself off in Emilia, driving a new car every week, hanging around the Line, knowing everybody will cater to you because you're Cotton Hargrove's daughter. Don't you?"

She didn't answer, but he went on as if she had.

"Well, I like that, too."

Elizabeth stared at him. He took a bite of the chicken. For a moment she thought she'd be sick, but she shook the feeling off.

"You don't want to know how much we're the same. That's all right. The main thing is, you want to keep right on being rich."

"We are rich," she said, suddenly afraid. "Those wells—"

"Don't make as much as you think," he finished for her. "And business hasn't been good. The boom's playing out. Those Fort Worth bankers I work with are starting to look pretty hard at their loans. If they called them in right now, we'd be back to shirttail ranching."

Elizabeth closed her eyes. She remembered things as they'd been, before the oil came. Now, it would be worse. The Hargroves wouldn't just be trash; they'd be trash who'd overreached themselves, had put on airs, had gotten what they deserved.

"What do you want me to do?" she asked.

Cotton Hargrove smiled. "That's better," he said. "Temple. I want him to work for me. If I talk to him straight out, I doubt he'll listen. I want you to bring it up to him."

"Work for you?" She opened her eyes. "Like Roy?"

"Damn it, that was an accident! I felt as bad about it as you."

"Like hell you did!"

He pushed back his plate and folded his napkin neatly on the table. "It's up to you. I don't mean him any harm. I've got a plan to bail us out, put the Hargroves back on top. But if you don't want Temple in it—"

"Why Lee? Why does it have to be him?"

"I need somebody to watch my back—somebody I can trust. He's the one I want."

"Somebody shoot at you again?"

"No. But somebody will. Don't worry about it."

Elizabeth realized she wasn't worried about it. She ought to be sad that she wasn't. She was not sad but angry. And afraid.

"And you think Lee can protect you? Why?" She stood up suddenly, hands on the table. "You know something about him. You have since that first night. What is it? What do you know?"

He smiled at her, a sly, horse trader's smile. "I'll make you a bargain. Tell me what you know about him, and I'll tell you what I know. What happened on the Line? What did you get Temple into?"

She started a sharp answer, then bit it back. He was right. She was tired now, too tired to fight anymore. Without thinking she sank back into the chair.

"All right," she said dully. Seeing it all reflected in the polished wood of the tabletop, she told about collecting money on the Line, her meeting with Temple, the robbery attempt, the fight.

"He seemed—funny," she said. "Like he was in a dream. And he was hurt. I didn't know what to do. So I brought him home." She looked up at Cotton. "Lucky for you, huh?"

He missed the irony. "Damn straight." He nodded, smiling to himself. "Yes, sir. Just like I thought."

"What do you mean? Tell me what you know."

Hargrove rose. "A bargain's a bargain," he said. "Come along. You can read it yourself."

Like a child, she followed him down the hall and into the room he used as study and office. The big desk between them, she stood as he opened a drawer in his oak wood filing cabinet.

"Meant to find this earlier," he murmured. "That's not it. Knew Matt Temple in El Paso, back in the eighties. Texas Ranger, he was then. Kept up with him when we both moved on. Here." He straightened, pulling out a folder. "Fifteen years ago, just like I thought."

He spread it open on the desk before her. She reached out, hesitated. At last she snatched it off the desk and turned away to the light. It held a single newspaper clipping, datelined New Mexico Territory, 1899.

"'Notorious pistoleer claims last victim,'" she read aloud. "'Retribution overtakes murderer of Blevins and O'Grady.'" She frowned. "Is this about his father?"

"Keep reading."

"Outraged Justice avenged herself last evening upon a self-professed killer, despite his acquittal on murder charges earlier in the day. A little before midnight, a legion of indignant citizenry stormed the Bastille where Matthew Temple was held for investigation of other charges. Overpowering Jailer Vega and Deputy Marshal Jameson, the avengers dragged Temple from the jail in Tularosa Town to the Southern Pacific Railroad bridge on Sheep Camp Draw. There the hangman's noose exacted its swift and final retribution.

The reader will remember Temple stood trial for the shooting deaths of Joseph Blevins and Martin O'Grady, both well known in the county. The defense claimed his victims attacked him with intent to kill, at the instigation of Arthur Blevins, father of one victim and employer of the other. Temple and the elder Blevins had been personal and political enemies since the Temple clan settled adjacent to the Blevins family's Coyote Peak ranch four years ago. Witnesses attested to repeated quarrels between the two men. Mr. Arthur Blevins indignantly denied the charges of instigation; but Lawyer Pittsfield, with zeal and energy worthy of a better cause, pressed the argument for self-defense so skillfully as to sway the jury in its judgment.

Temple, about thirty-five, was a fine figure of a man, tall and erect with fair hair and beard. However, he was cursed with a killer's eyes and a killer's heart. He often displayed a violent temper, especially when drinking. His skill with any type of firearm was widely known and feared, and he was never without his Colt's .44–40 revolver. He once served as a Texas Ranger, and later as a regulator in the range wars on the Maxwell land grant near Wagon Mound. Popular gossip attributed to him at least six other killings."

She looked quickly up at Cotton, then went back to the story.

"Temple met death with a degree of resolution that excited the admiration even of his enemies. Denied his request to write a final message to his wife and son—"

"Lee."

"—he stood composedly while the fatal rope was adjusted, disdaining to answer the taunts of the mob. Asked if he had final words before he swung into eternity, he replied that he would reserve them for the Eternal Judge, reminding his hearers that they would someday answer to the same tribunal."

There was more, but she'd seen enough. She stood up away from the desk, her eyes on fire. "That's why you want

Lee," she whispered. "You think he'll handle a gun for you, watch your back, shoot your killer before he can shoot you."

"If he's his father's son."

"Like Harry is *your* son?"

She heard her own words and could not understand what she had tried to say. She kept seeing Lee Temple's face as he'd come so close to beating the robber to death. *The eyes and the heart of a killer.* Cotton seemed to understand. He shrugged.

"At the least, he's a man I can trust, and those are scarce enough. Will you talk to him?"

The fire had gone liquid at the edges of her eyes. "Yes," she said, hating herself, hating him because he understood her so well. "Yes. I'll talk to him."

"That's good." Cotton Hargrove pushed back from the desk and stood up. "I'm going to bed. You can sit up with Temple, if you're minded to." He picked up the glass and started for the stairs. "Chances are, he won't remember much about today when he wakes up. But you never know. Good night, Eliza."

"Good night," she whispered, hating him. When she was sure he had gone, she crept up the stairs to Temple's room. He was still sleeping heavily. The light from the hall fell on his battered face. He looked like a mischievous boy.

The eyes and the heart of a killer.

Elizabeth shivered in the warm night. She wished Harry were there, or Roy, or anybody to tell her what to do. But she knew. She knew she would do exactly what her father wanted.

Alone, miserable, locked within herself, she stood for what seemed a long time. Temple stirred, murmured something. She bent to touch his forehead, and his lips formed a smile.

Chances are, he won't remember much about today when he wakes up.

Elizabeth bolted the door. Standing in the middle of the

room, she unbelted her kimono and let it slip to the floor. Then she drew back the sheet and crept softly in beside Temple, drawing to herself the warmth and comfort of his body.

Chapter 15

"ELIZABETH SAID YOU WANTED TO TALK," TEMPLE SAID. "SOMEthing about a job?"

"Damn straight!" Cotton Hargrove rose from his rocking chair on the unpainted porch. He set aside his first glass of whiskey of the young day and waved toward the Pierce Arrow. "I'm driving out to my new well site in a minute. Ride along. I'll tell you what I have in mind."

"I'm supposed to be at work."

"I telephoned Bremerton this morning, told him you were under the weather. Took the liberty." He squinted critically at Temple. "With that eye closed, you've got no business working in the field today. Probably you don't feel any too pert, either."

Temple touched his forehead above his right eye. It hurt. Come to think of it, he hurt just about everyplace he could put a name to. He leaned back against the porch railing and tried to smile at Hargrove. That hurt, too.

"I've been worse," he said, "but not much. I appreciate your hospitality."

Hargrove waved a hand. "My house is yours," he said. "Eliza told me what happened on the Line last night. I want to thank you."

"Por nada."

Temple tried to think just what *had* happened the night before. He remembered leaving Watson's and starting for the Line. In no special order, he remembered the Ballard boys, and having a drink at Mel's, and himself on a chair before a group of people, and Elizabeth, her face haloed by blond hair, looking up into his eyes. Then there was a red haze of fury, wind howling over the Mercer's hood. Finally, there'd been sleep, with a slow, warm, lazy dream about—who? Amy?

"Too modest, son. Just like old Matthew, when he was about your age."

"You've said you knew my father. I'd wanted to ask you how."

"Everybody around El Paso knew your father—knew of him, anyhow. Had himself quite a reputation, even then. Toughest—" He broke off as the screen door opened. "Eliza. Come on out, girl. I was talking old times to Temple."

Elizabeth stepped onto the porch. She wore the green dress she'd had on when Temple first met her. A light linen duster lay over her arm. She looked tired, he thought, or sad. It didn't suit her.

"Good morning, Papa," she said, as quietly as a dutiful daughter. She looked at Temple without a smile. "Hello, Cowboy."

"Hello, lady."

They'd talked at breakfast, though his mind had still been hazy. While Laurel Jean served hotcakes with syrup, Elizabeth told him about taking up the collection and the robbery attempt. When she got to the part about the fight, her voice dropped so low he could barely hear.

"It was scary," she had said, like a little girl.

"Sorry." It all seemed familiar to him, but not like anything that had really happened—more like the moving picture he'd watched one night in Forth Worth.

"No, don't be!" She'd put her hand on his. "You're a hero, Cowboy," she teased. "My hero!"

His dream had hung like a mist in the hollows of his mind. It had been so real that when he woke in the Hargroves' upstairs room, not knowing where he was, he'd imagined her scent still clung to the sheets around him. Amy?

"My pleasure, ma'am. Any time."

"I hope so. It would be—nice—to have you around more

often—in case I need rescuing again." She'd hesitated, biting her lip. Then she released his hand. "I meant to tell you," she said, all teasing gone from her voice. "Papa asked if you'd talk to him today. Something about a job."

Now, Cotton Hargrove said, "Better come along with us, Eliza. I and Temple are just about to go pick out the new well site. Be glad to have you along."

"No," she said quickly. She motioned with the arm that held the duster. "I mean—I have some things to do in town." Her voice regained some of the bite Temple was accustomed to. "Besides, I wouldn't want to come between you and that damned dog. I'll be back before dark. Stay for supper, Cowboy?"

"I don't—"

She started toward the yellow Mercer. "Good. I'll see you then."

"We'll stop by the field office and pick up Pop Wooster," Hargrove called over the rush of wind. "He's my top driller. I want him to see the location, too."

Temple nodded, wishing the big man would keep his attention on the road. Hargrove slung the heavy Pierce Arrow around the rutted ranch trails with the same abandon the rest of his family seemed to feel. At least the makers of the touring car had provided a couple of built-in handgrips for passengers who wanted to stay on the inside. Temple hung onto one of them, fitting his body to the bounce and sway as if the car were an unruly bronc. Rotten panted softly in his ear, reminding him he'd taken the black dog's seat.

"Picked the spot out myself," Hargrove said. He released the steering wheel to gesture at one of the windmills that dotted the upland plain. "Climbed those towers to see the lay of things. Not as flat as it looks. Mapped the shape of the rises. Followed the creeks up to their sources. I figure where the land rises, the formation must rise up underground, too."

"Makes sense to me," Temple said, not sure whether it did or not. At times he liked Cotton Hargrove.

Hargrove snorted. "Those fancy college geologists don't believe it. Call it creekology." He spun the wheel to miss a sudden dropoff, then swung back into the ruts. "Too much education and no horse sense. I don't need them."

"But you do need a weevil like me?"

The older man glanced at him. "What I do need," he said, "is somebody to watch my back."

Temple smiled. "Dog can't do that?"

"Rotten? He can't watch in front of me without chasing his own tail! No, I need a hand."

"And an eye." To watch your back, Temple repeated to himself. He was thinking about the times he'd disliked Hargrove, and the reasons. He wondered if his father might been like Cotton—if Matthew Temple had lived that long.

"A hand and an eye!" Hargrove laughed, tickled by the idea. "That's good. I want the whole man. And I'd pay him well for the service."

"Truth is, Mr. Hargrove, I already have a job. Brace Bremerton was good enough to hire me; I don't figure I could just walk off and leave him."

They were crossing through the Hargrove Hill oil field. Where the road passed by the squat redwood storage tanks, Cotton Hargrove spun the car to a halt. He crept ahead a little way, to park at the edge of the bluffs overlooking Oiltown-Emilia.

"Let's talk a minute," he said. "I like this spot. Used to come here to admire the town, back when I was just a kid. Figured one day I'd make them all take notice."

Temple nodded. It was one of the times he liked Hargrove. "Guess you've done that," he said, looking at the three big tanks with HARGROVE OIL painted across their bellies. A gauger was up on one of the tanks, getting ready to turn its contents into the pipeline that ran along the bluffs. Two roustabouts were busy scraping down the tanks to keep spilled oil from hiding their message.

"Thing is," Cotton said as if Temple hadn't spoken, "I'd expect the man I'm looking for to be loyal. That's half of what I'm paying for."

It was one of those times Temple didn't like Hargrove as well as he might. "I don't know as a man can buy loyalty. Not with money."

Cotton Hargrove looked at him approvingly. "Just what old Matt would've said! I'm with you. But there's a difference between buying something and paying for it when you find it."

"I can see that."

"Here's as fair as I can be. I'll pay exactly double what you're making now. If you say so, I'll go myself to old Brace, do whatever he wants to put things square between us. The only thing I'll ask is your word to stay till the job's done. Does that suit you?"

Temple thought about it. Could Hargrove buy him from Bremerton? Did he mean to threaten him? If some of the talk Temple had heard was true, Hargrove might mean to kill Bremerton.

"Remember," Hargrove said when he hesitated. "I'm the one sent you there in the first place. I and Brace, we've done right smart business together."

"Sounds fair to me." Temple was still trying to get his thoughts clear on the matter. "I suppose it's all right with me—if Mr. Bremerton agrees."

"Trust me," Cotton Hargrove said.

"I trust you. But I'll wait for Bremerton's say-so."

"And you'll stay until the well's on line?"

"Yes, sir."

"Done!" Cotton Hargrove shook his head. "Hardest man I ever saw to bargain with."

Temple grinned, carefully. He liked Hargrove again. "I don't know as I'd list you as easiest man I ever did business with, myself," he said.

Pop Wooster rode behind Hargrove in the touring car. The black dog sat on the other side, tongue lolling near Temple's ear. Temple leaned away from the dog, earning a low growl from Rotten and an amused snort from Hargrove. Hargrove stopped the car at a drag gate in a barbed-wire fence and waited while Temple got out to open it. Then he drove through and stopped in the open pasture.

"The property begins here," Hargrove said. "Four sections, right where my creekology says the field lies. I've had people buying it up or leasing the drilling rights under half a dozen names. Now I'm ready to put up my sign."

"Sounds like trouble to me," Wooster said.

"You get paid for trouble."

"I get paid for drilling."

Hargrove laughed. "Well, that's just fine." He gunned the motor. "Temple gets paid for trouble! Let's decide where we're going to drill."

The big car lurched across the uneven ground, scraping through patches of brush and bumping over exposed rocks. Hargrove drove with complete unconcern for both vehicle and passengers for most of a mile. Finally, Temple saw a flash of bright color ahead. Someone had driven a wooden stake into the ground and topped it with a strip of red ribbon. Hargrove saw it, too. He pulled to a stop and shut off the engine. Rotten surged past Temple and took off through the brush in a nervous, lazy lope.

"Survey marker," Hargrove said. He climbed out of the car and drew his stubby rifle from its scabbard. "This is the center of the property. What do you think of it, Temple?"

Temple didn't think much of it. The soil was thin and rocky, covered with short, tough grass. Stands of mesquite and catclaw and dark green scrub cedar struggled for a foothold.

"Not much grass."

"That's not why we're here. If it was yours, where would you site the well?"

Remembering what Hargrove had told him about creekology, Temple looked for the shape of the land. Sure enough, it fell gently away from them in three directions. The survey stake marked the spine of a long, gently sloping hogback, dotted with cedar thickets. Around its base strips of darker green marked the draws and creek beds where the grass stood tall and green and mesquite grew more thickly.

A quarter mile to the north the ground rose sharply to a series of knobby hilltops crowned with post oaks.

Temple pointed toward the hills. "There," he said.

Pop Wooster spat tobacco juice. Hargrove chuckled.

"You were listening, all right. But those hills are a lot younger than the rest of the land—so the schoolboy geologists say, anyway. This big hump we're on, it goes plumb back before the Flood."

"Okay," Temple said. "Right here, by the stake. Does it make a difference?"

Wooster pushed back his hat. His laugh was sharp as a nighthawk's cry.

"All the difference there is! Difference between a well that booms in and one that's a duster."

"Where, then?"

"Can't say, boy. What we've got to do is look around us. Look for a sign. There's always a sign, for them that knows how to read it."

"Let's find it, then," Hargrove said. He waved his arms widely. "Spread out. Look around you. Biggest treasure hunt you ever saw, Temple."

Wooster got out, stretched, started walking. Hargrove cast a little way off to the left. Out of his depth, Temple moved to the right. He wondered what a sign would look like. Probably it wouldn't be anything so simple as oil bubbling to the surface, though he'd heard of that sort of thing. He searched the area for a tall tree, a horse skeleton, a big rock, a buzzard's roost. He wondered if Hargrove and Wooster were crazy.

"Look there," Hargrove yelled. Ahead of him the big dog had stopped in a clump of mesquite and hunkered down.

"You're kidding," Temple said.

Rotten finished his business and dug at the dirt with his hind feet to cover his work. Satisfied, he barked and raced away after an inoffensive rabbit that had emerged from the brush.

"That's it," Hargrove said. "There's your sign."

The driller rubbed his forehead and frowned. "Well," he said finally, "I've seen sites chose in worse ways."

Temple started to ask what some of them were, but Hargrove was already pulling up the survey marker. Carrying it like a spear, he waded into the mesquite and planted the stake right in Rotten's tracks.

"All right," he said. "Back in the car! Wooster, we'll want the rig builders in here soon as we can get them lined up. Temple, get your things. You'll be moving to the ranch—and I'll see Bremerton's satisfied. Rotten! You worthless mutt, get in here. Let's get cracking."

Temple barely managed to get his door closed before Hargrove sent the Pierce Arrow roaring away. He'd signed on until the job was finished, he reminded himself. Given his word.

He felt a touch on his shoulder. Turning his head, he looked squarely into Rotten's wet muzzle. Wooster and Cotton Hargrove were talking loudly, making plans, congratulating themselves on getting the project under way. Temple leaned a little closer to the dog.

"They're crazy," he whispered confidentially. "You, too."

Chapter 16

HARRY HARGROVE STOOD AT THE SIDE WINDOW LOOKING OUT OF the library into an empty roadway. The lot across the road had once been the town park. Now a tall wooden derrick stood where the bandstand had been. A chuffing steam engine drove the walking beam up and down, pumping oil steadily into a stained redwood tank. The seams of the tank were crusted with leaked oil.

No one to keep the tank scraped down and painted, he thought. No big Hargrove Oil on the side. Aloud, he said, "I thought you'd understand."

Harriet crossed toward him from the main desk. "I want to understand, sweetheart," she said. "But I don't. This isn't like you." She waved a hand. "All this about business, and your father, and loans and wells and things. That never interested you before."

Two boys came into the roadway on a bicycle, one pumping, the other sitting sidesaddle on the crossbar. A small black and white dog ran flat out, trying to catch the bicycle. "I have to take hold," Harry said.

"Why do you say that? You've taken hold! Just this week that editor said he wanted to see more of your stories—that you might be another Jack London!"

He watched the dog scoot around the corner, his paws digging in the dirt.

"Then, we have two important people lined up to speak in our lecture series next month. And in another week you were going to have our first real theater troupe signed to come to town. Are you just going to forget all that?"

"No. But I can't work on it now. Not for a while."

"Is it something I've done?"

"No."

"Then why are you shutting me out?"

"I'm not shutting you out. I told everything to Betty last week. I've been thinking on it ever since."

"Without telling me!"

"It's a family problem."

"But—I thought you wanted me to be your family."

He turned to Harriet. A tear had caught at the bottom rim of her glasses. It flooded loose to run down her cheek. He took her in his arms, but she wouldn't look at him. Instead she pressed her face against the front of his coat.

"Listen, Hare, it's just for a little while. Until the well's down. Then they won't need me anymore."

"I need you *now.*"

"Then we can get back to work on the lecture series. And I can finish that story I started on the train. It's just a little while."

"Oh, Harry. What can you do to help him? That isn't your kind of work! And he's hired that friend of yours—Lee Temple. Won't that be all the help he needs?"

Harry released her and turned toward the window again.

The street was empty now, but he didn't notice. "Temple isn't superhuman. You shouldn't think he is, just because he can knock Frank Loman down and I can't."

"Harry!" The tears came more steadily. "You know I didn't mean that."

"Besides, Temple may change his mind." Harriet wiped at her eyes, turned away, bit back a sob. "You can keep up with what I've been doing."

"I can't! You know it takes a man to make those things work."

Harry Hargrove let her words hang in the air a moment. No one had ever said anything he liked better. The words made him feel like a man, for that little moment. He put his hands on her shoulders, turned her around, embraced her. "You will always be my sweetheart," he said.

She put her face against his chest and cried without restraint. "Why do you say that? You make it sound like you're leaving me!"

"No," he said. "No, not for good. Not at all, really. I'm just going home to help out. I'll never be any farther away than that."

"You already are farther away than that!" She lost her voice then in a series of deep racking sobs.

Lee Temple cinched the straps on his new leather valise. He set the bag by the door of his room and went down the hall to Mrs. Watson's dining room. The room was crowded. Most of the boarders who worked evening tour were just up and having their breakfasts, while a fair number of workers whose jobs were in town had stopped in for lunch. Ace High Ballard motioned Temple down toward the end of one long table. Slick Porterfield was down there, too, as usual arguing world affairs with Bull.

"You're not making a lick of sense!" Bull made room for Temple on the rough bench without missing a word. "You think just because some crazy man shot this archbishop—"

"Archduke."

"—away over someplace in Siberia—"

"Serbia."

"—that all them European countries are going to fight one another? Why, that'd be like us fighting Mexico just because some damn cowboy—no offense, Temple—got himself shot in a Matamoros whorehouse!"

"Now, look, Bull," Porterfield said patiently, "it's these alliances, see. Agreements. If Austria invades Serbia, then . . ."

"You ain't no special treat to eat with, Temple," Ace High growled under his breath as Porterfield went on. "But you're some relief from listening to these two. What do you think? Are they fixing to start a war?"

Temple helped himself to two pieces of fried chicken and a dipper full of red beans. "I couldn't say, Ace. To tell the truth, I haven't read the papers. What's up?"

"Some arch-something got himself shot dead over southeast of Austria. Try those potatoes, they're right good. That kind of thing happens every night on the Line, but everybody's hollering like it's the end of the world when it happens over there."

"Just might be, unless Wilson's smart enough to keep us out," Porterfield said. "Hello, Temple. Sorry to lose you."

Bull blinked. "Is Temple lost?" he asked. "Looks like he's right here."

"Not lost," Temple said. "Changing jobs. I'll be moving out to Hargrove's place today."

Ace High frowned. "I might have knowed it!" he said. "You're just the sort would work for that son of a bitch Hargrove. But I can't figure why you'd give up this grub."

Bull laughed. "Might be I can think of a reason, Ace. Might be you could, too." He nudged his brother. "Stands about five-foot-four, wears dresses about two-foot-two."

"Listen—" Temple began. Then he broke off. Tommy Ellis had stepped through the door of the dining room. He searched around until he caught Temple's eye, motioned to him with a jerk of his head, then backed out.

"I have to go," Temple said. "But I'll be seeing you all around."

"Not around Hargrove," Ace High said.

"I expect I'll see you boys every few days."

"All the worse for us."

"And down at the Line."

"He does still owe us a drink. Or two."

"He ain't bought us that drink yet. He won't. He ain't a drinking man's man."

"I will."

"We'll give you the chance. Wait and see."

"Not me," Ace High said. "Pass them potatoes before you eat the rest of them!"

Tommy was waiting outside, lounging behind the wheel of the big Nash Quad when Temple came out with his suitcase.

"Throw that in back. Mr. Bremerton asked me to bring you out to Hargrove's." Talking Tommy chewed on a toothpick until Temple had climbed into the cab. Then he threw it aside. "No, the truth is, I asked him. So you're truly going to go over, are you?"

Temple looked at the little man, surprised. Tommy put the truck in gear and let it grind away along the road.

"Going over?"

"Going over to Hargrove."

"I'm going to work for him, true enough. Bremerton said it suited him all right."

"Did he? Did he say he was happy to give you all the experience you've had and then turn you over to Hargrove?"

"I didn't ask him that exactly."

"No," Tommy said. "You just followed that Hargrove girl's—"

"Listen," Temple said. "I've heard about enough of that today. If you don't want to carry me out there, I can damn well walk."

Tommy set his jaw and said nothing for a mile. Finally he sighed and shook his head. "I'm worried about you, Lee," he said. "You're getting mixed up in something you don't understand."

"I can look out for myself."

"Hargrove's a killer."

"So was—" Temple bit his lip. He sat still while Tommy's glance searched him. "That's nothing to me," he said finally.

"Have you ever killed a man?"

"No. And I don't plan to. Have you?"

"Maybe Hargrove hasn't, either." Tommy shifted the big truck down into low gear. All four wheels churning, it started up the steep climb below the Hargrove Oil tanks. "But most of the town thinks he did."

In his mind Temple saw the line of type from the yellowed clipping he carried. *Popular gossip attributed to him at least six other killings.* "Maybe most of the town's wrong," he said.

"Cotton Hargrove grew up here. Wasn't worth much, and neither was that scrubby ranch his stepfather owned. When the old man died, Cotton took it over. Left town for a while, came back about 1890, with money."

"I don't see—"

Tommy held up a hand. "You've listened to many of my tales," he said. "Indulge me once more."

"Once."

"Cotton's uncle—his stepfather's brother—was living on the ranch. Said he figured Cotton had lost his claim to it. There was some hollering back and forth, some threats, some legal goings-on. Then one night, somebody shot the old man right off his front porch."

"Cotton?"

"The authorities never proved it." Tommy shrugged. "A young woman—respectable—swore he'd spent the night with her. It would have ruined her reputation, but he married her. That was Harry's mother. And Elizabeth's."

Temple didn't want to ask the question, but couldn't help himself. "What happened to her?"

The long-legged man wrestled the Quad's wheel as the truck heaved itself up over the edge of the bluff onto the tabletop that was Hargrove Hill. When the Quad settled into the ruts again, he shrugged.

"Nobody knows, exactly. Mr. Hargrove says she died in an accident while they were back East one year. Gossip says she ran away with another man. Whatever happened, happened about ten years ago."

They rode in silence for a while, Temple thinking over what he'd heard. Finally, he grinned at Tommy Ellis. "For a feller that talks so much, you sure find time to listen," he said.

Tommy nodded soberly. "That's because I never ask a question. Ask, and people clam up. But look interested, let it be their own idea, and they'll tell you anything." He glanced over at Temple and smiled. "Thought you should be aware of some background. It might help you in your new job."

"Thanks," Temple said. "But you never answered *my* question."

"Oh?"

"Maybe if I wait until it's your own idea, you'll tell me yourself."

Frank Loman finished his books for the week. He came out of his office and shouted for Clancy. Clancy didn't answer. Loman roared the name again. The back door slammed, bounced open in the wind, shut with a solid bang. "Clancy! What the hell! Is that you trying to tear the door off its hinges?"

Clancy shuffled into the big front room of the warehouse. "It's just me," he said.

"Where've you been?"

"Outhouse."

"I ought to forward your paycheck to the outhouse. You spend half the day out there."

"Learnt something."

"I expect."

"That cowboy—Temple. He's going to change jobs. Going to work for Cotton Hargrove."

Loman stopped, turned to look at Clancy. He'd been having fun, riding the clerk in a way neither of them took too seriously. Now he was completely serious.

"Say that again. Slow."

"Cotton Hargrove. You've heard the name? Old friend of yours. Big fellow, runs around with a dog."

"Shut up. No, talk. About Temple."

"Left Bremerton's with old Brace's blessing, so they say. Going to work for Hargrove, riding shotgun. The word on the street is that Hargrove's got some big deal cooking, going to put something over on everybody."

"The hell you say!"

"The hell I do say. Heard Tommy Ellis talking to the measuring woman. He was plenty peeved, it seemed like."

Loman beckoned Clancy into his office and waved him to a chair. He pulled the bottle from its drawer and poured himself a shot of rye, forgetting his rules far enough to offer one to Clancy.

"Shotgun?"

Clancy poured an inch of the liquor into his cup, then glanced at Loman and added another inch. He set the bottle down.

"So I heard—not from Ellis. Word is, Temple's there to guard that son of a bitch. Of course, we don't know whether he meant Cotton or Rotten."

"I don't like it."

Clancy drank. For a moment he was silent. Then he said, "I just figured you might want to know is all."

"Oh, you figured that right. Yes, I sure as certain did want to know. That's good work, Clancy."

"Thanks, Buff."

Loman was too preoccupied even to notice the use of the nickname. "Ride shotgun, you say? Well, now." He blinked, then glared at Clancy. "You. See if you can't get a little work done while you're indoors!"

"Sure thing." Clancy looked hurt, but not too hurt to finish his rye. Then he got up quickly and went to the door. "Just thought you ought to know. I'm always looking out for the company's interests, Buff."

"Don't call me that."

Alone in the office, Loman considered the information. Hargrove was up to something. He needed to find out what it was.

Temple was with Hargrove, after the damned cowboy had

stood right square in his own store, Loman recalled, and denied having anything to do with the Hargroves.

Liz, he thought. He'd bet Liz had a hand in Temple's change of heart.

No. Loman chuckled. No, not her hand.

Hargrove. And Temple. Thing to do's catch both birds on the same limb and kill them with one stone! I know Cotton's going to be shipping materials to his new location. To that wildcat he thinks nobody knows about.

But I still can't do without Hargrove while his whelps are alive. Liz and Harry. I'll run over them like a steamroller over a pair of daisies. Both of them'll lie down in their own way. Ha! And I can sure do without Lee Temple.

Loman closed the door of his dark little office and reached into the corner to retrieve his rifle. He found his cleaning rod. Then he unloaded the rifle and began to clean it without a thought to the job. He was lost in a fresh plan to destroy Cotton Hargrove. In the middle of his plan he forgot his surroundings entirely. "You dirty son of a bitch!" he shouted at the phantom of Hargrove.

From the front desk Clancy sang out, "What? Did you call me, Buff?"

Harry Hargrove drove the Reo into the yard and parked next to his sister's roadster. The ground in front of the porch bore the deep marks of a truck's ribbed tires, and Harry wondered who had dared drive up to Cotton's door. He took the steps two a time, swung open the door and strode into the house.

"Betty!" he sang out. "Where are you, girl? Your prodigal brother's home! Betty!"

He was halfway up the stairs when his sister came out of her room, pulling the door closed behind her. "Hi," she said. She put up a hand and straightened her short hair.

"Betty! Are you sick? You never take naps." He ran up the last steps to the second floor hall.

Elizabeth twisted at her skirt, shook her head. "I was just resting my eyes, Harry, trying to keep this headache from settling in."

He looked at her. She hadn't been asleep. Her face was flushed, her lip rouge smeared. "Betty," he said, "what are you doing?"

"I don't know what you mean."

"There's someone here. Have you brought a man home with you?" He stared at her, remembering what someone—Loman—had said. "One of them. One of your men?"

He expected her to hit him. At the least, he thought her eyes would blaze and she'd answer with the same heat. Instead her eyes showed hurt—the same hurt he'd felt at the idea of her and some stranger in their own home. Her look reminded him of a puppy who has chewed up his master's best shoes.

"Betty?"

"Lee is here," she said at last. "Not to see me. He's come to work for Papa."

"Where is he, then?"

"Right here," Temple said.

Harry looked beyond his flushed sister. Lee Temple stood in her bedroom doorway. At least he's dressed, Harry thought; and he has his hat in his hand. Maybe it isn't what it looks like.

"Lee," he said. He stepped around Elizabeth, who didn't move. "It doesn't look right for you to be in my sister's room when there's nobody home like this."

"Sorry," Temple said. "I guess we didn't think how it looked. We were talking."

"Sure."

Elizabeth gathered herself, turned to look at her brother. "Are you your sister's keeper?"

"Betty—"

"Harry, hush."

"—behave."

Temple walked past them toward the top of the stairs.

"Lee."

Temple stopped, looked at Harry. "You're making a mistake," he said.

Harry Hargrove felt his face flushing. Hell, here I've done

it again, he told himself. Here I stand letting these two make me feel like a boy, just when I was determined to be a man.

"Am I?" He wasn't happy with it, but it was the best he could do. He couldn't find a way to express the cold anger he felt. He couldn't understand it himself. *Betty! How could you?*

Betty gave him a quick hug. "You are," she said, laughing. "Lee was waiting for Papa to get home from the new well. Why don't you run him out there in your car? The three of you could make some plans, have a drink, smoke a cigar."

"Betty."

"I'll just sit home like a good girl. Maybe Laurel Jean will teach me to knit."

"Betty."

"That's it. Knit." She grinned up at him, reached up to muss his hair. "I'll knit you a new winter cap."

Harry put an arm around his sister, looked at Temple, made his decision. "All right," he told her. "That's a good idea." At the very worst, he would get Temple away from her for a while. He knew he had caught her in something. Betty—Liz—hadn't hugged him that way since she was ten years old. "That suit you, Lee?"

"Suits me square."

Harry pulled loose from his sister. "Wipe your mouth, then, and we'll go find Cotton."

Temple wiped at his mouth with the back of his hand, looked at the red smear, made no change in his expression. "All right," he said. "Ready when you are."

"Damnation," Harry said, starting down the stairs. He felt his sister's eyes on him, but he didn't look back. "I can see that."

Chapter 17

LEE TEMPLE STOOD WATCH IN THE PREDAWN GLOW OF THE GAS flares while a caravan formed up in Oiltown's already crowded main street. In front of Bremerton's, half a dozen workmen loaded a motortruck with personal gear, a week's worth of food, and a heavy iron cookstove. Others harnessed teams of mules to a pair of rickety wooden bunkhouses set on wheels.

"We'll have a watchman out for the first night or two," Hargrove had said. "Once we get to drilling, I figure on keeping what hands we need on location. Less confusion that way, and less chance of trouble on the road."

Low, heavily built wagons held the long timbers and stringers that would become a derrick, loads of sawn boards for the floor and decking, spools of wire rope, and scores of other things Temple had seen before but couldn't put a name to. Wagons and trucks from another supply yard funneled into line carrying the steam engine and boiler. A truckload of shouting, laughing rig builders sat in the middle of the confusion, yelling abuse at everyone and demanding that the parade get started.

Temple mostly kept out of the way while Pop Wooster, Tommy Ellis, and Slick Porterfield tried to pull things into some kind of order. Apparently needing no guarding himself, Cotton Hargrove holed up in his office and worked at his books. Along toward sunup Harry Hargrove hooked Temple's arm and fell in beside him.

"Hello, Harry. Didn't see you come up."

Harry laughed. "Small wonder. I had to leave the car away over near the library." He looked over the confusion. "How's it going?"

170

"I'm the wrong one to ask," Temple said. "Whatever your pa wanted me for, this isn't it."

"Your part comes later," Harry said seriously. He scanned the crowd again. "Where is he? Father, I mean."

"In his office. He—" Temple broke off as someone called his name. "I'm over here!"

Brace Bremerton trotted up, running a hand through his bushy hair. "Temple. Morning, Harry." He waved an arm in a wide, imperious gesture. "Got to move this. Bring the rest later. No room to load more. You going to tell Hargrove?"

"Surely. When can we get started?"

"Started? Soon. Now. Whenever he's ready." Abruptly, his voice rose to a shout. "You! On the truck! That's no way to lash down that bull wheel!"

He darted into the crowd again, Temple and Harry forgotten. They looked at each other, and Harry laughed.

"Well, I wanted an interview with Father. I guess this is the time. Lead the way, Lee."

Temple knocked on Hargrove's door. "Mr. Bremerton says it's time to move out," he said. "Do you want me to go out with the trucks or stay here with you?"

Hargrove glanced up from a big green ledger. "They finally ready?" he growled. Then he caught sight of Harry. "So."

Harry said, "I've come to help out. Told you I would."

"What the hell do you think you could do?" his father asked him.

"Anything you can." They stared at each other, the glint in their eyes as identical as full moons in a mirror. "Maybe a little bit better."

Cotton stared at him for a dozen seconds more, then gave his abrupt laugh. "Why hell," he said, "maybe I've got myself a son after all!" He pushed up from the desk and whistled for his dog. "We'll all go. You bring my car around and ride with me."

The Pierce Arrow liked the road. Hargrove led the trucks out, Harry beside him in the front seat. Temple and Rotten sat in the rear, watching their flanks and listening to the ribbed tires sing crisply on the gravel. The tires sprayed gravel against the underside of the fenders and threw stray pebbles back in the face of the lead truck. Hargrove drove like royalty, indifferent to gravel or the difficulties it caused for common folk.

The mule teams with their awkward loads lagged at first, opening gaps in the column. One of the trucks broke down and had to be shoved off into the pasture to be retrieved later. Hargrove stopped often, sending Harry or Temple back to see that the column was closed up. Temple wished for the loan of Chief's motorcycle, or for a good horse.

Finally, the procession reached the drag gate marking the property line of Hargrove's leases. A black buggy drawn by a matched pair of gray horses stood near the gatepost. As the Pierce Arrow approached, an old man with a long moustache stepped down from the buggy and marched out to stand in the road. The buggy looked as new and shiny as when it had rolled out of the coach maker's shop, twenty-five or thirty years before. The man was tall, but that was all Temple could tell about him. A white duster wrapped his body, sweeping almost to the ground, its folds hiding his hands.

Hargrove slammed the Pierce Arrow to a stop and stood up behind the wheel. "Morning, Mr. Wilkes," he called. "Better stand aside. I've got equipment coming through."

Wilkes didn't move. "I was warned about you, Hargrove," he said in a thin, angry voice. "You can't bring your oil field trash here."

"Like hell I can't!" Hargrove rummaged in the pocket of his coat and pulled out a sheaf of papers, holding them aloft. "I've got the lease papers and the right of access."

"This is my land!"

"The surface is yours. I own drilling rights and an easement for a road and location. You signed them yourself."

The old man's face reddened. "I was made a fool of!" he cried. "If I'd known you were behind this, I'd never have agreed to let some back-shooting upstart set foot on my ranch."

Cotton Hargrove snorted a laugh. "Too damn bad you didn't know." He turned abruptly. "Temple. Open that gate."

Temple hesitated, then stepped down from the car. "Mr. Hargrove," he said, "are you sure you're in the right?"

"Damn straight! Legal and proper." Hargrove looked back at the rancher who barred his way. "Listen, Wilkes, I'd enjoy calling the sheriff out to handle you, but I don't have time to waste. Move aside or we'll move you."

A chorus of agreement came from behind Temple. A dozen or more of Hargrove's men had dismounted from the trucks and come ahead to see what was happening. None of them looked happy, and Temple saw that some of them were armed.

"Temple," Hargrove said.

"Yes, sir."

He took a step forward as Harry swung down from the car beside him. "I'll go, too," Harry said.

Temple started to argue, then changed his mind. He walked toward the gate, Harry at his side. The rancher stood waiting. Temple eased a little away from Harry, trying to see the rancher's right hand. The duster was still in the way.

"Harry, be careful."

Harry glanced at him, then turned back to the rancher. "I'm sorry about this, Mr. Wilkes," he said.

"I'd thought better of you than this, Harry," Wilkes said. "I thought you'd rose above your kin."

"The papers are legal," Harry said. Temple heard the hardening of his tone. "We're coming through. But I'm sure we can reach a settlement, if you'll work with us."

"Settlement? Money, you mean?" Wilkes shook his head. "I was wrong about you. You're a Hargrove, right enough. Don't touch that gate."

Harry stepped past him and reached out to release the gate. Wilkes wheeled around, his right hand at last coming clear of the folds of the duster. The stubby barrels of a stagecoach-model shotgun glinted for a second in the morning sun as he swung them up toward Harry.

Temple had been waiting for that movement. He drove forward, grabbed for the shotgun, caught it by the barrels and forestock, forced it downward. His shoulder hit the old man and flung his slight body back into the fence. Rotten broke into furious barking. A bullet chipped wood from a fence post a yard to Temple's right, but the sound of the shot was lost in the roar of the shotgun.

Fiery pain lanced through Temple's hand but he kept his hold, wrenched sideways, twisted the shotgun away. He stepped back, holding it by the barrels.

"Damnation!" Hargrove cried, struggling to hold the frantic dog and to draw his rifle from its scabbard all at the same time.

"My God," Harry breathed at the same time. He stared at the torn patch of turf where the shotgun's charge had gone.

Wilkes pulled himself upright, away from the fence. White scraps from the duster stayed on the rusty barbs. The recoil of the shotgun and Temple's rough handling had injured the rancher's wrist. He cradled it in his left hand and glared at Temple like a hawk with a broken wing.

"Better let me look at that," Temple said.

The old man drew back from him as if he were a snake. "Damn you, sir," he said. He walked to the buggy, tried to mount to its seat. On the second try he made it, gathering the reins into his left hand. "We're not done with this, Hargrove," he said.

"Hey," somebody yelled from behind Temple. "You ain't just gonna let that old buzzard drive away?"

Temple turned. The shotgun's blast had pretty well scattered the Hargrove men, but now they were gathering again, moving to hem in the rancher and his buggy. Temple strode toward the middle of their line.

"Who fired that shot?" he asked.

The men looked at each other. After a moment one pushed forward. He was one of the Hargrove hands, older than Temple, unshaven, loud and cocky. Temple had noticed him with a gun earlier. He still held it in his hand, waving it in the general direction of Wilkes and the buggy.

"I did. That old bastard was trying to shoot somebody. Sorry I missed him."

"You're about half drunk. And you're fired. Head for town."

The man blinked. "Like hell!" He tightened his grip on the pistol, not quite pointing it at Temple. "I take my orders from Mr. Hargrove. You can't—"

Temple hit him. He put behind the blow all the anger he felt, all the bitterness over what he'd done, all the frustration that came from being on the wrong side. He felt the flesh of a knuckle split against hard bone. The man staggered back, tripped, went down flat. Shaking his head, he rolled to the side, looking for Temple, trying to bring the pistol to bear. Temple took a long stride and brought his boot down on the wrist of the hand that held the gun. As the man tried to pull free, Temple leaned down and hit him again.

"That's enough!" Cotton Hargrove said sharply.

Temple looked up at him. "Just about," he said. He took the pistol from the man's unresisting hand and stuck it into his belt. Straightening, he faced the rest of the crew.

"When he wakes up, he can walk back to town. Any of you that feel the way he does, go with him." He looked at Hargrove again. "Any objections, Mister Hargrove?"

Hargrove laughed. "Not a one, Lee," he said. He waved impatiently at Harry, who still stood beside the gate. "Get that gate open, Harry. Time's money."

The caravan stopped within twenty-five yards of Hargrove's location marker. Rotten immediately ran right to it again. The workers got out, stretched, complained, smoked, and began to unload the trucks. Hargrove bounded out of the car, as energetic as his dog, and began shouting orders. Temple stayed where he was. Harry, his face still pale, stood beside the car.

"I seem to say this a lot," he said. "You saved my life. Thanks."

"Por nada." Temple was tired. His hands hurt. He turned up his left palm. The shotgun's barrel had left blisters, some of them torn open when he twisted the gun away from Wilkes.

"For nothing?" Harry smiled a little. "Well, maybe you're right. Here, let me put something on that hand."

Temple squeezed his fist closed. It hurt. He wished it hurt more than it did. "It's all right," he said.

"Sure it is. But let me put something on it."

Temple didn't argue. Harry delved through the big leather-strapped trunk on the Pierce Arrow's back bumper and came up with a medical kit. He spread yellowish ointment across the palm of Temple's hand.

"What's holding you two up?" Cotton Hargrove strode up to look over Harry's shoulder. The black dog tagged at his heels, its tongue lolling. "Oh. That was good work, Temple. You need to be armed."

Temple grinned without much humor. "I am," he said, touching the pistol in his belt. "Now. There's a shotgun on the seat, too, but I don't have any shells."

Hargrove threw back his head. "Ha! Should have asked that old man for some!" He grew serious at once. "Listen, old Wilkes has lunch with the judge twice a week. He'll be swearing out warrants on us, filing for injunctions, calling out the militia and the Texas Rangers. I need to get back to town and get our lawyer busy. Can you boys handle things here?"

Harry finished wrapping Temple's hand with gauze and snipped off the end. "I expect so," he said. "Try that, Lee."

Temple flexed his fingers. "All right." He looked at Hargrove. "Listen, I'd better go back with you. I can't watch your back from here."

"Watch Harry's."

"I don't need watching," Harry said quickly.

Hargrove and the dog barked together. "Hell you don't," Hargrove said. "If old man Wilkes can take you, there's lots of others that can."

Harry's face flushed. He started to say something, then bit

it back. "Maybe you're right," he said. "Come to that, I guess I ought to be armed, too."

Cotton Hargrove thought about that. Then he nodded abruptly. "Good enough. Come along, both of you."

He led them to one of the trucks. A long bundle lay half opened in its bed. Temple counted the varnished stocks of a half-dozen rifles. Hargrove gripped the nearest one just behind the trigger guard and lifted it clear.

"Just like mine. Winchester autoloader, shoots a big .401 cartridge. Shells in that crate there, all you'll need."

He handed the rifle to Temple. It was heavier than it looked, short in the barrel, with a curious guppy-bellied bulge in the forestock. In shape it reminded Temple of the Winchester shotgun Tommy had taught him to use, but it had a clip magazine, and its barrel did not recoil.

Harry picked up another of the rifles. Hargrove took it away from him, showed him how to release the clip and where to load, then handed it back.

"You cock it with that plunger. Reach up there with your left hand and pull it to you till it stops, then let it go. That's right. You'll want to practice some, but don't do it here. These idiots will scatter like a flock of geese."

"All right."

"Now, the other rifles—" Hargrove began. Temple laid a hand across the smooth stocks.

"The other rifles will go where I say," he cut in. "I'll pick the guards. Nobody else on location carries a gun. Have Wooster pass the word."

Hargrove growled, "Making the rules now, are you?"

"It's what you hired me for. If somebody gets shot, I mean to be damn sure it's on purpose—not like today."

"Ha!" Cotton Hargrove waved a hand. "Right. Your call. Anything you need, order it on my bill." He looked at Harry. "Think you can handle things here?" he asked again.

"Sure. And I'll have Temple to watch me."

Cotton started back toward the car. "Watch your back," he said. "That's your job, Temple. Watch the back of whatever Hargrove you happen to be with."

Temple watched as Hargrove heaved himself up into the car and whistled for Rotten. Beside him, Harry stirred.

"You watch my back and his," he said. "Only those two. I'll watch Betty's."

Chapter 18

LOOKING AT IT IN THE FIRST ORANGE RAYS OF THE MORNING SUN, Temple didn't like the location. Anyone who felt like it could slip within shooting distance at a dozen spots and from almost as many directions. The chain of hills to the north was the obvious spot, but it was a good four hundred yards away. Closer and potentially more dangerous were the creek bottoms and the innumerable clumps of brush, still lying in deep shadow.

"It would only depend on the wind," he said to the dog, who had come trotting back from the brush, "where somebody would choose to shoot from."

The dog did not reply.

"How am I going to cover every one of them at once?"

The dog ran away barking, chasing a butterfly without any apparent interest in Temple's question.

Behind Temple, the location resembled a busy anthill. Work had started at first light. Truckloads of timber, cable, lumber, bolts, nails and the like lay stacked on the far side of the site. Like worker ants, the rig builders moved steadily between the pile and the cleared area where two halves of the derrick were taking shape on the ground. Hammers and hatchets chunked steadily, driving home the long spikes that held the timbers together.

Other workers were busy setting the boiler, leveling the steam engine, lashing together the hoisting works that would lift the finished derrick legs into place. Smoke rose from the cook shack, one of the two bunkhouses that now sat along the west side of the location. Behind them a roustabout gang was digging privies.

Mules milled inside a rope corral, pawing at the ground to get at the last sprigs of trampled-down grass. A water wagon was just pulling into location. Wooster met it and waved the driver toward the feed tank for the steam boiler.

Temple walked through the organized confusion until he reached a pile of supplies covered with heavy oiled canvas tarpaulins and so far untouched by the builders. A lean old man sat on top of it with a jug of coffee and a Winchester pump shotgun beside him.

"You're the watchman?"

The man stretched himself down and held out a bony hand to Temple. "Silas Gibbs," he said. "Show me a whoreson oil supply thief, and I'll catch 'em!" His words tickled him. He bent over laughing, then straightened up to stare at Temple with a more somber slyness. "You're Temple? Look right over here, where it happened."

A two-by-eight plank leaned against the stack a little way from the spot Gibbs was sitting. He pointed to it. Temple saw a scatter of angular splinters strewn across the tarpaulin behind the plank.

"Did you see anybody?"

Gibbs slapped the stock of the shotgun. "Had I seen him, the whoreson would still be here," he said. "But he shot at me right enough."

Temple peered at the board. It had a mill pattern stamped into its wide side, the outline of a pine tree in red ink. Within the pattern were three round holes laid out in a triangle no larger than a decent apple. The splinters had come from the back of the board.

"And you figure he was shooting at you?"

"Who else could the whoreson bastard be shooting at? Wasn't I sitting right here beside that board?"

The quick ring of Gibbs's insistence made Temple wonder. Why would anybody fire three times, hitting in the same spot every time, if he meant to shoot at a watchman three feet to the left of that spot? Wouldn't the watchman have been out of the way before the second shot came singing?

"What time was this?"

"Early on last evening, maybe an hour after the last crew left. It was might near dark."

If the shooter had wanted to scare the watchman, one shot would have done it. Three might have been better, but they would never have been so calmly set in the same spot. Temple couldn't picture that at all.

What he could picture was the watchman off napping or whatever out of the wind when the shots came. What Temple could picture was a watchman with sense enough to keep out of sight once the shooting started.

What I can picture, Temple thought, is a shooter testing the sights on his rifle without ever suspecting there was another soul in a hundred miles. Practicing, like a hunter that's put out corn for a deer.

Temple stood, shaded his eyes and looked north. The line of hills was clearly visible above the intervening brush and trees. He got down on one knee and looked through the holes in the back side of the board. The shots could have come from the highest hill. Or from a lot of other places.

"Well, what do you think of a man that'd do a thing like that?"

Temple stood, absently brushing dirt from the knee of his jeans. "I think," he said, "that he's a whoreson back-shooting bastard."

Temple found Cotton Hargrove at the rough planked-in shack that served as an office. Hargrove was right in the middle of things, watching, giving orders, criticizing. Each time his voice rose to a shout, the big black dog lifted its nose to bark out in chorus with his master. Harry trailed at his side, quieter, making notes on a clipboard as Cotton ticked off things that still needed doing. Hargrove broke off in the middle of a shout and came over to Temple.

"Lee. What about the shots?"

"Three bullet holes in a board. Tight pattern. The watch-man didn't see anything."

Hargrove snorted. "The inside of his eyelids, probably. Where was the shooter?"

"I'm about to find out." He looked past Cotton and grinned at Harry. "Harry, if that's a list of things we need, put down a couple of good saddle horses."

Harry looked at him as if he'd requested racing camels or dancing girls, but he made a note. "All right," he said. "But you can use any of the cars—"

Temple shook his head. He'd learned enough from Tommy that he could steer one of the big Quads, but he didn't intend to make a habit of it. "Might want to go where a car can't take me," he said. "I'll see about the tack next time I can get to town. Sure wish I'd kept my saddle."

Cotton Hargrove nodded, his eyes and his mind on the rig builders at work. "Fine, Temple. Hurry up and get some guards out. Time's money." He waved a hand in dismissal. "Harry, you'll have to take over. I've got business in town."

"What kind of business?"

"Lawyer business. Come on. I'll talk to Wooster. Tell him you're in charge."

Harry smiled. "Don't bother," he said. "He'll know I'm in charge."

Temple got a pair of binoculars from the car and hung them round his neck. Hefting the heavy little Winchester rifle in his bandaged hand, he started walking toward the hills to the north. Mockingbirds sang in the mesquite, and tiny nondescript gray birds fled from bush to bush just a jump ahead of him as he walked. He flushed a cottontail and a jackrabbit before he reached the shadowed slope of the first hill.

He was ten or twelve pounds heavier with his rifle and ammunition. Still, the climb was not strenuous and the sun was still low. Temple figured he'd come across a job that fitted him well. He liked being outdoors. Though he tried not to think about it, he also enjoyed carrying the rifle. It was almost like hunting.

Hunting. Man-hunting, he heard his mother's voice saying. *Oh yes, Lee. They're paying you to hunt. They paid your father for that. Pretty soon, they'll be paying you for man-killing—just like your father!*

Temple frowned. She'd never spoken those words when she was alive. He wondered how he could hear them now exactly in her voice, with her cadence and diction and severity.

He breathed deeply, climbing more slowly, but enjoying the animal energy it cost him, enjoying the smells of grass and bushes and dirt that people had not yet fouled. Toward the top of the hill the slope grew steeper, with exposed patches of gray-black rock splashed with scaly growths of lichen. Temple slung his rifle and freed his hands for the climb around to the ridged back of the hill. A quarter of an hour later he walked easily out along its spine to a comfortable flat spot overlooking the location. A few stunted oaks with mistletoe in their branches crowned the summit. Beneath one of them, glistening in the morning sun, lay three finger-long brass cartridge hulls.

Temple knelt to read the signs. A man had lain on the hilltop for some time. He had piled rocks to make a rest for his rifle. Each shell had a little dent in its side near the rim. The bright brass was wet with dew, showing they'd been there at least overnight, but they were too shiny to have stayed long in the open. He held their open ends to his nose. The burned powder smell confirmed they'd been fired recently.

Standing on the hilltop, he scanned with binoculars. The rig site, almost a quarter mile away, spread before him like a map. The sounds of heavy hammers drifted up from the floor, coinciding more with the workers' uplifted arms than with the moments when the hammers actually fell. It made Temple wonder how much faster a bullet would reach them than the sound of the rifle that sent it.

The shot was much too long for Temple's short-coupled rifle. The hulls he'd found, though, were marked .30-06. A military cartridge, made to shoot even greater distances than four hundred yards. He looked again at the cartridge cases, thinking their necks would probably match the holes punched in the timber. But a rifleman would have to be a dead shot to hit from such a distance, even with a telescopic sight.

He put one of the cartridge hulls in his pocket and laid the other two back as he'd found them. That way, he told himself, if he comes back looking for them, he can figure a squirrel or a crow got this one; he won't need to know I found his shooting spot.

Moving back along the ridge, he smoothed out his own tracks as best he could while he followed those of the rifleman. He lost them on the rocky slope, found them again in a small oak grove. A horse had been tied there. The prints leading to the grove and away from it were first parallel and then intermingled as the rider returned in the way he came.

He couldn't prove the shots had been fired at the rig, Temple told himself. Maybe somebody was out to poach a deer. The owner of the land—old man Wilkes, say—might have shot at whatever he pleased, whenever he pleased. But someone had fired at the rig site all the same. The hilltop would be a good place to post a guard.

"If he was trying to hide, why did he leave the cartridges?" Elizabeth Hargrove asked.

"Beats me. Maybe he didn't think anybody would come looking. If he didn't see the watchman, he might figure nobody would ever know about the shots."

"Hm." She bit her lip while she considered that. Then she shrugged and straightened gracefully away from the porch railing. Coming across to Temple, she perched on his lap as he sat in Cotton Hargrove's big rocking chair. "Just see you're not in the way the next time he starts shooting, Cowboy."

Temple reached up and stroked the short hair on the back of her neck. "I'll try," he said.

"You'd better." She snuggled against him like a kitten. "What's New Mexico like?"

Temple thought about it—the ranch headquarters backed into the shelter of a red-rock lava crag, the broad, rolling, green-brown-yellow sweep of the high plains before it, the clouds piled halfway up the eastern sky, a wide curtain of rain painted rose by the setting sun and holding a fragment of rainbow in its heart.

"It's all right," he said.

Elizabeth laughed against his neck. "Eloquent."

"It's hard to talk about things."

"I know." She sat up and looked at him seriously. "Do we have to be like our families—like our fathers? Is that what you think?"

The change of subject didn't surprise Temple. "You don't seem very proud of your father," he said, to keep from answering. "Considering that he's made a fortune for you."

"Not for me," she said quickly. "Not for any of us."

"You must have wanted something more than money."

Elizabeth laughed. "Is there something more than money?" Looking into his eyes, she said, "Are *you* proud of *your* father?" Then she put her hand to her mouth as though wishing she'd cut off the words.

Temple looked steadily up at her until she could no longer meet his eyes. At last he said, "I don't know. I never knew him, except for what I've been told—and I don't know what to believe about that." He stopped, not wanting to say anything else, but finally he asked, "Are you ever afraid you'll turn out to be like him?"

"No." She said it too quickly. Then she raised her eyes to his again. "Yes," she said. "I *am* like him. Harry's the one who doesn't have to worry."

"Harry doesn't have to worry about what?" Cotton Hargrove pushed open the screen door and barged out onto the porch. He saw the two of them in the rocker and barked a harsh laugh around his fresh cigar. "Damnation! A man never knows what's going on in his own chair!"

Temple made to get up, but Elizabeth settled herself more firmly on his knees. "Hello, Father," she said. "Harry doesn't have to worry about me, I meant."

"Looks like somebody had better," Hargrove murmured. "Eliza, I need to talk to Temple. Don't you have something else to do?"

Elizabeth grinned at him and put her arms around

Temple's neck. "Nothing I like better than this," she said. "Besides, I'm part of the family business. I want to know what's happening."

Hargrove stared at her for a couple of seconds. "Eliza," he said.

She pouted her lip at him. "All right, Papa, dear. I'll leave." She stood up, leaning to kiss Temple quickly on the mouth. "I'll see you later, Lee."

Hargrove watched her as she slipped through the door, closing it behind her. Then he switched his glare onto Temple. Temple held his ground in the big chair, and finally Hargrove leaned back against the porch railing. He took the cigar from his mouth so he could sip from his glass.

"Harry's still down to the location, looking after things." He said it abruptly. Then he pointed the cigar at Temple. "I was thinking you ought to be there, too."

"I've got two good men on guard." Temple said. "Price has the drag gate and Mickey Dolan's on that hilltop north of the rig. I figured I should be here to watch your back."

"Some truth in that." Hargrove puffed his cigar. "Sheriff Quinlan was in today. Wilkes wanted to charge you with stealing his shotgun."

Temple flexed his bandaged hand. "Should I give it back?" he asked.

"Not yet. I got to talking about attempted murder, and the sheriff backed off a little. He's trying to tiptoe through this without making anybody mad." Hargrove chuckled and took another sip of the liquor. "I contributed a little to his election campaign, too. That may have helped."

"How well did you know my father?" Temple asked.

Hargrove blinked, then focused on Temple. "Pretty well," he said. "Like the fox knows the hound."

"Were you friends?"

"Not exactly."

"Tell me about him."

Hargrove set the glass aside. He took a deep puff on the cigar, then breathed the smoke out and watched it rise on the still evening air.

"Matthew Temple," he said, more to the smoke than to Temple. "That was a time for you. El Paso. Matthew had a lot of friends there. Hell of a wild town in the eighties. Not much different now."

Temple waited. Cotton Hargrove smoked thoughtfully. Once, he reached out for the glass, picked it up, then put it down untasted.

"That was a time," he said finally. "I'd heard there was money to be made running cattle in the border country. I needed to make some in a hurry, so there I came. Took up with some fellers I'd been told about, and we ran cattle."

"Did you make money?"

Hargrove chuckled. "I was a young buck, probably five years older'n you are now. Had money and a woman to help me spend it and thought I was smarter than anybody." He winked slyly at Temple. "Anybody excepting old Matthew, maybe."

Again Temple kept his silence, waiting. Hargrove was lost someplace inside his thoughts, looking out toward the dark oaks that surrounded the house. His cigar tip glowed.

"Texas Ranger, Matthew was then," Hargrove said. "There was people smuggling stolen cattle across the border, and his job was stopping them, him and the rest of the Rangers there. Seemed like he took a special interest in me."

"Were you running stolen cattle?"

"Nobody ever proved it. Matt had me in his jail twice and couldn't hold me. The last time I got out, he told me friendly-like that the Rangers were tired of fooling with me. Next time out, I'd likely get shot resisting arrest." Hargrove shrugged. "So I pulled my stakes. By that time I'd put enough money by to come back here and get the ranch going."

Temple had already heard about that from Tommy. He waited, but Hargrove seemed to be finished. "My father?" he asked. "Was he—like you?"

Hargrove took a sip of whiskey, considering. "Some ways he was," he said finally. "Some ways not. He was a youngster, about your age, but he knew his onions. Couldn't buy him and couldn't scare him. Good lawman." He shrugged. "He took out for New Mexico about six months after I left. I kept track of him as long as I could."

"Some say he was a killer."

"He'd killed two that I know of, both shooting at him when he dropped them. Probably there were more."

"Any of them shot in the back?" Temple asked.

Cotton Hargrove finished his drink and set the glass aside. "Wouldn't know," he said to Temple. "This killing business ain't like you think. If a man's after you, you do what you have to. It doesn't make much difference where he's facing if you're trying to save your life."

"I see."

"You don't. But you will if you have a man after you with the intent to kill." Hargrove straightened away from the railing. His cigar had burned down to a stub. He tamped it out on the porch railing and tossed it toward the trees. "Best get some sleep," he said. "Early start tomorrow. We need to be drilling by Thursday, and we're not through having trouble with old man Wilkes."

"I hope nobody decides to shoot *him*," Temple said.

"It's not our side doing the shooting," Hargrove reminded him evenly. "Not yet."

Chapter 19

HARRY HAD DONE A GOOD JOB OF SELECTING SADDLE HORSES. THE dappled mare that Temple rode was lean and bony as a fence rail, but she was sure-footed and accustomed to working around the racket and motion of a drilling rig. Temple could trust her to pick her way around the location, while he concentrated on business and on his own delight at being in the saddle again.

That morning, the rig was unusually quiet, without the deep, muffled boom of the drill striking rock. The big walking beam was still. On the rig floor, Pop Wooster and his tool dresser were sharpening the drill bit. The dead clunk of sledges striking glowing iron echoed across the location, stopped while Wooster checked the diameter and heated the bit again in the forge, then started again. From the doorway of the office shack Cotton Hargrove watched impatiently.

Turning his back on Hargrove and the rig, Temple rode down to the drag gate. Silas Gibbs sat with his back against the gatepost, his Winchester shotgun across his knees. He peered out from beneath the brim of his hat and gave Temple a snaggletoothed grin.

"Ever'thing's quiet, cap'n. Not a whoreson soul's stopped by to visit since you came in."

"We're expecting a convoy from Bremerton's, bringing in casing for the well. Should be here before noon. Anybody else, you take him straight to Mr. Hargrove."

Gibbs chuckled. "Which Mr. Hargrove would that be?"

"Whichever is around. If either one catches you sleeping down here, you'll likely be looking for a job."

"Don't you worry about that." Gibbs waved a bony hand. "Listen, cap'n. I've hardly slept a wink since that whoreson dry-gulcher took those shots at me!"

Temple swung wide of the drilling site so that he could let the mare stretch her legs in a trot. At the base of the rocky hill to the north, he dismounted. He unbitted the mare to let her graze, then took his rifle and binoculars and climbed up through the scattered prickly pear. On the edge of the caprock, Mickey Dolan scrambled to his feet, his freckled face splitting in a smile as he recognized Temple.

"Morning, boss."

"Morning, Mickey. Everything quiet?"

Dolan grinned. He claimed to be twenty, and maybe he was, but his open, boyish face with its bridge of freckles across the nose made him look much younger. "Pretty much," he said with studied casualness. "Took me a prisoner last night."

"What?"

"Some yokel clumb up here in the middle of the night. Sounded like a cow on a marble staircase. Don't know why he didn't get snakebit. Anyway, when he blundered to the top, I was there to meet him." He laughed and slapped the stock of his autoloader. "Looked right surprised. He was set to mortgage the farm and buy me off, but I marched him down to Mr. Hargrove."

"Which Mr. Hargrove?"

"The young one. Turned out this yokel was an oil scout, decked out with field glasses and a camera and a notebook and probably a rocking chair and an umbrella. He was fixing to watch what we was all doing." He laughed. "Mr. Harry sent him packing. Said next time we'd shoot."

Temple heard the excitement and suppressed laughter in Dolan's voice. "Don't," he said.

"How's that?"

"Have you ever shot anybody, Mickey?"

A hint of a frown touched Dolan's unlined brow. "No," he admitted. "But I can, boss, if it comes up. Honest."

"I know you can," Temple said. "But you did just the right thing last night. That's good work."

"Thanks, Lee—boss."

"I'll take over here. Get some breakfast. Take the mare if you want."

Dolan grinned as if Temple had offered him an elephant ride. "I got my own legs," he said. "Take care, boss."

Temple stood at the edge of the cap, his hand resting on the gnarled trunk of the nearest oak, watching Dolan stride toward the location. The young man carried his rifle with jaunty confidence. Temple thought about being on the hilltop in the night, hearing someone coming, moving to challenge the intruder. Had Dolan been nervous, afraid? If so, he'd never admit it.

Mr. Harry sent him packing. Said next time we'd shoot.

Temple frowned. That wasn't like Harry. Saying things like that was dangerous. If Harry wasn't careful, somebody might think he meant it.

* * *

Harry Hargrove stood on the second-floor porch of the Jergin house, looking out across a green roof of trees toward Emilia's main street. The street itself was hidden, but a thick haze of dust combined with the smoke of the flares marked it as surely as a signpost.

"Looks like a dry day," he said. "I hope the rain holds off another month."

"We need rain pretty badly," Harriet said. "If the farmers don't get some soon, they won't make a crop this fall."

He turned toward her. It was her day off from the library. She wore a simple yellow housedress that brought out highlights in her eyes and hair. "I forget, from one time to another, how pretty you are," he said.

"Thank you."

"Farmers or not, we need for the roads to stay dry. If it turns off muddy, we'll have the devil to pay getting the well down on time."

"Sometimes you talk like that's all that matters."

He frowned, turning back to the porch railing. "It matters quite a bit to me," he said. "Father's got everything staked on it. His bankers are getting restless. If we don't get it down, then it'll matter a lot."

"Because of the money? Harry, money's never been important to you before."

"It's only important when you don't have it." He turned toward her. "Listen, Hare," he said, much more abruptly than he'd intended. "We'll be drilling close to another month. I'll be out there most of the time. I think . . ."

"Yes, Harry?"

"I think we'd better postpone the wedding."

He'd expected tears, an argument, maybe a bitter scene. Instead Harriet merely lowered her eyes and looked at the scuffed paint of the porch decking.

"All right."

"It's just for a little while."

"Of course, Harry."

"As soon as the well is down, we'll be married, just as we planned."

"If that's what you want."

"It's not what I want."

Then don't do it, her eyes said to him. *Don't throw away everything you are. Take me away from here and we'll live together and you'll write and we'll have money or not and it won't matter.* But she didn't say any of it aloud.

"I have to," he answered her anyway. "It's family."

Looking at the floor, Harriet nodded. "Harry," she asked, "what if the well doesn't come in? What if it's dry?"

He laughed sharply. "Then the Hargroves are back to being trash," he said.

"I see." She let him take her hand, even looked up at him as he said good-bye. "I'll be praying, Harry," she said.

"Thanks, Hare." But as he walked down the cracked sidewalk outside, he wondered which result she'd be praying for.

Cotton Hargrove was standing in front of the office shack, hands on his hips, when the green Reo pulled up and Harry got out. Pop Wooster had his sharpened bit back on bottom. The muffled thump of steel on rock throbbed like a heartbeat.

"About damn time," Hargrove grunted. "What were you doing in there? Any sign of that damned convoy with our casing?"

"It was forming up in front of Bremerton's when I came by." Harry held up a newspaper. "I brought this out for the men to see. It's war in Europe."

"It'll be war here if we don't get that casing right damned quick. I'm going to see about it." Hargrove grabbed the paper and glared at it. "Damned fools. Austria and Serbia and Russia and France and Germany, all invading one another."

"England's not in it yet."

"They will be. And they'll want oil. It's good for us— drive up the price!"

"That's one way to look at it."

Hargrove snorted. "Name me two other ways to look at

191

it!" he said. "You take over here. See the men don't get so busy reading about the war they forget to work."

"Don't worry," Harry said. "Most of them can't read. Where's Temple?"

"Up there keeping watch, we'll hope." Cotton threw an arm up in the direction of the nearest ridge.

Temple saw the gesture, thought of waving back, let it go. He couldn't make out what they were talking about, and he was supposed to be on guard. He wouldn't wave at them like a schoolgirl. He kept his glasses on them for a minute longer, then returned his attention to the space around him.

He'd looked at the land at first with an eye for its highs and lows. By now he'd located its places of concealment. One by one he scanned shallow gullies or stands of brush or rocky outcrops where an ambusher might hide. It came to him that a great deal of the fun had gone out of his comfortable new job the moment he saw those empty rifle cartridges.

Temple had his glasses on the farthest grove of cedars when he saw a bit of bright color. It might have been a bird's wing, a wildflower, a woman's dress. He adjusted the glasses. Almost hidden by the trees, he made out a yellow automobile. Not far away from the car, her short hair whipping in the wind, stood Elizabeth Hargrove.

Lee Temple watched her until she slipped down into a long gully out of his sight. He took a last sweep of the ridges, then slid down along the side of the hill. Leaving the mare where she was, he began circling toward the place he'd last seen Elizabeth.

It took him half an hour to make his way far enough around to catch sight of the young woman again. She was no more than forty yards away from him. She stood in the slanting sunlight watching the men work. If any of them saw her, they paid her no mind. Then Temple saw that one had seen her. Her brother Harry Hargrove had also flanked her and was moving toward her from behind. Temple started to call out to them. Then, instead, he went down on one knee to watch.

Elizabeth waited until Harry was almost near enough to touch her before she turned. "Hell, Harry," she said with a laugh. "Are you playing cowboys and Indians, trying to sneak up on me?" She saw that he was wearing a holster at his belt, its leather flap buttoned down over a heavy revolver. "You even look the part."

Harry ignored her teasing. He looked angry. "This is no place for you, Betty," he snapped. He sounded angry, too. "What are you doing out here anyway?"

None of your business, brother dear. You're not my keeper. But she didn't want to say that. Nor did she want to tell him the truth.

"Can't I just want to see what you're doing? I'm next in line, you know. I might be running this operation someday."

Harry snorted. "Sure you will," he said. "You know a woman's bad luck on a rig. If Father sees you, we'll both have the devil to pay."

"I've already paid. Anyway, he's gone. I saw him and the car and that bastard of a dog."

"Don't say that. You talk like a cheap Oiltown whore."

She was surprised and a little hurt and a little angrier than she'd been, but again she bit back the first answer that came to her. "You sound pretty rough yourself," she said instead. "You'd better not let Harriet or Aunt Minnie hear you talk that way."

She was surprised again when he grabbed her arm hard enough to hurt. "Get back down here out of sight," he said. "I'm not kidding around with you."

She sat down at the rim of the gully. "I agree. You haven't made me laugh yet."

He took her by the elbow and jerked her down to the bottom of the little gully. "What is it you want out here? Are you vamping for Mickey Dolan again? Answer me."

This time she did say it. "Mind your own business, Harry. You're not my keeper."

"I'm your family. I thought I knew you, until I came back and started hearing the stories about you."

Her eyes burned. She felt a tightening in her throat and was afraid she'd cry if she tried to answer. She turned her back on him while she got out a cigarette and lit it.

"And you believed them all," she was able to say then.

"I didn't want to."

Then why did you? But she knew if she said that, she *would* cry.

"Listen," he said. "It's about time you quit trying to disgrace the family and did something to help."

"I've been more help to Father than you have."

"More help? You? How?"

"I brought him Lee Temple."

For a moment Harry just stared at her. Then he laughed. It was an ugly sound. "I see what it is," he said. "You're not here for Mickey. You're vamping for Lee Temple!"

"What do you care? He's been a good enough friend to you, hasn't he?"

"He's not our kind."

She laughed. She thought it sounded ugly, too. "I know that. But there's still some chance he'll have me."

"You don't know anything about him."

"I know *all* about him."

He hit her with a short quick slap that caught her on the jaw just below her ear and rocked her head sideways. She put her hand up to her jaw, staring at him in disbelief. *No!* She was surprised she hadn't said the word aloud. *Papa, sure. But not you, Harry!*

He looked almost as shocked as she. For a second she thought he would apologize, would hug her the way they'd comforted one another as children. But he turned abruptly away.

"Temple's father was a killer," he said.

She laughed, though she thought she would never want to laugh again. "I know that!" she called after him. "Harry, what the hell do you think *your* father is?"

He turned. She thought he meant to hit her again, and she

dropped her hands, ready, defenseless. But he stood motionless, staring past her. She threw a quick glance over her shoulder and looked into Lee Temple's eyes.

Temple stood at the far rim of the gully. His new Winchester hung muzzle up at his shoulder and his hands hung loosely at his sides, but Elizabeth Hargrove was frightened anyway. She was frightened by his eyes. She'd seen that expression in them before, and she knew what it meant.

"Lee," she said.

Temple jerked his head toward Harry. "Up at the rig, Harry, they're looking for you."

"Are they?" Harry squared himself around toward Temple. His hand dropped to the flap of his holster. "I don't know how much you heard."

Temple said, "I have pretty good ears."

"Then I won't need to repeat it."

"Just the slapping part," Temple said. He came sliding down the far bank and on across the silty bottom toward them. When he was a couple of feet from Harry he stopped, leaned toward him. "Make that sound on my cheek," he said.

Harry Hargrove did not turn from him nor flinch. "I'm not afraid of you," he said.

Elizabeth knew it was true. More, she knew that in a few seconds, one or the other of these two was going to die. Desperately, she threw herself between them, facing Harry. She swung with all her strength, smashing the back of her hand across his mouth.

For a moment she was afraid he wouldn't even notice. Then he blinked, tore his eyes away from Temple's, looked at her with the same hurt bewilderment she'd felt when he slapped her. He took his hand from the butt of the pistol, pressed the back of it to his lips, stared at the blood he saw there.

"Betty?"

"Tough guy," Elizabeth said to hide her relief.

Hargrove spat out a little blood. To Temple he said,

"You're away from your post." Then he turned, scrambled up the bank, and headed back toward the rig walking very fast.

Elizabeth sighed. "Lee," she said. "God, I'm glad to see you."

Temple said, "More than Mickey Dolan?"

It caught her up short. She remembered what she'd told Harry. Had Lee heard, too? "You *do* have good ears," she said.

"As good as Mickey's?"

"I went out with him a few times. That was all."

She knew that wouldn't satisfy him, and it didn't.

"Was it?" he asked. "What does that mean—you went out with him?"

"To the Line. Dancing. Like that."

Temple turned to watch Harry Hargrove walk to the office shack. Harry paused in the doorway, looking back toward the gully before he went inside.

"I'm away from my post," Temple said. "Come on if you want to talk."

She started to speak, but he set out walking at a pretty good clip. For a moment she hesitated, but she knew she was going to follow him. She caught up, kept up. Neither of them spoke for the time it took them to climb back to the flat hilltop. Once there, he lifted his binoculars and studied the rig site. They were standing in the open. Elizabeth started to move back out of sight, then changed her mind and stood at Temple's side where Harry, or anybody, could see her.

"Is this your lookout?" she asked, keeping her voice light. She hoped it was over. "What a beautiful spot. Can I look through your glasses?"

He glanced at her, then handed the binoculars across. She looked at the rig site, searched for Harry, finally raised the glasses to look at a flight of sandhill cranes winging in toward the creek in the late sunlight.

She felt him looking at her. It wasn't over. Holding the glasses tightly to her eyes, she said, "I don't care anything about Mickey Dolan, nor him about me."

"What about the others?"

She lowered the glasses but kept her eyes on the sky. "What others?"

"All the others. People say there were quite a few."

"Is that what people say? It doesn't matter. I didn't care anything about any of them——"

"You just used them?"

He had heard. "——except the first one. Roy. That was his name. Roy Allison."

"You cared about him, did you?"

She nodded.

"Well, which one is he? How does he feel toward all the others? Do they sometimes get in a gang fight and tear up the town? Where is he?"

She turned her face away. She wasn't going to cry. "He's dead." She wiped her eyes savagely with the heel of a hand. "On a rig. Just like this one."

"You're not the crying kind," Temple said.

"No." She tried to stop, cried harder. He put out a hand, touched her hair. She shook her head angrily. "You must have heard about it. That first damned well. The nitro shot."

"I'm sorry," he said, and his voice was gentle. Somehow, she was more afraid of that than of his anger.

"It was my fault," she told him quickly.

"What? Don't be silly." He put his hands on her shoulders, tried to get her to look at him. "What did they tell you, that women are bad luck around a rig?"

"Don't humor me, damn you!" She wanted more than anything to collapse against him, safe in his arms, to cry until she couldn't cry anymore. She shook him off. "He thought I had to have money. Because my family never really had any. Not until the oil came."

"Listen——"

"Oil field jobs paid a lot better than farming or ranching or town work. Shooting wells paid the best of all."

"Not your fault," Temple said again, gently. *"He* saw it. *He* wanted it."

"No. He—He wanted me. And I—We—He was the first boy I ever—cared for." She didn't wait for him to answer, even if he intended to. "I was watching," she said in a hard, bright tone. "I saw the whole thing, just like a play. One second he was pouring that stuff into a torpedo. He finished, smiled over toward where I was, set down the can."

She looked up at Temple, her head cocked to one side. "Then he was gone. The rig, everything. All gone. Just fire and dust and things rising up in the air, tumbling over and over and over."

After a time, Temple said softly, "Not the worst way to go." She thought he wasn't talking to her at all.

"They never found—anything," she said. Then she shrugged. "Anyway, they didn't tell *me* what they found. That's why there's no grave. Not even a place for flowers."

"We could put up a marker," Temple said. "Someplace he liked. If you want to."

She laughed at the idea. "It won't help him."

"It might help you."

"Daddy was watching. It was our—his—first well. When the explosion came, he laughed. I've hated him ever since."

"For that? For laughing?"

She stared into his eyes, searching to see how deep he ran, to see whether he understood this thing that was the most important thing in the world to her. "Wouldn't you?" she asked. "Wouldn't you hate him for that?"

"I don't know," he said slowly. "Maybe I would. What else did he do?"

She tried to remember. "He caught a horse. They all took off running," she said. As she spoke, it seemed to all play out before her, the things she'd been too numbed to see as they happened. "Everybody was running away. But he spurred that white-eyed horse down there, and went into the fire and smoke and came out holding a burning hat."

"Hat?"

"I'd forgotten that," she said in wonder. "I hadn't thought of it in all this time. It was Roy's hat."

"How much time?"

She heard the change in his tone, heard what he was thinking. He was wondering how many *others* she'd had time for.

"A year. A year ago next Wednesday."

"It's a long time to hold something against your father."

"*I* didn't laugh," she said.

"Did you cry?"

"I'm not the crying kind."

"Maybe if—"

"Shut up!" she shouted. She stood up, took two or three steps away from the rim. She was going to cry again, and damned if she'd let him see it. "You weren't there. You don't know anything. You didn't know him. You don't know *me.*"

He came to stand behind her. His hands were warm on her shoulders. Fighting herself the whole way, she let him draw her back until their bodies touched.

"I don't quite see why you'd hate Cotton for that. You make it sound more like he did everything he could."

"I do hate him!" she said, too quickly to think about it. She couldn't analyze it, couldn't think about who she hated. "I hate him all the way through."

For a long time he didn't say anything. Then she felt one of his hands move away. He pointed at something on the ground near her feet.

"Then maybe these are your cartridge hulls."

"What?"

He pointed to the two brass shells that lay where he had left them that morning. She knelt to pick one up, turning it in her fingers. "Frank Loman," she said.

"What?"

"What? Father taught me about guns. Loman has a rifle like that. Has he been up here?"

"How do you know that?"

"Know what? About the caliber? I told you, Papa taught me to hunt. Said even a girl ought to know some things."

"Not that. How would you know about Loman's rifle? Was he one of the *others?*"

Kneeling on the ground, she raised her face and looked at him. "To hell with you, Cowboy," she said, low and clear. She wasn't crying now. "You aren't my keeper, no more than Papa or Harry. If that's how it's going to be, to hell with you."

She rose, swiftly but without hurrying, and started down

the hill. He didn't come after her. All the way across the pasture to the Mercer, she knew he was watching, but she didn't look back. When she reached the car, she clung to its fender, bent over by racking sobs that shook her body until she retched. But it was all right. Hidden by the arms of the cedars, she was certain no one could see.

Chapter 20

"HOW LONG CAN YOU GET FOR VIOLATING A COURT ORDER?" Mickey Dolan wanted to know. "What kind of rap is it?"

Seated on either side of a wooden crate, Talking Tommy Ellis and Slick Porterfield looked up from their blackjack game. Ellis smiled.

"Not so deep as a well nor so wide as a church door, my young felon," he said. "But 'tis enough, 'twill serve."

"Listen, mister, you shouldn't drink before you go out like this. You need a clear head."

Lee Temple broke off pacing the fairway of Bremerton's warehouse. "The trick," he said, "is not to get caught."

"On the contrary, friend Temple." Tommy dealt Porterfield a card. "Thirteen showing. The trick, indeed, is to avoid such a deplorable situation. I'm surprised this mishap should befall a man of Cotton Hargrove's experience."

"Hit me," Porterfield said.

Hargrove had been surprised, too, Temple remembered. It had been far past midnight when Hargrove and Rotten had gotten back to the well site the night before. It had been later still when Temple and Harry and Pop Wooster and the dog crowded into the office shack with him to hear the news.

"I had to leave the car away up north and walk in across the hills," Hargrove told them. He glared at Temple in the light of the hissing gasoline lantern. "That guard of yours came within an ace of shooting me."

Temple said, "Maybe he'd been told to shoot first."

"Damnation!" Hargrove slapped his hand down on the makeshift desk hard enough to make it shudder. Rotten barked. "I knew we'd have trouble with that old man."

"Mr. Wilkes?" Harry asked, covering a yawn.

"Hell, yes, Mister Wilkes. Got a restraining order to stop us using the road across his pasture. There's deputies out past the gate thick as yellowjackets in a watermelon patch."

"I thought you'd taken care of that," Harry said.

"Everybody's gone back on me, the damned judge and the sheriff, too. Our lawyer can get the order vacated the first of next week. We'll have to make do until then."

Pop Wooster stood for a moment listening to the throb of the drill. "Ain't no making do." He spat a stream of tobacco juice through the shack's doorway and into the night. "We'll have to shut down. Tomorrow night, day after at the latest."

"Shut down, hell!" Hargrove lunged to his feet, crowding the tiny space still further. "We're supposed to have everything we need to operate for a week, people and supplies and all."

"Would have, too, 'cepting maybe water," Wooster said calmly. "But the deputies turned back our load of casing." He nodded toward the drilling rig. "Listen how mushy that bit sounds. Come noon, we won't be making a foot of hole."

Temple listened. To him the rig sounded the same as always, the squeaks and rattles and the hissing chuff of steam punctuated every few seconds by the thump of the bit. "I don't understand," he said. "I thought the casing was meant to keep the hole open after you finished drilling."

Wooster spat. "Right, so far as you go," he said. "That's the production string. What we have now is a water flow down underground, coming in faster'n we can bail it out. We have to case it off so's we can keep drilling." He turned to Hargrove. "If'n we shut down, I won't promise there'll be a hole to come back to. We'd likely have to start over."

"No time," Hargrove growled. "Nor money, either. Damnation."

"I don't see what we can do," Harry said. "You can't go up against the law."

Cotton Hargrove sank back down on the nail keg that served as an office chair. "No," he said. "We surely can't go against the law." He rubbed his chin, looking at Temple. "But maybe we can go around it."

"What we do is go around it," Temple said. He spread the map Cotton Hargrove had marked for him on the crate. "We leave the main road just past Cedar Creek and go north about three miles. Then we follow this draw back west. There's no road, but Hargrove's Pierce Arrow made it through."

"Then two wagonloads of casing ought to be all right," Porterfield said. "Simple enough."

"If not entirely legal," Tommy added.

Temple looked up. "We don't get onto Wilkes's property until we turn west. Up until then, we're legal enough."

"Maybe," Tommy said gently. "But whose property *are* we crossing?"

Temple hadn't thought of that. "Harry's going to keep the deputies busy at the main gate," he said. "Cotton's in town, telling people he's going to raise Cain with the judge tomorrow. The sheriff shouldn't be expecting us." He stood up, folding the map back into the pocket of his khaki shirt. "Nobody has to go that doesn't want to."

Slick Porterfield laughed. "With what Hargrove's paying, I don't intend to back out."

"Me neither," Mickey Dolan put in quickly.

Temple was sure Tommy Ellis cared nothing about the money, and less about Cotton Hargrove. "Talk?" he asked.

The long-legged man walked to the double doors of the warehouse and shoved one of them back. He looked for a moment at the hazy twilight that was Emilia's night.

"Until it's delivered to location, it's still Mr. Bremerton's casing," he said. "I believe I'll ride along and see to the transfer. Shall we go?"

Temple and Porterfield harnessed eight-horse hitches to the low, eight-wheeled wagons. Each wagon was piled with lengths of steel pipe. Mickey Dolan stood watch at the doorway.

"Beats me why you want to use horses," Dolan complained. "We'd make better time with those gas buggies."

"Too much noise," Temple said. "And horses can haul more. Ready, Tommy?"

Ellis came from Bremerton's office with two long guns over his arm. He put the Winchester shotgun on the seat of one wagon and handed Porterfield a short Marlin carbine.

"Ready. You've got those odd autoloaders of yours? You'd better let Slick and me take the lead. The shotgun'll cut more ice if anybody tries to hijack us."

Temple thought about it, then shook his head. "No, we'll go first. I know the way." He looked at the others and tried a smile. "I doubt we have to worry about hijackers. No way anybody could know we're doing this."

He saw Tommy tap his fingers against the wood of a wagon wheel. "Lee, I've known you since your first day in the oil patch," the talking man said, "and that's the first truly foolish thing I've heard you say."

From the window of his darkened store Frank Loman watched the two wagons creep away. Temple was in the lead. That was good. It was just like Hargrove to try a backdoor stunt like this. Old Cotton always thought he was just a little smarter than anybody else. Before daylight he'd find out who was smart.

"Buff?" Clancy's voice was a whisper, as if the men on the wagon might hear him. "You think it's true? You think Hargrove's really about busted?"

"Huh? No. That old buzzard's got money enough to burn a wet dog—even if he's wasting a pile of it on this wildcat."

"But everybody says—"

"Hell with what everybody says. Listen, when Billings gets in from this, tell him he's earned a bonus. You, too. Y'all have done a good day's work bird-dogging Temple."

"Thanks, Buff. But—"

"Shut up. And don't call me Buff."

* * *

At the edge of town Temple checked his heavy little rifle and racked a cartridge into the chamber. He kept it standing beside him while he worked the lines to drive the team. As the lights of Emilia fell behind, he watched the ditches and the trees along the way. He took comfort at first in the bright moonlight, until it came to him that anyone hiding in the shadows could see him even better than he could see the countryside.

"What do you really think?" Mickey Dolan whispered. "Any chance of hijackers?"

Temple glanced at him. Dolan held his rifle tensely. In the moonlight his eyes shone with the excitement of a boy playing at pirates.

"I doubt it, Mickey," Temple said. "There's a better chance we'll end up in jail when some deputy jumps us."

"Aw. You don't think that." Dolan grinned. "Goes to show," he said. "I almost quit a couple days before you picked me as guard. Look what I'd've missed."

Temple licked his lips. Everything should be quiet, he reminded himself, at least until they left the main road. "Why'd you want to quit?" he asked Dolan. "Trouble with Cotton?"

The boy shook his head. "Cotton's okay," he conceded. "But I figured it was time to move. Nobody's brought in a well for over a week, and the whole town's taming down. Boom's about dead here."

"Dead?" Temple wanted to knock on wood the way Tommy did. He clenched his hands on the reins. "I thought it seemed pretty lively."

"You ain't seen so many boomtowns as me," Dolan said. "Anyway, I've done about all there is to do here. Worked for all the bosses, drank at all the bars, kissed all the girls."

"I went out with him a few times. To the Line. Dancing. Like that."

"All of them?" Temple asked.

"All I could afford."

They came to a bend in the road, overhung with twisted oaks. The shadows beneath the trees were silky black, moving and shifting as the wind shook the limbs. "Watch it," Temple murmured. He didn't speak again until both wagons had passed through the shadows.

"Ever go sparking the town girls?" he asked then.

Dolan laughed. "Not likely! I can tell you ain't, either. Best stick to the oil doves on the Line." He shook his head. "Some papa would put the sheriff on you quicker'n scat. Folks don't like oil field trash sniffing at their daughters."

"I hear Hargrove's daughter is different."

"Liz? You're right." Mickey Dolan chuckled. "She's different, sure enough." He looked sideways at Temple. "I figured you knew all about her, cozy as you seem with all the Hargroves—not meaning any offense."

"I hear she hangs around the Line."

"Looks like a dream. Dances like one, too."

"Drinks too much."

"Don't we all?"

"Runs with a fast crowd."

"There's nobody real slow on the Line."

"Sleeps—"

He broke off. The team had stopped, the lead horses shying at a dark shape in the road ahead. Temple realized they'd reached the Cedar Creek bridge. He saw the bridge was blocked, knew he'd been so busy with damned foolishness that he'd forgotten his duty. Cursing himself, he slacked the lines and grabbed up his rifle.

"Who's there?"

A slender figure drew out of the shadow beside the bridge. It took a long stride forward, swaying in the road almost in front of the snorting horses.

"Stand and deliver!"

"Hell!"

Mickey Dolan swung the autoloader up and onto the shadowy target. As his finger closed on the trigger, Temple thrust hard with his own rifle. Its barrel clashed against the forestock of Dolan's Winchester and knocked the gun upward just as it fired.

"Don't shoot!" Ears ringing from the bark of the rifle, eyes dazzled by the muzzle flash, Temple scrambled down from the wagon. "Don't shoot. Don't shoot, Mickey. It's her."

For a moment he couldn't see anything. Then the dark shadow slipped toward him. Elizabeth's arms slid around him. Her body pressed against his and her throaty laugh sounded beside his ear.

"Hello, Cowboy."

"Thank God." Relief surged through Temple like a wave, to be washed away an instant later by an even greater wave of anger. "You idiot, we damn near killed you." He held her away, peered at her face in the moonlight. "You're drunk."

She pushed away from him. "What the hell's it to you?" Turning away, she reached out for Dolan, who had come down from the wagon. "Mickey. Hi." She snuggled against him. "You're not mad at me, are you?"

"Liz!" Dolan hesitated, uncertain what to do with her. Finally he shifted his rifle to his left hand and put his arm around her shoulders. "What in—"

"What in hell's going on?" Tommy Ellis demanded. He loomed out of the darkness behind them, the shotgun ready at his hip. A second later Porterfield came around the front of the wagon from its off side. "Hold it right there!"

"Slick, Tommy, it's all right," Temple said. He drew a deep breath. The anger had subsided in him. Now that the danger had passed, he felt himself begin to shake. If Dolan had been just a little faster, or himself just a little slower . . .

He clenched his hands on the rifle to keep them steady. "It's all right," he repeated. "We have a visitor, that's all."

"So we do." Tommy came closer, peering at Elizabeth as she huddled against Mickey Dolan. "Miss Hargrove. If it's not unduly curious on my part, could you tell us just what in hell you're doing out here?"

"Came to see Cowboy," she said, pouting. "Heard everybody on the Line talking about you sneaking around. Thought I'd surprise him. But he's mad at me, and my bastard of a car won't go."

Tommy Ellis winked at Temple. "There's your secrecy."

Porterfield stood fingering the Marlin carbine and staring anxiously into the night. "Look," he said over his shoulder. "I hate to break up a reunion, but we need to get the hell moving."

"I'll see about the car." Sounding relieved, Dolan passed Elizabeth across to Temple, who didn't particularly want her. "I need a light."

Porterfield brought a lantern. The Mercer sat at an odd angle. One front wheel had dropped off the road into a deep cut just at the end of the bridge. Dolan looked at it, then dropped to the ground and slithered under the car.

"Axle's broken," he called. "Ain't going anywhere, not unless we tie the team onto it."

"Bastard," Elizabeth muttered.

"We can't leave her here," Temple said.

"Helluva sight safer than taking her with us." Porterfield told him. "Sounds like every thief and hijacker on the Line knows where we're going."

"We have to turn back," Ellis said.

"Not me." Dolan joined them, bringing with him the pool of light from the lantern. "If we don't deliver, Hargrove don't pay."

"Put out that damn light," Porterfield growled. He turned to Ellis. "I'm with him. We go on."

"We don't have to. It's not life and death," Ellis said. "It's only oil."

"It's money."

Elizabeth stirred against Temple's chest. "Me, too," she murmured. "Go on. Got to have that casing. Time's money."

"Lee?" Temple felt the weight of Tommy's eyes. "It's your call. What do you say?"

"No time," Cotton Hargrove had said. *"No time. Nor money, either."*

Temple looked at the night sky, the bridge, the huge shaggy horses standing patiently, the long pyramids of stacked casing on the wagons. He tightened his hands on the cold metal of the Winchester.

"Shove that car out of the way," he said. "We need to be there by daylight."

Porterfield and Tommy Ellis took the lead wagon north from the bridge. Elizabeth squeezed onto the seat of the second wagon between Temple and Mickey Dolan. Giggling, she put an arm around each of them.

"Midnight ride," she murmured. "Always liked midnight rides."

Temple shook her arm away. "Keep quiet," he said.

"Grouch." She turned, putting both arms around Dolan, laying her face against his chest. "Mickey. Just like old times."

Dolan couldn't decide whether to push her away or pull her closer. Hanging onto his rifle with one hand, he looked across at Temple.

"Listen, boss—"

"It's okay, Mickey. Just keep her quiet."

Dolan did his best. Finally Elizabeth put her head down in his lap. Apparently she went to sleep.

"Boss, I—"

"Shut up."

Temple listened for the night sounds, for anything out of the ordinary. He heard the rattles and squeaks of the wagon, the soft clop of hooves in the dust, the leathery creak of harness. Elizabeth's hip pressed against his, firm and warm. She stirred and said something softly, something ending with Dolan's name.

"Here." Temple passed the lines to the younger man. "Drive the damn thing. I want to see we don't miss our turn."

He took his rifle and dropped off the wagon, stumbling ahead as fast as he could manage in the darkness. Abreast of the first wagon he began searching the ground, glad now of the bright moonlight. They couldn't be sure just how far they'd come, he told himself. He needed to be here, needed to watch for the tracks of Hargrove's auto. It didn't have anything to do with Elizabeth, nor with Dolan.

There was a barbed-wire fence to their left now, one that he remembered. The road topped a low rise and started down into a draw. Its bottom was thickly grown up with mesquite and underbrush.

"Hold up," Temple called softly. "It's right along here."

The lead wagon trundled to a stop, and a moment later

Dolan reined the second one up. Temple cast ahead a few yards until he came to a barred wooden gate. Kneeling to examine the ground, he saw the faint tire marks of the Pierce Arrow.

"Right here."

"We can't turn that sharp." Tommy was beside him, though Temple hadn't heard the long-legged man come up. "We'll have to swing wide to the right and come back. I'll send Dolan through first."

"Go."

Tommy slipped back to the shadowy wagons. After a moment the second one began to swing out of line. It turned wide and came across in front of the other. Temple pushed the gate back on protesting hinges. For a second he saw Dolan's head and shoulders outlined clear and sharp against the stars.

"Straight through, Mickey. Stop on the other side."

"Don't worry, boss. I—"

Whatever he'd been about to say ended in a welter of sounds that came all at once. Later, Temple was able to sort it out: a hoarse warning shout from Porterfield, a rifle's sharp crack an instant ahead of the boom of Tommy's shotgun, a startled grunt from Mickey Dolan. But at the moment it all happened, the only thing he heard clearly was Elizabeth Hargrove's scream.

Chapter 21

TEMPLE LEAPED FOR THE WAGON SEAT AS THE EIGHT BIG HORSES spooked into a lurching run. The handhold jerked painfully at his shoulder, but he swung himself up. Mickey Dolan was a huddle of shadow. Beside him, Elizabeth knelt on the seat, both hands to her mouth, still screaming. Temple fought down his instinct to grab for the trailing reins. Instead he got

Dolan by one arm and caught a handful of Elizabeth's dress, throwing himself backward and dragging them along.

He kicked back hard against the wagon, pushing to get clear of the wheels. Fabric ripped under his hand. A bullet went past with a droning buzz. Another slapped into some part of the wagon, and a third struck the load of pipe and whined away into the night.

Then he was falling, the stars before his eyes, the wagon and its load of pipe between him and the guns in the draw. He hit hard and rolled with the forward momentum of the wagon. The impact drove air from his lungs in a rush. Through a roaring in his head he heard Elizabeth's scream cut off in an agonized gasp. Something from the wagon fell across his head and shoulder like a club. He pushed with a belated hand to ward it off, touched the cold barrel of Dolan's rifle and pulled it to him.

The wagon lurched uphill, slowing as its weight dragged at the frantic horses. Temple lay in the open, a dozen yards from the gate. Elizabeth was somewhere to his right, breathing in sobbing gasps. To his left Mickey Dolan was still and quiet.

The slam of a rifle and a lance of flame from the mesquite thicket at the bottom of the gully told him the fight wasn't over. Temple tensed, but the fire wasn't aimed his way. From the direction of the first wagon, a horse screamed. More shots came from the gully, to be answered by the deep voice of the shotgun and a rapid bap-bap-bap that must have been Porterfield's carbine.

"Art! Get around to the side! Get 'em!"

The hoarse voice came from the shadows of the thicket. One of the men in there fired again, the noise partly drowning the answer.

"—that first bunch?"

"They're out of business. Get moving!"

At first the voices rang without meaning in Temple's aching head. Then the shadows before him thickened into something solid, and the words thickened into meaning. As he shoved the rifle forward, the shadow became a man in a crouching run, a long gun in his hand.

"Billings—"

Temple squeezed the trigger. The autoloader's steel butt plate punched back hard against his shoulder once, again, again. As if he'd hit a clothesline in the dark, the running man jerked upright. His head and shoulders flung backward as his legs, still running, went out from under him.

"Art! What the hell—"

Temple was up before the man fell. He swung the rifle toward the voice, fired twice, heard the shout turn to muffled curse. Then he was running, tearing down the slope, firing into the shifting shadows as he ran. He heard the sounds of men in the thicket. Later he would remember them as sounds of distress and anger. He put three more streaking bullets into the grove, heard the Winchester click empty. Before he could turn it as a club, his foot caught on something and he fell.

"Lee! Lee Temple!" He thought the voice might be Tommy's. The boom of the shotgun confirmed it for him. "Lee! God's sake, Lee, stay down!"

Somewhere nearby a man was screaming. Others yelled, cursed, scrambled through the brush. None of them seemed to be worried about Temple. The few more scattered bullets seemed to be aimed loosely toward the wagon. Temple lifted his head far enough to see above the grass.

The shadows were moving. He rolled on his side and groped for a new clip for the autoloader, tore a fingernail getting the empty one out, fumbled with the clumsy action. By the time he was ready to fire again, he heard horses running flat out through the low scrub.

From the wagon, Porterfield emptied the Marlin's magazine in a long rattle of shots. The screams had stopped, but something still thrashed madly in the thicket. Cautiously, Temple rose to his feet.

"Temple?" Talking Tommy Ellis's shout came immediately. "Lee, if that's you, sing out."

"It—" Temple choked on the word, coughed, tried again. "Tommy. Are you all okay?"

"More or less."

"Mickey's shot. See about him. I'm going in."

"Wait," Ellis called, but Temple eased ahead, holding the rifle ready. He wanted to know about Elizabeth, to find out how bad Mickey Dolan was hurt, but first he had to learn what was in the thicket.

He went up the hill through the scattered trees and came back to the thicket from above. The sound turned out to be a horse, shot down in the fight, thrashing out its last breaths in bloody foam. Another horse reared and plunged against tied reins, fighting to escape the smell of blood.

Filled with a relief he couldn't identify, Temple moved clear of the flailing hoofs, took the best aim he could manage in the shadows, and fired once. The fallen horse shuddered and was still. Trailing the rifle, Temple turned slowly and started back toward the others.

A sound stopped him, the slow, solid sound of a steel hammer clicking into cock. Sweat broke out on Temple's face and seemed to freeze on his skin. He dropped, boneless as a hangman's sandbag, just as the heavy handgun went off a few feet away in a blast of heat and noise. The bullet cut the air a foot above him.

He brought the rifle up, ready to fire. It wasn't needed. The man on the ground didn't move again. Temple approached him carefully, kicked the pistol away from a limp hand, knelt over him. He couldn't find a pulse. In the moonlight that filtered into the draw, the man's blood showed dead black.

"Lee?"

"Here, Tommy."

Temple was still kneeling there when Ellis crashed through the brush to stand above him. The long-legged man looked down for a moment at the hijacker's body, then put a hand on Temple's shoulder.

"You'd better get back, Lee. Miss Hargrove's—"

Temple had been looking at an image his mother had left him, the image of his father standing gun in hand above the body of a man he'd just killed. Now Lee stood inside the image, filling his father's boots, holding his own gun, looking down at the still-warm body of a man freshly killed.

Tommy's words jerked him back to the present, and he shook the image off.

"Is she hurt?"

"Not shot, but she's pretty upset. Dolan's dead."

"Mickey? No, he can't be. He was just—"

The hand tightened on his shoulder. "Come on, Lee."

Temple rose. He let the hand propel him out of the thicket, up the slope, past the fallen body of a second man.

"That one's yours," Tommy said quietly.

Temple remembered his first shots, remembered the man's kicking legs.

"Slick! It's us. Don't shoot, they're gone."

"Come on."

Porterfield lighted a lantern. In its glow Mickey Dolan lay rolled up like a pill bug in the sparse grass. A dark, oozing spot like a bruise showed through his sandy hair. Elizabeth huddled on the ground near him. Blood, Dolan's blood and some of her own, spattered her face and stained her dress. When Temple lifted her to her feet, she grabbed at him as if she were drowning.

"He'd just talked to me. 'Rest easy, Liz,' he said. Then he spoke to you, and—" Hard, jolting sobs shook her thin body. "But after—I crawled to him—but—he couldn't—he was—"

Again Temple saw the image, himself and the man he'd killed. Standing now in his father's boots, he saw the rest of the picture. He saw the man who had tried to kill him. He saw the slumped form of his driver and heard the agony in Elizabeth's voice. And within the image he found a new understanding.

"I never knew about that part of it," he murmured.

"What?"

Holding Elizabeth, he looked across her at the two other men. Porterfield had a deep, ugly burn along the side of his left cheekbone and a bloody compress of rags bound over his ear. Tommy Ellis held the shotgun at port, his face wholly grim.

"We've got to get her out of here," Temple said.

Tommy said, "No. We have to report this."

"How?" Porterfield asked.

"There's a horse in the thicket. One of us can take her home while the others get the wagons in."

"Lee, listen," Tommy said. "Violating a court order is a misdemeanor. Running off from a killing is a lot worse. Don't make the mistake—" He stopped, then finished, "—that mistake."

"We'll report it when we get to the rig," Porterfield said. "Plenty of deputies there." He looked at Temple. "You're the rider. Talk and I can handle the wagons."

"I'll meet you there soon as I can." Temple raised a hand when Tommy started to protest again. "That's how it's going to be. Tell them all about me, but she was never here. Got it?"

Tommy's hands clenched on the shotgun, but finally he nodded. "Better get rid of those bloodstained clothes, then. Get her cleaned up." He turned away. "Help me, Slick. We'll take Dolan in with us."

By the time Temple got the horse gentled down so that he and Elizabeth could mount, the wagons were already on their way. Temple turned back toward the main road. He didn't know the country well enough to cut across pastures, and Elizabeth couldn't help. At first he had to hold her on the saddle, curled against his chest like a child. Within the first mile, she stopped crying and held herself more erect. A little way past the creek, she had to get down to be violently sick.

"Lady, you ought to give up drinking," Temple said as he helped her up in front of him. "You sure as hell ain't very good at it."

"Damn you," she muttered. For a moment he thought she would cry again, and he felt her muscles grow rigid under his hands as she fought against it.

"I didn't know what it would be like," she murmured. "Killing somebody. I didn't know." Her voice grew stronger. "Stay away from me, Cowboy," she said then. "I'm bad luck. Get you killed."

"I'll take the chance."

But she meant it. "Roy. Now Mickey Dolan. My fault." Her body tensed again. "He was—sweet. If I hadn't—"

"If you hadn't been along, it wouldn't have meant a thing to that bullet," Temple said. "Nor to the man that fired it." He felt as if he were repeating someone else's words—his father's, maybe. "The one to blame for Mickey is the man who shot him. It was his choice to pull the trigger or not."

And I hope to God I killed him for it, he added in his mind. Elizabeth said nothing more, but he felt her despairing headshake. They rode on in silence until he brought the horse up at the edge of the oak grove, looking at the dark bulk of Hargrove's house. He waited to be sure Rotten wasn't about to charge down on them barking, then rode around to the wash house at the back of the building.

"Come on," he whispered. "You need to clean up before anybody sees you."

"It doesn't matter."

"It does. Get in here." He fastened the door behind them, then groped for the lantern and lighted it. "I'll pump some water for you. Get out of those clothes."

He filled the basin, then turned to see her still standing bloodstained and forlorn in the flickering light.

"Do you want me to undress you?"

She looked at him with a hint of spirit. "Didn't think you wanted to," she said. She stood a moment longer, then moved a hand abruptly to the buttons of her dress. "I'll need something to put on."

"You can have my—"

Temple stopped, almost laughed. He hadn't taken inventory of himself before. Even the pain he felt had seemed generalized rather than individual aches and hurts. Now he realized his own clothes were ripped and ragged from his fall, dappled with blood from skinned knees and elbows, dirty beyond salvage.

"Well, maybe not. I'll see what I can find."

What he found was a man's shirt in the saddlebag of the hijacker's horse. He brought it back inside. Elizabeth was in the tub, using the soap vigorously. She made no effort to cover herself when he hung the shirt on the faucet above the tub.

"Good," she said. Her eyes and her voice were firm and level, with no trace of the teasing he'd come to expect. "I'm all right. You'd better go."

"I'll see you safe inside first."

"Damnit, Lee, go." When he didn't move, she stood up and stepped out onto the floor, reaching for the rough white towel. "I told you, I'm bad luck. Get away while you can."

He grabbed her, towel and all, and pulled her close to him. "I don't know what I'm going to do about you," he said roughly, looking down into her face. "But I'm sure as hell not going to run away."

"Lee—"

Something crashed against the door of the wash shack. "Who's in there?" Laurel Jean's voice demanded. "Open up or I'll shoot."

Elizabeth caught her breath and Temple thought she was going to cry again. Instead she began to laugh, deeply, helplessly. Temple released her, staring as she buried her face in the towel to muffle her giggles.

"Every time!" she gasped finally. She raised her voice. "Don't shoot, Laurel Jean. Lee will get the door."

Temple obeyed. Laurel Jean was outside, gripping a pistol that Elizabeth's grandfather might have carried in the Civil War.

"Good lands! Prowling around at all hours of the night and frightening a poor woman to death and all skinned up from rolling in dirt! What in the world . . . ?"

She looked past Temple. Elizabeth, still trying to decide between laughter and tears, was buttoning the shirt across her breasts. Laurel Jean's mouth dropped open in utter surprise.

"Sorry, Laurel Jean," Temple said. "We had a little bit of trouble."

"Well, I just expect you did. Good lands. And about to have a little bit more, I'd judge."

That decided Elizabeth in favor of laughter. "Don't

worry, Laurel Jean," she said. "With him, it's the same every time. Every damned time!"

The sun was just shouldering into sight when Temple reached the drag gate. He dismounted from the tired horse, holding to the saddle skirt for a moment when his legs didn't want to support him. A polite young sheriff's deputy was waiting to take the reins. Another drew the Winchester autoloader from the saddle boot, frowned at it, then tucked it under his arm.

"Mr. Temple? Been expecting you, sir. The sheriff'll be with you in just a minute."

It took longer than a minute, but Temple didn't mind. He squatted with his back against the gatepost and tipped his hat down, letting himself relax for the first time in more than a day. He'd watched Laurel Jean burn the bloodstained dress and underclothes in a rusted trash barrel. Then she'd insisted on frying him a mess of bacon and eggs, which he'd eaten while she put Elizabeth to bed. Now he was content to wait.

He was asleep when the county police car rattled up from the direction of Hargrove's rig. The polite deputy woke him opening the gate. Sheriff Quinlan and Harry Hargrove piled out of the car, followed by Silas Gibbs and Tommy Ellis.

"Temple, where in hell have you been?" Harry demanded.

Sheriff Quinlan frowned. Quinlan looked more like a farmer than a lawman, especially his knobby, sunburned hands. He looked at his hands and said, "Mr. Temple, we need to ask you a question or two."

"Questions, hell," Harry said. "Somebody tries to hijack your load, and there's a fight, and then you go running off without a thought for that casing." He waved a hand at Tommy. "Now Bremerton's people won't say anything except you had some business to attend to. What business?"

Quinlan cleared his throat. "I'll tell you, Mr. Temple, we've got pretty much the same questions," he said.

Temple pushed back his hat. "How's Slick?" he asked Tommy Ellis.

"In the hands of the physician," Ellis said. "His left eye's all swollen shut, but he'll recover."

"Then everything's fine," Temple said, and saw Tommy understand.

"Fine—" Harry began, but the sheriff cut him off.

"Maybe it'll be better if you come with me," he said. "Providing you've got no objection."

"Is he under arrest?" Ellis asked quickly.

Quinlan looked annoyed. "Not exactly. Not unless he wants to be. But we do need some answers."

"So do I," Harry Hargrove said. "Temple, did you think what would've happened if that casing hadn't gotten through? What if the hijackers had tried again? I thought you knew this run was important."

Temple had been stooping to get into the car. He straightened and looked squarely at Harry Hargrove. "Important?" He thought about Elizabeth, about the man he'd killed, about Mickey Dolan lying with the side of his head shot away.

"Go to hell, Harry," he said. "Go right plumb to hell."

Chapter 22

ON HORSEBACK AGAIN, LEE TEMPLE WAS FREE TO ENJOY THE outdoors and the hot fall morning. He reined his horse off to the south along a road with a grassy middle between ruts worn smooth by the tires of Shooter's nitro truck. Letting the horse pick its way and pace, he studied the distant buildings.

A couple of sheds and an outhouse lay on the eastern slope no more than twenty yards from the small shotgun house that jutted out of an unmown two-acre pasture. Farther out in the pasture, away from everything else, sat a low, squat structure roofed and timbered with square twelve-by-twelve derrick sills. Built without benefit of foundations or studs, the buildings leaned in their own directions like scattered children's building blocks lost in the yard. A thin gray haze of smoke rose bravely from the stovepipe, then dissipated in the higher breeze.

Parked in the midst of the buildings, Shooter's truck might have been a cast-iron toy left to rust in the dew. A new Harley-Davidson motorcycle leaned against the house a couple of feet from the only door.

Temple tied his horse to the ring of an iron post off to the far side of the house. He knocked at the door, hallooed them, and waited. A crow sailed across the pasture behind the house, wings pumping hard to outdistance a scissortail. Quicker and more nimble, the smaller bird swooped above the clumsy crow, then dived to give him a peck every few flaps. Temple felt himself a part of that drama, but he wasn't sure whether he was the pursued or the pursuer.

"Come in, Cowboy!" Shooter shouted. "The latch string is out."

The house was bright inside, lighted by two or three lamps and sunshine at the uncurtained windows. Lingering odors suggested that the occupants had eaten fried steak for lunch. Little else in the one big room hinted that anyone went through the normal animal motions of living there.

No dirty dish or pan littered the kitchen cabinet or heavy iron stove. Two narrow, crisply made bunks stood neatly against other walls. Temple saw that the floor was swept as clean as a billiard table, but he saw no broom. In one corner a kerosene iron rested on an ironing board, with three starched and creased khaki shirts hanging over it.

Shooter looked up from a checkerboard on the unvarnished wooden table. "Be right with you, Cowboy." He smiled like a contented frog. "Soon's I'm finished scalping the Indian here."

He turned back to the board, frowned, made a move.

"Ah," Chief said. He pushed back his silver-banded hat and studied the board intently. "Oh-ho." Lifting a red king, he danced it across the squares in a sweeping zigzag that claimed every remaining black piece. "Ha."

Shooter said, "*Ha,* hell. No need to gloat like a savage. It's just a children's game." They performed a ritual handshake above the board and turned to face their company. Shooter offered Temple a salute. "You boys got the hole ready?"

So much, Temple thought, for the small talk. "We think so. You might want to take a look."

Shooter shook his head. "Hargrove may not be quite civilized, but he knows his 'taters. He says it's ready, I take his word. I guess you'll want to be my helper on the floor this time."

"Well, I hadn't—"

"Tell us about the well."

"Listen, I'm just a weevil—"

Chief finished putting away the checkers and board. "Then your impressions are unprejudiced by experience," he said. "Tell us what you know and what you've heard."

"Well, Hargrove set casing on top of the Gunsight Lime. His geologist says we're thirty-five feet into it now. He's afraid to go deeper because of water. The well sort of hisses and hiccups, but it won't settle down and flow. Pop calls it—"

"Kicking?" Shooter suggested when Temple hesitated. "Flowing by heads?"

"Both of those."

"We'll have to look sharp, Cowboy. Wouldn't do to have her kick and blow a torpedo out of the hole." Shooter grinned and spread his pudgy hands like an opening flower. "Boom! Toothpicks everywhere."

"Listen—" Temple said.

Chief rubbed his hooked nose. "I don't like it," he said. "People are not happy about the well. Some stand at the gate with guns."

"Not our lookout," his partner answered. To Temple he said, "We've been thinking about moving on. The boom's dying down here. Can't decide if we ought to go now or see how Hargrove's wildcat comes in."

"White man no decide. Indian decide."

Temple said, "I'll need to tell Hargrove one way or the other. He doesn't know you're still making up your mind."

"Minds," Chief said.

Shooter said, "We're even up on checkers for the day. I'll play you one more game. Shooting Hargrove's wildcat'll be the winner's choice."

"No. It's too important to leave to chance."

"You don't believe in chance?"

"I'll race you to the road."

Shooter laughed. "I couldn't beat you to the road if I was riding a camel!" He thought a moment, then said, "Tell you what. We'll race from the door to the rock and back. The cowboy can be our judge."

"What rock?"

Temple tried to imagine explaining the scene to Hargrove. He grinned, picturing Cotton's reaction when he learned he'd have to find somebody else to shoot his well.

"The hen's egg rock you found in the creek bed."

Chief looked suspicious. "Who throws it?"

"Temple."

"Me?"

"It'd be only fair to let the judge throw the rock."

Temple said, "I don't think—"

"Done," said Chief. He rose from the table and went across to take something from the pie safe. Then he removed his hat and went outside. Shooter followed as solemnly as if they were about to duel to the death. Temple followed the two of them as solemnly as if his job depended on the outcome, which he figured it did.

Chief held out his treasure to Temple. It was a smooth, stratified, brown and black stone that did indeed look like a hen's egg. Temple hefted it. "I don't think—"

"Here's the rules," Shooter said. "You throw the rock down the road as far as you can. Soon's it hits the ground, we'll go after it. The one that brings it back to you is the winner."

Chief asked, "Are you sure this is the best way to decide?"

Shooter said, "Flip a coin."

"That's worse yet."

"No, I mean to see whether this is the best way."

Chief sighed and bent toward the road, ready to run.

Shooter began limbering himself, stretching his arms. "All right," he said, crouching down as if he were about to hop. "Ready, Cowboy?"

Temple balanced the rock in his hand. It was perfect for throwing. He aimed down the road and threw overhand as hard as he could. The stone egg flew like a cannonball, glinted in the afternoon sunlight, crossed the edge of the meadow and sailed on to strike the grassy middle of the road forty yards away. It bounced and rolled across the west rut into a stand of arrow grass. Shooter and Chief were gone before it quit rolling.

Shooter shot out of his stance. Short legs pumping, he scooted away like a terrier after a rat. He had covered ten feet before his partner got his lean body uncoiled. The Indian swung into a long-legged, ground-covering stride as he reached the edge of the lea and started downhill. Shooter was already out of sight down the slope.

When they reappeared in the road below, the Indian was five yards ahead and holding the inside track. He plunged off the road at the spot where the stone had hidden itself. After a moment he came out with the rock.

Ten yards behind, Shooter slid to a stop, scrabbled for footing and started back up the road, digging out dirt with short, quick steps. When they disappeared again, the Indian had not yet reached his full speed nor caught up to Shooter.

Temple saw that he could never explain it to Hargrove; there was nothing to do but tell him he needed someone else to shoot the well. He was startled to see Shooter top the hill with his digging stride.

Shooter came a few steps closer, losing steam, his wide mouth gaping for breath. Chief topped the rise in a full flowing stride, eating up the grassy ground toward the victory that would seal all their fates. Ahead of him Shooter looked back, stumbled, and fell. Temple gave it up.

Shooter hit the grass, bounced over in a roll, and came up with a shoulder aimed right in the Indian's belly. The collision tumbled the two of them eight feet closer to Temple. Temple saw the rock come bouncing toward him in halfhearted skips. Nimbler than the greyhound, the terrier scrambled out of the tangle of bruised limbs, snatched up the rock and fetched it to Temple two steps ahead of the vengeful Chief.

Shooter went to his knees straining for breath. "We'll—shoot—daylight—tomorrow," he wheezed. "Tell—Cotton—ready. You—help—Cowboy?"

Chief stood over him, his dark face reproachful. "That part wasn't in the rules," he said.

"Nothing—against—it." Shooter rolled his eyes up toward Temple. "How many—quarts?"

Harry Hargrove was coming out of the lease gate in the green Reo when he met Temple lazing along the road toward him on horseback. "How'd it go?" Harry said in greeting. "We've been waiting half the day to hear from you. Can't you learn to drive a car?"

"Absolutely not," Temple said. "The deal's all set. Shooter'll be here well before sunup tomorrow."

Hargrove drove his car onto the road, leaving the gate open for Temple. "Better tell the old man. He's down there at the rig waiting for you. You might put that horse into a trot getting there!"

He let out the clutch and roared off toward town, leaving Temple in a cloud of white dust. Harry was impatient. At first he'd been unhappy that he'd let Betty talk him into returning to the ranch. Now he saw it was the best thing she'd ever done for him. *Even though it wasn't—it was for herself.* He chuckled at the thought. Little sister didn't know how good a turn she'd done him—and as much time as she was spending on Temple, she wasn't likely to notice.

Harry still didn't know much about the oil business. But he was learning. He liked running the risks. He liked the game of wits with bankers and leaseholders and suppliers. The only part he didn't like was working beside his father.

But being Cotton's son had advantages. It meant power, the power of being something between the boss's son and a full partner. After days of watching him narrowly, Cotton had started shifting more and more of the day-to-day burden of business onto Harry. Some of the hands didn't much like taking their orders from a weevil, but Harry didn't care. They knew he was boss just as Cotton was boss.

For the first time, he had his father's respect. Harry had never thought that was important to him. Now he found that it was. He still didn't care about the money—not much, anyway—but the power was important, too. He liked being in charge, calling the shots, bearing the responsibility for how things turned out. Beside that, the things that had filled his life before didn't seem important.

I can write a hell of a book about it once this is over, he thought, and smiled. He'd been away from his writing over a month, hadn't even kept up his journal. But that was all right. He meant to get back to it, just as soon as things let up. And he was learning. He would have more insight into people, into men like his father. Power. That would be his theme. Power and how it worked on a man, built him up, gave him a moral strength. A hell of a book, he thought.

He threw the car into its final gear and gave the engine more gas. At the edge of town he passed Talking Tommy's house and barreled on into the town proper. Slowing to a barely civilized pace, he tried again to plan what he wanted to say to Harriet. He noted Tommy's truck in front of Measuring Alice's store, but forgot about it as he turned the next corner.

Alice Mayfair and Tommy Ellis watched Harry pass. "We'll never run out of Hargroves in Emilia," Alice said, setting down her cup. "Not while the breed runs so true."

Tommy Ellis started on his slice of pie. "I'm slowing down," he said. "Getting old."

She smiled, her eyes downcast. "I hadn't noticed."

"Shameless." He laughed, then turned serious again. "Harry, I mean. It was a thing I didn't see coming, him turning into Cotton. It worries me."

"It worries us all to see another boll worm in the cotton." She bent over the counter and laughed.

He laughed with her. "We haven't seen one of those for a while, have we, Al?" He chewed another bite of pie. "What worries me is that I didn't see it coming. If I've become that slow on the uptake, somebody's liable to sneak up on me. Frank Loman, maybe."

"Loman hasn't bothered you again, has he?"

"He hasn't been back. But he bothers me. He's sitting on some secret that won't let him rest. He's like—" He considered. "—like having a can of Shooter's soup sitting in the closet, waiting for something to jar it. He worries me."

She reached over to take a bite of his pie. "His secret hasn't anything to do with us," she said.

"It might."

"After all this time, Rad?" She sighed. "Some days I get to believing maybe we're free. Maybe we don't need to look over our shoulders anymore."

"I'd like to think so. But I'd feel safer if things hadn't begun to sneak up on me without my noticing."

"You don't still want to move on, do you, dear?"

"No. But I've never felt it as strong that we ought to."

She turned away to look out the side window. Harry Hargrove had turned off the main street toward Aunt Minnie Jergin's house.

"I see. I guess you could find another job. I guess I could get another shop. Someday."

He shook his head.

"Sure we could. Unless you'd like to go back to practicing—"

"You know better than that!"

She stared at her feet.

"I ask for your pardon," he said. "I would not have snapped at you for anything in the world. But it's better not to think about that life."

"About that life you lost on my account."

"I didn't mean to sound that way."

She wiped back a tear, bit at the twisted corner of her mouth. "You didn't make it sound that way. It *is* that way. I know it. I ruined your life, robbed you of the profession you loved, caused you to come all the way out here to this godforsaken, uncivilized—"

"Listen," he said. He stood, put his arms around her.

"Not in the daylight, Rad! There's no telling."

225

"In the daylight. In the dim. In the closet and on the porch and out in the middle of the street—I love you, anytime. Anywhere."

Anywhere except in the church! hung unspoken in the air between them.

"Would you tell me—"

"Yes, Al, would I tell you what?"

"—that it isn't all my fault, that I haven't ruined your life . . ."

Tommy laughed and hugged her. "Miss Alice, ma'am, I wouldn't trade this life with you for any other life in the world."

"Really, Rad?"

His chin on her shoulder, he nodded strongly.

"Then I'll never ask anything else of you again—not even to stay. If you think we should go, I'm ready. We'll just lock up and pack a bag and be gone before dark."

He nodded until he bruised her shoulder. Then he turned her around to face him, looked into her eyes. "You're the one, Al," he told her. "The only one there's ever been in this world. You'd really leave all we have and go, wouldn't you?"

She nodded.

"I think we ought," he said, "but I don't want to. Let's wait to see what happens to Hargrove's wildcat. We'll let that do our deciding. An omen."

"All right." Alice smiled. "I didn't know you believed in omens."

"Oh, yes. I'm just never sure which way they point."

Minnie Jergin stood in her upstairs room looking down through her chinaberry trees at the street, a book of poetry forgotten in her hand. She had heard a car coming. She was right, too. It was Harry Hargrove's green Reo. It made too much noise in their quiet street because it was going too fast, and it was stopping before her door.

Two months ago she would have welcomed his visit for the chance to talk with someone young and alive. Six months ago, before his return, she would have given anything for a visit, to see the pink back in Harriet's cheeks and the smile back in her eyes. Now the visit wasn't welcome. She'd seen Harry change shape and color almost before her eyes, and it frightened her.

That's silly, she told herself. Silly old woman. You've known it all his life. You've seen it in him, in his blood. It had to come out one day. If you hadn't known, you'd never have said to the boy the things you did that day he asked Harriet to marry him.

She watched him get out of his car. He strode across the yard as a man now. The change had not been flattering. He was hard, unsmiling, all business. Gone from him were his boyish ways, his concern for his fellow folk. Even his warm animal love for Harriet had been transformed. Minnie was not surprised. She'd known. But she was frightened for Harriet.

She went into the shadows of her curtained upper hall and stood like a high judge as Harriet came hurrying to answer the impatient ringing of the bell at the front door. Minnie was out of sight in the shadows of the landing, but she could see and hear everything. She saw Harriet's face high and bright and hopeful when she opened the glass-paned door. Harriet wore the new yellow dress that just suited her hair and eyes.

"Harry!" she said. "You did find time!"

He laughed, the sound sharp and confident. "You never *find* time," he said. "I made time. Had to come straight here from the well. But you're worth it."

"Why—thank you, Harry. Here, let me take your hat." She took it, looked at the begrimed hat, couldn't think where to put it. "Let's go back into the kitchen. I have some coffee for you."

He sat at the kitchen table, one elbow resting on its white cloth, careless of the dust and grease that clung to his clothing. "Thanks." He took the cup and saucer, drank deeply. "Ah. That's good," he said. "Beats rig coffee."

Harriet stood before him like a child saying her lessons. "Can you stay for the lecture at the Woodmen's tonight? I thought we might go together. It's about—"

"Can't go," he said. He put down cup and saucer hard

enough to rattle the porcelain. "Either Cotton or I've got to be at the rig. Can't leave those fools on their own for a minute." He looked up at her, then reached out to catch her hands. "I tell you, Hare, it's hard to find somebody to depend on these days."

"I know."

He didn't understand. "Even Temple. Thought he was one man I could trust for anything." He laughed at himself. "Wrong again. But I'm learning."

"But you told me he was your friend."

"Oh, I like Lee," Harry said. "Fine fellow. Helped me out a lot that time on the train. But he's just a cowboy. No idea of responsibility. He's apt to be out riding horseback or chasing after Betty just when I need him most."

"I see." Harriet whispered. She did not resist when he drew her closer, so that she stood between his spread knees. "Do you still want him to be our best man?"

He looked up at her. "That's what I needed to talk to you about, Hare," he said. "We're going to have to put off the wedding for a while."

"Again? Oh, Harry—"

"Now, it's just for a little while—a few months, say. I thought I could leave as soon as the wildcat was down, but I can see Cotton's going to need somebody around if it comes in." He stood suddenly, sweeping her against him. "I tell you, Hare, it's going to be great for us, though. Once I have his business back in shape, your husband'll really be somebody."

"But—you're important *now,* Harry. Your writing—"

"Oh, I'll get back to that, soon as I have the time." He bent to kiss her hair, then to nuzzle against her neck. His hands tightened on her back, pressing her tightly against him. "Ummm. Wish I could stay. You smell good enough to eat. Hey, don't cry."

"But Harry, our wedding!"

"Don't worry, Hare. Before I'm done, I'll buy you the biggest wedding anybody in Emilia ever had. But this is important." Over her shoulder, he glanced at the kitchen clock. "Gotta go—I have a meeting with Bremerton. But I'll see you next chance I get."

He kissed her hard enough to bruise, scratching her chin with his bristly face, then set her loose and turned away.

"Here, no need to see me out."

Already thinking about the well, he didn't see Harriet stumble out toward the back porch, her face forlorn with tears, her pretty yellow frock rumpled and grease-stained. Miss Minnie did. She'd found what she needed in her cupboard while they were talking, and she was ready as he came into the hall.

"Harry Hargrove."

Harry tilted back his head in the dimness. She waited halfway up the grand staircase until his eyes found her.

"Aunt Minnie. Listen, I'm in a hurry right now—"

"Be quiet," she said. She cocked the hammer of her Civil War Colt with one thumb like a man. "I have something to say to you."

He heard the noise, stared as she lifted the gun and pointed it straight in his face. "What the hell?" he asked.

"Your memory isn't that poor," she told him. "You will remember my telling you I would shoot you dead if you wronged my Harriet."

"I haven't wronged her. I just—"

"Hush, you vermin. I know what you've done. I heard what you've said. And I know what you are now that your spots have begun to show."

"Don't point that gun—"

"Hush. Your last task in this house is to listen. I'm not going to shoot you for disappointing my girl. It would be wasted on you, because you would not understand. But I *will* shoot you if you ever set foot on my porch again or ever speak to my Harriet again."

"But—the wedding—"

"There will be no wedding." She moved close enough for him to see the lead bullets in the cylinder. "And I will shoot you if you say another word now. Get out."

Harry opened his mouth, saw her eyes, and got out. On

the porch, he jammed his hat down to his ears and strode straight toward his car.

"Now what in hell was that about?" he said aloud as he pulled away in the Reo. But he didn't spend long wondering about it. He had to plan for the meeting with Brace.

Chapter 23

LEE TEMPLE FINISHED HIS BREAKFAST. LAUREL JEAN TOOK HIS plate and poured him another cup of coffee.

"Thank you."

She ignored him, silent as a graven image, and went back to the kitchen. Across the table, Elizabeth Hargrove sipped her milk. "I'm glad," she said.

"About what?" He was in a hurry. While he'd slept, Harry and Cotton had gone out to the rig. Temple didn't know why they'd left without him.

"That Papa changed his mind."

"About what?" he asked again. "Not about me."

"About putting off the shot. Not doing it today."

"What?" Temple hadn't been looking forward to working with the nitroglycerine, but he didn't expect to get out of it. "What are you doing?" he asked. "He would have told me."

"I'm telling you. Don't you believe me?"

"No. Even if he didn't want me to work with Shooter, he'd want me on the job. Time's money."

She made a face at him, came around the table to stand at his side. She put her hands on his shoulders. "He didn't decide until this morning," she said. "Then he looked at the clouds and said we'd better wait."

"Clouds?"

"Too much danger of lightning around the nitroglycerine. Everything's called off. Papa and Harry went out to get ready to shoot tomorrow. They gave most of the hands the day off." She leaned over his shoulder and kissed him at the edge of his mouth. "You especially."

He turned toward her. "Why didn't they tell me?"

"I promised to tell you." She put her arms around his neck. "I'm better at it."

Temple laughed. "Come on, Liz. Either one of them would rather have me dead than alone with you."

"They thought *I* was dead," she said. "But I fooled them. Come on, let's get started."

"To the rig?"

"Later. There's a place I want to show you first—my special place. It's a little bit of a drive." She leaned down and kissed him like she meant it. "There. Does that satisfy you I'm telling you true?"

"No." He pulled her down onto his lap and held her there. "But I'm willing to be convinced."

Cotton Hargrove stood on the drilling floor, watched the dark clouds that hung over the mast of the derrick, and waited. It wasn't something he did well. Things had to go right today, and they'd already started going wrong. He spun quickly as Pop Wooster stumped up to the floor.

"Well? Where's Temple?"

"Ain't seen him." Wooster spat. "Was it me looking to get blowed to glory, likely I'd be pretty scarce myself."

Hargrove swore. That damned girl. If she didn't keep her word to have Temple there in time, he'd see she never spent another dime of his money. Not that he'd have any money! Unless the well blew in big, he'd be up to his ass in Fort Worth bankers wanting to be paid off right that minute.

He heard the whine of an engine soft as an owl crossing a meadow. That would be Shooter. Hargrove came down from the platform and looked at his watch. Where the hell was Temple? The soft-sprung Ford truck rolled toward him like a baby buggy full of eggs. Shooter braked, backed it carefully around, and squared it up right at the edge of the drilling floor.

"Took you long enough," Hargrove called.

Shooter looked at him with wide sleepy eyes. "Pretty near

didn't get in at all," he said. "Mr. Wilkes is down at the gate with the sheriff and a whole crowd of folks. Said he aims to keep you from shooting off all this hell juice on his land."

"Damnation! That's not legal!"

"I expect the sheriff agrees." Shooter gave his happy frog smile. "But he's running for election pretty quick and doesn't need any enemies. Harry and old Silas are keeping them out, but probably they'd appreciate a little help."

"Well, hell." Hargrove looked swiftly around the location, caught sight of a tall young man carrying a rifle. "You, Price! Get over here."

"Yes, sir."

"Report to Harry down at the gate. Take the evening drilling crew with you. We've got trespassers."

Price pointed toward the hills. "But Mr. Temple told me——" he began.

"Hell with what Temple told you. Hell with Temple," Hargrove roared. "I'll get this well down if every panhandling son of a bitch on my payroll goes back on me. Do what I tell you!"

"Yes, sir."

Price hurried away. Hargrove cursed him silently, cursed Wilkes, cursed Elizabeth for whatever she'd done with Temple, and Temple for letting a damned girl lead him by his nose. Couldn't any of them realize how important today was? Today, Cotton Hargrove would bring in a wildcat field as big as Spindletop, or know the reason why!

But he knew the reasons why. He'd just recited them in his curses. He swung around to look at his crew. They had drawn away from the rig and the Ford truck. Pop Wooster was fifty yards away, watching Shooter's truck like a mother hen eyeing a skunk. The whole bunch could be sitting in a tavern in Fort Worth for all the good they were.

"Well," Shooter asked, "do we wait for Temple to bring her in?"

What Hargrove wouldn't consider was the possibility the well might be a duster even after it was shot. It was not in him to consider that. He had fired a hand the day before for using the word *duster* in his hearing. Others probably needed firing, but none had owned up to thinking the well might not come in.

"She's going to come in," he said aloud, "if I have to bring her in myself."

Shooter shrugged. "Suits me. You did pretty good that last time." He grinned. "Though I wouldn't suggest you take up nitro work regular. Too excitable."

Hargrove started to answer, then heard a motorcycle putter to a stop somewhere behind him. He turned to see the Indian set his machine on its stand and lean his own form against one of the bunkhouses.

"How about him?"

"We never work together."

"Damnation. Then it's me."

"That's good." Shooter stretched. "Don't suppose you could take time for a cup of coffee first? I loaded this batch at two forty-five, and I'm ten years older than when I started. I could use a few minutes to think through the job and enjoy being alive this morning."

"Time's—" Hargrove began. Then he stopped. Time was money. But he had time now. He could afford a little more anticipation before his well came in. "Hell, yes," he said. "Coffee's in the office. We'll have a cup and enjoy the morning. Invite your Indian, unless you're afraid to risk rig coffee together."

Experience had taught Temple to check the gasoline and oil in Elizabeth's car, since she never did. To his surprise, both tank and crankcase were full. He got down on his knees and peered beneath the front of the car. Because it was neither rusted nor muddy, the new axle showed up at a glance. Temple was satisfied. "Everything's ready," he said.

Coming down the front steps, Elizabeth said that she was ready as well. She had a scarf around her head, a linen duster across her arm. She stowed a basket behind the seat. "Laurel Jean even packed us a lunch. Would you like to drive?"

"No." He slipped the Winchester autoloader into the boot Harry had mounted on the running board. "I'm a guard, no matter which Hargrove I'm with. I'll ride shotgun."

She drove out of the yard with the usual Hargrove disregard for life, limb, or machine. At the first corner, she turned west and plunged into a tangle of ranch roads with perfect assurance. Temple touched her shoulder to get her attention.

"Listen," he shouted. "We have the day. Let's live to enjoy it."

Elizabeth laughed, shifted down, and flung the car down what seemed to be a cattle trail overhung by tall spindly mesquites. She had to slow down when the mesquites gave way to real trees, oaks and cottonwoods hung with thick green vines. Temple knew they must be near the creek, but he couldn't see it. Finally Elizabeth pulled up where the wheel ruts ended at a rocky shelf. She killed the engine and sprang out, reaching back for the picnic basket.

"Let's walk."

Temple stretched himself, picked up the Winchester and came around to join her. He took her outstretched hand. They picked their way down a steep, rocky cut with the sound of flowing water at the bottom. Handing her down the steepest part, he wondered how often she had led others down that same hill to her special place.

"Just ahead," she said. "Close your eyes."

"I'll break my neck."

"Coward."

He opened his eyes onto a grassy bank at the foot of the bluff. The creek curved into a deep, lazy pool below the sheer rock of the opposite wall.

"Did you bring any fishing gear?" he asked.

"We used to swim here," she said, "when we were just children."

"Did you?"

"Mother brought us."

He liked that better. "Did she swim?"

"Not a lick, but she loved the water." Elizabeth smiled at

the memory. "She'd load Harry and me in the wagon early in the morning and drive over here. She'd have a lunch fixed. In this very basket. We'd all three of us play in the water until time to eat."

"Your father didn't come with you?"

She shook her head seriously. "He may never have known we came. He was usually off to . . . wherever he went. Sometimes he was on one of his cattle-buying trips when he'd be away for weeks and come home without any cattle."

They walked across the bank until it broke in a gentle slope down to the sandy margin of the creek. "Here?"

She nodded. "We sat here to eat our lunch. Harry loved to jump off the bluff up there. There's a hole below the rocks, six or seven feet, deep enough to swim. Mother and I would splash around in the shallow part."

"I wish I'd been here then."

She wrinkled her nose at him. "You wouldn't have liked me. I was a brat." She put the basket down and took his free hand. "We could wade in, you and I."

"Wade?" He'd made it a practice all his brief adult life not to get into running water when he could avoid it. "No."

She sat in the grass to take off her shoes. "Come on, sissy."

"I'll watch you."

"Are you afraid?"

"Not of watching. I can watch all day." He sat beside her, laying the Winchester carefully on the grass. "The only thing I'm afraid of is you getting your skirts wet."

"I can take care of that."

"Just be sure to hold them high enough to keep dry."

She put in a foot to test the water temperature, drew it out and shivered. "It's cold."

"Now who's afraid?"

She studied the creek, looking for holes or rocks. Then she lifted her skirt and stepped into the water. "Is this high enough to suit you?" she asked.

He shook his head somberly.

"Well? Does this look safer?"

He grinned. "Better and better." Her legs were slim,

well-turned, bare of stockings. But he couldn't help wondering how many others had sat where he was sitting, had looked at her as he was looking.

She waded on out toward the middle, looking every bit the tomboy she must have been a dozen years earlier. Deep enough to get her skirts wet, she turned and came back. She kicked a splash of water at him and laughed.

He wiped water out of his eyes, not laughing. "What do you usually do now?" he asked.

Slowly her laughter died away. She came out and sat beside him. "'Usually'?" She did not look at him.

"Did your others wade with you?"

She rubbed her feet dry and slipped her shoes back on. "This is how it would always be," she said flatly. "Those others of yours—"

"Of yours."

"—would always be around, wouldn't they?"

He didn't answer.

"There for a minute . . ." she said.

"Yes?"

"There for a minute, I thought you liked me, wanted to see me, wanted me."

"I did." He wanted her all right. He wasn't sure about the rest. "I do. I don't know."

Her laugh was flat and metallic. "I know. I've known from the start." She twisted to put her back to him. "Since you ask so nicely," she said, "there was only one."

"I didn't—"

"Only one of my 'others' came here with me. Only the very first one. I told you about him."

"Ray—no, Roy. Roy Allison."

"How sweet of you to remember! Yes, Roy Allison. Yes, he did wade with me. And swim with me. And we lay on the grass and talked. And then we—"

He caught her by the shoulders, pulled her around to face him. "All right," he said.

"And a week later, Roy died. And I never came here again. Not with anyone. Not by myself. Never until today."

He thought she was going to cry, but she didn't. He'd seen her cry only once, over Mickey Dolan's body. He wondered if she'd cried the time Roy Allison died.

"Then, today, I brought you here." She gave him a crooked grin. "Pretty—Pretty damned silly of me, wasn't it?"

Temple nodded. "I guess so," he said. "But it's not your fault. You had no way to know how dumb I was. I didn't know myself until right now."

Her laugh sounded almost natural. "Is that an apology?"

"Must be." He released her shoulders, got up to his knees. "I'll drive you back—or you can drive me."

"Lee?" She put out a hand to him. "Is that what you want?"

"No."

The hand tightened on his arm. "Then stay."

Still kneeling, he turned toward her. She raised her face blindly, her eyes brimming with tears, her face wet, her lips slick and salty when he bent to kiss her.

"There's nobody here," she whispered. "Nobody to bang on the door. No door to bang on."

He didn't answer. Instead he sought her mouth again, sinking down with her on the bank as her arms tightened around him.

Frank Loman tied his horse a half mile from the low hills that overlooked the drilling site. He was late. He'd had to swing far out of his way to avoid being seen by the crowd around Hargrove's gate. That had been a bad break, but the overcast was a good break. Since he had to move in daylight, it would make him harder to see.

He climbed the deeply shaded slope, holding his rifle horizontally, keeping his eyes on the thickets and the lighter grays where the rising land touched the sky. He expected to find a guard on the hilltop, somebody he'd have to deal with. But what if there was more than one? He had the feeling every Hargrove man on the location was waiting to shoot him down the minute he showed his head.

At the crest he went to his knees, crawled a few feet, and lay on his chest to peer down toward the rig. No guard. Another good break. It was his day. Every dog had his day. So he'd always heard, and this was his.

Through the rifle's telescopic sight the rig floor was dark. He could make out Shooter's squat shape, though the light was too poor to show his face. Shooter was pouring nitro into a long torpedo. Another man was helping, his figure only a deeper shadow beneath the derrick. Loman chuckled. He knew who it was. He knew Lee Temple was swamping for Shooter today. That was one reason he'd come.

Frank Loman blew steam on the lenses of his telescope, wiped them clean, and laid the rifle carefully in position. He flipped the safety off and put his cheek to the stock. When he had everything lined up the way he wanted it, he put the sight on Shooter, who was lifting a last can of nitroglycerine. Ever so slowly, Loman moved his sight until the crosshairs centered on the torpedo. He chuckled again, waited until it had passed, waited until he was solid and steady on the target.

Then he squeezed the trigger.

Robert L. Randall, grandson of Comanche chief Blackpowder Musket, had just lit a cigar. He'd put out of his mind the Line girl with feathers like a war chief. In his place against the bunkhouse wall he was thinking of his conversation with Shooter that morning, of their notion of leaving Emilia. They'd talked of buying tickets for the Pullman car and heading for California, where the crude was sweet and the weather warm all year around. That would be a different life, wearing white man's clothes and living in a white man's house. He'd heard that was possible in California.

Watching his partner pour out the last dregs of an old life, he began singing in his mind an Indian litany he'd heard his grandmother chant when she dreamed of her youth and of sending her man off to war. Perhaps because he was between the rifle and the rig or perhaps because he was the grandson of a Comanche chief or perhaps because his senses would have been as keen if he'd been born Eskimo or Chinese, he alone heard the boom of the rifle some tiny part of a second before Frank Loman's bullet hit the torpedo.

Everyone within a mile heard the vast thunderclap of the explosion. All of them saw the fireball that began with a flash, spread out to hide forever Shooter and Cotton Hargrove and the lower structure of the derrick, boiled up in a fire-shot cloud of smoke and dust and flying wood and metal. All of them felt the earth tremble like a frightened horse.

Two of the rig crewmen never saw nor heard nor felt anything past that moment. One was smashed down in his tracks by a massive wooden beam that flew at him like a spear, the other beheaded by a hissing scythe of metal that had been part of a Ford truck. The others ran. No one heard their cries or their silence.

Far below the surface of the earth the concussive power of the blast thrust down the cased borehole and out into the rocky strata below the casing. Rocks crumbled under the counterthrust of released pressure. A black torrent pistoned up the hole, smashed aside the debris that blocked the wellhead, and roared high above the splintered wreckage of the drilling rig.

All but one of the survivors saw the column of oil blowing in, bringing in the field that would make Emilia famous. Chief Randall did not. In that brief part of a second, he had given over his new life, set aside all thought of California. He had already turned in the direction from which the bullet had come, toward the hilltop where the least puffy haze of white smoke was dying in the air.

Chief was neither surprised nor excited. He had expected the powder mist to be just where it was. He went after it with a smooth, swift stride. Behind him, Rotten recovered from his quivering and threw up his nose to howl a dirge. The smell of light sweet crude touched Chief's senses, but he no longer cared. He skimmed the hill like a dark-skinned shadow, leaping rocks and dodging through the clusters of cactus that studded the steeper slope.

At the top he dived over the rim into a stand of needlegrass, rolled, and came up running. He heard another shot, but there was no time to dodge. The bullet split the air a foot from his ear. He fell as if he had been pole-axed and remained in a tumble.

He was certain he had seen a man. He was certain that man had fired the shot that touched off the nitro. He had no idea who the man might be, but he knew in the ancestry in his bones that the killer was still looking back up the slope to see if he'd killed his pursuer. Chief lay prone in the foot-high grass, motionless as a long dark stone.

Only when his bones told him that the killer had done watching and taken again to running did he get to his feet and start down the slope. He ran no more than twenty yards along the top of the ridge before he angled down into a shallow ravine. Bent at the waist, he ran downhill as devilishly invisible as a timber wolf.

The ravine bottomed out onto the main slope before he came to the trees. But he had been listening as he ran, had been looking, had been smelling the rushing air. He ran across the last clearing and into the trees with no fear at all. The assassin was running hard. The few boot prints told Chief that a big man was running. He took a deeper breath and ran faster. No white man could outdistance him over a mile course. He knew that.

He was in time to hear the hoofbeats of the galloping horse. But Comanche Chief twice removed Robert Randall didn't get even the briefest glimpse of the assassin. He had waited too long at the rim, he thought, had been too concerned about his own red skin. He knelt to examine a place where the killer had stopped. Among the leaves lay a long, shiny, empty brass rifle case, still a little warm from the barrel.

Randall stood with his feet apart, staring the way the killer had gone, wishing for his motorcycle, or better yet, for a strong war pony and his grandfather's lance. Only then, at the end of the trail, did he allow himself to think of Shooter.

Eight miles away, Lee Temple sat up quickly, uncertain what had waked him. "What?" he said.

Elizabeth murmured something and turned in her sleep. Temple sniffed at the wind, listened. He heard nothing, felt nothing. But something had happened—a dream, maybe, but he didn't think it was a dream. It was almost as though the ground had shifted beneath him.

Carefully, he shifted Elizabeth's head off his lap and onto a pillow of discarded clothing. He let his hand linger for a second on the curve of her breast, then got to his feet. As he began to pull on his jeans, he heard the heavy, rolling rumble from the east.

Elizabeth stirred, reached out, found him gone. She opened her eyes. "What's that?" she asked.

"Thunder, I guess."

"Mmm." She stretched out a lazy arm. "C'mere, Cowboy."

"In a minute." Temple slipped into his boots and scrambled to the top of the bluff. The clouds had closed down while they slept. Above the trees the sky was a uniform gray. Back generally in the direction of town, he thought he saw a darker cloud rising against the overcast. But he wasn't sure. Thunder rolled high above him.

"We're going to get wet," he called down to Elizabeth.

She sat up, smiling. "I don't mind." She shivered and draped his shirt over her shoulders. "It's gotten cool. Was that thunder?"

"Sure." He came slowly back down to her side. "A sign, maybe."

She came easily into his arms, letting the shirt fall away. "Sign of what? Why did you put your clothes on?"

"A sign for us. Sign of luck maybe. Sign we're doing the right thing." Or the very wrong one.

"What is?" She let her eyes close again.

"That thunder or artillery or maybe the earth opening up to reveal her dead."

She opened her eyes wide. "That's very poetic. I didn't know you were poetic."

"You felt the ground shake?"

"What? Maybe."

He smiled. "We dreamed the same thing, I guess."

"That's poetic, too." She snuggled against him. "Let's go tell Papa we're getting married."

"All right."

"As easy as that, are you?"

"That easy."

She pulled away, sat up, covering herself with the shirt. "Don't worry, Cowboy, I'm only teasing," she said. "You don't have to make an honest woman of me. But find me a cigarette."

He didn't move. "I wasn't teasing."

She kissed his cheek. "I was. But it would be fun to see his face."

"We'll see it." He held her away at arm's length and looked into her eyes. "I'll tell him. I said I'd stay until this well was in. The minute it flows, I'll tell him."

She looked at him in wonder. "You really would." Her lips formed her teasing half pout, but there was no teasing in her eyes. "There's still the others. What about them?"

He reached for her and drew her down beside him again. "What others?" he asked.

Chapter 24

HAD THEY NOT BEEN SO ENTWINED IN EACH OTHER, THEY WOULD have sensed the tragedy as soon as they turned into the yard. The bare space in front of the house held a light spring wagon and a landau, three automobiles, and a shiny black buggy drawn by matched grays. The front door of the tall unpainted house stood open.

"Something's happened," Elizabeth said.

"What?"

"I don't know."

She clung to Temple's arm all the way to the foot of the steps. Then she realized that some unknown event had shaken the earth, had changed the steps, the porch, the house, her life. She sensed as well that whatever it was could not be bargained with.

"Wait here, Lee."

She released Temple's arm and flew up the four steps like a stricken young doe. If at the top she thought of Temple, she did not look back, but ran on across the porch and into the house.

She was right. Everything had changed since she left home that morning. Laurel Jean was wearing a flowered dress, a starched apron, and a white lace cap that her grandmother must have made. She shuffled in shiny black high-button shoes that Elizabeth had never seen before.

Open, bright, dusted—the parlor was crowded with people who had never been in the house, as far as Elizabeth could remember. The Baptist preacher, the Reverend Paul Sandow, stood when Elizabeth passed the open, arched doorway. She saw others on the couch, in the chairs, at the window: Miss Minnie Jergin, Banker Myers, Buster and Mrs. Carstairs, the widow McCandless, old Harlan Wilkes and his wife. Elizabeth knew then. Only one thing could explain their presence. She hesitated, then rushed past the doorway without a word.

In the kitchen she waited for Laurel Jean to come in. "Which one was it?" she asked.

Laurel Jean stared straight at her young employer. "They say it was your father, child," she said with none of her usual deference.

Elizabeth's eyes closed. She leaned against the huge iron range, found it too hot to touch, and stood straight as a schoolgirl. "They say? Where is he?"

"There was an accident with the well," said the cook. "An explosion—"

"Did it shake the ground?"

"—and they can't find him."

"Can't—find him?" She thought of Roy. They'd never

243

found him, as they put it, either. He went out to work that day. Now here it was again. It seemed so appropriate that she hoped she wasn't smiling. She really did not feel like smiling.

"Good lands yes, it shook the ground. Rattled all the pots and pans, made the china dance, cracked your mother's good Bavarian teapot. Then the noise, just like thunder. They say he was working right there when it happened."

Elizabeth swallowed. She thought of a dozen questions whose answers would determine her course for the rest of her life. But she couldn't put words to them, and Laurel Jean couldn't have answered them anyway. "And Harry?" she asked, holding her breath. "Do they say Harry was with him?"

"No. Mr. Harry was down at the gate, talking to some people. He hasn't been home. He's still out there, out to that place where it happened."

"Why?"

The cook had no answer.

"What are you baking?"

Laurel Jean brightened. "They have eaten already two batches of cookies. I'd just put in some fresh when you came home." She bent to the stove, opened the oven door and looked at her cookies. They were not done.

On a back burner the big coffeepot was bubbling merrily. Elizabeth saw the kitchen table covered with trays and serving pieces, cups, cream, sugar, napkins, spoons, little saucers. Elizabeth caught Laurel Jean's arm.

"What are you doing? This isn't a party. Papa—my father—Mr. Hargrove—is dead. How can you be doing these things?"

"There's people out there, Miss Elizabeth," Laurel Jean said, as though explaining to a child. "People come to pay their respects to your pa." She pursed her lips. "Likely most of them think he didn't amount to much. Likely he didn't, by some lights. But there's none going to say they weren't treated right in his house."

Elizabeth stared at her for a moment. Of course. The

ground had not shaken for nothing. She had begun a new life. She was going to live it properly. "Thank you," she said.

While Laurel Jean went to see to the guests, Elizabeth moved as if in a dream. She climbed the back stairs to the upper hall, went into her room and stripped off her wrinkled, dirty clothes.

She found her best and longest black dress, black stockings, black shoes. She looked critically at a black hat with a veil, but left it lying on her bed. As quickly as she could, she got into the mourning clothes, asked her mirror about her hair, brushed it to be sure no stems of grass remained. Then she started downstairs. Not once had she thought of Lee Temple since she left him at the porch steps.

At the head of the stairs she changed her mind, went back along the hall and down the same back stairs to the kitchen. It was empty. She put dirty cups and saucers in the sink and began arranging the latest batch of cookies on a serving tray. She was still busy with them when Laurel Jean returned with an empty tray.

"Thank you, Laurel Jean," she said again. "I appreciate all the work you've gone to. I'm sure Harry will, too."

"Good lands, child, it wasn't anything. Here, I'll do that. You go and see to your guests."

Elizabeth took the other way out of the kitchen to enter the parlor from the little-used east door. Her guests did not conceal their surprise. She greeted each of them in turn and by name. When they offered their condolences, she thanked them graciously.

"I'm so sorry I wasn't here when you came. Yes, it was such a shock. I didn't know," she said in such a piteous and fetching manner that the ladies and gentlemen alike reached out to her in spirit and in flesh with waiting arms and kind hands and teary eyes.

For her part, Elizabeth did not cry, did not think of crying, did not think of her father or brother or beau. No, she told them, she had no idea. "I just don't know what I'll do without him."

They had ideas. "God will provide, Elizabeth," Pastor

Sandow said. "We can't always see it at the time, but things happen for the best. If you'd like me to pray with you . . ."

Oliver Myers mentioned neither money, debt, nor interest. But the words were on his breath, behind his eyes, in the overtones of his polite phrases. Elizabeth heard them but could not decipher them. She decided that time would bring him back with clearer words. She was astonished to learn of herself that she, who had never had any patience at all, could wait. Worse, she saw that it was the ugly sort of patience her impatient father had shown.

"We'll help out any time you need us," Mr. Wilkes said, turning his hat in his hands. "I can't change what I've done in the past. But you can count on Dorothy and me now. We'll want to help." Elizabeth thanked him, knowing he meant it.

"Time heals your wounds," Buster Carstairs said, apparently searching for physical signs of them with his eyes until his wife drew him away.

Mrs. McCandless would take another cookie, yes. She had certainly not come to eat or to be entertained but, rather, to offer her sympathy to Elizabeth. Mrs. McCandless had lost her own father—did Elizabeth realize that?—it would soon be twenty years ago. And, of course, her husband. He had left them some twelve years earlier. "Why, you must have been just a child then, dear?"

Elizabeth could see the widow fingering a set of merchant's beads in her mind, calculating the young heiress's age. "I'm nineteen," she said, and in her bluntness saw that she had not changed entirely.

Well. The widow certainly had not been inquiring into Miss Hargrove's age. But that was very young indeed to come into so much . . . "But no one's thinking about such things today, my dear," she said. "We're all just so sorry about your poor father."

So, Elizabeth thought. So much? So much of what Mr. Myers would not name today. *Have you come because you don't yet know there's no more money?* She didn't know that the well, still blowing wild, was spoiling Mr. Wilke's grass with a hundred barrels of oil an hour. *Is that why you've come, all of you?*

She looked at Brother Sandow, at the solemn faces of Harlan and Dorothy Wilkes, Miss Minnie, and knew better. Those good people would have come, money or no. So would some of the others. Tomorrow she might again be Liz, unwelcome in their parlors, but today they would pay their respects and offer their help. She smiled graciously at the widow and went to greet the guests who had just come in.

Laurel Jean was coming along the hall from the kitchen with a fresh tray of cookies, coffee, jellies, and a small, warm cake when Harry Hargrove banged his way through the front door and came jamb up against her.

"What the hell are you doing?" he demanded. "Has no silly old biddy told you yet that my father lies scattered in a thousand little pieces over his whole lease?" He grabbed the cake and crushed it in his hand. "My father's not dead half a day and you're entertaining guests in his house!"

Harry's clothes were oil-stained and grimy, his hands black, his face streaked with grease. About his waist he wore a military-style pistol belt. A heavy revolver slapped against his thigh as he walked. He pushed tray and cook backward until the tray tilted and the coffee spilled.

"Good lands, young Harry," Laurel Jean said.

Brother Sandow put his head out of the parlor. "Well, Harry," he said, as if nothing unusual had happened. He stepped out into the hall, Wilkes and Buster Carstairs following. "We didn't mean to cause you any upset. It's just some neighbors, dropped over to show their respect for your father."

"Respect!" Harry turned on him, his voice choked with tears or anger. "They could've damned well shown it while he was alive, then. You, Harlan Wilkes. You're not welcome here."

The old man took a step forward. "Harry, I'm heartily sorry you feel that way," he said. "I've spoken to your sister already. I'd hope we could put our troubles behind us and—"

Harry laughed sharply. "I'll just bet you would, now that the well's come in and—"

"The well?"

"—the Hargroves are on top again. Suppose you get out of this house—"

"Harry! Good lands!"

"—before I set Rotten after you."

Harlan Wilkes turned his hat in his hands, looked at it, set it firmly on his head. "I guess that won't be necessary, Harry." He looked back toward the parlor. "Dot! We're going!" To Laurel Jean he said, "Thanks for your hospitality, ma'am. Tell Miss Elizabeth the same."

Quietly and without fuss the others found reasons to leave. "I'll call in a few days," Brother Sandow said. "This sort of thing is often a shock right at first." Harry nodded and saw him out. Then he turned on Laurel Jean.

"And just where is *Miss* Elizabeth?"

"Good lands, Harry, I'd be ashamed if—"

"Where is she?"

"Up—Upstairs. She felt faint and went to her room. "Asleep, when I looked in on her, poor lamb." She took a tentative step toward the stairs. "Do you want me to wake her?"

"No. I'll talk to the poor lamb later," he said. "Right now, where's Lee Temple? Where is that low, sly, slithering snake that took my father's money and left him alone and unguarded to do the hired work himself?"

Trembling, Laurel Jean leaned back against the wall to let him by. She nodded toward the end of the hall, toward the door to the spare bedroom. "He went in there."

Harry Hargrove went on along the hall in steps that rattled the bowed joists and loose underpinnings of the house. He did not knock at the far door, but flung it open, went through it, and slammed it behind him.

Lee Temple had waited for a few minutes where Elizabeth left him hanging at the altar of her front porch steps. He saw that she understood something he didn't know for certain.

He looked around him. He saw no hearse but he smelled death.

He hadn't been around it too often, but he knew the signs. Who could it be? Laurel Jean? Why would this many townspeople be out for that? How would they even have heard about it?

What had made the ground shake? Then he knew all the answers at once, and he closed his eyes in despair.

Today, you silly ass, was the day to shoot the well! Today was the day you were supposed to help with the nitro. Today was the day Elizabeth told you there would be no nitro after all.

He should have known. Elizabeth had intended to protect him from the nitro. He should have known.

You did know. But you were willing to be convinced. Willing to let a pretty girl pull a sack over your head—again!

He realized, finally, that Elizabeth was not coming back. She'd forgotten him, left him to die in the yard. He walked around the short side of the house to the back porch. There should have been men there talking, smoking, drinking weak, sweet coffee. The porch was empty.

Temple went into the kitchen. Laurel Jean was taking cookies out of the oven. Maybe he was wrong. Or maybe they did things differently in Texas. The round little woman glanced at him and went back to her work, scooping fresh hot cookies off the tin and onto a silver tray.

"Listen," he said. He felt like a beggar at the back door. She looked up again, then back to the tray she was preparing. Temple asked the same question as Elizabeth. "Which one was it?"

"They say it was Mr. Hargrove." She saw he was waiting. "Mr. Cotton Hargrove."

"How? When?"

"There was an accident with the well. An explosion, and they can't find him." She put on a face of horror. "They say he was exploded. There is no more of him."

Temple let it rest. He went on past her into the main hall, turned toward the back of the house to his room, went in, closed the door. Putting aside the Winchester, he lay facedown on the tightly made bed. Well, there it was.

A man hired you to keep him alive. He paid you well. Or promised to. And you couldn't rest until you didn't show up for work. And the minute you didn't show up for work, he had an accident. Sure he did!

What were the chances of a man who hired a bodyguard suddenly having an accident, for God's sake? No court in the world would believe that. Nor would they believe his reason for not being where he belonged. In fact, they'd probably hang him on that basis alone.

Just one job. You promised to watch the man's back until he brought his well in. He gave you one job to do, and that was one more than you could be trusted with!

Temple sat up. He started to take off his boots but thought better of it. He wasn't going to be there that long. He started to rise, but then a new thought struck him.

There's another side to it.

Sure there was.

No. The other side is that I'd be the one dead if I'd been there. He didn't want me to be his guard today. I was going to work with Shooter.

So Elizabeth had been right. She'd loved him and feared for his life and lied to lure him away and given herself to hold him there out of harm's way. If he believed that, then he owed her his life.

If.

There was another way to look at that, too. He was Hargrove's guard dog. So Elizabeth had whistled him off and thrown him a bone to keep him busy. And while he was busy, someone had killed "poor Papa."

No. She couldn't have known it would be Cotton on the floor with the nitro. It might have been Price, or Pop Wooster. Or Harry. She wouldn't let anything happen to Harry.

Unless he was in on it, too.

No! She loves me.

She hadn't said so. And even if she had, what would it mean? Wasn't she the same cunning little whore who'd said the same to God-knew-how-many others?

"This is how it would always be," she'd said. "Those others would always be between us, wouldn't they?"

Temple reflected. The first of the *others* that came between them in his mind had half his head blown off. "Hell!"

Temple came to his feet. He would find Elizabeth, talk with her, get things straight between them. There was nothing now to hold her to Emilia. He would ask her to leave with him, come away with him to New Mexico, marry him. Then he would know. He'd know if he was more important to her than the money, than all the *others* that tied her memories to Emilia.

He reached out for the doorknob, then straightened and stepped back. Footsteps came down the hall like rolling thunder. Temple knew the gait. He hadn't failed entirely at guarding the Hargroves; Harry Hargrove was still alive.

Harry slammed into the room, almost colliding with Lee Temple, who was just moving away from the door. Without breaking stride, Harry took another step forward and threw an overhand right that had all his weight behind it. The punch caught Temple backing up, snapped his head around and bounced him back on the bed. Temple blinked. He raised himself on one elbow, pressing the back of his hand to his bloody lips.

"Get up," Harry said.

"No," Temple said. His voice was thick, but his eyes were steady on Harry's. "I don't want to fight you."

"That makes you a coward, too."

Temple's eyes changed, but he didn't move. "I'm whatever you want me to be, Harry. Let it go."

"He paid you. God damn you! He paid you money to stand beside him."

"Money didn't figure in it."

"He thought he could trust you." Harry Hargrove laughed without smiling. *"I* thought so, too." He put his hand on the flap of his holster. "I ought to kill you."

"I hate it I wasn't there."

"The hell you do. He was doing your job! If you'd been there, you'd be dead instead."

251

"Did you see what happened?"

Harry hesitated. "No," he said finally. "I was down at the gate when it—happened."

"Then you weren't there either."

"Shut up!" Harry yelled. "It's you that's responsible! Why weren't you there?"

"Why weren't you?"

"I had a reason! I was doing what he told me!"

"I thought I was, too."

Harry Hargrove swung at Temple, clubbing down with his arm as Loman had done that day on the train. Temple rolled, came to his feet on the far side of the bed. Harry fell heavily to his knees and slumped across the edge of the bed on his face. Temple waited for him to rise, but Hargrove did not move. Instead he began to sob quietly, desperately. After a moment Temple turned. He hadn't brought much with him. He swept his few things into his grip, strapped it shut, and left.

The house was quiet, the guests gone. Temple wondered where Elizabeth was. He looked into the kitchen. Laurel Jean sat at the table, her head resting on her crossed arms. She didn't answer when Temple spoke to her.

He went out the back door and around to the yard. Harry's Reo was parked by the hitching post, its body so plastered with oil and mud that the color was hardly recognizable. Temple could have taken it. No one would have stopped him, but he didn't want to owe the Hargroves anything more than he already owed.

The road was not the closest way to Emilia. Temple walked away from the house and up the wooded slope along a path worn by boots and hooves in the days before the automobile. At the top of the hill he resisted an impulse to look back. They weren't following him, wouldn't ask him to stay, were unaware that he had left.

Or that I was ever there, he thought. They may never remember me.

Around him the birds were singing, flitting from tree to

tree ahead of him. A squirrel ran halfway down an oak trunk, stopped, looked briskly at the man on the trail, and disappeared behind a limb. The overcast was still heavy. A drop of rain splashed on Temple's hat, then another, then a few more before the shower stopped.

At the upper fork of the creek the path gave way to an ancient arched wooden bridge. He left his bag at the edge of the bridge and eased down the grassy slope to the water. He knelt, laid aside his hat, and drank more than he needed. After that he washed his hands and his face. He had an urge to walk out into the water and bathe the dust of the place off himself for good. But he didn't.

Half an hour later he came out of the woods on the outskirts of the Line. In the clear gray light after the shower, the Line looked almost innocent. Not many people were around. Swampers were at work cleaning out the tents and shanties. Temple stopped at the bar he had first seen between the Ballard brothers. At the bar, Mel was polishing glasses with his bar towel, holding them up to the light to find the worst spots.

"Afternoon, Cowboy. Glad to see you still with us."

"Light crowd today?"

"Everybody's out to the Wilkes place, watching the Hargrove gusher. Did you hear about it? And about the big explosion?"

"I heard."

"Funny thing." Mel squinted at the glass he was working on. He moistened a particularly stubborn spot with his tongue and went back to polishing. "Boss was all set to move out. The boom was playing out and we'd heard there was a new strike at Burkburnett. But now Emilia'll have a brand new boom. Good for everybody."

"Maybe not for Hargrove and Shooter."

"Maybe." He frowned at Temple as if a spot on his nose needed polishing. "Taking up another collection, are you?"

"No."

"A drink, then?"

"Not for me, thanks. But I owe the Ballard boys a drink

253

apiece." He slid a silver dollar across to Mel. "Give them one on me when they come in this evening." Thinking about it, he added a second dollar. "Have a couple yourself."

Mel smiled, took one of the coins and left the other. "I don't drink," he said. "Against my principles. But I appreciate the sentiment."

That was all the debts Temple could think of. He was square with Emilia, maybe a little ahead. He walked on up to the depot and found the station agent.

"Tickets, mister? Sure, where to?"

Temple hadn't thought of that. There was nothing much for him in Wagon Mound. He thought of the boom at Burkburnett, then remembered something Cotton Hargrove had said.

"El Paso. Matthew had a lot of friends there. Hell of a wild town in the eighties."

"El Paso."

The stationmaster chuckled. "Good choice. You won't have no trouble spending up your wages there." He stamped a ticket and gave it to Temple. "Five-fifty, please. Train's due in at seven o'clock, departs at seven-ten. If you want to leave that suitcase, there's a good place for supper just a few streets down."

"Thanks," Temple said. He thought about Widow Watson's place. "It seems like the right place to go."

Chapter 25

FRANK LOMAN MADE IT BACK DOWN THE SLOPE AND INTO THE shelter of a cedar brake before the echoes of the explosion died away. He stopped there, knelt to rest, looked back. A pillar of smoke and dust reared above the hills like something out of the Bible. Some large object—Loman thought it was part of the bull wheel—spun out of the cloud and fell ponderously back to earth. Loman laughed.

He stopped laughing a second later when the figure of a man came over the crest of the hill in a long dive. No, that couldn't be right. Nobody could have seen him. But the man rolled to his feet and sprinted across the hilltop, coming his way. Working the rifle bolt frantically, Loman rammed a fresh cartridge into the chamber, then threw the weapon to his shoulder and fired.

The running man dropped, disappearing into the brush as if the earth had swallowed him. Loman jacked another shell into the rifle and searched the area with the telescopic sight. Nothing. He didn't think he'd hit his pursuer; he hadn't had time to get the sights on, even if he hadn't been shooting uphill. For a moment he considered going back, afraid he might be leaving behind a witness who could identify him. But it was too risky. Others might be on the way, or the man might be armed. He might be lying up now, just waiting for a shot.

"Hell," Loman muttered. There had been no one nearer than the well location. No one could have recognized him. He was certain of that. Almost certain.

He snapped the safety on and ran down the narrow gully. Though the morning was still cool, he felt the sweat slick on his body. His breath burned in his lungs and his legs felt as if he were running in water, but he didn't slow down. His horse threw up its head and shied away when he burst into the clearing where he'd left it. Loman seized the reins, jammed the rifle into its scabbard, and heaved himself into the saddle. He rode out fast without looking back.

After a hard mile he let the animal drop back to a trot, then a walk. He had to think. Behind him he heard a steady, sustained roar. He had heard it from the beginning. It took him a few minutes to understand what it was, and when he did, he almost turned back. The well had blown in! Hargrove's wildcat was flowing!

"Damnation," he said aloud. Then he realized that was Cotton Hargrove's word and cursed himself again. The laugh was on him after all. He'd figured to break Hargrove, to buy up the big man's assets cheap. Instead he'd done him a favor. Now Loman had to cover his tracks, and fast. Almost at once he thought of a way. He chuckled and kicked the horse back into a gallop.

Frank Loman rode into Oiltown at a dead run, shouting and waving. People stopped what they were doing to turn and gape at him. Some decided he was drunk and turned back to their business, but others, enough, gave him their attention. Calculating the effect, he was relieved to see he'd been right. He'd guessed the survivors at the rig would need a while to recover from their shock, and longer to get to the nearest telephone and call for help. Loman had hurried, and it looked like he was first with the news.

"My God!" he shouted, his voice hoarse. Heads turned. "Hell's broke through. All hell's loose at the Wilkes place."

In front of Bremerton's, Talking Tommy and a balding man with a scarred ear leapt out into the muddy street to head the horse.

"Whoa! Hey! What the hell!" Tommy Ellis got hold of the reins and looked up at Loman curiously. "What's the matter, Frank?"

"Hell!" Loman echoed. "On the Wilkes place. Hell's loose!"

They pulled him out of the saddle and let the horse go. "Talk sense, Loman."

"It blowed up. The Hargrove wildcat blowed up! There's no telling how many poor bastards's blowed to hell with it. Temple and the Shooter for sure."

"Temple!" Ellis and the other man exchanged looks. "You saw it happen?"

"Heard it. Felt the ground shake. Saw the cloud of fire. It was that home-brewed nitro. And the well's blowed in!"

A pretty good crowd had gathered. "I told you," somebody said. "I said I felt the ground shake!"

"He did say that."

"We heard him."

"The well's in? Hargrove's wildcat? It's a new strike!"

Tommy Ellis turned away from Loman. "Round up a crew, Slick," he said. "And tell Bremerton. I'll get hold of the sheriff and the doctor. We've got to get help out there."

They had come from every building and street in town. They filled cars and the backs of trucks, rode motorbikes, horses, whatever would move. Many wanted to help. Many wanted to learn about friends who'd been on the site. The rest stampeded in gold-rush excitement, wanting to see the disaster site or the site of the next oil boom or both. They barreled out of town in a choking cloud of dust and exhaust fumes, jamming the narrow road.

"Blamed idiots," Tommy Ellis muttered. He pressed the button for the electric horn repeatedly, but the sound was lost in the cacophony of shouts and bleating horns and backfiring engines. "Don't know how so many got ahead of us."

"Like buzzards," Porterfield said. He and Brace Bremerton crowded into the seat of one of the Quads. Four other men clung to whatever support they could find. The bed of the truck had been loaded hastily with tools, shovels, a new wellhead and master valve. "You think it's true about Temple?"

Ellis shrugged, looking at the road. "Hate to think so." He hit the brake and the horn button again. "Hey, you, watch out!" He glanced at his passengers. "Loman didn't sound like he was close enough to see what really happened. We'll hope he was wrong about Temple."

"Loman." Brace Bremerton said. "I wonder. Must have been snooping around. Had every oil scout and spy in town asking questions about the well."

"They should be settled now," Porterfield said grimly. He grabbed for a handhold as a truck pulled past, swerved sharply in front of them. "What the hell!"

"Loman again," Tommy said. "In a hurry to get to town, and in a hurry to get back. Wait, here's the ambulance, following him." Tommy crept to the edge of the road to let the ambulance past, then accelerated to keep just on its tailgate. "Well, if Frank wants to break trail, let's us just follow him."

Dr. Thornton and his helper were loading the ambulance when Loman found them. Thornton threw in a last duffel of supplies.

"Burns. Fractures," he said. "Wounds and blows from flying objects. We're ready for all those." He patted at his pockets. "I have to get cigarettes. Get us started."

The helper spun the vehicle's crank, managed to get the engine to catch, fire two or three times.

"Here," Loman said. It was a kind of engine he knew about. He stepped up into the ambulance cab and adjusted the controls. "You'd got the spark advanced enough to break your arm!" He backed off the spark and gave the engine a bit more gas. "Spin it!"

The helper brought the crank against the compression, laid his weight into it and turned the engine over. It started. Loman laughed and set the controls at a good, strong, steady warm-up level.

"Best hurry out there," he said. "I'll go for the sheriff."

"Sheriff's already out there," Thornton said, coming back to the cab. "Quite a crowd of people at the gate, apparently, when it happened. Several injured." He frowned Loman's way. "I thought you said you were there. Never mind. Let's get going."

Loman left the medical people with their ambulance. His horse was still at the rail, too tired to hold up its head. The town mob had taken every other animal and vehicle in sight. Loman led the horse across to his business and turned him loose in the yard. Clancy was already rolling out the black Bulldog motortruck.

"What the hell are you doing?" Loman asked him.

"Big accident out at Hargrove's. He's dead, they say. I was going to—"

"Shut up. Who's dead, they say?"

"Hargrove. The old one. Cotton. Blowed up with his own nitro, him and that guy that looked like a frog. I—"

"Hargrove's not dead. It was Temple working the shot."

"You sure, Buff? I got it from the deputy when Quinlan telephoned for more help, 'bout a minute ago."

For a dozen seconds or more Loman merely stared at him, his mouth open. No. Hargrove wasn't dead. That couldn't be right. It wasn't time for Hargrove to die. Loman wasn't ready. For reassurance he lifted his hand to the money belt in which he kept his most valuable possession; it was still there. But Hargrove couldn't be dead.

"Hell, Buff, I thought you'd dance a jig on Hargrove's grave," Clancy said. "You look like you lost your best friend."

"I got to see about this," Loman muttered.

"Sure. We can—"

"Not *we.*" Loman unstrapped the rifle scabbard from his saddle. He threw his heavy, booted rifle into the truck cab. He reached under the seat, found a gun belt, strapped it around his waist. "Me. You keep watch on things. The way things sit, somebody could come in and steal the whole damn town." He leaped to the truck cab and started off, leaving Clancy staring. "Look after that horse!" Loman yelled back at him.

He caught up to the ambulance at the edge of town. It had slowed in the midst of a scattering of wagons and men on horseback. Loman honked for the road, roared through the ditch to pass the ambulance and took the lead. He stayed on the horn and began crowding less forceful traffic off the road. He knew he was causing horses to spill riders, forcing automobiles into the ditch, making enemies. He heard a crash behind him as a light truck he'd sideswiped smashed into a lumbering farm wagon, but he didn't care. He had to see for himself who had been killed at the rig.

The ambulance followed him, but Loman didn't notice. Nor did he notice when Tommy Ellis swung the Bremerton truck in behind the ambulance. He was thinking about the conversation he had rehearsed so often, the conversation he would have with Hargrove just before he killed him. Now he would never be able to tell him, not if Hargrove were already dead. He rehearsed the conversation again.

"You killed my mother. Now I'm going to kill you."

"Put down that gun, you crazy bastard. And that's a lie. I've never killed any woman. Not even that bitch I married, though God knows she deserved it. Why would you want to kill me!"

"You called me 'bastard' just now. People called me that when I was just a runny-nosed kid. The day I found out what it meant was the day I made up my mind to find you and kill you for the words they called my mother."

"You are a crazy bastard. I never knew your mother!"

"You knew her all right! You left her alone and pregnant. You might as well have killed her with your own hands."

"What? Left who pregnant! Look at me—here in the light, you bastard. Damnation, you're Lupe's kid."

"Yes I am, you miserable son of a bitch. I'm Lupe Castro's son—and yours."

Touching the money belt again, he smiled. Men driven to the ditches in front of him saw the wide, wild grin and cursed him as he roared past them. Impatient with the traffic, he left the main road just past the pileup at Cedar Creek bridge and followed the back way in. The ambulance followed him as naturally as a coal car follows its engine, and Bremerton's truck followed like the caboose. Loman didn't notice. He had no thought but getting to the well site as quickly as possible. He would find Hargrove there. Hargrove couldn't be dead. Hargrove had to learn who he was.

A fence loomed up on his left, blocking the way to the well. He swung the wheel hard over and drove through it. The nearest poles ripped up by their roots. Strands of barbed wire stretched, sang from tension, parted with the twang of a fiddle string snapping. The broken ends whipped back like angry snakes, one of them lashing across Loman's shoulder, tearing away a patch of shirt and flesh. He never felt it. The roar of the wild well grew loud enough to hear over the engine. A black mist seemed to cover the land ahead, a mist made of fine droplets of crude oil.

Loman drove into the mist past the wavering, ghostly

shapes of mesquites. Men and mules moved here and there, to some plan not immediately obvious. The ground was strewn with all kinds of things—lumber and timbers of all sizes, curling lengths of wire rope, an intact yellow-dog lantern sitting upright beside the rear axle of a Ford truck. Fifty yards farther along, someone had gotten a tent raised and staked for a field hospital. Loman went past without a glance. The ambulance peeled off and stopped, Dr. Thornton out with his bag and running before the vehicle came to a stop.

Loman drove on until he was as close to the flowing wellhead as he dared go. He stopped his truck on the high side and got out. For the first time he realized that Bremerton's truck had been right behind him. Porterfield and Tommy Ellis were supervising the men unloading it while Bremerton stared like an eager terrier into the mess of wreckage that vaguely resembled a drilling rig.

Men were working amid the wreckage and the thunderous roar of the flowing well. Oil had half filled the lower ravine and was pooling back toward the rig. Loman saw mule drivers dragging things away from the wellhead while other men, half seen, labored at the base of the column of oil. Bremerton darted into the heart of the noise and returned, drawing with him a dripping black scarecrow. The scarecrow pulled an oil-soaked handkerchief from its face and became Harry Hargrove.

"—like a big doodlebug hole where the wellhead was," Harry was shouting over the noise. He gestured with the wrench he still held. "We got the crater cleared, but we have to stab on a new wellhead and master valve."

"Wellhead. Valve. On the truck," Bremerton answered. "More hands coming. Held up in that mob at the gate."

"Glad you got through."

"Mr. Loman helped." Tommy Ellis had come up. He was looking thoughtfully at Loman. "He led us on a shortcut that not too many people know about."

"Hey—" Loman began, but Harry Hargrove cut him off.

"Loman! You son of a bitch, get off this property!"

"Now, Harry," Bremerton said, "he brought the ambulance. He—"

Harry paid no attention. He took a step closer to Loman and jabbed the wrench at him. "Hear me? Clear off, or I'll have you arrested! And if you come back, I'll damn well have you shot!"

Red anger shot through Loman. He started to raise his fist, but then remembered where he was. Other men had gathered around the little group. Hargrove's men, or Bremerton's. Loman had no friends here, and that damned Ellis was still looking at him strangely.

"Sorry you feel that way, Hargrove," he called, trying to smile. "Just wanted to be of help. Maybe if I could speak to your pa—"

He didn't see the blow coming. Likely Harry Hargrove didn't think about throwing it. He simply lashed out with the hand that held the wrench. Fire exploded along Loman's jaw and through his head. For a moment he thought the well had exploded. Then he was on his hands and knees, looking at his blood dripping into the oily grass.

"Price! See that the Buffalo finds the gate," Hargrove yelled. "Tommy, Brace, let's get cracking with that wellhead! My men have about got the pipe cut-off level. We don't have time to visit."

Chapter 26

DAZED AS MUCH BY HARRY'S REACTION AS BY THE BLOW, LOMAN let young Price boost him up into the seat of his truck. He drove a wavering path down to the drag gate. Four sheriff's deputies stood guard there. A dozen more men, Hargrove's or Bremerton's, strung out along the fence line to keep the crowd back. One of the deputies opened the gate. The others pushed out to clear the road and wave him through. Then the gate closed behind him and everybody forgot about Frank Loman.

That was how it seemed to Loman, anyway. They'll remember before long, he swore. Rage pounded in his aching head. Young Harry and all of them. They'll remember, all right.

Bullying his way through the press of people and vehicles, he parked the truck beside the fence a hundred yards from the gate. Everybody in Emilia—and probably in Eastland and Sipe Springs and Desdemona as well—seemed to have gathered to watch the show, to gossip about the explosion and the new strike, to gape at the ambulance coming out and the trucks loaded with men and equipment going in. Oil scouts and lease buyers sifted among the crowd, looking for information, making deals in the excitement of the moment. The moment Loman stopped, a half-dozen men gathered around his truck, shouting questions.

"How's it look in there? Is the well burning?"

"Is it true she's flowing ten thousand a day?"

"You're hurt. Look at the blood. Was there another accident?"

"If it was an accident. Hargrove had as many enemies as a skunk has fleas."

That cut through the fog in Loman's mind. He put his hand to his throbbing head and looked at the blood.

"I'm okay. I was—helping them make up the wellhead. Wrench sprung back and hit me."

"Pretty damned cold-blooded, young Hargrove hustling you out that way," somebody said. "Should have got you to the doctor. That's a bad cut."

"Yeah, well, nobody said a Hargrove had any gratitude." Loman began to see his way more clearly. "Anybody got something to tie this up?"

Several of the group offered handkerchiefs or rags. Loman let them urge him down from the truck's high seat. He perched on the running board while one of the men tied a rough bandage around his head.

Up to now his thoughts had run to "What?" and "Why?" and "Are you sure?" Now he began to understand what a bad turn he'd done himself by killing Hargrove too soon. He'd intended it to be later, after the other heirs were out of the way. Then he would have been able to produce his proof and claim his due as the long-lost son. But it had all happened too early. He didn't even know if Cotton had left a will. Without a will, Loman thought, he might still own a proper third of Cotton Hargrove's empire.

Loman shook his head violently. "Here, hold still," the man with the bandage said.

No. Loman had known from the beginning that he could not be happy with his third. He wanted it all.

Hargrove's chicks would be easy enough to handle now that the old rooster was dead. And a lot more fun, maybe, he decided, thinking of Liz. She was his sister—halfway, anyhow—but nobody knew that. Nobody alive. *I've eaten the cake and saved the frosting for last!*

Loman jumped to his feet as soon as the bandaging was done. "What happened to that bastard Temple?" he demanded.

His audience had begun to lose interest. That got their attention again. "How's that?"

"Temple. That hired gun of Hargrove's. Was he up close enough to go in the blast?"

"Haven't heard about no Temple. There was old Hargrove and the kid they called Shooter and Ralph Fiske and Nort Norton killed. Pop Wooster and about six more hurt, but no Temple."

"I don't think he was here."

"What!" Loman hadn't considered that. His information had been that Temple would be on the floor that morning. He looked behind him, then all around the area. Off to his right a single figure moved. Loman fixed his stare on a lean, dark man riding a motorcycle. It was not Temple.

It was the Indian. Something moved in Loman's memory. But he couldn't place it. "Young Hargrove," he said. "Where was he when hell broke loose?"

"Right here by the gate," one of the men said quickly.

"We saw it, me and Wes. Harry and the sheriff was talking, and then this big boom shook the ground and I—"

"It sounds damned odd to me."

"What does?"

"Both them young bucks just happening to be out of the way, so's Cotton would just happen to help with the nitro the one time the whole home-brew batch just happened to blow up!"

They looked at each other, then at him. "Why, hell," one said. "What're you saying, Frank?"

"Yes, Mr. Loman, what *are* you saying?"

Loman almost jumped. He hadn't seen Chief come up, but the Indian was standing just at the edge of the group. Behind him the motorcycle chugged gently on its stand.

"Well . . ." Loman scowled. "Well, all I'm saying is there's a lot of *just happen* in there. It seems almighty strange that there would be just such an accident at just such a time."

"I can set your mind at rest on that," Chief said. "It wasn't an accident."

All of them stared at him with their question, Loman hardest of all. "How do you know?" the boldest of the spectators asked. "Was you here?"

"You saw me arrive on this cycle. When the explosion came, you dived under the pipe rack. The pipe spilled off, but not on you."

"Damn lucky for me, too." The man nodded to Loman. "He was here, all right, if he seen that."

"You're saying you could tell what touched it off?"

Chief looked at each of them individually. He looked across the rough road to Loman's truck. He nodded his head.

"What then?" Wes asked for all of them.

"Could you not tell?"

"No, we could not tell!" The bold one said. "Listen, mister, are you sure you're an Indian? You talk like—"

"It's no time for joking," Chief interrupted. "You did not hear the bullet in the air?"

"Bullet?"

Several of them chorused the word together. Loman put a hand on his revolver again.

"A man shot from the hilltop to the north. He got away on a horse."

"How would you know that?" Loman all but lifted the revolver from his holster. "It sounds like you—"

"I know because I followed him."

"Maybe you know because you was the one did the shooting," somebody called from the back row.

"No, he didn't."

"Couldn't have."

"But maybe he saw who did."

Loman looked around him. There were a couple of dozen men gathered around now, all listening. He lifted his revolver free of its holster, stood staring plainly at the Indian. "Did you see who it was?" he asked.

"No." Chief seemed not to notice the pistol. "He shot at me, slowed me down. When I got down the hill, he was gone."

"I didn't hear no second shot," Wes muttered.

"Hell, you didn't even hear the well blow in. After that big boom, you couldn't've heard it thunder."

"Yeah. Can't you see the Indian's telling the truth? It weren't no accident."

"That's right, boys!" Loman had turned half away from them to slip the gun back in his holster. Now he grabbed the lead again. "That's what I've been telling you. Didn't any of you wonder where was Temple? Didn't anybody ask yourself how that soup happened to blow up?"

"I wondered about it. I just hadn't said nothing."

"Me either."

"I'm thinking about it now."

"Well, hell, there you are! I'm telling you, you ought to be looking at those boys."

"Looking at them? Why, Harry's right out there getting the well killed. He's been here the whole time."

"Then Temple must have fired the shots," Loman said.

They exchanged uncertain glances, all but Chief. He was

looking at Loman. "What kind of rifle does Temple have?" he asked.

Loman felt a twinge of doubt deep in his gut. "Why would you ask that?" Unconsciously, he rested his hand on his revolver again. "What's the difference?"

"It's a quarter mile from the hilltop to the rig. Not everybody could make such a long shot." Chief put his hand to his shirt pocket for a moment, then frowned and took it away. "Not every rifle could reach so far."

"Well, the devil knows Temple made it. Him and Little Hargrove are the only ones riding horses around here and carrying guns." Loman swept an arm around his head. "Listen, boys, some of y'all climb on the back of my truck. Let's us see if we can't just track Temple down and ask him."

Some of them moved, then a few more. Still uneasy, Loman looked around to see if Chief was following the rest. He didn't find him, but he did hear the roar of the motorcycle fading into the distance.

Lee Temple finished his pie and asked for one last cup of Irma Watson's coffee. "I declare," she told him, "but I believe us four are the only souls left in town."

Temple drank some of the coffee. "Give me about five minutes and there won't be but three souls left in town," he said.

"Are you sure what you're doing?" Bull Ballard asked for the third time. "It hasn't been but a little while since you thought you was right in going out to work for Hargrove."

Temple nodded. "I had reasons. Or thought I did."

"That's just what Bull's getting at!" Ace High said. "I mean, hell, I never much liked you, but I hate to think you'd be stupid enough to pull stakes the very day your little skirt inherited all that oil money."

Temple started to answer, stopped when somebody banged on the front door. Irma Watson bustled away. A few moments later she came back leading a very quiet Tommy Ellis. His eyes were red and swollen and he'd lost the bounce Temple had come to expect. Though he'd had the chance to clean up and change clothes, he brought a strong odor of crude oil with him.

"Here's another soul," the widow said.

"Just back from hell, looks like," Ace said. "What's happening out at the well, Tommy?"

"We got her killed." Ellis reached toward a chair, then drew back. "Still a lot to do. Stuff scattered hell to breakfast. Hargrove sent me in to get supplies." He looked at Temple. "And to find you."

"Hargrove?"

"Hargroves. Elizabeth. And Harry."

"I didn't see much sign they were interested."

"Here, Tommy, sit before you fall." Irma Watson spread a cloth on one of the kitchen chairs. "Ain't the first time somebody's come in a little greasy. I'll pour your coffee."

"Thanks." Tommy sank down, still looking at Temple. "Well, they are. One of them in particular."

"Temple's told us he's leaving," Bull Ballard put in. "Got his train ticket. Is that wildcat as good as they say?"

"Better." Tommy drank deeply from his cup. He closed his eyes for a moment. "Lee, is that right? You're leaving?"

"That's right."

"I think you ought to wait."

"Tommy—" Temple stopped. The others were looking at him, friendly, interested, wanting the best for him. He couldn't explain. He couldn't tell them it was his fault, his failure, that he should be dead instead of Cotton Hargrove. "I'm going." He looked at the big clock on the kitchen wall. "Right now, if I expect to make the train."

Tommy Ellis said, "Whatever the question is, Lee, running away isn't much of an answer. I'm in a position to know." He looked at Temple a moment longer, then rose and offered his hand. "But if you're set, you are. So long."

"Reckon we're not worth much for friends." Bull looked as if he would like to cry but didn't remember how. He stood when Temple did and stretched out a huge paw in parting. "See you next boom."

Temple shook his hand, clapped Ace on the shoulder, then

turned to say good-bye to Mrs. Watson. She ducked inside his arms and hugged him hard enough to break a frailer man's ribs. He was awkward in embracing her. At last she turned away, told him to go. He went.

Past the corner he turned into an alley toward the depot. This time he'd had money enough to buy a ticket. If I'd had that much money when I left Fort Worth, I'd never have stopped here at all, he thought. The idea had its appeal.

Hargrove hadn't gotten around to paying him for the past couple of weeks. Now he never would. The money would've been a pretty good stake right about now, but he couldn't in good conscience ask for it. Hell, he'd been off fooling around with his girl instead of doing his job. *Yes, you're one hell of a bodyguard! You're lucky they haven't brought charges against you!*

"Lee! Lee Temple!"

He knew Elizabeth's voice. His first temptation was to keep on walking, but he couldn't do it. He turned. She had just stepped down from the yellow roadster.

"Lee!" she cried again, her voice filled with joy. "They said you were leaving. Thank God I caught you."

She started toward him, arms outstretched. Then a giant shadow stepped in front of her, a man Temple couldn't recognize in the evening's yellow twilight.

"Lee Temple!" The voice stood between him and the depot. "Just stop right there and put down your tote."

Temple thought about the short autoloading Winchester he'd left at the Hargrove house. Right that minute he would have given a month's pay for it. But then, he hadn't been drawing his pay. It made him smile.

"Stand easy. You don't want to give us an excuse to shoot you down." The big shadow still had no face. "That's better. Get him, boys."

"Wait!" Elizabeth screamed from somewhere behind the shadow. "You can't—"

Her voice cut off in a choked struggle. Temple dropped his bag and took a step toward her as a dozen men poured past the buildings on his left and into the alley all around him.

They laid rough hands on him, banged him around when he tried to fight them off. He felt someone going through his pockets, and then a man held up his ticket.

"Looky here! He's riding the evening train to El Paso!"

"Skipping out. We've got our killer," the big man said with satisfaction. "Over here! Who's got a rope?"

Temple understood the word *rope*. He began to fight in earnest, getting a hand free and smashing a hard punch into the nearest man's face. Then others closed on him. Somebody hit him on the side of the head, maybe with a blackjack, and his legs went rubbery. He recognized the men who were dragging him, some from the field and many more from the Line.

"Wes, Sam Fisher, listen—" But he smelled the raw bite of liquor on them and heard the leader shouting orders and knew they wouldn't listen. In the background he heard Elizabeth's frantic protests.

One day you'll end up at the end of a rope—just like your father.

The words rang in his mind as the men holding him slammed him up thump against the side of a building. Squirming, still trying to fight, Temple saw the giant shadow turn into Frank Loman. Loman had a coil of rope in his hand. A noose hung off to one side of the coil. The big man threw the heavy noose up over the iron frame of the building's fire escape. Then he dropped the noose over Temple's head.

Temple realized that Loman had been talking the whole while, that the others had pretty much quieted down. "He's the one they paid to do it," Loman was saying. "He hasn't ever denied it."

"Yeah."

"He hasn't."

"He can't."

"He won't if he don't hurry!"

They stepped away from him. He struggled, found his hands were tied. Loman took up on the rope, dragging him upright. He looked around the half circle of faces, saw nothing but hostility and anger. Elizabeth Hargrove, her face white, struggled in the grip of two men.

"Let him talk," someone said.

"Yeah! Confess! Who paid you to do it?"

The rope slacked a little and he drew in a ragged gasp. "Do—what?"

"Hell, don't pull that. We know you killed Hargrove and them others."

"You blew up the nitro. Did Harry pay you?"

"He didn't!" Elizabeth screamed. "He was with me!"

"Yeah, sure."

"She's in on it, too."

The faces told Temple. They meant to hang him. Nothing he could say would change their minds. He swallowed to wet a suddenly dry mouth and whispered, "Get her out of here."

"What? What did he say? Did he come clean?"

"Get her out of here for God's sake," Temple said, louder this time.

"Lee! No!"

"Go on, get away," he told Elizabeth. "Go back to Watson's!" He looked at the men holding her. "Please," he said. "You don't want her to see this."

An uneasy ripple ran through the crowd. "Hell," Loman cried. "Probably she's part of it. Let her watch!"

The man who'd been at the location stepped out of the group, faced Loman. "No. It ain't right," he said. A couple of the crowd, anonymous, murmured agreement. "Maybe we ought to wait for the sheriff."

"Wait, hell!" Loman shouted. "Give the Hargroves time to get him off some way?" He waved an arm at the rebel. "Hell, take her away, then, if it suits you. Likely you're too delicate to watch yourself!"

Temple released his breath when he saw the man lead Elizabeth away. His legs were trembling, but the noose held him erect. He knew now how it had been with Matthew Temple, why his father had spoken the words he had at the end of his life. He understood, and knew bitterly that it was the last thing he'd understand on earth.

"Last chance, Cowboy. What do you have to say?"

Temple swallowed again, tried to keep his voice steady. "I'll explain it to the Lord," he said. He figured those were about the words his father had used. "You boys will have to do the same sometime." He turned his head, looked at Frank Loman. "All right, you son of a bitch, get it over with."

Chapter 27

"HERE, HOLD THE BASTARD A MINUTE." LOMAN HANDED OFF THE rope to a couple of men from the crowd. "We'll do this right."

Held as he was by the noose, Temple couldn't see where Loman went, but when the big man came back, he was leading a saddled horse.

"I reckon nobody will mind if we borrow us a horse for a minute," he said, getting a laugh from the others. He took the rope and flipped a hitch over the saddlehorn. "No room to drop our killer proper, but when I put the spurs to this nag, it ought to swing him up just fine."

Temple clenched his jaw and tried to keep his face blank. Loman was enjoying himself. Temple knew there was nothing he could do about it. If Elizabeth had heard what he was telling her, he might have a chance. If not, he would finish it out as best he could.

Somewhere up the street Temple heard the roar of a motor. The sound drew nearer. He concentrated on it, knowing it might be the last thing he heard, trying to think about it rather than the rough prickling of the noose at his throat. The warm wind plastered his sweat-soaked shirt against his body. Loman started to mount the horse.

The motor's sound changed, dropped off to a lower-pitched popping. A motorcycle slid into the alley between

Temple and the waiting men. Chief slipped his goggles up on his forehead and looked without emotion at Temple.

"You caught him, then."

"Sure did." Loman had paused, one foot in the stirrup. He stepped down and faced the Indian. "Got him just before he skipped town. You're in time to see the finish."

Chief glanced at Loman, then at the others. "Did he confess?"

"Nope. But we know enough."

"Let me talk to him."

"We're wasting time," Loman said. He backed toward the street. "We don't want to get interrupted before we're done."

"It was my partner he killed." Chief reached back to his hip pocket, drew out a long folding knife. He flipped the blade open with one hand. "I'd like to hear him confess."

"Makes sense," somebody said.

"Yeah, let the Indian have him."

"Make him tell!"

Loman started to protest again, but Chief had already moved forward. His eyes, hard and black and with none of the humor Temple remembered, burned into Temple's.

"Did you do it? Did you kill Shooter?"

"No," Temple said without hesitation. This wasn't like the questions from the mob. Chief wanted to know. "What could make you think I would?"

"You've been riding a horse lately."

"Yes."

"You've been carrying a rifle."

"Yes."

"And this morning you left your horse while you crept up and fired this—" The Indian opened his other hand to reveal a spent .30-06 brass hull. Temple saw the crimped nose. "—at the torpedo while Shooter was filling it."

"No."

"Now you've begun to lie. I see the sweat in your hair."

"I'm afraid. Of hanging. Of you and that knife. But I'm not lying."

273

"I think you are." Chief held the knife so its blade glittered before Temple's eyes. "Why should I believe you?"

"Two reasons. I wasn't there. And I don't have a rifle like that." He dropped his voice to a whisper. "But I've seen a shell like that one before."

Chief paused. "Your rifle?" he asked.

"You saw my rifle—the Winchester. If somebody hasn't taken them, I'm still carrying a cartridge or two."

Loman said, "Get back, Indian. We're going through with this thing."

Chief ignored Loman in the way that he would have ignored any man at that moment. He stepped in close and put a hand in Temple's pocket. He needed only a touch to know the cartridge was different. "Who then?" he said softly.

"I've got a guess. But—"

A tug on the rope cut him off. Loman swung into the saddle. His hand rested on his holster as he stared at Chief.

"That's enough lies," he said. When a couple of the men started to protest, he raised his voice and overrode them. "You'll start believing him, next. I'm going to put an end to this. Step back, Indian."

"No. I want to hear—"

At the outer edge of the crowd men began to shuffle and turn. Then a big voice parted them like the Red Sea rolling back, and Bull Ballard barged through the opening.

"Move back or die, by God. It's that plain."

They moved back. Bull held a shotgun, its muzzles upright like a flagstaff. Ace High stopped at the edge of the group where he could cover his brother. His shotgun was steady at waist level, and no one doubted his willingness to use it.

Bull said, "You, Indian, stand away or state your intentions. I mean business."

Loman meant business, too. He kicked hard at the horse's flanks and whirled him away. Temple had just started to relax, thinking he'd been saved. Then the first big leap of the horse swept him off the ground like a doll. The noose clamped on his throat like an iron collar. He thought the jerk must've broken his neck, but that was wrong because he still felt the agony in his throat and trapped blood pounding in his head and the awful need for air and his body beyond his control flopping on the rope like a catfish on a hook.

The horse came straight at Tommy Ellis. He didn't flinch, and his heavy Colt automatic didn't waver. He shot the horse in the forehead. With his left hand he shoved the rearing animal backward. Frank Loman got his boots out of the stirrups in time to keep the horse from falling on him. Tied to the saddle, the rope held taut as a fiddle string.

No other man in Emilia could have been quick enough with knife or prayer to stay that hangman's rope. But Chief Robert Randall had grabbed it above the noose as it tightened. He rode it up for the height of a breath before he could slash the knife in his other hand across it. The rope parted with a twang, and he and Temple fell into the dirt like two bags of laundry.

Immediately Chief had the knife to Temple's throat. "Who?" he demanded.

He might have meant the knife as a threat, or he might have been trying to cut through the noose that still bit deeply into Temple's neck. Temple, half conscious, fighting his bonds and strangling, never knew. Before Chief could do whatever he had in mind, Bull Ballard swung the shotgun barrels level and across all in one motion and clubbed him senseless. The Indian rolled away and lay still. Ballard kicked the knife away.

Then he knelt over Temple like a clumsy child. His big fingers pulled the noose apart. "Temple? Are you all right?"

Temple wasn't. His face nearly purple, he put both hands to his throat and breathed in great whooping gasps. It was more than a minute before he could quiet himself and open bloodshot eyes to look up at Ballard.

"Hell," Bull said. "You about scared me to death."

Temple nodded. He tried to speak, but nothing came out except a hiss. He rubbed his throat and tried again. "Had—the same effect—on me," he whispered.

Behind Bull a babble of voices mingled in loud confusion. Then a single speaker rode over them, loud and oratorical, someone Temple had never heard before.

"Be still, you white trash! Lower those guns and stand back while you still look like men!"

Temple tried to sit up, made it with Ballard's aid. Talking Tommy Ellis stood facing the mob, flanked by Ace High and his shotgun. Another big Army Colt had appeared in Tommy's other hand, but it was his voice that held the crowd.

"You look like men, but what kind of men would hang a helpless victim without a hearing? What kind of men would be swayed by gossip to commit a cowardly murder by dark of night? Stand still, or we'll shoot you like the animals you are."

"Aw, Tommy, it wasn't so bad as that."

"Yeah. It sure sounds like he's guilty."

"Guilty? The guilt would've belonged to you—to you and your children and all your blood."

"Lee!"

Temple heard Elizabeth's voice. She came plunging through the mass of the lynch mob. Men moved aside for her, their eyes on the ground.

"Lee, are you all right?" She knelt beside him, across from Bull. "What have you done to yourself?"

He coughed—he thought he'd be coughing for the rest of his life—and whispered, "Tried to commit suicide, I guess." He reached out for her hand, marveled that he could feel it, warm and real, in his. "Nearly made it."

"I came in to find you. Harry had to go back to the rig, but he'll be here as soon as he can." Her laugh was shaky. "We—I—We decided we need you around, Cowboy."

She put her arms around his neck. One of the men standing nearby said, "Don't love on him, Liz. He killed your daddy."

Elizabeth glared up at him. "He didn't," she snapped. "He was with me when the explosion came. I tried to tell you, but you wouldn't believe me."

"Maybe you were in it, too."

"Like hell," Ace High said. "We know Liz, Bull and me. She'd never do a thing like that. Not even Temple would. You say a second thing like that, and I'll maybe just shoot you and whoever's close to you when I touch this thing off."

Temple said, "Chief has a cartridge the man used." He had not realized what had happened to his rescuer. "Ask him!"

"Easy," Bull said. He put out his lip like a naughty child. "I was maybe a mite rough on him, but I'll swear I thought he was going to cut Temple's throat. I'll see about it."

He checked the pulse in Chief's throat, found that he was alive, and smiled. "Here's the cartridge." He pried his hand open and held up the brass hull. "Looks like a .30-06. Temple, you shoot one of them new little automatics, don't you?"

"That's right. Mine's a .401 caliber." He felt for a pocket. "Here's one."

The men examined the empty and the new cartridge, saw that they were not similar. "Listen, then," Wes called out, "who shoots a rifle like this?"

"Lots of people."

"Hell, I got one myself—but I didn't shoot at Hargrove."

"That's fine," said Bull. "Now, how many has an extractor that causes a little dent in the case like this?"

"I guess we'd better start checking to see!"

Tommy Ellis said, "You're not checking anything. We'll turn the evidence over to the sheriff. As for you curs, get yourselves home!"

"You can't talk like that to us, Tommy," one of the men groused. "You ain't no law."

Tommy turned on him, and his new voice boomed out again. "Law? Here's law you'll understand!" He brandished the Colt, then fired it into the ground at the man's feet. Shocked by the noise and the flash, the crowd surged back. "Get out of here! Move! Go home and kneel down and give thanks that God saw fit to save you from your folly. As for you, Frank Loman—"

He swung around, pointing the right-hand Colt toward the place Loman had been, but the big man was gone.

"Your leader has slunk away. It's time you all did the same. Move! If a single one of you is in sight in thirty seconds . . ."

He didn't need to complete the threat. Grumbling and muttering among themselves, the men broke up, drifted away. One or two looked back toward Tommy or Ace, but nobody stayed to see what would happen in thirty seconds.

"I better get this Indian to Doc Thornton," Bull said. "What about Temple?"

Elizabeth tightened her grip on Temple's shoulders. The mark of the noose seemed to be burned into his skin like a brand. "I'll take care of him," she said.

Bull looked at the two of them and chuckled. "Yes, I just expect you will," he murmured. "But is it okay if Ace High helps in case you need to carry him someplace?"

"Why, hell—" Ace High began.

"I—can walk," Temple husked.

"Sure you can," Elizabeth told him. "But not just yet. You stay right where you are."

"Where's—Tommy?"

Bull turned. "Why, he's right—" He stared. "No, he ain't. I swear, he comes and goes just like he's somebody's ghost."

Tommy Ellis slipped away from the lynch scene the moment he saw that Temple was safe and the crowd had dispersed. He had been thinking about Frank Loman off and on since the night Loman had come to his house. Now he could not ignore his conclusions any longer. Loman was almost certainly a killer, and he had orchestrated the attempt to lynch Lee Temple. Damn nearly succeeded, too.

Ellis slid into the shadows, trotting along easily in the direction he thought Loman must have gone. Loman was nowhere in sight. Ellis put away one of his pistols and walked slowly, listening. In the distance a heavy door closed. Ellis made a turn, moved in that direction, looked across an empty alley. The closest door was the rear entrance to Cotton Hargrove's office. A light showed in the cracks around it.

Ellis didn't like the possibilities. He'd shown too much of himself to the mob. He'd never been able to resist the urge to make a speech, to sway a crowd or convince a jury. They wouldn't talk much, but they would remember. He should go home to Roxanne, maybe move on. But Loman was loose, still a menace to him and Rox, and probably to a lot of others.

He made up his mind. Three long-legged strides took him across the alley. Two more quiet steps and he stood on the low porch. The doorknob turned easily in his hand.

He threw open the door, stepped into the room and pointed his heavy pistol at the man going through the drawers of Hargrove's desk. "Frank," Ellis said.

Brace Bremerton was still bent when his face popped up into the light of the candle that stood on the desk. "What?" he cried. "Who the hell? Is that you, Tommy?"

Tommy Ellis put the gun in his coat pocket. "I'm sorry, Brace. I was looking for Frank Loman."

"Loman? Last place he'd be."

"Maybe. But it seems the last place you'd be, too."

Bremerton looked at Ellis. "Nothing wrong with me being here. Business."

He straightened and took a step toward Ellis. He stopped when Tommy drew the pistol from his pocket again.

"Sorry, Brace," Ellis said again, gently. He held the Colt in sight, angling its muzzle toward the floor. "I'm afraid I'll have to know a little more than that."

Bremerton licked his lips. Finally, he nodded. "All right. Partners. Hargrove and me." He slapped a hand on the desk. "The truth of it is, Hargrove's been backing me."

"You fronted for him?"

"Wouldn't put it like that. He lent me money. Back when I needed it and back when he had it."

Tommy dropped the gun back into his pocket. Chuckling, he leaned against the door. "You mean I've been working for Hargrove all this time?" he asked. "After all my warnings to Lee, I've been doing the same as him!"

"In a way, Tom. But not as much as you'd think." Bremerton put out a hand in quick, desperate appeal.

"Listen, Tom. Cotton holds some of my paper. The way young Harry's been acting lately, well, I don't want to be in his debt. Not if I can help it."

"Against the law, Brace."

For the first time, Bremerton smiled. "You're not wearing a badge, Tom. And there've been those times when I wouldn't swear to it you weren't looking over your shoulder yourself." He sat down in Hargrove's chair and leaned back. "Now, if you was to want to get back to your own rat-killing, why, I might help you find your rat."

Ellis considered. "All right," he agreed. "Which way'd Loman go?"

"He took out in that black Bulldog of his not ten minutes ago. Saw him as I was coming here. He didn't see me. Going like devils were after him."

"They are," Tommy murmured. "You wouldn't know where he was headed?"

"No idea." Bremerton tapped the desk. "Listen, Tom—"

"What kind of rifle's he shoot?"

"Rifle? He hunts with a .30-06. Why the hell would you want—" But Ellis was already gone.

Chapter 28

FRANK LOMAN LEFT TOWN DRIVING TOWARD HARGROVE'S WILD-cat like an honest man in flight from the devil. As soon as he was out of sight and sound of anyone that might care, however, he slowed his pace. Soon he turned off the main road. He opened a five-barred wooden gate, drove through, and closed it behind him. Crossing a hill pasture where there was no road at all, he finally bounced back onto a road that would take him to Hargrove Hill.

Loman was thinking hard. People knew things now. Not

just that damned Ellis, but Temple, too, if his neck wasn't broken. And the Indian would surely show that cartridge he'd picked up. Loman had hunted with Brace Bremerton and several others in town. He knew that some of them might have noticed the dent his rifle's extractor put in the shells.

Hell, they might already be printing posters on him! What he was going to need was a good lawyer. But not to defend him. No. What he would do, he'd go to another state. Then he'd have the lawyer make his claim on Cotton's estate, using his real name. And he'd have the proof to back it up.

The proof. Loman touched the money belt and chuckled. He had the proof, and there wouldn't be a thing anybody could do to stop it! Not a blessed thing!

All that I got to do before I go is to be good and damn certain there's no heirs left to make a contest of it or to divide with. I suppose I could ask them to move to South America and never come back.

He laughed a good long time.

Half a mile from the Hargrove house, Loman drove the truck headlong into a thicket of oaks and brush to hide it from sight. Reaching under the seat, he drew out his rifle.

He worked his way along until he reached the grove of trees around the house. The rifle ready, he moved carefully through them. The house was dark. No cars stood in the open space before the porch. Loman thought of circling to the shed where Cotton had kept his Pierce Arrow. Before he could make up his mind, a dog started its deep-throated barking from the porch.

"Damned mutt," Loman muttered. "Wish I'd blowed you up along with the rest."

A light came on back toward the kitchen. Loman couldn't see the window, but the glow lighted the porch pillars on that side. Probably the maid or cook or whatever she was, but the word was she could shoot as good as any man. Not to mention that damned dog!

All right. Growling to himself, Loman drew back. His birds weren't in their nest. But they would come home sooner or later. From the top of the slope he could cover either road into the Hargrove place. All he had to do was wait.

"Sure you don't want to take a poke at me, Lee?" Harry yelled. "You have one coming. More than one, if you like."

Temple shook his head. His throat still wouldn't let him talk much. "It's okay, Harry," he said.

"Not everybody's so forgiving. When you needed me, I was out at that damned well."

"It's all right." Temple was thinking about the rope recently round his own throat. Above the roar of the engine, he called, "Listen! What makes you think you can take the law in your hands?"

Hargrove downshifted and bullied his car roughly around another bend. "The real law's out at the well," he shouted back. He broke off while he swung into the opposite curve of the switchback. "I've sent them word. But Tommy figures Loman's gunning for me. I call it self-defense if I get him first."

Cotton had said much the same thing once, Temple remembered. "You think he'll be at the house?"

"He didn't come to the rig, and he has to be someplace. Laurel Jean's alone out there except for Rotten."

He stopped talking to concentrate on the road. Harry Hargrove was driving hard, pushing the light but powerful Reo. He'd chosen the shortest but worst route back toward the ranch, the road that zigzagged up the bluff by the Hargrove Oil tanks. The car skidded alarmingly on the unbanked curves while Temple clung to his Winchester with one hand and gripped the dash with the other.

Temple started to shout a caution, then let it go. Nothing was going to slow Harry tonight. He had it in his head that Frank Loman had killed his father and blown up his wellhead. Looking back, Temple saw Tommy and Chief herding one of Bremerton's Quads, its lights haloed by the dust Harry was raising. Tommy had slowed more dramatically to make the curve.

The Reo was losing momentum on the grade. Harry

downshifted again and opened the throttle. Temple had not learned much about motor cars, but he knew what effect that treatment would have on a horse.

"If you don't ease off, you'll run it in the ground!" he shouted. "If Loman's at your place looking for you, he'll wait until you get there."

Hargrove started to answer, then shut the throttle back to a merely punishing engine speed. "Sorry, Lee. I'm in a hurry to get this over with." He flung a glance behind him. "We'll let the truck catch up a little."

"Good."

"Lee, listen." Harry didn't have to shout now to be heard over the motor. "The way I've been acting—"

"Forget it, Harry."

"—don't know what was happening. Earlier tonight, talking to Betty, it was like—" He thought for a moment. "It was like I realized for the first time Cotton was dead. I saw he didn't have a hold on me anymore."

Temple nodded an understanding he didn't feel. "It's okay."

"I hope so." Harry laughed—his own laugh, not someone else's. "I'll believe it when I convince Harriet and Aunt Minnie that I'm not—"

He brought the Reo over the rimrock and onto the gentle slope that led to the top of the hill. The Hargrove Oil tanks loomed ahead in the lights.

"—that I'm not Cotton," Harry finished. And then he cried out in pain and shock as the Reo's windshield exploded inward on him.

Car and truck had been out of sight for a couple of minutes on their steep climb up the bluff, but Loman knew where he wanted them. If they were stacked up the way he hoped, he would stop the car and let the truck run over it. Then he could pot any survivors before they figured out where he was.

Everything had fallen into place for Loman. He'd seen the lights like fireflies on the steep face of the bluff. Their slow climb had given him time to take a position in the shadows around one of Hargrove's oil wells. The rhythmic creak and rattle of the walking beam covered any noise he might make, even if anyone were around to hear. A flickering gas flare near the Hargrove Oil tanks offered plenty of light for shooting.

The car came out by itself. Loman could hear the truck still laboring up the slope. He put the scope on the car. It was coming almost directly toward him, so he wouldn't have to worry much about a moving target.

The truck wallowed over the rim. The car had been waiting. Now it came on like a Hargrove was driving it.

Loman almost hurried his shot. But the truck too began to accelerate on the milder slope. They'd come some distance past the point where he had meant to hit them, but now they were bunched together. He fixed the sights as well as he could on the bouncing windshield and fired.

He saw the driver rocked back against his seat, then forward onto the steering wheel. Accelerating, the car made a sharp turn, hit the graded row of gravel at the edge of the road and bounced completely off the ground. The passenger went flying out onto the roadside.

When the car came down, the driver was fighting the wheel, still alive, trying regain control. Loman fired again. He couldn't tell if he hit, but the car's engine roared under a full throttle. The Reo shot forward. Behind it the truck had steered sharply left to avoid the man on the ground. It was correcting with equal sharpness when one of the front wheels hung on a rock. The top-heavy vehicle teetered a moment, then fell slowly over on its right side.

The Reo's passenger had tumbled up onto one knee, still holding a long gun of some kind. He made it to his feet and started to run after the car. Loman sent a third bullet at him. The man went down, rolled over the bank of rock and gravel, and lay still on the other side.

A figure was trying to climb out of the wrecked truck, but Loman was more interested in the Reo racing toward him. He got it back in the scope just as the little car left the road to rip through the fence around the storage tanks. Out of control, it bounced over the low earthen retaining dike, plowed through the sludge in the shallow moat, and plunged nose first into the middle tank.

Loman's reaction was instinctive. He forgot the men in the truck, the stray passenger, even his determination to wipe out the Hargrove name. As the Reo's headlights died in the sweeping tide of crude oil that poured from the tank, Loman sprang up and ran. Behind him was a noise like a sigh, so deep and loud that he felt it through his bones. Hot air struck him like a giant fist, almost knocking him down. A great blossom of orange-yellow flame flowered over the tanks, illuminating the hilltop like a new sunrise.

In the dawning light, a big bullet came roaring up the slope at him. He heard it pass within a foot of his head. He dodged into cover by the base of a derrick and looked back. Flames were spreading, the oil cresting the wall of the dike and slopping over in tongues of flame. Thick, choking black smoke rolled upward like a thundercloud.

The rifleman was up now, running for his life as liquid fire poured down his way. Safe for the moment on higher ground, Loman would have enjoyed shooting him. But someone was firing an automatic pistol from the area of the truck, the .45 bullets coming closer than he would have thought possible from that range. An arm of fire threatened to cut off his escape. It was time to go. He was sure he'd gotten Hargrove, and Hargrove was the one that mattered.

He scrambled away from the derrick, keeping low, circled the hill and lumbered back to his truck in the thicket. Behind him men were shouting. The iron bands reinforcing the right-hand tank began to part, snapping with reports like gunshots as heated oil bulged the tank's sides. The wooden slats collapsed and thousands of barrels of fresh fuel cascaded out to overflow the dike. Loman got the Bulldog started and backed it onto a road lighted brighter than day.

A bullet spanged into the truck's body, but only one. The men back there would be too busy staying alive to give him too much thought. Loman fed gas and clattered down the road, away from the fire. He wanted to find Elizabeth

Hargrove. Since she had not come up the hill with her brother, she must still be in town. Loman saw that the town would be in confusion over the fire. It would be his chance to slip in, kill the girl, and get out of town while people were still occupied.

He laughed, thinking of the day he could lay claim to everything that had Hargrove written on it. He did not take time to realize that much of Hargrove's assets were pouring in a river of fire down the slope toward the sleeping town of Emilia.

"Christ!"

Temple didn't know if Harry meant it as oath or prayer. In that first instant, he didn't understand. He heard and felt the glass come in, felt himself splattered with warm liquid, saw Harry flung back and then forward. He turned to reach for Harry, knowing now what had happened. Then the engine roared and the car heaved itself up like a bronc loosed from the chute.

"Harry!"

By the time he was able to shout, Temple was already flying through the air. He tumbled in the road for a dozen bruising yards, stumbled to his feet, tried to run after the Reo. A muzzle flash bloomed from the floor of a pumping rig. The bullet struck rock in front of him, glancing off with a shower of sparks and a whizzing moan. Temple dived for cover. In a moment he realized he still had his rifle, and he fired once in the general direction of the rig.

He heard the tearing crash as the Reo hit the fence, and an instant later the louder and more destructive noise of the car smashing into the wooden tank. Forgetting the rifleman, he turned toward the tanks. The night seemed to catch its breath. Something came that was deeper than a sound. A pillar of fire shot up, showering everything around with burning oil.

"Damn you!" Temple's scream ripped at his raw throat. He threw himself down again as the bushwhacker broke from cover. Temple sent a bullet straight at him in the sudden glare. He wanted to keep shooting, to bring the man down and kill him, but a tide of moving fire was sweeping down at him from a weakness in the dike.

"Run, Lee!" Tommy shouted from the truck. The long-legged man was firing steadily. "I'll cover you."

Choking from the smoke and slapping at smoldering patches on his clothing, Temple ran. The muscles along his backbone crawled, anticipating the impact of a bullet, but none came. Apparently the ambusher had found more resistance than he'd expected, or had been unnerved by the fire—or maybe he'd accomplished what he intended.

Though his right ankle pained him at every step, Temple made a good pace back toward the Quad. The truck had turned on its side, then slid another twenty or thirty yards along the edge of the road. Temple called out to Tommy and Chief as soon as he got close enough to be heard above the roar of the fire.

Tommy Ellis called out a hoarse response. "Here." He was hanging out the driver's side—now the top—with a big Army Colt in each hand. He didn't move as Temple came up.

"Are you all right?"

"Hard to say," Tommy replied. "I've got a leg that won't work. I can't get forward or back."

"Hang on. I'll help you over the edge."

"Just don't overbalance this big can. I don't want to roll the rest of the way down the slope. Where's Harry?"

Temple swallowed the sickness in his throat. "Harry didn't get out," he said.

Ellis looked at the roaring furnace within the dike. His face set, but all he said was, "We have to get away from here. Those other tanks are going to go. Chief—"

Temple swung up onto the side of the truck so that he stood over Tommy. "You first. Give me those pistols." He remembered to set the safeties, then shoved the guns into his belt. "I'm going to get you under the arms. Now."

"Easy! God of mercy. I said that leg didn't work; I didn't say it doesn't have any feeling."

As gently as he could manage, Temple hauled Tommy up to a sitting position on the edge of the cab, then lifted him down. Tommy folded up on the ground, holding his leg with both hands.

"Damned thing's broken. No, don't be easy. Drag me the hell out of here and get Chief."

Temple half carried, half dragged the smaller man up the slope toward the forest of Hargrove derricks. The dike around the tanks was washing out on the far side, most of the burning oil starting to find its way down the bluff. Temple picked a spot he thought would be safe and let Ellis down. Tommy had groaned once when his leg caught on something. He seemed to be unconscious, but as Temple started back toward the truck, a strong hand caught at him.

"Leave me those pistols. Look out for yourself, Lee."

"Yeah."

The second tank had collapsed and fire was flooding over the dike. The heat seemed to have doubled in intensity. Temple shielded his face with his arms as he hobbled back to the truck. He hitched over the side to look down into the cab, then dropped down and kicked the windshield in, smashing the glass aside and wriggling through.

Chief lay curled in a ball, part of the seat and a lot of odds and ends on top of him. The bandage Doc Thornton had put on his head earlier in the evening was askew and soaked with fresh blood. He didn't respond to Temple's shaking. Temple didn't know how bad he was hurt, and he didn't have time to find out. Burning oil was beginning to pool in the trench the Quad had dug during its slide. In the orange glare, Temple saw the paint start to blister on the truck's sides.

Breathing a prayer, Temple grabbed the Indian by the shoulders and dragged him through the windshield area and into the momentary shelter in front of the engine. He crouched there until he could work the limp body across his shoulders, then broke into a lumbering run back toward Ellis.

The moment he was clear of the truck, the heat struck him like a blast from the gate of hell. He stumbled on his bad ankle, fought for balance, knowing if he went down he'd never be able to get up again. He could feel the shirt blaze up on his back, feel his skin blister.

Behind him the truck's gasoline tank exploded, the sound barely audible over the greater roar from the fire. The blast swept him along like a leaf in a storm. He couldn't breathe, his lungs were filled with the same fire that followed him, the weight on his shoulders was too much, he was going to fall and die after just one more, one more step, one more—

The shadow of the derrick fell across him like a gift from God. Tommy had crawled out as far as he could to meet them. Temple swung Chief down and collapsed into the sheltering blackness beside him, while Tommy beat with his hands at the flames that licked their hair and garments.

At first Temple could only pant, trying to breathe the thick, hot air that swept around them. As the pain in his chest began to subside, he pushed himself up and blinked at Tommy. The long-legged man leaned on one elbow over Chief, gently touching his legs, his arms, his chest.

"Nothing much broken. Can't tell if he's hurt inside. But it may only be another crack on the head."

Temple nodded. He got to his knees. His ankle hurt viciously. His back wasn't so bad, but he had an idea how it would feel later.

Tommy Ellis looked up at him. "What you'd better do is take one of these pistols." He held one out, butt first. "I'll keep the other. Here, take an extra clip. Get to town."

"I'll get help back to you just as soon as I can."

"Never mind us and never mind this oil. Look."

Headlights were coming along the road from the east, at least two cars.

"Some of Hargrove's hands must've seen the fire," Tommy said. "They'll take care of us." His lips skinned back in a grin of pain or humor. "More important, they'll shut the wells in so we quit pumping fresh oil onto the fire. You have to get to town."

"Town."

Temple risked a look back into the blinding center of the tanks. Up until now he'd been grateful the flood of oil and fire and death had gone away from them, down the hill. Now, for the first time, he realized where that river of fire was going.

"My God. Liz."

"And Alice. And the town." As Temple started to rise, Tommy caught his arm. "Look sharp, Lee. I don't suppose we have to ask what son of a bitch did this."

Temple stood up, checked the clip in his Colt, shoved it home. "I'm going to kill Frank Loman for it and ask who did it after I've finished," he said, and started for the road down.

Chapter 29

FOR THE SECOND TIME, ELIZABETH HARGROVE FELT THE EARTH tremble beneath her. She leaped up, her first thought that the wildcat had exploded again. Sound came right behind the shock, a single deep-throated boom. The kitchen window of Irma Watson's boardinghouse lighted as though from an early dawn.

"What . . . ?"

The others in the kitchen—Measuring Alice, the Ballards, Mrs. Watson herself—were all on their feet, all asking the same question. They crowded through the back door and stopped on the porch, staring in disbelief.

A tower of fire reared above the bluff, as solid and enduring as if it were made of bronze, spreading wide and intolerably bright at its base. For five, ten, a dozen seconds it stood, while smoke poured up to hide the stars. Then the column collapsed onto itself in a hail of sparks. Fiery orange threads unraveled down the hillside, exploding scrubby cedars into balls of flame. Maybe it was imagination, but Elizabeth felt a breath of heat in the wind that touched her cheek.

"Great God Almighty!" Bull Ballard whispered.

"It ain't done," Ace High said.

"What?"

"It ain't done." The younger Ballard pointed where the fire was thickest. "That's one tank gone. The others will blow surer'n—" He glanced toward the women. "—surer'n Christmas."

"The dike—" Elizabeth's voice died with her hope. The dike was already giving way. She bit her lip. "Lee. And Harry. Do you think—" She couldn't finish.

"No reason to think it has anything to do with them," Ace High said. "Bull, I and you'd better round up some hands and get up there. Somebody's got to shut them wells in."

"Now, wait," Bull Ballard said. "Tommy said to watch over Alice and Liz until him and Temple and them got back."

There was no second explosion, but the flaming tower shot upward again. When it fell back, the orange trickles on the hillside widened to streams, flowed together as they tumbled along. Halfway down the bluff they spread into a single sheet of moving fire, studded with black islands of rock and sand.

"Tommy didn't know the world was going to end," Elizabeth said. "We'll look after ourselves. You have to get those wells shut down. We'll be safe. We'll go up the hill to the school if it gets bad in town."

"But Loman—"

"Loman won't be chasing after anybody down here. Hurry! That's Hargrove oil."

The Ballards wanted to argue, but Elizabeth shooed them on their way. Down toward the courthouse a bell was ringing. The bell in the Baptist church joined it, followed by others. From the depot a locomotive's whistle broke into short, urgent hoots. Then the steam siren on top of the volunteer fire station added its howl to the racket. Other boarders were crowding onto the porch to gape at the spreading fire. Irma Watson bustled off to start coffee and to wake anyone still asleep.

"I'm going to the shop," Alice said. Her voice was steady, but Elizabeth saw in her eyes the same fear she herself felt. "I've got to wet things down."

Elizabeth stared at her. The fire licked along the base of the bluffs, momentarily held up by the broken ground there. A gully leading to the creek became a river of burning oil, the brush along its sides vanishing in fresh spurts of flame. Birds circled, crows and hawks and songbirds all together, some speeding desperately away, others plunging straight into the smoke and glare. The fire found one of the streets leading into town and flowed along it.

"You can't fight this!"

"I can try," Alice said. She pulled away from Elizabeth. "It's ours, Tommy's and mine. If—Until he comes back, I'll do what I can."

Elizabeth hesitated only a moment. She couldn't let Alice go alone, and she couldn't sit and do nothing. Anything would be better than waiting to hear if Lee or Harry were dead.

"I'll help. We'll take the roadster."

From the store things didn't seem so bad. The sky was bright, streaked with smoke, but no current of fire had swept that way yet. Across the street men trickled into Bremerton's yard like ants to sugar, organized into work gangs, drove out with Quads or teams of frightened horses or big waddling steam tractors. One gang stopped briefly, helped the women carry water to pour along the lower walls of the store.

"We've got it held near the courthouse," the pusher said. "We're intending to shut in the wells in town. Slick's gang is trying to cut a firebreak between here and the Line. If it breaks out anyplace, you'll have to get out fast."

"We'll be fine," Alice told him. Elizabeth agreed, but she felt herself tremble when the truck pulled away.

"Help me with the ladder," Alice said. "I want to get some water on the roof. Then we'll go."

Her arms and back aching, Elizabeth carried pail after pail of water to the foot of the ladder for Alice to haul up and pour on the shingles. Cars and wagons began to move along the street, loaded with dirty, smoke-grimed men and women. A horse pounded by furiously, its tail on fire.

From Emilia's side of town a pillar of fire rose suddenly, followed by the shock of an explosion—a well or a storage tank, Elizabeth guessed. Drops of oil fell like burning rain, driving her to cover while Alice stamped out those that fell on the roof. One of the cars stopped and a man waved frantically to Elizabeth.

"It's broke out down by the Line," he shouted. "Ragtown's gone, and the Paradise's burned with near everybody inside. You got to leave."

"Where?"

"Doc Thornton's up in the school. Needs help."

"Alice!"

"I heard." Alice was standing at the edge of the roof. "You go with him. Send those buckets up first. I'll be done in a minute and follow in your car."

"All right."

Elizabeth and the driver passed the buckets up to Alice. Then the man hustled Elizabeth into the car and sped away. Looking back to the tall woman bending over her work, Elizabeth felt she was leaving a place of safety for the unknown.

Frank Loman picked his way through refugees and victims, driving slowly and deliberately. The Line had been hit hard. Flames rose from the tents, and the three-storied Paradise burned like a bonfire. People stacked up against the fence surrounding the Line, trying to fight their way over or through. A wagon passed Loman, the driver lashing his horses furiously to distance himself from that hellhole so that no one would know he'd been gambling. But the wagon was on fire, was burning faster all the time.

Loman shouted something to the work gang that tried to wave him down, and drove into the lower end of Oiltown. A man with his clothes on fire rushed into the street. Two more men pursued him, dragged him down, beat with their hands at the flames. Farther on, two workmen had fallen into a dispute over a topic neither of them remembered; they faced each other, taking turns with their punches—hitting, being hit, hitting again.

Loman found the yellow Mercer in the street beside Alice's store. He parked the truck on high ground across the street, got out and went across to look for his half sister.

Instead he saw Alice on the roof. "You," he called up to her. "Where's the Hargrove girl?"

Alice looked down at him. He saw a trace of fear, all but hidden by anger and loathing. "I would hope she's at home," she called in a close to normal voice.

"What's her car doing there?"

"Is that her car?"

"Bitch!" Loman grasped the ladder, put a foot on the first rung. "You're lying. Tell me, or I'll come up there and squeeze—"

Alice emptied her bucket of water down into Loman's face. "You're a foul-mouthed, low-moraled man, sir." She brandished the empty bucket. "And if you've hurt Tommy—"

Loman spat water. "You're a no-moraled, kept woman, ma'am." He jerked at her ladder and threw it out into the street. "Mind you hold tight to them skirts when you jump down from there."

He searched Alice's store until he found the rear door bolted on the inside. Certain Elizabeth wasn't there, he headed off to look for her. In the chaos of the town, nobody paid him or the Bulldog any mind. He steered away from the worst of the fire, judging she would be in some safer place. Soon he found people crowding up the hill toward the school. He left the truck and followed their current.

He was standing on the cement steps by the back door, assessing the progress of the fire, when Dr. Thornton stepped out and emptied a basin of water over the railing. The doctor was talking to someone inside.

"—short on everything. We'll need more blankets," he said harshly.

But Loman's eye had fallen on the people inside. He saw Elizabeth Hargrove straighten up from some figure on a cot and answer the doctor. Loman didn't hear what she said, but he recognized her. The doctor went back inside; the door closed.

Loman thought of a plan. He opened the door a slit and peered into the makeshift hospital. The doctor was up to his elbows in other people's misery. Liz was talking intently to a young boy. As Loman watched, she finished her instructions and gave the boy a little push on his way.

Loman had hoped she would go after the blankets herself. That would have made things easier. He cursed his luck, changed his plan. After a moment he saw her take up another basin of bloody water. He stepped to one side and stood three feet from her when she emptied the pan.

"Liz," he said.

She jumped, dropped the basin. "You!" she cried.

"Listen," he told her. He got a grip on her arm. "Harry's been hurt. They've got him over here a ways. Afraid to move him. He's calling for you."

"Where?"

"He's been burnt. Wanting to see you bad."

She drew back, doubtful. "Bring him here where we can care for him. I'll find someone to help you."

"I can't do that," he said. "Come on. It's not far."

She took a step or two before she threw herself away from him. "No!" she cried. "He wouldn't send you!"

Loman quit trying to persuade her. He struck her a sobering blow across the jaw and dragged her down toward where he'd left the truck with a grip that threatened to break her arm if she did not keep up his pace.

The creek was burning. Temple crossed the bridge, scorched by the heat rising from the oily water. Flames were lapping at the support timbers, gaining footholds where oil gathered in the eddies of the current, mounting to the decking.

A dozen unattended horses milled on the far side, bunched up and white-eyed. Temple caught one, a streaky roan, and fought his way into the saddle. The horse bucked and shied, but Temple's weight and sure hands seemed to quiet it. He was glad to have a horse under him, even one so frightened and sweat-soaked. The pain in his ankle had dropped to a numb throb, but he felt his boot cutting into the swollen flesh of his leg.

Keeping to the streets on higher ground, he avoided the worst of the flowing oil. Where the streets were paved with brick, fire rilled down the gutters, building into an unbroken square around the courthouse but not invading the center. In the dirt streets of Oiltown it was different. The flaming liquid filled ruts, puddled in low spots, spread to fill the streets and eat at the foundations of the buildings.

Temple's first thought had been to go after Loman. He'd thought Elizabeth safe with Alice, but a glance at the town told him no place was safe. He tried first to reach Irma Watson's, but the street was blocked. He caught at a man helping a crew rig dynamite charges in the buildings up from the depot.

"How about the boardinghouse?"

"Gone. Miz Watson's burned bad. Tried to sweep the oil back with a broom. The broom caught, set her skirts on fire. Listen, better get away. We're blowing this block for a break."

"Did you see the Hargrove girl?"

"Liz? Went with Measuring Alice to her store. Can't be anybody in there now, though."

Nothing Temple could do would make his horse go deeper into the burning town. He released it, hoping it would find its way out, and hobbled along the fire-strewn street to Alice's store. Fingers of fire were beginning to inch their way up the wooden walls. Alice called down to him from the roof.

"Where's Elizabeth?" he shouted up at her.

"She went off to the hospital. Bring me that ladder!"

"Hospital? Is—"

"She's not hurt. Bring the ladder."

He saw the ladder, brought it back to the building, held it while she climbed down. "Where is she?"

"Doc Thornton's got a hospital in the school up the hill. She went to help. I meant to follow her, but that damned

Frank Loman threw down my ladder. Thought I was going to have to jump for it."

"Loman? Did you tell him where she was?"

"Didn't tell him anything."

"We have to find her."

Alice looked at the store, at the flames that had gained purchase and were nibbling at the roof. She nodded.

"It's gone, that's all. Her car's over there. Your foot's hurt. Let me drive."

Alice didn't have the Hargrove disregard for life and limb, but she quickly threaded the Mercer through deserted streets where closed businesses burned with no one to tend them. Tall derricks stood as fiery skeletons before the weakened timbers collapsed and sent the crown blocks crashing down.

Things were better up the hill. The town below looked like something from the Pit of Hell, but only smoke invaded the wooded mall around the school. Survivors milled around the grounds, lay on the grass, huddled at tents set up to serve soup and coffee. Alice parked the car amid a tangle of other vehicles.

"She could be anyplace. I'll look outside. You see if Doc Thornton's seen her."

Inside the school, people were moaning, crying, dying. The smell of burning hung over everything. Dr. Thornton was moving from cot to cot. Two men helped him. Elizabeth was nowhere in sight. Temple asked about her. One of the men glanced up, tossed his head toward the back door.

Temple went through to the concrete steps. In the yard below, a big tin basin lay half buried in the mud. Temple ran haltingly along the rear of the building, stopped at the corner to look around. Off to his left a block or more away, two figures in conflict passed through a shaft of firelight and turned off to the south.

Temple ran. Dodging through the smoke and flame, he glimpsed the struggling pair beside a truck. By the time he got there, the truck had pulled away. He followed as best he could. When he came to the warehouse yard at Buffalo

Supply, a black Bulldog truck was standing there, its motor running.

In the garish twilight a rear door stood open. Inside, someone lit a lamp while Temple was getting his breath. He went to the door, listened, stepped through with Tommy's gun in his hand. From the office area Loman's voice rose in an angry shout.

"That's right, whore, I'm your blood brother! Here, I want you to see it writ legal on official paper. No, you sit. You're going to see it!"

Temple glided through the poorly lit storage area, staring at the dark floor, listening hard.

"That's my name. This here's my mother's name. And that right there, see it? That there's yours and my father's name!"

Crossing the sales area, Temple edged up to the open door of Loman's office. Loman stood in front of his desk with the paper in one hand and his unfurled money belt in the other. Elizabeth slumped in a chair, staring at the paper.

"But why . . ." she said.

"Why what? Why am I showing you? Ha! I'm showing you so you'll know what you died for. I'm showing *you* because I didn't get the chance to show Cotton Hargrove who I am."

"Cotton?"

"I've waited these many years for the moment when I'd show him. To show him and see the fear in his face when I killed him for abandoning my mother and me. To show him I was going to inherit every penny he had!"

"You did kill him. Harry's sure you did."

Loman snatched the paper away from her, laughing. "Is he now? Well, he was right. I killed them both!"

Her voice changed. "Killed who both?"

"Your father and your brother. And you're the last one living between me and my inheritance."

"You—killed—Harry?"

He laughed. "Sure, I did. And—"

She came out of the chair in a dive, striking Loman chest-high, driving him backward by sheer fury. A flurry of blows stung his eye and cheekbone, cut his mouth. He blocked the knee she drove at his groin, cuffed her hard on the side of the head, turned her, and pinned her hands with one strong arm.

"You fight better than your brother," he said, laughing. With his free hand he reached around to grasp her throat. "Sorry we don't have a little more time."

"Go on and kill me!" she said. "It won't get you anywhere. As soon as you show that paper, they'll hang you for what you've done!"

"We'll see."

"I doubt it." Temple stepped into the room and pointed the heavy Colt automatic at Loman's back. "Let her go."

Loman whirled, still holding Elizabeth in front of his body. "You, Cowboy," he said. "You've got between my feet from the first! Throw that gun down."

"Not likely."

"I'll kill her."

"You won't live half a second longer than she does." Temple lifted the gun until he and Loman stared at each other along the top of the barrel. "You're a head taller. I'll take you right between the eyes."

"Do it!" Elizabeth screamed.

Loman choked off her cry. Tightening his grip until her eyes bulged, he lifted her off the floor, holding her as a shield before his face. Temple raked the gun down sharply and shot him in the foot. The buffalo-shaped man roared in pain. Still roaring, he swung Elizabeth like a doll.

Her legs struck Temple and knocked him against the wall. He fell, holding onto his gun, trying to bring it to bear on Loman. But the big man was already in the doorway, still holding Elizabeth between himself and Temple. In one hand he gripped a wrinkled sheet of paper.

"I'll be back for you!" he screamed.

He ducked through the door, dragging Elizabeth by her throat, leaving bloody prints with one foot. She beat at his arm with both hands, fighting for breath. By the time Temple regained his feet, he heard the outer door slam.

He stumbled through the darkened building, tripped over a spool of cable, fell headlong. He lost the gun, but couldn't take time to hunt it in the dark. He scrambled up, kept running.

Outside, the heat and glare and noise struck him again. Half dazed, he searched for Loman. The Buffalo was beside the truck, struggling with Elizabeth. He slung her into the cab, shoved his paper into his shirt, and found his pistol. He sent two quick shots at Temple.

The bullets bit at the wall on either side of Temple's head. Before the next shot came, Temple dived to the side and limped along the loading dock into the shadows. Loman emptied the revolver at him and got into the truck, his every other breath a great roar of indignation at his foot.

The truck kicked, started, grated into gear, and jumped toward the gate. Temple saw that it would pass within a few feet of the dock. He got a start and ran headlong, ignoring the pain of his leg, toward the end of the dock. At the edge he leaped as far out into the darkness as he could.

He landed in the littered bed of the truck, twisted his bad ankle again, and fell hard. As he was trying to rise, the truck shot forward with new speed. Temple went on over in a backward somersault. He crashed against the tailgate, his legs slipping over to drag almost to the ground. Desperately he clawed at the bed, got hold of a corner stake, and dragged himself up as Loman ran through the gate.

Elizabeth lunged up off the floorboard, throwing herself at Loman again. Her nails raked at his eyes, missed. She got a grip on his shirt and ripped it open. As he batted at her, she jammed her heel down into his injured instep.

"Damn you!" Loman roared and shoved her away. Unguided, the truck careened off downhill, slewed sideways, and teetered on two wheels, threatening to overturn. Loman got a fresh purchase on the wheel and brought the truck down flat. But by that time he was committed on a narrow downhill street that led straight into the middle of the fire.

Loman cursed his foot, his fate, the Hargroves, the fire. But the fire came on, rising to meet the truck. At last he cursed his father and drove full throttle into the fire, steering around bodies, dead horses, burning wagons. Half strangled by the thick smoke, Temple rolled onto his stomach and covered his head, unable to do more than hang on as Loman raced the Bulldog straight through the worst of the flames.

Ahead of them the bridge across the creek stretched like the road to hell, even the rails on fire. Now screaming, Loman headed the truck onto the bridge, trying to shift gears, determined to reach sanctuary on the far side. The truck caught fire from the flooring, its wooden bed flaming around Temple, fire flaring up the sides of the steel cab.

Halfway across, above the blazing lava flow of the creek, the wheels found a spot where the beams were burned through. The bridge gave way. The nose of the truck dived, stopped against a solid beam with the cab submerged in fire halfway up the doors.

Temple had slammed into the back of the cab, Loman into the steering wheel, taking the wind out of him. Elizabeth, wiping blood from her face, struggled to get out the window. Her screams brought Temple around. He saw that the doors were jammed against the timbers. Leaning across the top of the truck, he caught her wrist. She screamed again as he set his feet and pulled. Fire danced and leaped as high as his head, but at last he got her out far enough to get a hand under her shoulder. He heaved her free, felt her dangle above the river of fire as he lost his footing.

He fell back, holding onto her with all his might. The two of them tumbled off the end of the bed onto the smoldering timbers of the bridge. As Temple pulled her to her feet, a bullet smashed into the blazing rail beside him.

"Temple!"

Frank Loman was halfway out the window on the driver's side, his gun in his hand. He squirmed a little farther, started to level the pistol again. As he brought it down, a white square of paper slipped from the open front of his shirt.

"No!" Loman bellowed. He grabbed for it, but only managed to knock it away. Caught by the eddying winds of the fire, it fluttered back into the truck's cab. "No!"

He disappeared back into the truck. For an instant, even as Temple dragged Elizabeth away, he saw Loman moving, a black shadow against orange flame. He caught something, held it up in triumph, turned again for the window.

Behind him the truck's gasoline tank reached a boiling point, ruptured, exploded into a rising ball of flame. Burned almost through, the support beam collapsed and the truck shuddered, slipped, fell slowly into the boiling creek. Loman screamed, a sound Temple figured he would hear on his deathbed, but there was nothing to do.

Nothing except run. The center span of the bridge was gone. Now its whole structure started to give way, a pillar at a time like a roofed row of dominoes.

Shaking himself free of his horror, Temple dragged Elizabeth to her feet. She screamed and went limp in his arms. He took her up, got himself balanced, and ran as fast as he could manage. He heard the collapse coming, chasing them, opening its mouth to engulf them. He saw he wasn't going to make it.

With his last strength he hurled himself toward the bank, fell over a twisted, burning timber, lost his hold on Elizabeth. He floundered after her, reached her where she lay in a shapeless tangle of bent limbs and smoldering cloth. He crawled to her side as the bridge went down in thunder behind him. She might have been breathing. He couldn't tell.

Chapter 30

LEE TEMPLE STOOD OVER ELIZABETH'S BED WATCHING HER breathe as she slept. He was uncertain on his feet. Both hands were bulky with bandages, smeared with burn ointment and extending well up his arms. He had dressings on a dozen other places, too, and his tightly strapped right ankle was swollen the size of a small watermelon.

"Not your fault it isn't broken," Dr. Thornton had scolded when he finally had time to deal with such things. "The sprain was bad enough. Then you had to run around on it all night. Pretty well tore everything loose. Hold still!"

"How's Miss Hargrove?"

"Shock. Nervous exhaustion. Some burns, mostly superficial—those on her legs will leave scars. Possible concussion." He washed his hands, dried them on a bloody towel. "Lots of people did worse."

"What should we do?"

"Do? With her? Take her home. Keep her quiet, let her sleep. Change those dressings daily. Yours, too." He paused at the door, looking back at Temple. "The hard part for her's coming after she wakes up," he said in a gentler voice, and went out.

If she wakes up, Temple thought. Beneath its bandages, her face was gentle in sleep, just as it had been that day at the creek, the day that seemed so long ago.

"Mr. Temple."

He turned. Laurel Jean stood in the bedroom doorway, a basket of knitting in her hand. "You have visitors downstairs in the study," she said. She drew a chair to the edge of the bed. "I will sit with Miss Elizabeth for a while. You go along."

The study was a corner room on the first floor. Its ceiling was high like the others, and its tall windows looked out onto the porch in two directions. One inside wall was covered with bookshelves finished in dark mahogany varnish.

Temple could have counted the books on the fingers of one hand. The only one he recognized was a leather-bound family Bible. Chief sat in a big leather chair across from the desk. Beneath the white bandage around his temples, his swarthy face was bloodless. Bull and Ace High Ballard stood nearby. They looked uneasily out of place amid the bookshelves as they sipped coffee and ate Laurel Jean's fresh cookies. The fourth man was slender and blond-haired, someone Temple hadn't met before. He nodded and raised his cup, but it was Bull who spoke first.

"We come to inquire about Liz—Miss Hargrove, that is," he said.

"She's fine, far as we can tell. She's showed some signs of coming out of it, but she's still—resting. Laurel Jean says she'll wake up when she's ready."

Bull nodded. "Laurel Jean knows. Damn shame." He looked out the window for a minute. "Things are all right out at the wildcat. We got that seepage stopped at the new wellhead. It ain't so good in town, though."

Temple remembered the last he'd seen of Emilia and Oiltown, dirty and burned over and smoke-stained, with the fire brigades from Eastland and Desdemona helping to contain the last bad spots of the blaze. "I expect not," he said. "You all look like you should be in bed. You especially, Chief."

"Damn well should be, according to Doc," Ace High snapped. "Don't know why he'd get out just to visit with a lizard like you, but he wouldn't have it any other way."

"Had to be sure." Chief turned his head and looked at Temple with black eyes. "Loman. He did it?"

"He did. Most likely the action of his rifle's at the bottom of the creek now. Along with him."

"You got him?"

Temple nodded, closed his eyes. "Yes," he said, "I did." And now he knew he'd been right. He would hear Loman's last cry for a long time. On the other side of the ledger—thinking about all the ones Loman killed—he wished he'd gotten Loman sooner.

He shook his head. "Look, I'm sorry about Shooter. If you want a job, I'm pretty sure Miss Hargrove—"

"Nope. I'm going back in the nitro shooting business. Got me a new partner." He nodded toward the blond man, who stepped forward and held out a hand.

"Jack Murchison." He smiled. "Never got to meet you, but I understand we shared a room."

Temple stared at him. "Mad Dog Jack?" he asked.

Murchison shrugged and looked at the floor. "Guess I been called that," he said.

"Look here," Bull said hastily. "Reason we come is to find out what you mean to do. I know you were planning to move on before they took you out to hang you, but we been talking—"

"Not me," Ace High growled.

"—us and Tommy—"

"How's Tommy?"

"In a real hospital over in Eastland. He'll be all right. Alice is sitting over him like a mother hen. But we think you should stay on."

Temple hesitated. "Won't have much choice for a while," he said carefully. "Doc says take it easy on this leg for two or three weeks."

"Yeah, but after that," Ace High said. "Liz's gonna need some help running this operation. If we're working for her, we need a boss who's not as big a bastard as some." He jerked his head at Bull. "Tell him about the deal, Bull."

Bull Ballard put three cookies in his mouth, chewed on them a minute, washed them down with coffee from a cup whose handle was too small for his big fingers. "Well, I and Ace had about decided on this. If you'll stay on, I'll keep about half sober, and I'll work at keeping him about half drunk. That way we'll both be on our good behavior."

Chief laughed. "I don't see how you can pass that up, Lee," he said, "for all our sakes!"

"I'll think it over."

"Fair enough," Bull said.

Ace High put down his cup with a clatter. "All right, that's enough time wasted here." He waved the others off, helped Chief up as gently as a mother cat lifting her kitten. "Some folks got work to do, even if Temple can sit around all day."

Temple went out to the porch to see them off. After they'd gone, he stood for a time, looking out at the trees and beyond. A gray pall still hung in the sky over toward Emilia. It would be a long time before all the scars were healed there—if they could be healed at all.

He flexed his hands inside their bandages, grimacing from

the pain of raw, seared flesh. He would have his scars, too, as would Elizabeth. The ones on the surface would heal. He didn't know about the others.

"This is how it would always be," she had said. "Those others would always be around."

Even then, a lot of things had separated them. Now there would be more—death and the guilt that went with it and Hargrove money. Temple hadn't known how to answer Bull, because he didn't know how to answer himself.

"Mr. Temple." Laurel Jean had come to the top of the stairs to call down. "Mr. Temple. She's awake."

He went up the stairs slowly on his bad leg. Elizabeth was awake, her eyes drowsy until she saw him in the doorway. Without speaking, she held out her arms.

He came across to her, knelt beside the bed, put his arm around her shoulders.

"What—" she said, then stopped on that single word.

In her eyes he saw the memory come back, each part like a separate blow. Pain, loss, sadness, the horror of the fire, and the desolating shock of Harry's death all showed there. And at the last, through her tears, he thought he saw the beginning of an answer to his questions. And he liked the answer he was beginning to see. She looked up into his face, slipped her arms around his neck.

"Hello, Cowboy," she said.

About the Authors

Successful Writing Team Puts Up with Hassles for End Result

by Georgia Todd Temple

Midland Reporter Telegram

"'He has to die! There's no two ways about it!'"

"The words rose in the still air of the judge's chambers to resonate in the iron-framed skylight . . ."

Thus begins *Manhunt,* Midlanders Wayne Barton's and Stan Williams's third co-authored novel.

"We thought it was a good way to start a book—the old nail-them-in-the-first-line approach," Barton said.

The book was released in November 1992 by Pocket Books, yet Barton traces the inspiration for it to a brochure he was browsing through some years ago.

"I saw a Fort Stockton tourist brochure which mentioned the fact that at one time several of the town's leading citizens had drawn lots to see who would murder the county sheriff," recalled Barton, an engineer with Atlantic Richfield Company.

"I collected some more material on that and intended at the time to do a magazine article on it and took a trip down to Fort Stockton to see what more I could find out.

"And I found out enough to see that I could not write it as nonfiction because there was not enough background

307

material available. But I decided it would make a heck of a novel, and after a couple of false starts, Stan and I finally turned it into one."

The two writers remember first being introduced at a meeting at the University of Texas of the Permian Basin. They did not see each other again until years later, when they found themselves serving on the same jury.

"We realized that we had seen each other at some writing function and we were both writers," said Williams, who has spent the past twenty years teaching English at Odessa College.

"For several years we talked about his writing and my writing. Wayne had had maybe fifty stories published. He then had two Western novels published."

At the time Barton asked Williams to co-author a novel, his agent had cut a deal with Pocket Books for four novels from Barton. The first two were reprints of his previous novels—*Ride Down the Wind* and *Return to Phantom Hill.* The others were written by the two-man team, who first wrote two stories together before tackling a novel.

"We really get together and talk over what we intend to do, and then I do a rough draft—just a chapter at a time," Williams said of the process of co-authoring books.

"And he then does a second draft staying about a chapter behind me so that I will know what changes he's making that will affect my rough draft.

"We really don't sit down and write together. We sit down and talk about it together, but we write separately."

Having two minds work together has its advantages.

"We each bring something a little different to the book—a different approach and a different way of looking at things," said Barton, who, with his wife Margie, has two children—Charles, twenty-five, who manages a theater in San Angelo; and Kristin, twenty-one, a senior at Texas Tech.

"It's pretty good discipline for a writer because one of

you is always around to keep the other one on track. Also, I feel that we get better stories than either of us has done individually.

"Stan is responsible for a lot of the depth that goes into the characters and a lot of the narrative density that goes in the plot, and I have a lot to do with—for want of a better word—the directness for getting from point to point in the plot and the sense of place in the story."

The problem of limited time also is addressed when a writer has a partner.

"If you have limited time to devote to this, it's much more effective to have more than one person work on the project," said Barton, who has received the Spur Award and the Medicine Pipe Bearer's Award from the Western Writers of America.

Of course, working as a team also has its down side.

"The greatest dilemma is the tendency sometimes to fall over your own ego," Barton said. "I will undoubtedly come along and cut out some of Stan's most treasured passages, and sometimes when I see what he's doing ahead, the character of the situation is working out a little differently than I think it should.

"You have to be prepared to compromise and make concessions and see what the other person is doing, but the results have been more than worth the hassle."

"I imagine sometimes I feel the way he does," said Williams, who has been married for thirty years to Jill Williams, chairman of the English Department at Lee High School. The couple have two grown children—Midlander Wendy Tomlinson, and Stan (not junior), who is working on his master's at New York University.

"There's this or that I would have done a little differently if I had been doing it by myself," Williams said. "But when I was doing things differently by myself, no one would publish them. So, I'm really quite pleased about the whole process of getting to work on some that are published."

Although both enjoy writing, Williams said he had

previously "never really gotten quite the sense of fulfillment from it I had hoped for.

"The last time I went back to school, I decided what I wanted was to be a writer, and so I studied creative writing. That was what I intended to teach, then there weren't any jobs in teaching creative writing. I was more interested in doing the writing anyway.

"And so I have been intent upon writing fiction for twenty-some-odd years now. I never had gotten very much of it published until the opportunity to work with Wayne came along."

The way they address the discipline of writing is different, Williams said.

"I work in spurts and fits and starts," he said. "Wayne probably works a little every day."

The most important aspect of working as a member of a team, Barton said, "is to have a very clear understanding of what each person's role is."

For those considering a larger effort than two writers working together, Barton said he recommends talking "to a lawyer and getting a contract drawn up. I can see how this would be very complicated for more than two people."

Writing as a team has worked successfully for Barton and Williams, who are currently working off a six-book contract with Pocket Books for co-authored stories.

"Very few professional writers make their living entirely by writing," Barton said. "My intention has always been to get paid for doing this, but there's a lot of truth in writing for the love of it."